IMMINENT
THREAT

Books by Jeff Gunhus

SILENT THREAT

IMMINENT THREAT

Published by Kensington Publishing Corp.

IMMINENT
THREAT

JEFF
GUNHUS

KENSINGTON
PUBLISHING CORP.

www.kensingtonbooks.com

KENSINGTON BOOKS are published by

Kensington Publishing Corp.
119 West 40th Street
New York, NY 10018

All Kensington titles, imprints, and distributed lines are available at special quantity discounts for bulk purchases for sales promotion, premiums, fund-raising, educational, or institutional use.

Special book excerpts or customized printings can also be created to fit specific needs. For details, write or phone the office of the Kensington Sales Manager: Kensington Publishing Corp., 119 West 40th Street, New York, NY 10018. Attn. Sales Department. Phone: 1-800-221-2647.

ISBN-13: 978-1-4967-2624-7 (ebook)
ISBN-10: 1-4967-2624-3 (ebook)

ISBN-13: 978-1-4967-2623-0
ISBN-10: 1-4967-2623-5
First Kensington Trade Paperback Printing: January 2021

10 9 8 7 6 5 4 3 2 1

Printed in the United States of America

For Nicole
Because they are always for you

CHAPTER 1

Jacobslav Scarvan realized too late that his countrymen meant to kill him. The surprise wasn't that the entire voyage out to the middle of the Aegean Sea on a godforsaken fishing trawler had been an elaborate trap, but that his comrades had possessed the imagination to pull it off.

Which meant they'd had help.

And if they had, it meant the list of men he would need to kill after this was done was going to be long indeed.

The trawler heeled to the side as it dipped into the trough of a wave. Water broke over the bow as it plowed through, hurtling a sheet of cold seawater across the deck. The three men in front of him staggered from the force of it.

Scarvan didn't move.

"Jacob, this is ridiculous. Let's go inside and talk." Viktor Belchik looked pathetic, clutching his sopping wet coat at the collar, squinting as the wind from the storm whipsawed around them. His thin hair, usually dutifully combed over to cover his spotted scalp, was pasted over his ear and cheek. Scarvan had once thought of this man as mentor and father. Part of his heart broke that his own personal Judas would be the one person in the world he trusted most.

"Let's do it here," Scarvan said, spreading his feet wider, a strong base to compensate for the violent rocking of the deck.

He turned his body into a side profile to offer less of a target. At six foot three inches, this was no mean feat. He was broad-shouldered, still muscular from his grueling daily workouts even at the age of fifty-two. His gray hair was cut short so it didn't obscure his vision as the rain and wind buffeted him. He knew his dark Serbian features—heavy brow, thick lips, brooding eyes—would work to his advantage as he scowled at the men facing him. Anyone from the world of espionage knew to fear him. The two particular men standing in front of him had worked with him before. They knew enough to be terrified.

The men took a position on either side of Belchik and reached for their firearms holstered at their sides. They didn't pull them out.

Scarvan knew these men, Demetri Acha and Sergei Kolonov. They were good operatives, fast and accurate, lethal killers. They should be. Scarvan had trained them himself.

"You're paranoid!" Belchik shouted. "Just as I taught you to be. But this is madness. Why would I want to terminate my most powerful asset? What sense does it make?"

Scarvan felt nearly embarrassed for his old mentor. They both knew how the game ended for men like him. He possessed too many state secrets, knew where too many of the bodies were buried, both figuratively and literally. Eventually, Mother Russia would want her house put in order. Men like him either timed it right and disappeared one day to live out their lives in some remote village or island, or they were terminated.

Looked like his timing had been off.

And, in retrospect, as he stood on the bucking deck in the middle of a storm, he had a good idea why.

"It's because of the Americans, isn't it?" Scarvan asked.

Belchik's eyes betrayed him. His demeanor changed, a man who'd made a decision.

"Yes," he said.

Scarvan gave a slight nod, acknowledging the honesty. A bolt of lightning cut across the sky, followed immediately by a crash of thunder that shook the boat. Scarvan took notice of the reactions from both Acha and Kolonov. Any advantage he could spot was going to count in the next few seconds. Unfortunately, neither man flinched at the thunder.

"Who gave the order?" he asked.

"What does it matter?" Belchik said.

"To me, it matters."

Belchik lost his balance as another wave hit and he staggered backward. Once he regained his footing, he was next to a metal support column for the balcony on the second-floor deck. He slid his body over so that his vitals were protected. The movement had been orchestrated and perfectly executed. Scarvan had to admit it was a nice move by the old man.

"Was this your decision?" Scarvan asked.

"I follow orders," Belchik said. "We all follow orders."

"Look around," Scarvan replied, gesturing to his surroundings. "You can see where that gets you."

He'd spent a lifetime following orders. Who to kill. Who to maim. Who to take apart piece by piece until they spilled their secrets. He'd killed for his country for three decades. And now she wanted to kill him.

"This comes from the highest levels," Belchik said. "After the operation in America, reprisals were demanded."

Scarvan nodded. He'd been the sacrificial lamb offered for the slaughter. Again, the only surprise he felt was that he hadn't seen it coming. He'd resisted the idea that at age fifty-two he'd lost his edge. But tonight was proof that he'd not only done that, but he'd somehow turned dull, inured by overconfidence and ego that had made him think he was beyond this kind of treatment.

Killing the two American agents on their home territory hadn't been the mistake. That part was fair play in the dangerous game in which they all played. It was making the two men watch as he tortured their wives and children alive that had been a step too far. There had been poetry in the act, a Biblical sense of eye-for-an-eye given the operation the two agents had executed in Bulgaria. A bomb where innocent women and children had been killed. Why were these men's families any more important than those killed in the collateral damage from their bomb? But he should have understood that the act would be taken as too personal, too outside the convoluted rules they all followed.

"The children. It was too much, Jacob. There was nothing I could do," Belchik said. "You were not authorized to do such a thing."

Scarvan took note of the denial. It was bullshit, they both knew it. He never had limits put on him and his handlers had always encouraged his ruthlessness. Demanded it. Belchik was speaking to someone else.

Scarvan raised his eyes to the balcony one story above the back deck where they stood. The lights didn't penetrate to a spot in the center. He didn't think it was an accident.

"I'm sorry, Jacob. It's over," Belchik said.

The old man looked to Acha and Kolonov as if it were their cue to complete the task. But they didn't move. Scarvan didn't mistake their hesitation for compassion or internal conflict about killing their teacher.

No, they hesitated because they knew his capability. If they both pulled their weapons, they would be able to kill him. But at least one of them would die in the process and the other would likely be wounded. Whoever drew first would be the one Scarvan would kill.

Neither wanted to go first.

That was a fatal mistake.

Scarvan timed his move with the next big wave that slammed into the ship. As it crashed over the bow, he ducked down and rolled to his right, his Sig Sauer out of its holster and in his hand as the wall of water hit them.

Acha and Kolonov jumped toward cover, guns out.

Scarvan took aim but waited. The ship's nose dipped into the next trough, sending his targets downward. In the split second before the trawler climbed back up the next wave face, the deck was flat and stable.

He squeezed the trigger and Acha's head jerked back, the spray of blood visible even in the storm. He turned to look for Kolonov.

Then the unexpected happened.

Searing pain shot up his arm as his gun flew from his hand. He clasped his wrist. It felt like it was on fire. He had been shot enough times to know the feeling. But where had the shot come from?

He reached for his backup weapon strapped to his ankle. The Glock 22 was not as effective as his Sig Sauer. Before he could grasp it, another bullet tore into his calf, shattering bone and flesh.

He cried out. He could take the white-hot pain, he'd endured far worse, but he knew he was now in real trouble. The problem was the precision of the shooter. Whoever it was had placed two perfect shots in a row on a moving deck in the middle of a storm. That wasn't good.

Scarvan grunted as he pushed back the flap of skin that used to be his calf, digging for his gun. Triumph surged through him as he felt it on the deck next to him. He wrapped the fingers from his good hand around it and lifted it toward the balcony.

The shooter had to be there. It's where he would be if—

Scarvan's shoulder exploded. This time he saw the muzzle flash come from the balcony. The riot of pain a small consolation for being right.

He dropped his weapon and it skittered across the deck.

Unarmed and shot three times, Scarvan fell to his knees in the center of the deck.

He saw Kolonov train his weapon on him, but then a new voice called out.

"No, wait."

Scarvan raised his head to see a man step out from the shadows of the trawler's cabin. He was similar in age to him, wearing a black trench coat and a hat pulled low. Still, he knew immediately who it was. James Hawthorn. CIA.

Scarvan glanced up to the balcony. He saw the shooter now,

covering him as Hawthorn approached. If Hawthorn was here, in person, he knew the identity of the shooter.

Scott Roberts.

It had to be. He was the best Hawthorn had and it explained the precision of the shots so far. One move and he'd get a bullet in the head, he had no doubt.

Hawthorn stopped short of him, far enough to be safe. Close enough to gloat over his pain.

"The agents you killed, they were my friends," Hawthorn said. "But we all understand the risks of our profession. But you tortured their families. Burned them alive one by one. You brought great dishonor on your country."

Scarvan spat on the deck between them. "I'm going to kill you," he said. Then he cried out, "I'm going to kill all of you, I swear it!"

Hawthorn sneered. "You'll have to come back from the dead to do it." Without taking his eyes off Scarvan, he said, "Kill this miserable piece of trash."

The trawler hammered into a wave. The ship shuddered like it'd glanced off a solid wall. It was the chance Scarvan had been waiting for. He jumped to his feet and ran. A shot fired and he heard the round zip past his right ear. He didn't think he would be as lucky with the next bullet.

He reached the port side of the trawler and dove headfirst over the railing. As he fell, another shot slammed into his leg.

Then he hit the cold water.

His body reacted with a sharp inhalation. He sucked down seawater and then coughed it back up. A wave crashed on him and he was underwater, struggling to swim with his damaged leg and blown-out shoulder.

He fought back to the surface. When he came up, he saw searchlights from the trawler stretching like fingers across the water. But he was already far away from the ship. There was no way they were going to find him.

But it felt like an empty victory. As another wave pushed him back underwater, he felt like he'd accomplished nothing more than to choose the manner of his own death.

If it was meant to be that way, then so be it.

But if he did survive somehow, if he made it through, he was going to enjoy punishing each one of the people on that boat.

Like Hawthorn said, even if he had to come back from the dead to do it.

CHAPTER 2

Father Spiros climbed daily down from his home high over the water, navigating the rope ladder to the rocky landing twenty feet below. It was his daily habit of several decades to walk the stretch of stone shoreline beneath his skete, the ancient hermit dwelling built into the cliff rising from the Aegean.

Sometimes the sea delivered useful items to him. A length of fishing net. A fish stranded on the rocks that became his supper. A piece of castaway clothing.

He'd been a fit, athletic man, a soldier in the Greek army during the war against the Nazis. At seventy years old, he was a *gheronda*, a respected elder among the monastic community. He was fit for his age, wiry and lean, stronger than his long gray beard and wrinkled face indicated. His daily walks on the uneven ground kept him healthy. He enjoyed it most after a storm, interested to find whatever the sea had delivered from the depths after it had raged.

On his regular path he'd found a length of good rope, two bottles of a beautiful blue color in which he would put flowers. It was much farther up the shore than he normally walked when Father Spiros found the body.

At first, he didn't think the shape on the rocky shore was a man. Certainly, it was something out of place. A pile of dark brown seaweed perhaps. Or some trash from one of the tankers that passed by the shores. But as he came closer, he made out the outline and knew what it was.

The body was on its side and had its feet pointed toward land with its head near the water. The man had not crawled out, but rather had been washed ashore. Clear evidence he was likely dead.

And it was a man. Even sprawled on the rocks in wet clothes, one arm bent back at an impossible angle, clearly broken or separated at the shoulder, the figure's muscular bulk was apparent.

Spiros walked to the other side of the body to look at the face.

The man appeared Slavic, with a heavy brow and high forehead. Thick hair pasted to his scalp. His mouth hung open, revealing teeth covered in blood. The man's eyes were closed, which gave Spiros pause. He'd seen more than his share of death and he'd expected to see the man staring blankly into the sky.

Unless . . .

Carefully, he kneeled beside the man and placed his hand near his mouth. He thought he felt the barest hint of warm breath but couldn't be sure.

He reached to the man's neck and pressed his fingers there, digging for a pulse.

As he did, the old man's other hand pulled back the man's shirt. It was soaked red with blood. He looked quickly back up to the man's face.

The eyes were open.

Spiros cried out as the man snapped at him with his teeth. Gnashing at him like a wild animal.

The man's feet kicked. He groaned and vomited a foul-smelling mix of blood, bile and seawater. Then his entire body spasmed, shaking violently. Spiros placed a hand on the man's shoulder and gripped it tight.

"Isychia. Isychia," he said. *Quiet, quiet.*

The man's eyes rolled back in his head, closed, and he went still.

Spiros reached again for the man's neck, ready this time in case the man tried to bite him again.

There was a pulse. Thin and ragged, but a pulse.

Spiros made the man as comfortable as possible and then set out to fetch some of the younger brothers to help him carry the man back to his skete.

As he clambered over the rocks, hurrying as fast as he dared, he marveled at the ways God revealed Himself. For years, Father Spiros had prayed for God to send him an instrument, a divine weapon to help him realize the vision his Lord had sent to him throughout his life. A world that was to be reborn, baptized by fire. Destroyed so that it might be renewed.

Certainly, this man on the beach could be the fulfillment of prayer.

Or a challenge to his faith.

He could not have known on that day that the Lord would take twenty years to answer that question. And, true to the nature of his God, the answer would be *both*.

CHAPTER 3

Twenty years later

Scott Roberts felt no sympathy for the sniveling terrorist on the floor in front of him. Sure, the man was someone's son, maybe someone's brother, maybe even some poor woman's husband. It didn't matter. Whatever rocks life had thrown at Hassan Abbas, there was no excuse for what he'd done. Ultimately it was his own decision that had led him to leave behind a duffel bag of explosives in a Christmas market in Munich, Germany.

Just like it was Scott's decision to take a detour from his mission in Prague to lend a hand in finding the scumbag.

Hawthorn had denied his request to divert but Scott had ignored him. Six months of hunting Omega had yielded nothing but dead ends and dead informants. Both Scott and his team were restless, ready for a win, ready for anything that didn't feel like pissing into the wind.

The counterterrorism unit of the German intelligence service Bundesnachrichtendienst, or BND, was already working the case. Nineteen dead, seven of them just school kids not much older than his grandson Joey, meant the manhunt was going to receive every resource available. Still, Scott had old contacts in Munich. Contacts that owed him favors that he'd held onto for a long time. He'd had a hunch they might just prove useful.

He'd been right.

A few phone calls on his scrambled satellite phone during the train ride from Prague had put him on the trail. Once he arrived, he'd gone into bloodhound mode and rooted the man out. Fortunately, when Scott arrived, Abbas had tried to run from his hideout in an abandoned warehouse in the northern borough of Hasenbergl. Scott had taken great pleasure in shooting the man in the leg to bring him down.

Now it was a matter of what to do with him next.

"I'm not afraid to die," Abbas said, speaking German.

"Why don't I believe you?" Scott replied, his German rusty but passable.

Early reports accessed by Jordi Pines, Alpha Team's tech extraordinaire back in Washington, DC, showed that the BND had been able to determine the bomb had been an explosive vest put into a bag.

"You know nothing about me," Abbas said.

"I know you chickened out," Scott said. "If you're going to blow up a bunch of women and children, you could at least have the decency to blow yourself to hell, too."

"You're American," Abbas said. "You'll never understand martyrdom. Ascendancy to paradise where I will be eternally rewarded."

"Then why'd you take off the vest?" Scott said. "Paradise sounds pretty good. Isn't there supposed to be a bunch of virgins? A land of milk and honey and all?"

Abbas shifted uncomfortably, gripping his bleeding leg. Judging from the amount of blood, the femoral artery hadn't been hit so he didn't have a lot of risk of bleeding out. Pity.

"My master has greater plans for me."

Scott was suddenly more interested. If this little rat had information about other planned attacks, he wanted to get it out of him. "Really? And what's that?"

"You are an infidel. You wouldn't understand," Abbas said.

Scott raised his gun and pointed it at Abbas's other leg. He made a show of tracing up his leg until the barrel of his Glock was pointed at the man's groin. "I suggest you tell me, otherwise when you get to Paradise those virgins will be mighty disappointed with the crater you have between your legs."

Abbas swallowed hard. Beads of sweat had formed on the man's forehead and brow. Scott was well versed in how to get people to talk, even hardened operatives. He planned to crack this guy open like a walnut. Soon he'd have the guy admitting to every wrong thing he'd done in his life since he'd been a kid.

But then Abbas grinned, and Scott saw the fear in the man's eyes click off, replaced by resignation and moral indignation.

"Are you a religious man?" Abbas asked.

"No. How about you?"

This brought a small chuckle. "The end of the world is coming. Caused by man. Caused by God. It doesn't matter. Because in the end, only the righteous will be saved."

As Abbas spoke the last words, a white foam appeared at the corners of his mouth.

"You better not have just done what I think you did," Scott said, dropping to a knee.

Abbas convulsed with a choking cough and foam and spittle poured out down his chin.

"Allah Akbar," Abbas mumbled, his eyes shining bright. "Omega Akbar. Omega Akbar."

Scott froze in disbelief at the words, thinking his mind was playing a trick on him.

Abbas repeated the words. "Omega Akbar." *Omega is great.*

Scott turned Abbas on his side and stuck a finger down the man's throat. It worked and he gagged and then vomited a thin green bile. Stuck in it were pieces of a fake tooth. The delivery system for the poison Abbas had taken.

Scott grabbed the man by the collar of his jacket and pulled him up to him. "What do you know about Omega?" he said. "What do they have to do with this?"

But the only response he got was the brutal choking sounds

of Abbas's airways constricting and shutting down. His face turned red and then purple as his oxygen depleted. His eyes bulged and his body went rigid in a final back-arching spasm.

And then he was dead.

Scott threw him to the ground.

"Shit!" he shouted, the word echoing through the warehouse. He felt like an idiot. He should have checked the man more thoroughly. Would he have caught the fake tooth? If he was being honest, probably not. His own fake tooth loaded with cyanide was indistinguishable from his other dental work except with an X-ray. Still, he hadn't even checked. Maybe it was lazy, but it also didn't fit the MO of a radicalized Islamist to be fitted with a suicide tooth.

But he wasn't just a radicalized terrorist. He'd somehow known about Omega. Somehow, they were connected to the attack. And he'd lost the first good lead they'd had in months.

He turned back on the coms he'd switched off a few hours earlier and reinserted his earpiece. After a series of clicks, the signal bouncing through a series of secure satellites, the system came back online.

"'E's back, Director 'Awthorn," Jordi said, the computer genius's exaggerated English accent dropping the H's. Even though the man was born and raised in Jersey, the accent was one of his many unexplained quirks. Mara had vouched for his technical genius and she'd been right. The personality was just an added benefit. "Someone's been naughty."

"Jordi, I need you to relook at the list of victims at the Christmas Market attack," he said. "Omega's involved."

"How are they involved?" It was Jim Hawthorn, ex-director of the CIA and legend among operatives. It was widely assumed Hawthorn had retired from the game. But those in the know had been briefed about his new position as director of Alpha Team, an elite group tasked with finding and eliminating the shadowy organization known as Omega. A task at which they'd all failed miserably so far.

Scott bent down and started to rifle through Abbas's pockets. "I found the bomber. Hassan Abbas wasn't very talkative, but what he did say was interesting. He knew about Omega."

A long pause. He imagined Hawthorn standing next to Jordi's workstation, a horseshoe of computers and large monitors that he played like a virtuoso. He knew Hawthorn would be incredulous Scott's side trip had actually turned out to involve Omega.

"Explain," Hawthorn said. He was obviously still not happy with him.

"He said 'Allah Akbar' once. But then he switched to saying 'Omega Akbar.' "

"Jordi, is there an alternative word in Arabic or in any dialects for Omega?" Hawthorn asked.

"No, Mara explored that months ago," Jordi said. "Before she took 'er leave of absence."

Leave of absence. Is that what they were calling it now?

"All right," Hawthorn said. "Bring him in. I'll inform the BND you have him in custody. They want to have him after you're done, so be quick about it."

"There's going to be a problem with that," Scott said.

Another long pause on the com-link. He was glad he couldn't see Hawthorn's face.

"Daddy's not very happy with you right now," Jordi whispered.

"I didn't kill him. The guy cracked a cyanide pill in his mouth," Scott said. "Fake tooth."

"That's unusual," Hawthorn said. "Anything else? Anything on him? Any markings? Tattoos?"

Scott pulled back the man's clothing. No ink. No scars.

"Nothing."

"Jordi, let our friends at BND know the location of their bomber."

"Get me clearance to join them on the investigation. I want

to see Abbas's apartment and see if there's anything that ties him to Omega."

"Negative. I need you on the next flight out of Munich back to DC."

"But we—"

"Scott, I want you—"

"Just a couple of days is all I'm—"

"Dammit, Scott. Will you just listen to me?" Hawthorn said, raising his voice. The sound shocked Scott. Hawthorn was always in control. There was a pause on the line. Hawthorn had his attention. The next two words sent chills through his body. "Jacobslav Scarvan."

Scott pressed his earpiece in more firmly. "What did you say?"

When Hawthorn responded, his voice was calm, but Scott heard the stress still there. "Scarvan's back. I don't know how it's possible after all these years, but he's back."

Scott felt his stomach turn over as the implications hit him. No wonder Hawthorn was on edge. "Okay, I'll be on the next plane," Scott said. "And Jim. We'll sort this out. I promise."

"I'm waiting to brief the president when you arrive," Hawthorn said. "And Scott."

"Yeah?"

"We need Mara for this."

He nodded, not sure how he was going to pull that off. But he knew he had to.

"Are you there?" Hawthorn said.

"I'm here. Have Jordi send me her location when I land. I'll take another shot at her. She's not going to like it."

"She may not have a choice," Hawthorn said. "See you stateside. Be safe."

Scott terminated the connection. Standing in the middle of the abandoned warehouse, Abbas's dead body at his feet, he had a sudden feeling of being watched. He spun around, gun raised, checking the shadows. Nothing.

He laughed nervously at himself, the sound coming across

hollow and scared in the large open space. Jacobslav Scarvan. It didn't seem possible.

If it were true, then the world had just gotten a lot more dangerous.

As he left the building, he wondered what it was going to take to make Mara understand that simple truth.

CHAPTER 4

Mara's ass hurt. She shifted her position in her saddle for the hundredth time that day only to find a few seconds' worth of comfort before the ache started again. She'd endured covert ops in the jungles of Southeast Asia, the tundra of Mongolia, and the desert sands of Yemen. She'd trained with Navy SEALs and Force Recon Marines. She was going to be damned if a horse named Buttercup was going to get the best of her.

"You doing okay?" Rick Hallsey asked. He handled his horse like he'd popped out of the womb right into a cattle drive.

"No problem," Mara said. "Buttercup here is great."

As if on cue, Buttercup lowered her head to the ground and munched on a full mouth of grass. Mara pulled up on the reins, but the mare ignored her.

"Yeah, you're really showing her who's boss," Rick laughed.

Mara didn't mind Buttercup stopping. She was enjoying the view, and not the majestic Grand Tetons that stretched in front of her against a perfect bluebird sky. The sight of Rick was enough for her. Gone was his Secret Service tailored suit, replaced with jeans, light denim shirts, and a tan leather jacket with a shearling collar. He looked like an African American Marlboro Man, if the Marlboro Man had an extra twenty pounds of muscle and was an expert marksman.

"We've achieved homeostasis," Mara said.

"Homeostasis," Rick deadpanned. "Do tell."

"Didn't they teach that word at Yale?" she said. Kidding him about his Ivy League education and his academic prowess was a constant riff between them. He was likely the most educated agent on the president's protective detail. His mind was what most attracted him to her. The handsome face, wide smile, and stacked muscles didn't hurt, either.

"I know what it means," Rick said. "They finally got around to teaching it to us in the last week of getting my master's in Theology at Georgetown."

"Oh, you went there. I see how it is," she said, finally pulling Buttercup's head up and getting her going again. "Then you know what I'm talking about."

"Homeostasis. A relatively stable equilibrium between independent elements," he said. "Key words *relatively stable* and *independent elements*. While the independence remains, there's never total stability."

A pheasant flew out from a bush next to the trail. The sudden movement startled Buttercup, who reared back and then bolted forward. It was all Mara could do to grab on to the saddle horn to keep herself on the horse. Within seconds, Rick's horse was next to hers, slowing her down.

"You all right?" he asked once they'd stopped.

She patted Buttercup's neck and repositioned herself once again in the saddle. "I just want to know how much you paid the pheasant to make your point."

They shared a nice laugh together and the world felt better to Mara than it had in a long time. She still grieved her sister Lucy's death. Finding the right balance of sharing responsibility for her nephew Joey between her and his grandparents was still a challenge, but getting easier. But no amount of therapy was going to erase the bitterness from the events of last year. She and her father had an unspoken pact to leave what happened alone for now. Likely not the healthiest decision, but one they'd both been thankful for. And one she'd not found difficult to live by.

The blood on her hands from that night on the Arlington Memorial Bridge had washed off, but the demons were still alive and well, even six months after the fact. She knew she'd need to face all the implications from that night eventually, but not yet.

On top of all that, the sense of futility chasing Omega hadn't helped things. It wasn't until she'd begun her leave of absence from the nascent Alpha Team that her life felt like it was gluing back together again. She was finally seeing a path forward. And she was happy that path for right now included Rick Hallsey.

But it was becoming clearer that it didn't include Alpha Team.

"C'mon, we'll take a shortcut and head over to a dive bar I know. Half cowboys, half bikers. You'll love it."

"You had me at shortcut, but dive bar is where I really fell for you," she said.

They hadn't said *I love you* yet, neither of them in a hurry to do so. Even when kidding around, they were careful to avoid it.

"If you and Buttercup over there are back to your homeostasis, then we can kick this up a notch. The faster we go, the faster we're drinking . . . Hey!"

Mara laughed as she and Buttercup galloped past Rick and his mustang. Sore or not, she hated to lose. Rick might be ten times the horseman she was, but she knew how to get and exploit an advantage.

Besides, she was really looking forward to an ice-cold beer.

Buck's Saloon was, as advertised, a complete dive. If the use of the word *saloon* was meant as a nod to old-timey Western roots, everything else in the place missed the mark. It was a hodgepodge of rusted corrugated metal siding, chicken wire, and old metal street signs. The two-lane highway passed nearby, but the dirt parking lot was nothing more than a rectangle of mostly cleared brush.

It was Mara's kind of place.

"Come here much?" she asked as they tied up their horses next to a row of Harleys. This trip was all Rick. The ranch they were staying at belonged to his uncle, a man who'd made a fortune in news media. Rick had spent summers there as a kid, learning about the outdoors and work ethic.

"Been a few years, but yeah, my uncle used to love this place," he said. "You beat me here, so looks like I'm buying."

The inside of Buck's Saloon wasn't a disappointment. Dark and dingy, the seating area had mismatched tables and chairs. The bar was more ornate than expected, like something plucked out of a nicer building. Mara imagined it might have been something bought at auction from an actual saloon, or something found in one of the ghost towns out on the high plains. Behind the bar were the requisite neon signs for Coors and Budweiser and rows of cheap bottles of booze.

Rick went to get them two beers while she grabbed them a table.

Out of habit, she took stock of each person in the room and every possible entrance and exit to the place. Five guys in leather biker jackets played darts at the far end of the seating area. Two old men sat at the bar, eyes glued to an old TV playing a rerun of some college football game, hands locked on their mugs of pale beer. There was a pair of swinging doors to the left of the bar that led to the back, a kitchen maybe. Another two doors on the right were the bathrooms.

Nothing complicated. Nothing dangerous.

Still, she positioned herself with her back to the wall, so she had a view of the entire room. And she felt the reassuring bulge of her Glock resting in her shoulder holster. She wasn't looking for trouble, but trouble often found her. She didn't have to wait long for it to show up.

Rick delivered the beers and sat down. Surprisingly, they were in frosted mugs and cold enough that a thin layer of ice formed in the beer. Turned out ol' Buck had a nice touch.

"To getting away," Rick said, lifting his beer.

"To getting away," she agreed, joining her mug to his and taking a deep drink. She wondered if a beer had ever felt so good going down.

"How long do you think it will last?" Rick said.

Mara choked a little mid-drink and wiped her mouth. Rick's no-bullshit frankness was something she liked about him, but the question caught her off guard.

"Well, you're a great guy," Mara started carefully. "And think we . . . what?"

Rick was laughing and holding his hand up. "I didn't mean how long do you think we would last. Jesus, even I know better than to ask that question."

She felt a surge of relief. He'd been asking how long she was going to stay out of the game, away from the CIA. That question she could handle. "Thank God," she laughed.

"I did like seeing you squirm, though," Rick said. "And now I'm curious how you planned on answering."

"I was going to say it'll last as long as you don't turn into one of those guys always asking about how long it's going to last."

He raised his beer to her. "Then let's go with the question as it was intended. How long until you go crazy being on the outside? Two weeks and no visible signs yet."

From his position as part of the Presidential Protective Detail, Rick knew she along with her father and Jim Hawthorn had been regulars in the White House to brief the president. He knew she was CIA but part of some special directorate. Beyond that, it was all conjecture. But he was a smart man and, while they'd never discussed it directly, she was certain he'd pieced together that she wasn't a peace emissary.

"I was going crazy on the inside," she said. "All activity and no progress."

"That's the nature of the beast sometimes, isn't it?" he asked. "Things take time."

"What's going on here? Are you getting tired of having me around?"

"No, it's been great. It really has. You're not like anyone I've been with before. Smart, sexy. You kick my ass at everything."

"Except fly-fishing."

"It's a matter of time," he said. "I'm guessing you'll lose sleep practicing your cast until you nail it."

She shrugged. "I give you two months until I'm outfishing you."

"I bet it's faster," he chuckled. Then his demeanor turned more serious. "I don't know exactly what you do for the president, and I'm not asking. But I'd bet my pension that you're likely the best person in the world to do it."

She looked away, the weightless feeling she'd carried with her most of the day leaving her. She knew what would replace it. Obligation. Guilt. A sense of duty that waited for her back in DC.

"I wasn't fulfilling my promise to take care of Joey," she said. Rick had met Joey. In fact, Rick had been the Secret Service agent assigned to Joey after he'd been retrieved from the Omega kidnapping. It was his kindness to him that first caught her attention.

"Ted and Marie have a great home for him," Rick said. "You've seen it, he loves it there."

It was true. They'd visited Lucy's in-laws together many times to hang out with Joey. As much as Mara wanted to have him live with her, she wasn't blind. What she could offer him was nothing compared to a retired couple with nothing to do but dote on their grandson all day. And he was happy there. What right did she have to take him away from that? She was certain her sister would have felt the same way.

"I'm comfortable with my decision," she said, adding an edge to her voice she hoped he'd pick up on. "I'm not going back."

They fell silent, a rare awkward pause for them. Finally, Rick put his mug on the table and said, "That's my cue to hit the john. Another round?"

She nodded but didn't say anything. He hesitated and she tensed, hoping he wasn't going to make things worse. But he seemed to think better of it. She watched him walk across the bar and disappear through the bathroom door.

She took a deep breath, trying to shake off the last few minutes. The problem was that she knew he was right. Of course he was. But she couldn't think of going back. Not now.

As she sat there, she noticed one of the bikers slide off his tall bar chair by the dartboard and start the walk over to her table. His buddies laughed and urged him on, casting long looks in her direction. The man was early thirties with long hair to his shoulders. He was decked out in full Harley Davidson regalia: leather jacket, leather pants, wallet chain, silver rings on his fingers, tattoos on his forearms and neck. He was wiry and high-strung. She didn't like the look of him.

"Anyone sitting here?" the man said.

She smiled, deciding on a gentle approach instead of aggressive. "Yeah, I'm with my friend. He's in the bathroom."

"Your friend, huh?" the man said. Mara noticed the other bikers were drifting closer, listening to their buddy talk. "Figured that's all he was."

Mara felt a cool stillness come over her. "And why's that?"

"Cuz he's black, that's why," the man said.

"Oh shit," Rick said, walking up to the table. "And here I just thought I had a kick-ass tan."

Instead of being embarrassed at being caught mouthing off or looking intimidated by Rick's size, the biker's lips parted in a half grin, half sneer.

"I never seen a black cowboy before," he said. "Have you fellas?"

The other bikers laughed, spreading out discreetly on either side of their table.

Mara pushed back her chair, but Rick held up a hand to stop her, a gesture that said *I got this.*

"You boys never saw *Pale Rider*? With Clint Eastwood? Morgan Freeman was a great cowboy in that one," Rick said.

The biker looked momentarily confused by Rick's reaction. "I meant, I've never seen one out here. Where you people ought to know better."

"This is your unlucky day, you little piece of shit," Mara said. "You have no idea who you're messing with."

The bikers laughed at this, genuinely enjoying themselves. Mara knew that wasn't going to last long. She couldn't believe the next words that came from Rick.

"How about I buy you fellas a drink instead?" Rick said. "On me."

"How about you get the hell out of here?" the biker said. "And take your race-traitor whore with you."

Mara stood, her movement faster than the men expected, making them take a step back.

Rick's eyes were locked on the man in front of him, clearly fighting an internal battle to control his emotions. The cords of muscle in his neck rippled as they tensed up. He reached out to Mara. "Let's go."

She imagined he might think she found it weak for wanting to leave, but she understood. As a Secret Service agent, he couldn't be getting into bar fights with a bunch of locals, even if they were white supremacist assholes. She got it. She even respected the hell out of the emotional control on display.

She was just happy she didn't live by the same set of rules that he did.

"All right," she said. "If you think it's for the best."

"I do," he said. "Seriously."

"Yeah, get out of here, bitch," the biker said.

Mara had walked around the table, but now made a show of stopping in her tracks. She turned to the man. "Do you want to apologize now or after?"

He looked confused. "After what?"

"After I put each of you on the ground."

"Mara," Rick said, but it seemed halfhearted to her. At least that's what she told herself.

The biker walked up to her, his face a mask of hate now. "I'd put you on the ground myself and show you a real good time, but I don't go after no ni—"

Mara punched the man in the throat before the word was out. His eyes bulged with surprise as his hands went up to his neck. Mara followed up with a swift kick to the man's balls. A gargling sound came from his mouth, a cry of pain trying to pass through a damaged windpipe. He bent in half and dropped to the floor.

The biker's friends didn't rush to help him, but they didn't run away, either. Two of them pulled knives from sheaths attached to their belts. One pulled a bully stick. The fourth slid on brass knuckles, a set on each hand.

"Put the weapons down, now," Rick shouted. He pulled a badge from his coat pocket. "United States Secret Service."

"Secret Service?" one of the bikers said. "You protect that bastard Patterson. If he ever came up here, I'd shoot that son of a bitch right between the eyes."

Mara smiled. "You all feel the same way? You'd all like to kill the president?"

"Hell yes," came the answer.

"Agent Hallsey," Mara said. "The floor is yours."

Rick already had his jacket off. "Sorry, gentlemen. You can say what you want about me, because I don't give a damn what you lowlifes say. But threatening the President of the United States? That's something else altogether."

As if sensing what was on the way, one of the bikers with a knife lunged at Rick. He deftly sidestepped, trapping the man's arm against his side. With a twist, the man's arm snapped, broken at the elbow. The man screamed and dropped to the floor as his two buddies charged.

Mara resisted the temptation to join in the melee. She wanted Rick to have the satisfaction on his own. Besides, she got a rush out of seeing him in action.

The two attackers were smarter than the first. They took their time, getting on either side of Rick before charging, one with a knife and the other wielding a bully stick. Despite his size, Rick was fast. He waited until the last moment and then dodged the attack, throwing one man into the other.

The man with the bully stick screamed in pain as his friend's knife lodged in his shoulder. But the friend didn't have a chance to retrieve his knife or apologize for what he'd done. Rick's left hook connected with the man's chin and down he went.

The last biker had backed up a few steps and Mara thought he might turn and run.

Instead the man dug into his jacket and pulled out a gun.

In a second, Mara had her Glock out. She didn't give a warning. It wasn't in her nature.

The first shot hit the gun and sent it flying through the air. Once it thumped on the floor, she shot it again, sending it tumbling. She shot it again and again, making it dance. Finally, it skittered out of sight.

The biker stood there, holding his hand in shock.

"I ain't got nothing against the president," the biker said, his voice shaking. "Hell, I even voted for him. I swear I did." The man turned and ran from the saloon.

Rick surveyed the men in front of them. "Nice shooting, Tex," he said to Mara.

"I saw that in an old Western once," she said. "I think there were some black cowboys in it."

Rick laughed as he pulled out his cell phone. Mara pointed over to the bartender, who was on the phone. "I think he beat you to the punch."

Rick still raised the phone to his ear. "I'm going to make sure the locals don't come in guns blazing. I know all the law enforcement around here. Won't be a problem."

A deep rhythmic vibration rose up from outside. It built quickly, the saloon windows shook, and the corrugated metal walls shuddered like the whole place might fall in on itself.

Mara knew exactly what the sound was and likely what it meant.

She and Rick walked outside just as a wall of dust and gravel reached them. Rick ran to the horses and tried to steady them as the helicopter landed in the field next to the saloon.

The door opened and, as Mara had expected the second she'd heard the rotors, her father climbed out. He walked over to her, nodding in acknowledgment to Rick.

"You weren't answering your phone," he shouted. The helo pilot still had the engines going, indicating he didn't expect to stay long.

"Yeah, on purpose."

"We need you back," he said. "Something's happened."

"Something's always happening."

"Not like this," Scott said. "It's a threat to you. It's a threat to Joey."

Mara felt the rage flare inside her. "Omega?" she asked.

"No," Scott said. "It worse than that. I'll tell you on the ride."

Mara looked to Rick, holding the horses. By the expression on his face, he already knew what she was only slowly coming to accept.

Her leave of absence was over.

CHAPTER 5

Hawthorn was impatient. He'd always thought that age would provide him wisdom and forbearance; instead he constantly fought a nagging sensation that he was running out of time. At the age of seventy-four, it wasn't an inaccurate statement. He'd had a grandfather who'd lived to a hundred and four, but dementia had robbed him of the last decade so that didn't really count. Other men in his family had died early, but most of them in the service of their country.

Verdun.

Omaha Beach.

Chosin Reservoir.

Brave fighters who carried rifles and faced their enemies head-on.

He'd fought the wars of his country in a different way. The results were a mixed bag. The service medals and accolades applauded his victories, the ones the general public would never hear about. But all he seemed to be able to remember were the failures.

And the weight of them felt heavier on the scales as he neared the end of his life.

Hawthorn knew there was nothing he could do to absolve himself of the many errors of his past. The only way to bring the scales into balance, even tip them so that the good outweighed the bad, was to continue to fight the good fight. To find ways to protect his country.

That was what Alpha Team was all about. Finding the shadowy extra-national group called Omega and running them into the ground.

Only it hadn't gone that way. Their prey's camouflage had proven to be sophisticated and impossible to penetrate. Omega was like a windstorm and they were always finding its debris long after it had passed. The effects of the organization were discernable and real, now that they were looking for it. But using what they found to make any advancement against them had proven to be a problem.

And now, in the middle of it all, he had to deal with the apparent return of Jacobslav Scarvan.

He'd watched the man die twenty years ago. At least as close to dying without actually seeing the body and feeling for a pulse.

Hawthorn tipped back his glass of Macallan 25, relishing the smooth lingering taste of the single-malt Scotch. It was a rare indulgence, but he felt he needed it tonight.

If Scarvan was back, then their hunt for Omega would have to wait.

He reopened the letter he'd received hours earlier and went through the dossier for the tenth time. The proof was there, spread out in detail, but it still made no sense.

Twenty years.

Scarvan would be over seventy now. An old man like him.

Then why did every intelligence officer he'd reached out to have the same reaction he did?

Fear.

A knock on his office door. "Come in."

Jordi cracked the door open. "The family Roberts 'ave landed at Andrews. They're on their way up now."

Hawthorn waved the man in. He'd taken a liking to the odd computer genius after a bumpy beginning. He'd had to learn to accept the man's bizarre fashion sense that sometimes included wearing a bathrobe over his clothes when working on a challenging project. And his trash-heap of a workstation that included superhero action figures set up in fake battles, empty bags of Cheetos, and at least a dozen cans of Coke. Then there was the fake Cockney accent.

But he'd fast come to agree with Mara that Jordi was the best in the business at what he did. Then, once the two of them discovered their mutual love of *Downton Abbey*, they'd gotten along perfectly.

"Anything new to add to the dossier?" he asked.

"Not yet. Tracking down a few things, but it was very complete."

Hawthorn nodded toward a row of glasses against the wall and Jordi picked one up and brought it to Hawthorn's desk.

"Neat, I believe," Hawthorn said, pouring two fingers into the glass. Neat meant with no ice or mixers, the only civilized way to drink.

"You believe correctly," Jordi said. "What are we drinking to?"

"Killing old friends," Hawthorn said. "For a second time."

Jordi looked confused but didn't ask for clarification. He raised his glass and took a drink. Hawthorn eyed the clock. He needed to leave in fifteen minutes for the White House. It wasn't polite to keep the most powerful man in the world waiting. Especially when you were delivering bad news.

CHAPTER 6

"Here, try this." Hawthorn pushed a glass of Macallan across the table, nudging aside the shot glasses they'd been using for vodka since just before midnight.

Jacobslav Scarvan picked up the glass and held it to the light. "Hard to trust alcohol you can't see through." He tipped the drink back and chugged it down. His eyes lit up and he nodded appreciatively.

"See, Jacob," Hawthorn said, "sometimes trust pays off."

Scarvan laughed and reached for the bottle of Scotch and poured them both another.

"If such a thing only translated to countries," Scarvan said. "Me and you, we learned to trust through action. Through blood. Through survival."

"You saved my life," Hawthorn said, raising a glass to toast.

Scarvan raised his. "And you saved mine."

They drank silently. The moment was surreal. Scarvan was a legend in the KGB, a man whispered about and feared whenever it was suspected he'd been assigned to a mission. His ruthlessness was part of his legend. While he didn't doubt the tales were based in truth, what he'd seen of the man in their mission together in Afghanistan framed him differently. He was no madman. Hawthorn now saw him as no different from himself. A warrior willing to do what it took to get the job done.

"You are a good man. But your country. My country. They are run by idiots. You know this is true," Scarvan said.

"Not sure I'm with you on this one. I'll agree they are mostly idiots," Hawthorn said. "But some of them are just assholes."

Scarvan let out a deep-throated laugh that echoed in the low-ceilinged bar. Only the die-hard drinkers remained, and they didn't even bother looking over.

"True, true," Scarvan said. He grew quiet and then turned serious. "Tomorrow we return to being adversaries. Carrying out the orders of idiots and assholes."

Normally, Hawthorn would have used the moment to try to turn an asset, to offer a deal, use the man's dissatisfaction with his government as a wedge to break him free. It was something Hawthorn was exceptionally good at doing. Maybe even the best there'd ever been.

And that's why he knew it was pointless to try.

Hawthorn raised his glass and met Scarvan's eyes. "To a respected adversary and now friend."

Scarvan straightened his posture and raised his glass to meet Hawthorn's. "To a respected adversary and friend. May we never again meet on the field. If we do, let each not expect mercy from the other."

A chill passed through Hawthorn. It was not only the words, but the distant look in Scarvan's eyes that did it.

"No mercy," Hawthorn agreed.

And they both drank.

CHAPTER 7

Mara was no stranger to the Oval Office, having joined Jim Hawthorn on several of the briefings to the president regarding Alpha Team. Still, walking into the room filled her with a sense of awe. The room gave off an energy of its own, a mix of history and power and solemnity. It was as if the great weight of decisions that had been made in the room over the years had left behind a residual gravity that pulled on its occupants, forcing them to recognize the great responsibility imparted to them.

She felt that weight on her. Every part of her career had been in service to the higher cause that was America. Not some blind patriotism, but open-eyed knowledge that even with her country's terrible past mistakes and her current contradictions, she remained fundamentally the world's great hope for stability and peace. Knowing the weight of that burden for just her tiny bit of responsibility made her wonder at the stress the occupant of the office must feel.

To add to it, while presidents redecorated the Oval to their liking, they all kept the portrait of George Washington looking down from above the fireplace. She imagined Washington's slightly disapproving look had caused more than one president to feel they were letting the great Founding Father down. She liked the thought of that. Washington was a pretty damn good example to try to emulate.

Hawthorn walked up and stood next to her in front of the portrait.

"Lost nearly every battle," he said. "And yet won the war."

"He was exactly the man his country needed," she said, noticing her father take a seat on the couch to her right.

Hawthorn placed a hand on her forearm. "I'm very glad you're here, Mara. I wouldn't have asked unless it was important."

"It's always important," she said. Not angry, just stating the truth.

"Late-night meeting in the Oval, it better be important," President Kyle Patterson said as he walked in. Mara noticed the president appeared thinner than she remembered, his face gaunt. The office exacted its toll.

"Good evening, Mr. President," Hawthorn said. "Thank you for seeing us."

"It's never good news at this hour," the president said. "But you didn't give me much of a choice. You don't rattle very easily, so your phone call left me worried. Sit, everyone. Please."

They all took their seats, Scott and Mara on one couch and Hawthorn on the other. The president sat in a chair between them and accepted a thin briefing folder from Hawthorn. Each of them had a copy.

"At least Townsend isn't here," the president said, opening the binder. His predecessor to the office, a man who'd left the office in disgrace, had become an ad hoc member of Alpha Team since he'd been there at its inception. He'd helped periodically but was more interested in making money on the lecture circuit again since his newfound popularity after being kidnapped. In a way, he had Scott and Mara to thank for that. After all, they'd been the ones who kidnapped him. Not only that, but each had contributed a right hook to create his battered and bruised face that the TV audience had loved so much.

"I will need to brief President Townsend later, sir. He will also be on Scarvan's list. It's difficult to bring the ex-president on short notice. Especially since . . . well . . ."

"Since we don't like each other?" the president finished. He closed the folder. "Let's get on the same page here, Jim. Lay it out for me."

Mara liked Patterson. He was no-nonsense and appreciated that trait in others. Also, if he liked you, he trusted the briefing would get to the salient points in good order. Some people wanted to ask questions right from the get-go, forcing the briefer to jog around instead of laying out a case. Then again, if Patterson thought you were dragging things out, he'd pounce. More than one briefer had had both their first and last presidential briefing happen on the same day.

"Jacobslav Scarvan. If there's a single man most feared by intelligence agencies around the world, it's him. Ex-Russian Special Forces, then KGB, then FSB after the fall of the Soviet Union. He's a one-man army. He can infiltrate anywhere and kill anyone, regardless of the protection they have."

"I'm sure Mitch Dreslan would have an opinion about that," the president said, shifting in his chair uncomfortably. Dreslan was the head of the Secret Service Presidential Protective Detail.

"Sir, Mitch Dreslan is a good man. Once he fully understands the threat, he's going to want to put you on lockdown in the bunker."

The president laughed. "He'd prefer that every day. Wrap me in bubble wrap, too." No one else in the room laughed along with him. Mara considered how rarely that likely happened.

"Okay, so he was a very bad guy," the president said. "And he's supposed to be dead, right? How did we get that wrong?"

"That's on me, Mr. President," Scott said. "I filed the report that he was dead."

"On what evidence?"

"That I shot him," Scott said. "Four times. And then watched him fall over the side of a ship in middle of a monster storm in the Aegean Sea."

"Is that in the record?" the president asked.

"No," Hawthorn said. "Neither is the fact that I was on the ship with him. I saw Scott shoot him. Saw him go over. There was no way he could have survived."

"And yet here we are."

"Yes sir," Hawthorn said. "A little over twenty-four hours ago I received a letter from an old adversary, Viktor Belchik. I believe you are familiar?"

Unlike his predecessor, who had charged into the presidency on a wave of family money, ego, and backroom deals while managing to avoid ever becoming a student of anything, President Patterson had an inquisitive mind. In fact, he had done his dissertation on espionage during the Cold War while earning a master's in International Relations from Georgetown University. Belchik factored prominently into any such discussion. "I know about Viktor Belchik's role in Russian history. Learned a great more about it after taking this office and having better access to the files. Nearly as impressive as your role for us, Jim."

Hawthorn kept a poker face, not showing any reaction to the compliment.

"The letter he sent was very disturbing."

"Why a letter? Seems quaint, doesn't it?"

Mara spoke up. "You'd be surprised how well the simplest methods to avoid detection work. A letter given to a trusted person to be dropped off in the mail with no return address is far less trackable than email or a phone call."

"I'll keep that in mind the next time I want to circumvent the national security apparatus. How can you be sure it's Belchik?"

"He used an old cipher," Hawthorn said. "Something only the two of us knew from the old days when we were a back channel. It's him."

"And he says Scarvan is back."

"Yes sir," Hawthorn said. "He says the first hints came a month ago. Five different members of the old guard at the FSB met grisly ends. All made to look like accidents." He spread out photos across the coffee table in front of the president. They showed mutilated and burned bodies. "This one fell in front of a subway in Rome. This one was in a car accident with a propane truck. And so on."

"All these men were connected to the order to take out Scarvan," Scott said. "They were either in the chain of command or foot soldiers along the way. They are being eliminated one by one."

"Couldn't it be coincidence? Belchik is still alive," the president said. "Seems like he would be high on the list."

"He is alive and he was high on the list," Hawthorn said. "Belchik was in Spain under an alias, enjoying a retirement among the orange trees and good food of Seville, far away from the miserable winters of Moscow. Scarvan found him two weeks ago. Belchik says he spoke to Scarvan for some time before he left."

"It makes no sense," the president said. "If the working theory is that Scarvan has come back to kill those responsible, then why would he leave Belchik alive?"

"A man like Scarvan doesn't just want to kill those responsible," Mara said. "He wants to punish them."

"Mara is correct," Hawthorn said. "Not soon after he left, Belchik fell ill. Nausea, vomiting, tremors. The doctors missed the cause at first, but once Belchik told them what to look for it was clear. Polonium-210. Radiation poisoning. The same type used by Russian operatives a few years ago in the botched attempt in England. He's still in Spain, dying a slow, painful death."

President Patterson shut the briefing book. "So, we have a dangerous assassin out for revenge. I get it. But—don't take this the wrong way, Jim, because I know the two of you are contemporaries—wouldn't he be a decrepit old man now? In a world where entire nation-states pledge to bring down the great Satan of America and well-funded terrorist groups target me and my family daily, why all the fuss over this one man? Certainly, you and Scott can protect yourselves? Ramp up your personal security?"

Hawthorn took a second to answer. Mara had seen him use the technique several times before and had adopted it herself. The pause gave weight to the words that followed. Everyone, including herself, had chills from what he said.

"Jacobslav Scarvan is the most proficient killer in the world. Belchik says that he's aged, of course, but that he's in excellent physical condition. Lethal as ever. This isn't about him coming after Scott and me. Belchik's warning was that punishing those responsible for trying to kill him is only the opening salvo. After that, Scarvan plans nothing less than to make the world burn."

The president squirmed in his chair uncomfortably.

"The good news is that Belchik says he knows what Scarvan is planning, but he will only tell us in person."

"It could be a trap," the president said.

Scott grinned. He pointed to Mara and said, "And that's why they're sending us."

CHAPTER 8

Belchik's three-story townhome apartment was on Paseo de Cristóbal Colón directly across from the Guadalquivir River in the center of Seville's historic district. The Plaza de Toros, the bullfighting ring, was only two hundred meters to the north and the iconic Torre del Oro, the thirteenth-century military watchtower standing guard over the river, was a hundred meters to the south.

Mara thought the location was fitting, symbolic of Belchik's life. He'd stood guard over his country, from his perspective, fighting the good fight against her enemies, foreign and domestic. An enemy that included on many occasions the United States. But he was in the bullring as well. Part of a rough and brutal world of danger, violence, and blood. For decades, he'd been the matador in the center of the ring, waving his *capote de brega* at the fearsome men charging at him, deftly stepping aside at the last moment, relying on confusion and misdirection to keep his opponents off-balance.

But in the end, one of the bulls had hit his mark.

That was the other reason for the townhome's location. Attached to the same building was the Centro Médico Avanzado, a convenience for his medical needs.

"How many times have you met Belchik?" Mara asked.

"Only once in person," Scott said. They were standing opposite the apartment, their backs to the river. They'd been there for thirty minutes, watching.

"On the boat the night with Scarvan?"

"Even then, we didn't speak to one another directly," Scott said. "It was all Hawthorn. He had the relationship."

She felt the twinge again that perhaps it ought to have been Hawthorn to come make this contact. It'd been discussed in the Oval Office, but they'd decided against it. If Scarvan wanted Hawthorn dead, then what better trap to set than to bait him with the promise of information? If it was a trap, then whoever was there needed to be able to react and adjust tactically to any situation. Hawthorn chafed under the implication he wasn't up to the challenge, but he hadn't fought it. He was all too aware of his physical limitations.

The problem was that if it was a trap, it could just as well have been set for Scott as for Hawthorn. Scarvan had reason to kill them both.

"What kind of security detail do you think we're up against?" she said.

"The secrets in Belchik's head could rewrite history books, and not in a way that any nation would come out looking good. I'm certain our Russian friends have him on lockdown. For his own protection, of course."

"Not that it helped," Mara said.

A black SUV rolled to a stop in front of Belchik's apartment. Two men in suits climbed out of the backseats and surveyed the street. Scott held up the tourist map and Mara pointed blindly at it. They were both looking up through their dark sunglasses at the men. "Shift change," she said.

The two men rang the door and a few seconds later it opened, and they disappeared inside. Two minutes after, the door opened again, and two different men came out. They were having an animated conversation and let the door close behind them as they walked to the SUV, barely looking around them as they did.

"Sloppy," Mara said.

"They're guarding a dying man with a week or two to live," he said. "It shows."

"Don't suppose we can just walk up and ring the doorbell," Mara said.

"Hi, just your friendly CIA operatives, wondering if Mr. Belchik has some state secrets he'd like to share on the way out."

"Yeah, probably not the move."

Scott nodded back toward the building. "Just got more complicated."

Two women, one gray-haired and stooped over, the other middle-aged, holding the older woman's arms in support, had walked out of the medical center connected to the townhouse building and were now buzzing into Belchik's apartment.

"Wife and daughter?" Mara asked.

"Looks that way. Shit."

Mara felt the same way. Even though they weren't planning a full assault with guns blazing to overpower Belchik's guards, things sometimes went wrong. If and when they did, there was a good chance some level of violence was going to prove necessary to get an unmonitored audience with the old man.

Having civilians in the house wasn't part of the plan.

"Thoughts?" Scott asked.

Mara scanned the townhomes. There were eight units in a row, all three stories high, all facing the river. Each had a covered patio on the second floor. Where most units had the windows and doors open to capture that day's gentle breeze, Belchik's balcony had metal screens pulled down over all openings.

"How's your Russian?" she asked.

"Passable, but with a terrible accent," he said. "How's yours?"

"Strong accent. No way we're getting past as official visitors from Moscow."

They strolled upriver, taking stock of the building as they passed.

"We don't even know what floor he's on."

"We can rule out the first floor," Scott said. "Not defensible enough. Leaves second and third. Metal covers on those nice big balcony windows says security protocol to me. You saw his protective detail. They're phoning it in. Why be on the river unless . . ."

". . . you wanted to die with a nice view."

Mara glanced up at the two windows on the third floor. One was shuttered, but the other had curtains pushed to either side. The glass had a semi-reflective coating on it so it was hard to see anything else inside.

Scott continued, "I'd say most of the protection team, two or three men max, on the second floor. Maybe one guy on duty on the street level."

"Wife and daughter either in his room or the room next to him."

"Sounds about right."

They turned the corner and walked down the side street to get a look at the back of the building. There was a narrow alley behind the building, but it wasn't private. There was no back door or access point on the ground floor. The windows on the rear of the building were shuttered.

"We access the roof via one of the other units and traverse across to his unit," Mara said. "Wait until late so the guards are asleep or watching TV downstairs. Circle-cut the window, climb in, have our little chitchat, climb out, off we go."

Scott nodded. "I like it. Direct, simple. What could go wrong?"

Mara hated when he did this. They both knew there were a dozen things that could and probably would go wrong. "They might have the roof rigged with laser tripwires and pressure pads. The window might be bulletproof, which makes it impossible to cut. His room might have motion sensors tied into an overall alarm system. The wife might be in the room and raise the alarm. Belchik isn't expecting us, he might raise the alarm. Once the alarm is raised . . ."

". . . we've got to start hurting people," Scott said. "Sounds like maybe we need a better plan."

"All right, smart-ass. Let's hear yours."

"Food," he said.

They'd grabbed a sandwich on the train down. Seville was known for its amazing food but his sudden suggestion threw her off guard. But only for a second.

"Probably long shifts for the protection detail," she said. "Guys have to eat."

Scott painted a picture. "We intercept the food being brought in and add some night-night juice. We have what we need in the supplies. With radiation poisoning, he's not eating solid foods. We wait until they eat. When all the guards are out, we enter through the front door and just step over the sleeping bodies."

"I like it," Mara said, enjoying the opportunity Scott had given her to hand his own comment right back at him. "Direct. Simple. What could go wrong?"

Scott frowned. "Finding the food source being brought in might take a bit," he said. "And not everyone eats at the same time. Maybe the wife and daughter already ate. Maybe one of the guards brought his own food, he's not out when we come in. He raises the alarm. Once the alarm is raised . . ."

". . . we've got to start hurting people," Mara finished. "Sounds like maybe we need a better plan."

"Who taught you how to be such a smart-ass?" Scott asked.

"Pretty sure it's genetic."

They both smiled, but an awkward silence followed. The follow-up comment would have been something like *Yeah, your mom's side of the family was like that* or *That's not a very nice thing to say about your mom.* But they didn't talk about her mom. Wendy Roberts may not have appeared to either of them as an actual ghost, but she was still very effective at haunting them every day. It was like she was everywhere, permeating everything, as if the memory was the air she breathed.

Mara stopped in place. She pulled out her phone and brought

up the images of the town house she'd snapped. She zoomed in on them and smiled.

"I like that smile," Scott said. "I know what that usually means."

Mara showed him the photo and what she'd enlarged. It only took a few seconds for him to grasp her new idea. "Of course. Perfect. That'll work."

"Do we have what we need?" she asked.

Scott shook his head. "No, but we can get it by tonight. Good work. Kind of mad I didn't think of it."

"Don't worry, I'm sure when I'm your age I'll lose a few steps, too," Mara said.

"See, there's that charming hereditary trait kicking into gear again," he said.

Scott pulled out the satellite phone and, covering his mouth with his hand, ordered the exact materials they would need. He was told it would take at least eight hours, arriving close to midnight. That worked for their timeline. He hung up the phone and they started their preparations.

CHAPTER 9

Jacobslav Scarvan fought toward the glimmer of light far above him, knowing it was the surface. His lungs burned, his head throbbed. But no matter how hard he kicked and clawed, he made no progress. The gunshot wounds in his body sent electric bolts of pain through him with every move.

But he wouldn't give up. Couldn't give up.

With one final, excruciating effort, he gave everything he had. He blew out the stale air in his lungs in an underwater scream, forcing his damaged limbs to do his bidding one last time and reach, reach, reach . . .

Scarvan bolted up in bed, screaming with a ragged voice he hardly recognized.

Waves of pain crashed over him. From the gunshot wounds. From his head. From everywhere.

He fell back onto the mattress, fighting to stay conscious.

He took short breaths, fighting through the pain, something he was good at doing. Before long, he got control of it. Pushing it aside. Using the adrenaline rush of waking up in a strange place to give him strength.

With the pain pushed aside, something else rushed in to fill the space.

Confusion.

Where was he? What the hell had happened to him?

"I thought you had gone to meet our Maker," came a voice.

Scarvan instinctively pushed his body away, arms up covering his face.

"It's all right," the voice said. "Nothing to fear. Not from me."

An old man rose from a wicker rocking chair deep in the shadowed corner. He wore a plain black gown cinched at the waist with a length of brown rope. A curled, gray beard hung down to his chest, matching a shock of wild white hair sticking out from a tall black hat. Scarvan knew what the clothes and hat meant, but in his experience, anyone could be anything. A man dressed as a priest did not mean he was one.

"How long?"

"Four days," the old man said. "You are on Mount Athos. My name is Father Spiros. And you are . . . ?"

Scarvan swung his legs off the bed. The second he raised himself up, a brilliant burst of pain exploded in his head. The room tipped on its side and he collapsed back onto the thin mattress.

Father Spiros laughed, a low, rasping sound that produced a wad of phlegm that he spit into a handkerchief from his pocket. "That won't work. Not for a while, I think. Rest. You are safe here."

Scarvan took stock of his situation. If he had been out for four days like the old priest had said, then the fool could be right. If his enemies thought he was still alive, then the search would have turned him up by now. They must have thought there was no way anyone could survive the open ocean in the middle of a storm like that. Let alone with four bullet holes in him.

They'd underestimated him.

Like always.

"I'll make us some soup," Spiros said. "Avgolemono. Egg and lemon. Very good for you."

The priest bent slowly down and turned on the burner on a small propane stove. He moved stiffly, pulling ingredients off the shelves in the small corner of the room that served as a kitchen. His face was ancient, covered with deep lines and splotched with sun damage. Dark bags hung under deep, heavy-lidded eyes.

Out of habit, Scarvan surveyed the space around him, looking for both threats and weapons. He was in a rectangular room made of laid stone on three sides and a sheer mountain face on the fourth. He heard waves crashing against a shore nearby and tasted salt in the air. Two small windows had been left open in the rock walls, but these were covered with shutters that let in only slivers of light.

He laid back on the bed and closed his eyes. How could he have been so stupid? All the warnings had been there. The assignment information had been too perfect, too complete. That never happened. Not unless it was being made up out of whole cloth. But he'd trusted Belchik, a man he'd known for decades, a legend in the KGB, a man known to fight for his agents against the bureaucracy. Belchik had asked him personally to take the job, saying it was personal, promising he would come with him in the field.

All of it lies to isolate him on that boat.

But that wasn't all. They could have taken him out anywhere. A sniper rifle from two thousand yards could have ended it all without the need for the extravagant ruse. There was something more at work here. And he knew what it was.

The Americans.

They'd wanted to witness it. Be a part of the retribution for what he'd done.

He knew the CIA man, James Hawthorn. There was history between the two of them. A grudging respect; admiration, even. But the political capital he'd had to have expended to demand such an execution must have been incredible. Then again, perhaps his mentor would have agreed no matter what the Americans had on him.

And why? Because of the death of a single family? Burning them alive hadn't been his fault. The agent he'd been assigned to interrogate could have just told him what he needed to know early on. It was his own obstinance that led to his family's death. The American agent bore the blame, not him.

Besides, he'd only done what Belchik had taught him years ago.

Scarvan opened his eyes and stared at the stone roof above him. Moss lined the mortar joints, giving his eyes a crisscrossing pattern to follow. Everything was connected, just like all the men on the boat were connected. But more than that. There were others. People who had been briefed once the idea to kill him had been suggested. Approvals had been made. Help given to fool him along the way. He thought through all of them, connection after connection, until he ended up on the trawler, staring into the eyes of James Hawthorn.

And then down the barrel of a gun held by Scott Roberts.

Only one thing was clear to Scarvan, all of them had to die.

"Here, eat," Father Spiros said, holding out a bowl of steaming soup.

Scarvan grunted as he pushed himself up onto an elbow and then up against the headboard. He reached out and accepted the soup, his stomach growling in hunger.

The old man stood in front of him, watching. Scarvan lifted the spoon from the bowl and tried to bring it to his mouth. His hand shook violently, spilling the soup everywhere.

"Let me help you," Father Spiros said.

Scarvan shrugged him off with a scowl. He dropped the spoon on the bed and put a hand on either side of the bowl, slowly bringing it toward his lips. Halfway there, his hands trembled; his body wouldn't obey the command to execute the simple act.

"Shit!" Scarvan yelled, throwing the bowl to the floor. The dish shattered, sending soup everywhere.

Father Spiros turned, crossed the few steps to his stove, and filled a new bowl. His face registered no anger or judgment. He sat on the chair next to the bed, spooned out some soup and lifted it toward his visitor.

Scarvan tried to resist, but his hunger was too strong. He

opened his mouth and allowed the old man to feed him like a baby.

The soup tasted better than any food he could remember. Smooth and creamy, with a pleasant tartness from the lemon. The aroma wafted up to his nose and he breathed it in deeply. He opened his mouth a second time, expecting the spoon to be there. But it wasn't.

The old man held it just out of reach until Scarvan met his eyes.

"The Lord our God has sent you here for a great purpose," Father Spiros said. "He has revealed this to me. I have seen in visions how you will transform the world." He squinted his eyes. "So, you will not use such coarse language again. Is that understood?"

Scarvan nodded slowly, not sure what to make of the old man, but knowing he'd do anything for another mouthful of soup.

"Good," Father Spiros said. "Let's nurse you back to health. I have much to teach you before you go back out into the world."

Scarvan ate, savoring each bite, unaware that it would be twenty years before he set off to complete his task. But that when he did, it would not only be to execute a plan for his revenge, but to completely change the course of human history.

CHAPTER 10

Scott and Mara had two hours until the material arrived. All other preparations had been made, so they left the camera trained on the building to catch video of any new activity in the area, and then went down the street for a quick bite to eat. He was looking forward to a little downtime with his daughter before things got serious.

The tavern they selected was down a side alley, away from the tourist avenues where menus were offered in both English and Spanish. Both of them were fluent so navigating the menu filled with tapas was simple enough. They ordered several dishes, Scott staying conservative with piles of Iberica ham, gambas de ajillo and patatas bravas. Mara went with more of the local delicacies, ordering orejas a la plancha and callos a la Madrileña, pig's ears and a heavily sauced tripe, or the lining of a cow's stomach. Scott wrinkled his nose at her choices.

"Do you really like that stuff? Or are you just trying to ruin my meal?" he said.

She sipped her water. "You look like the waiter when we told him we'd drink water instead of wine with dinner. Total disgust."

"I'm with him," Scott said, taking a drink and making a sour face. Mara gave him an easy chuckle. It was the kind of thing dads did the world over to make their kids smile. He still loved making her laugh. He put the glass down and rubbed his hands together. "So, are we going to talk about this guy you're dating?"

"I don't see why we would," she said, tearing into some of the bread on the table. "And you know his name. Wouldn't doubt you've done a full background check on him."

Scott feigned shock but felt a small pang of a guilty conscience. Of course, he'd run a background check on the guy. What father with the full resources of the United States intelligence community wouldn't do that when it looked like his only daughter was getting serious about someone?

"Why don't you tell me about him?" Scott said.

"See if there's something that wasn't in his file that you might want to know?" she said, grinning. "A little ground truth. Want to hear how great he is in bed? Because there's a lot to talk about there, let me tell you."

Scott choked on the bread he was chewing on and had to take a quick drink of his water. He overdid it for comic effect. Mara smiled. Beamed really. God, he loved that. All kidding aside, he was happy she'd fallen for someone.

"I could have passed on that detail," he finally managed. "But thank you for sharing. And good for you."

"It really is," she said. "Incredible, actually."

"Enough! I'm an old man. You're killing me over here." The waiter approached with their food. "Oh, thank God."

The first of the food arrived on small, steaming plates. The gambas de ajillo were plump shrimp in a piping hot butter and garlic sauce and Scott dug into them, dipping his bread into the mix. Mara ate the orejas, munching on the pig's ears and making low sounds of appreciation. She offered one to Scott.

"I like eating most parts of a pig, but I'll pass on the ears," he said. "I suppose Rick is all about the pig ears?"

"It's not a contest, Dad," she said. She waited a few beats before adding, "Good thing, because he's smart, handsome, kind, empathetic, thoughtful—"

"—but can he take out a bad guy at a thousand yards?"

"Yeah, he can," she said. "He trains with the counter-sniper team for fun."

Scott already knew that part, but he enjoyed seeing Mara's pride in telling him. He turned more serious. "You both have hard jobs to make a relationship work. Just making sure you're keeping a clear head around this."

Mara leaned back, clearly surprised at his serious observation. "I know," she said. "We talk about it."

"And?"

"And we're making it work," she said. "For now, it's good and right now is all we're worrying about."

The rest of the food came. The waiter asked one last time if they'd like some wine or beer, looking bewildered when they both declined.

"Are all these questions really about Rick, or about my thinking about leaving Alpha?" she asked.

Scott liked that his daughter was direct and to the point. "Both, really. I figure he's part of the reason, so . . ."

"He's not," she said. "In fact, he's trying to talk me into staying."

"I like him better already."

"The problem is, it doesn't feel like we're getting anywhere," she said, leaning in and lowering her voice. "Omega is either so far ahead of us that we've lost their trail. Or they don't even exist anymore. Maybe they collapsed after DC."

"I don't believe they're gone," he said. "And neither do you. Not really."

"We keep finding small splinters, like this terrorist in Munich you told me about. Are those really part of some sprawling, powerful entity? Or just copycat wannabes that try to co-opt something they've heard whispered in dark places?"

"You didn't see this guy in Munich," Scott said. "He had the look of a true believer as he popped the cyanide capsule in his mouth."

"But what he did, the Christmas market bombing, it's terrible, but not the mission of an organization supposedly trying to restructure the world order."

Scott munched on his food. This wasn't a new conversation for them. Nor were the ideas she was expressing something he hadn't thought of before in his own mind. But in his gut, he knew Omega was still a threat. Still powerful. Still dangerous. And his gut was rarely wrong.

"Omega is still out there," Scott said. "And I need your help."

Mara leaned back in her chair, taking stock of the two men who were walking into the tavern. Her eyes searched each one, looking for any signs they were carrying guns beneath their clothes. Seeing none, she evaluated the way they carried themselves, the way they looked over the room, whether they stole a glance her way, whether they tried too hard not to look at them.

Scott watched her, knowing exactly what she was doing. He wondered if, like him, part of any threat assessment included a quick calculation of how to kill the target if it proved necessary.

They both reached the same conclusion. The men posed no threat.

"A few more months," Scott said. "After this business is done."

Mara shook her head. "I have Joey to think of, too."

"He's probably having the time of his life with Ted and Marie," he said. He knew the comment fell flat because he couldn't help the jealousy and guilt creeping into his tone. Ted Suarez was Joey's grandfather, but so was he. Sure, he was risking his life every day trying to stop madmen from destroying the world that Joey lived in, but Ted was actually there for the kid. Teaching him how to ride horses. Developing his work ethic by doing chores on their Wyoming ranch. Hunting rabbits in the afternoon. Fly-fishing on the river meandering through their property. Joey was having the best childhood possible. But it didn't change the fact Scott hadn't seen him in over two months.

"The whole reason to sacrifice the time with Joey was the imminent threat Omega represented," Mara said. "I'm just not sure that's the case anymore."

Scott finished the last of his food, sopping up the delicious red sauce that had drenched his patatas bravas with the heel of the bread. "Has nothing to do with Rick?"

"I told you, he wants me to stay in. Thinks I'll go crazy teaching at the Farm. Being near the action without really being in it."

Scott had to grudgingly admit he was starting to like this guy. Sounded like he was trying to look out for what was best for Mara and not just what would give them more time together.

"You really like this one, don't you?" he said.

Usually she'd make some kind of joke, a sarcastic remark about the failings of his own love life, or the complete lack of one. But she didn't. She just smiled.

"Yeah, I do."

Scott raised his glass of water and Mara did the same. "Then I'm happy for you."

"Thanks," she said, giving him a wink. "Now let's go take out a Russian safehouse."

"Now you're talking my language," he said.

CHAPTER 11

Scarvan watched from across the street as Scott Roberts and his daughter paid their bill and left the tavern. It would have been so simple to eliminate them both right there. Or just the daughter. That was how it was going to go down eventually. Making Scott suffer the loss of his child before he was allowed the mercy of his own death.

But not yet.

As much as seeing the man in person made him tremble with twenty years of pent-up rage, Scarvan had a role for the Roberts family to play first.

Old wounds ached as if sensing the man who'd fired the bullets into his body was nearby. This only added to Scarvan's anger. Even at seventy-one, his body had the strength and agility of a far younger man, but nothing compared to the physicality he once enjoyed. The pain that racked his body was a constant reminder of that fact.

Time had wrinkled his face, atrophied his muscles, and made his bones more brittle. Still, he was able to do his daily routine of one hundred push-ups, two hundred sit-ups, and a five-mile run. Even though the workout took longer than it used to, he was still able to complete it. His reflexes had slowed, but not much. He felt confident he could go toe-to-toe with anyone in a fight. But in the old days, he could have taken on five adversaries at a time.

Still, Scarvan's strength and endurance were unusual for a man his age.

Another sign that Father Spiros was right.

God was on his side.

It'd taken Scarvan years to accept this simple fact. Early on, he'd gone along with the old monk's wild ideas and bizarre prophecies. It was part of surviving any new environment. Adapt. Assimilate. Blend in.

But over time, Father Spiros's certainty had rubbed off on him. Slowly at first. Small, tentative steps. A small sign, something innocuous like a finch landing on his shoulder while he was praying. Or a premonition of when one of the brothers was about to arrive from the monastery with supplies. A rainbow over the ocean when there was no rain that he could see from the high cliffs.

All of these things the man Scarvan had been before being left for dead would have discounted. No, he would have never even acknowledged them to begin with. But something in him had changed. Father Spiros told him it was because he'd died and returned back to the world, like Lazarus or Christ himself. That in doing so, he'd been touched by divinity. Been held in the grace of God's light. And God had sent him back to do his great purpose.

Father Spiros knew with certainty what that great purpose was.

In fact, he'd known of it for years before he found Scarvan washed up on his beach, riddled with bullets. A damaged man both physically and spiritually.

It was a full year before the old man had told him the truth of what the purpose was. Years more before he'd shared the details of the visions sent to him by God. For all that time, Scarvan planned his departure from the community of monks, plotted his return to the world where he would exact his revenge on the people who'd betrayed him. No one tried to stop him, especially not Father Spiros. But as time went on and his injuries healed, the unexpected thing happened.

His soul began to heal as well. God became a possibility, an idea he'd abandoned as a child when the travesty of man's inhumanity made it clear to him that God did not exist. And if God did not exist, then what was the point of worrying about a soul? This conclusion, and the certainty with which he'd reached it early in life, had given him the license he needed to become the world's foremost killer. Ruthless. Heartless. Cruel. Completely without any moral compunction about the tasks he deemed necessary to achieve a goal.

Only a man without a care for his soul could burn children alive one by one in front of their father just to exact punishment.

But Father Spiros somehow showed him the soul did exist and, in the process, slowly led Scarvan to faith in God.

Not the New Testament God, the one Constantine had given the world with his New Testament curated to appeal to the masses. Not the God of light with the love and forgiveness that blessed the meek and the downtrodden. His was the true God, the Old Testament God that loved discipline and obedience, that exacted vengeance on those who violated his commands.

Time went on and on, Scarvan always planning to leave the next week, and then the next month, and then the next year. But each day he stayed, he fell deeper and deeper into his new monastic life. He became first a believer, then a disciple, and then an instrument of God's will as revealed to Father Spiros in his visions.

When Scarvan received a vision of his own, he fought against the idea of it. It was a simple thing, not the torrent of images and ideas Father Spiros received, just a clear instruction not to leave Father Spiros's side until his death.

No, it had been more than instruction.

It had been a commandment from God Himself.

Father Spiros had gently questioned whether Scarvan had understood correctly. Or whether he could have mistaken a dream for a vision. Father Spiros wanted desperately to see the transformation of the world predicted to him and that would be made manifest by Scarvan's actions. And he needed Scarvan to leave Mt. Athos for that to happen.

But Scarvan was sure of the message so they both accepted it. At that time, neither of them could have guessed it would have meant too long of a wait. But Father Spiros had not only been given the gift of visions of the future from his Creator, but the gift of longevity as well. Satisfying his obedience to God, waiting for Father Spiros to die, had meant Scarvan was now an old man.

But, like the God he served, he'd not lost his desire for vengeance.

As he watched Scott and Mara walk down the narrow street back to their vantage point across from Belchik's apartment, he felt the old version of himself flex against his self-imposed rules. He wanted their blood now. Could so easily have it. But they were part of a larger plan, so he would have to wait.

Just as he was about to move position, he saw another figure step from a doorway farther down the street. Instinctively, he drew back deeper into the shadow and watched. There was something immediately familiar about the way the person walked. But it wasn't until he passed by a streetlight that he could confirm his suspicion. The man turned his head away from the CTV camera that watched the road, a move that gave Scarvan a clear view of his face.

He frowned at what he saw. This complicated matters a bit. He knew this man, knew how dangerous he could be. And that reputation was from when the man had been only a boy. Twenty or twenty-one. Surely his skills and lethality had only increased over the last two decades. He wondered if he was there to shadow Scott and Mara Roberts, or to kill them.

If the former, he would need to be careful to work around him.

If the latter, then that was just unacceptable.

They were Scarvan's to kill, no one else's.

CHAPTER 12

A second-floor studio apartment in the building next to their base of operations was the drop point for the courier. Scott and Mara stopped outside the building, as close to the room as possible. Mara pulled out her phone and activated an app that opened the camera she'd placed in the studio. She panned it back and forth, knowing the tiny camera's movements would be barely noticeable from the light fixture where she'd hidden it.

The room was empty except for three duffel bags in the middle of the hardwood floor. They were laid in perfect order, one right next to the other, each bag's handles tented together. *Someone was a little OCD*, Mara thought.

She slid her finger across the screen and the image flickered as she sped back in time. There was a split second of motion and then the bags disappeared. Mara stopped and rolled the image forward until the door to the studio apartment opened. A man in a hat and long coat walked in carrying a bag in each hand and one strapped to his back. She knew what was in them and knew they had to be heavy, but the man moved like the weight didn't bother him at all. He placed the bags on the floor, then stood back and looked at them. He nudged the bags forward until they were in a perfect line, then leaned down and lifted the handles to tent them together. Once he was done, he pulled his hat down low over his eyes and walked to the door. At the last second, he pointed directly at the camera Mara had gone to great lengths to conceal and gave them a little wave.

"That's no usual courier," Scott said.

"An operator, by the way he handles himself," Mara said. "Hawthorn's taking no chances."

"Considering what's in the bags, I'm surprised he didn't send a tank to deliver them."

Mara turned her phone off. Together they entered the building, retrieved the bags, and returned to their apartment with the line-of-sight view of Belchik's place. Carefully, they unpacked the silver canisters, hoses, and other equipment and took inventory.

"They sent extra for good measure. That's going to be a pain to dispose of when we're done," Scott said. "But that will be someone else's problem."

"Maybe we should just use it up."

"Too much could be dangerous."

Mara nodded. They'd agreed this was to be nonlethal. The bodyguards weren't combatants. They were just men and women doing their jobs.

"If we're wrong about Belchik's setup, we're going to be in trouble," Mara said.

"I talked to the medical team stateside, they agree with our assessment of how he'll be hooked up overnight," Scott said.

Mara opened the laptop on the single table in the apartment. The image of the front of the Belchik townhome filled the screen with a timestamp on the bottom-left corner. Just as she'd done with the video of the studio apartment, she scrolled through time, checking over the last hour they'd been gone.

"No arrivals or departures," she said. "Looks like they're buttoned down for the night."

"Then let's get to work."

They repacked the supplies, this time fitting the items they needed into two bags, leaving the excess in the third. Scott tried to pick up both bags, but Mara stopped him.

"Oh please," she said, grabbing one of the bags. "That's all we need is you throwing your back out."

"Hey, be nice to your elders," he said.

They both knew he could easily carry the bags, just like they knew Mara wouldn't ever do less than carry her own weight on a mission. But the easy joking released the pre-mission tension.

"Right, off we go," Scott said. "Just father-daughter back-packers carrying chemical weapons through a major European town. What could possibly go wrong?"

"Everything and anything," she said, smiling as she double-checked her Sig Sauer P226 and her Sig Sauer P365 micro-compact backup weapon in her ankle holster. "Just like always."

They left the apartment and began the walk toward the bridge. The crowds were sparse compared to the tourist high season. Unlike the scorching heat of the midsummer, September turned cooler and more forgiving. Even well after midnight, there were still plenty of people out enjoying the night air and working off the heavy dinners and drinks that typically didn't start until ten o'clock at night.

They made short work of the distance to the Puente de San Telmo, a nondescript bridge connecting Triana with the old section of Seville. The Guadalquivir rolled casually beneath them, dark and silent, heading toward the port of Cadiz over fifty miles away. The narrow river was surprisingly deep and was the reason Seville had once been one of the richest cities in all of Spain. The trade ships from the New World, often carrying the spoils of the conquistadores, sailed the length of the river after making their long journey across the ocean. The port deep inland proved to be an effective protection from pirates and countries jealous of Spain's gold. Mara wondered if Belchik's affinity for the city was somehow driven by this idea of safe haven. She knew from his dossier that he was not only one of the greatest spy handlers of all time, but a serious historian as well. He would have known the history of this place as well as anyone.

On the bridge, she took notice of the hundreds of padlocks attached to the railings. It was a trend in nearly every European city now. Lovers would bring their own or purchase a padlock from one of the many stores around the bridge, write their names on it, then lock it onto the railing. After doing so, the key would be ceremoniously thrown into the river below. The idea was to show the permanence of the love. Although, like most relationships, permanence was more an abstract idea than a reality. Mara had read that the locks on the famous Pont Neuf in Paris had been removed when engineers realized that the padlocks were adding forty-five tons of weight to the bridge. All that love came at a cost. But Mara couldn't help but imagine being on the bridge with Rick, maybe drunk on good wine and each other's company, attaching a padlock and sending the key into the water below. The thought filled her with a warmth that made her smile.

"Head in the game," Scott said next to her.

She didn't bother objecting because he was right. She'd slowed down considerably without noticing it, looking at the padlocks. There was a balance between relaxing her mind to fight the tension and being complacent. She pushed Rick from her thoughts and focused on the matter at hand.

They left the bridge and turned left, keeping to the lower level of the pedestrian walkway along the river. The Torre del Oro rose up on their right, beautifully lit, showing off its eight-hundred-year-old stonework. They walked another two hundred yards before using a staircase to climb up to the Paseo de Cristóbal Colón, directly across from their target. They scanned for any protective detail positioned on the street but saw none.

They went right, skirting away from the entrance door, then crossed to the Calle dos de Mayo, the small street after the block of apartment buildings. Just behind the buildings was the small alley Calle Velarde. Deserted at this hour as they assumed it would be.

They paused at the corner and Mara pulled what looked like a small pen flashlight from her pocket. She took aim at the camera positioned above them and pressed a button. A powerful laser hit the wall next to the camera. She adjusted and shined the light directly into the camera lens for only a few seconds. That was enough. The lens would never work again.

They moved with precision, all business. Scott found the wires leading to the security system near the rear door and attached a clamp, bypassing the circuit before cutting the main feed. It was a low-quality system and easily fooled. Much easier than the system on Belchik's apartment would have been three units down from where they stood.

Once the wires were cut, Mara picked the lock and went in, Scott right behind her. This last unit of the building was a travel agency, making it the perfect entry point.

"Stairs are over here," Scott said.

They passed the desks and the walls covered with posters of exotic beaches and world capitals and headed up the staircase. From their long-range optics, they knew the upper levels were executive offices and storage areas so they didn't expect to run into anyone.

So, it was a shock when they saw two bodies sprawled on an air mattress in the middle of the first office on the second floor.

Two very naked bodies.

A quick look around the room told the story. An older man and a younger woman. Two bottles of wine. Clothes thrown around the room. A half-dozen unlit candles, which they'd at least had the presence of mind to extinguish before passing out.

Mara pulled a thin hood down over her face and saw Scott do the same. They couldn't leave them here, but they of course couldn't hurt them, either. She pulled zip-tie cuffs from her pocket and Scott pulled off two strips of duct tape.

"Hey, wake up," he said.

The man stirred first, groggy and disoriented. Mara shined a flashlight in his eyes, and he got clear in a hurry.

"Wh-what is this? Who are you?" he stammered in Spanish.

"Your wife sent us," Mara replied, noticing his wedding band. "She's not very happy with the hours you're keeping at the office."

Scott grabbed the man and shoved a piece of cloth into his

mouth and then duct-taped it shut. Mara threw him a zip tie and he secured the man's arms behind his back. The man whimpered pathetically, hanging his head.

Mara kneeled on the floor next to the girl. She was pretty, mid-twenties, and certainly could do better than an overweight guy in his mid-forties. Just to check her bias, she confirmed there wasn't a wedding ring on the girl's finger.

"Hey sweetie, time to wake up," she said.

The girl smiled but kept her eyes closed. She reached out like she might kiss Mara. But when she felt the mask covering Mara's face, her eyes bolted open.

"Hi," Mara said.

The girl drew in a deep breath and Mara knew a scream was coming next unless she hurried. A bit more forcefully than she wanted, she slapped a hand over her mouth, using her other hand to hold her down.

"Shhh . . ." she said. "No one's going to hurt you. Just relax, okay? We're here to teach him a lesson, not you."

The girl froze and then nodded.

Mara took a piece of tape from Scott and placed it over her mouth. She let her pull on a pair of pants and a shirt before sitting them together next to a desk and cuffing them to it as well.

"Your wife was suspicious, so she hired us," Scott said. "If you promise to get your shit together and be a good husband, we'll tell her we didn't find anything. Can you do that?"

The man nodded, still whimpering.

"You tell anyone we were here, we'll tell her the truth. Got it?" he said.

"Does this girl work for you?" Mara asked.

The man nodded again.

"She gets a raise. Fifty percent." The man's eyes went wide. "Really?" Mara said. "You want to bargain with me?" The man cowered and shook his head. Mara leaned in toward the girl. "You can't tell anyone either. Understand?" The girl agreed. "All right, someone will come let you out when we're gone. Just hold tight."

She followed Scott, who had already walked over to the stairs to take them to the next level. They both lifted their masks, so they rested on their foreheads, and shared a silent laugh.

"What are the chances?" Scott asked.

"I think that story will work, though. Keep them from talking."

"At least for a while," he said. "As long as they aren't being questioned in the investigation of a father-daughter strike team that was killed while entering the home of a former KGB boss, then I think we're good."

They climbed the stairs two more levels and came to the door that accessed the roof.

"Don't know if there's recon sat imagery locked on this place, so go mask," he said.

Mara pulled her mask back down and Scott opened the door onto the night.

The roof was empty except for a few storage sheds and two wicker chairs with a coffee can half-filled with sand and cigarette butts. Looked like the perfect place for the travel agency employees to take a break when they weren't sleeping with each other.

They made their way to the low wall dividing the units, giving the next rooftop some privacy. Scott jumped over the wall and Mara handed the duffel bags over to him before jumping over herself. This roof belonged to a private residence and it showed. Potted plants lined the edges of the roof and a small marble fountain sat in the center surrounded by comfortable chairs with thick cushions. A little oasis in the Spanish heat during the day.

They cleared this roof, repeating the process of climbing over and handing across their bags twice more before coming to Belchik's property.

Even though Mara had been keeping close count of which unit she was on, it wasn't necessary. His was the only roof wall with strands of razor wire across its top.

Mara dug into her bag and pulled out her night-vision goggles, an upgraded version of L3's ENVG-B, the "E" standing for "enhanced." This cutting-edge tech was a hybrid system that included a separate thermal channel for image fusion and thermal target-detection capabilities. With all the ambient light, she could see well enough, but it was the invisible light she was looking for. She switched the ENVG to a specialized setting and scanned the roof for laser trip wires.

Nothing.

These guys were sloppy.

While Scott clipped the razor wire, she pulled out a broadband RF scanner calibrated for 50 MHz to 3GHz. She doubted any cameras set up on the roof were hardwired when wireless models were so much simpler to use. The problem with those was that their communications exit linking them back to the network was simple to track. The encryption was likely state of the art, but Mara didn't need to see the image, she just needed to know where the cameras were located.

The scanner lit up and Mara was able to dial it in directionally to pick up four cameras. Scott armed the laser this time and systematically fried their processors. Depending on the man on duty, there was a chance that the roof cameras going offline could elicit an immediate response. But judging from what they'd seen of this crew on deathwatch, they didn't think anyone would rush up. But just in case, they crossed quickly and took a position next to the door. Mara stood guard while Scott set up the rest of their equipment.

She checked her watch. One forty-three. Thirteen minutes behind their predicted timeline, thanks to the lovers in building one. It was all right. There was no extraction team or deadline they were racing against. Still, out of professional pride, she hated being off-schedule.

Scott placed a canister next to each of the air-conditioning units on the roof. They'd counted four from their lookout point. Full building air-conditioning was uncommon in Seville; most relied on opening windows to catch the breeze off the river and maybe a window unit or two to cool a single room for the hottest days. Apparently, Belchik liked his comfort and his security. His home's massive system explained the shuttered windows. The creature comfort was going to cost his protective detail.

Mara grabbed a metal folding chair and wedged it against the door that opened onto the roof. She grinned, thinking of the tens of thousands of dollars of specialized equipment the courier had delivered to them, and that a chair was still the best solution to secure the door.

"What do you want me to do?" she asked Scott.

He stole a quick glance at the door. Seeing the chair brought a smile to his face, too. "Canisters are in position. I have the pumps and hoses on this one. You do the back two."

Mara scurried over to the air-conditioning unit nearest the back wall and got to work. The setup was intuitive and, in true military fashion, designed to be dummy-proof. The hose connections were marked with a shape that corresponded to the same shape on the unit it was being attached to. Mara appreciated the designer in some faraway lab who had thought to make the process as easy as possible.

The pump was small, a black rectangular box the size of a loaf of bread. The canister hose snapped into one end and the delivery hose snapped into the other. She made certain the connections were tight. Any leakage would bring the night's activities to an end real fast.

On the end of the delivery hose, she attached the last piece, a large bag of stretchy material. This she placed over the top of the air-conditioning unit, pulling it first across its length, then down its sides. Once it covered the entire thing, she tugged on a cinch at the bottom and then pressed all around the edge, knowing the adhesive inside the bag would create a strong, airtight seal.

She moved to the next unit and completed the same process.

Scott finished his two first and came over to help her.

"Ready?" Scott asked when they'd pulled the cover tight.

Mara nodded, pulling out her Sig Sauer. "Showtime."

CHAPTER 13

Demetri Isimov hated this assignment.

He'd been hopeful at first when his supervisor had informed him of the duty, whispering the name of the new protectee. Viktor Belchik was a monolithic figure not only in Russian intelligence but in Russian history. A man with hands that stretched into every corner of the world. Isimov had imagined getting to know the great man, being a sounding board for stories of the glory days of the KGB. Perhaps even gaining the man's favor in a way that could lead to introductions and advancement.

None of that had come true.

In two months of duty, he'd said only a few words to the man. Mostly in greeting or asking for instructions. The responses came back in either grunts or a short, barked order, but never with even a moment of eye contact.

And then the poisoning happened. No one was certain how, but suspicions had gone immediately to the trip Belchik had taken to the hospital clinic next door for an MRI. Everything else for the man's cancer treatment could be brought to the town house, but the MRI to see whether the immunotherapy treatment was having any effect on the lung cancer could not. Isimov had been off rotation that day, enjoying the sun in Cadiz. Lucky for him because the team that failed to protect him were now stationed in obscure facilities in one of the -stan countries watching over crumbling nuclear facilities in the middle of nowhere. Nothing said career end like being on post when one of Russia's greatest men was poisoned.

The investigation turned up minute traces of polonium in the hospital. Not enough to injure anyone there. Just enough to confirm that was where the assault had taken place.

And that's what it was, an assault. Isimov knew of the FSB's use of polonium as a weapon of assassination. After the events in England years earlier, the whole world knew it. But seeing the ravages of the radiation poisoning firsthand had been terrible. The sores. The hair loss. Bleeding gums. The rheumy eyes.

Not only that, but the idea of poisoning an already dying man seemed cruel and unnecessary. Then again, a man like Belchik had created his share of powerful enemies over his life. That one would want him to die a slow, painful death wasn't too surprising.

What had been surprising was the series of events that had followed the poisoning. Things had gotten so bad that some of them had started to lie to the old man, sheltering him from the terrible news from the outside world. It didn't take a genius to determine that whoever had poisoned Belchik had meant that as only the first step in his torment. What had happened afterward, and continued to happen every other day with numbing regularity, showed they were dealing with a sick mind.

Isimov just hoped whoever it was had moved on. And, in a reversal that surprised even himself, he wished the old man would just die and get it over with.

He walked into the kitchen and rooted around the refrigerator for something to eat. He was the only one still up. Demitri Golav was supposed to be on watch with him, but the older man was even more done with this assignment than he was. All of them had been lowered to being nursemaids to the old man when the medical staff was off duty, tending to him, assisting the staff cleaning his shriveled body when he defecated in his bed.

The two medical staff were sleeping upstairs, a man and woman who Isimov heard having sex earlier that night. The sounds didn't offend him, only made him horny and lonely. Five minutes alone in the bathroom got rid of the horniness but only made the loneliness more acute. Next time, he thought, maybe he'd see about joining the two upstairs. He knew it was a pipe dream, but it at least gave him something to think about to pass the time.

Golav could be heard snoring in the other room, sprawled out on a couch, a bottle of vodka half-stuffed into the cushion next to him. The other two men on the protection team were sleeping downstairs, but their shift started at six in the morning. Golav was a derelict, an embarrassment to the team.

And no one cared.

Belchik was a dead man. In fact, all of them had participated in a whispered conversation that if the old man tried to commit suicide again, they should just let him. They'd sworn a pact, but it was one Isimov knew he couldn't follow. Part of it was self-preservation. His orders were to keep the man alive. If Belchik were to kill himself under his watch, then it would reflect on Isimov's record forever. Apparently, the powers-that-be didn't want their hero's end to be a story of suicide. Bad for morale, Isimov thought glumly.

As if dying of polonium poisoning at the hands of a madman was any better.

But the other reason he couldn't bring himself to look the other way when Belchik tried to steal a length of cord or a scalpel from the visiting doctor's bag was his remaining affection for the man. Or at least the larger-than-life legend of the man. Isimov believed in God. He understood the penalty for suicide and, in his hero's moment of weakness, didn't want to think of him enduring everlasting damnation for a single act of cowardice at the end of a life of bravery and accomplishment.

So, he watched closely. Made certain there was nothing within Belchik's reach that he could use to do himself in. And, with the others, he waited for the radiation poison to do its slow, nasty work. Cringing every other day when the news inevitably came from Moscow of the next tragedy in Belchik's life. The tragedies he'd wanted to keep from him, but which Golav insisted they share whenever he got wind of them. It was the only part of the assignment the senior man enjoyed.

A loud beeping sound startled Isimov. A burst of adrenaline entered his system. An alarm. Someone was infiltrating the apartment.

But he quickly realized it was nothing of the sort. It was just the refrigerator door. He'd been standing with it open, absently staring at the contents, not really hungry, not really seeing what was inside. Just on the autopilot that happened in the middle of the night when the boredom set in.

He closed the door and opened the freezer. He pulled back the small bags of ice there to reveal three bottles of vodka. It wasn't a good hiding place, but the ice in front at least gave the appearance that they gave a shit if one of the medical staff happened to open the freezer.

He twisted the cap and took a long drink from the bottle, feeling the fire in his throat spread through his chest as a warm heat. It felt like coming home, even though it was laced with the sense of guilt from drinking while on duty.

Isimov put the bottle back and piled the ice back up in front of it.

He took a staggered step back, suddenly dizzy.

He laughed at himself. Maybe he should have eaten something. The single drink had hit him like he was a teenager.

Blinking hard, he shook his head to clear it, but that only threw him more off-balance.

His throat and nose burned.

It took him a second to recognize it as something more than just the vodka. The sensation was too strong. Too intense.

Something was wrong.

He tried to run to the living room to wake Golav but he only made it a few steps before his legs buckled under him.

He hit the floor hard, still in control enough to twist his body so that his shoulder took the impact instead of his face.

For some reason his arms weren't working.

He blinked hard again, his eyes tearing up. His throat constricting.

Poison.

The vodka had to be poison.

But that was impossible. He'd seen the others drink from the same bottle earlier.

Then something else happened.

He tried to lift his head to scan the room but was only able to move it a few inches.

Terror raced through him. There were two men in the room. Dressed in black. Gas masks covering their faces.

That was it. Why he was on the floor. They'd used gas. All of them would be out.

Isimov knew they were here to kill Belchik. And there was nothing he could do about it.

As he closed his eyes and lost consciousness, his last hope was that they would make it quick and painless.

The ending his hero deserved.

CHAPTER 14

Scott trained his gun on the bodyguard sprawled on the kitchen floor. There'd been a moment when it seemed like the man was going to have enough fight left in him to pull his weapon, but he'd succumbed to the gas and fallen to the floor.

He nudged the man with his foot. Totally out.

The GX gas was powerful, a variant of the knockout agent developed by the Russians. The public knew it from the 2002 Dubrovka Theater hostage crisis in Moscow. Chechnyan separatists had taken 850 hostages. After a long standoff, Russian Special Forces had piped an undisclosed chemical agent into the opera house. But it had two problems. The first was that it created panic as the separatists watched it come in and started firing wildly in reaction. Secondly was that while it successfully rendered all the occupants of the opera house unconscious, for over two hundred of the hostages, it turned out to be permanent.

Langley had taken notice and went to great lengths to procure exactly what the Russian Special Forces had used. After much testing and adjustment, they'd perfected a variant that was powerful enough to overwhelm an adversary quickly, but without the fatality rate or long-term effects.

GX had proven useful on a number of missions. The last time

he and Mara had used it had been to kidnap the ex-president of the United States, still a sore spot with the Secret Service.

Mara's voice came over the speaker in his left ear. "One on the couch. He's out."

That made four so far. The two medical staff upstairs, passed out in the same bed together. Two bodyguards here. One floor to go.

He and Mara worked their way through the room in a two-by-two cover motion. They each had guns drawn, fitted with a red-dot laser sighting unit that crisscrossed the apartment, searching every corner and behind every piece of furniture for an adversary.

Clear.

Mara went down the last flight of stairs first. "Careful," he whispered, knowing she would hear it clearly in her ear mic.

He knew the warning likely annoyed her, but she did slow down just a fraction.

The lower level opened to a wide foyer of marble columns. It was more ornate than the other levels, a formal entry to impress guests. A metal desk with two open laptops on it was positioned at the base of the stairs with only a narrow space through which someone might walk. The laptop screens were partitioned into grids, each box a different camera feed. Four of the boxes were black—the cameras they'd taken out on the roof. Clear evidence there was an issue, only there was no one monitoring the screens to raise the alarm.

Scott toggled through the other feeds, enlarging each in turn, looking for anyone else in the building. He paused on the image of Belchik's room, smiling as his hopes were confirmed.

"Moving to the last rooms," Mara said.

"Let me see if they are on the feed," he said.

From his peripheral vision, he saw Mara move across the room. He quickly stamped his fingers on the keyboard, trying to find the right room.

Just as he found it, Mara said, "Going in."

Scott squinted at the screen. It was sparsely furnished. Just a bed and a small table. There appeared to be a man asleep under the sheets, probably passed out from the GX. The door opened and he saw Mara step into the room.

But then Scott spotted something wrong.

The two windows above the bed were wide open.

The meant fresh air.

"Mara, wait!"

Scott shoved the table away and ran toward the room. As he did, he heard the first shot fired. Then another. The unmistakable hiss of a suppressor.

When he got to the door, Mara was locked in a grappling hold with a large man. He had her by the lower arm and one hand on her neck. She looked small next to the man's hulking frame, but Scott relaxed. Neither hand held a gun. Even with his size, he posed little threat to Mara.

"Need help?" he said, needling her.

The big man turned his head just a fraction on seeing Scott enter the room.

It was all Mara needed.

She shifted her weight and ducked down, at the same time landing a bone-crunching kick to the man's knee. He bent over in pain. But on the way down, there was more pain waiting for him. Mara's knee slammed into the bodyguard's face, shattering his nose and signaling to his brain that it was time to take a little break from the world. He fell back, out cold.

"No," Mara deadpanned. "I've got it."

They gagged and cuffed the man and cleared the rest of the downstairs.

"I saw Belchik on the monitor," he told her. "We're in good shape."

"Great," she said. "Let's go see what was so important that he couldn't just tell Hawthorn in a letter like a normal person."

They worked their way upstairs, opening windows as they did to dispel the gas. The bodyguards would be out for at least an hour, but they cuffed and gagged each of them as a precaution.

Once on the upper floor, they entered Belchik's room. Even through their masks, the smell of the room was pungent. It reminded Scott of walking into a public restroom that'd been recently doused with antiseptic cleaning fluids. Even the chemicals couldn't mask the smell of death and decay.

Belchik was in a hospital bed, inclined at a forty-five-degree angle. Monitors flanked each side, giving real-time readouts of his heart functions and respiration. Wires snaked from the machines, disappearing under the thin sheets to different parts of his body. Most importantly, as hoped, an oxygen mask was strapped to his face, covering both his nose and mouth.

Mara opened the windows in the room and shut the door behind them. The canisters on the roof were long finished dispensing the GX, so it wouldn't be long before the room was clear.

As Scott walked closer to the bed, he was struck by how old and frail Belchik looked. He remembered him clearly from the ship on the Aegean, the night he'd shot Scarvan, thinking him dead and buried in the sea. He'd been old even then, toward the end of his career. But he'd been sharp, calculating. A wolf walking in a world of lambs. Beyond that one meeting, he was a student of Belchik's operations, of his ruthless control of power inside first the USSR and then the Russian Federation. Even under the cult of personality of Vladimir Putin, Belchik had thrived.

But now he wasn't much more than a corpse. Without the monitor showing a weak heartbeat, Scott would have bet good money he was looking at a dead man.

In photos as recent as a year ago, Belchik had the puffy look of a man swollen from too much good food and wine. All that was gone now. His cheeks were sunk in, his blotched skin stretched tight against bone. His eyes, even closed, were dark pits. Almost glistening purple like a nasty bruise. His sheets had a spattering of blood on them and, on closer inspection, so did the inside of his oxygen mask. His hair was gone completely, revealing inky marks and sores that would never heal. His arms rested on top of the sheet. They looked like sticks wrapped in pale parchment paper, torn in places, bandaged with gauze wraps stained with yellow pus.

Mara pulled a gauge from her pocket, another nice present from the folks in the CIA labs, and measured the air. She nodded at Scott and pulled off her mask.

As was protocol, Scott waited as Mara breathed the air. If they'd miscalculated and she felt the effects of the GX, she would put her mask back on. If they'd really gotten it wrong and she passed out, he'd be able to carry her out.

After a full minute of deep breathing, Mara flashed the okay sign and he removed his own mask. He gave Mara a second to set up the small video camera to capture the interview with Belchik and then he gently shook the old man's bony shoulder.

"Belchik," he said, whispering into the man's ear. "Wake up, sir. Jim Hawthorn sent us to talk to you. Sir, can you hear me?"

The old man's eyes fluttered open. Scott winced at the sight of them. It was troubling enough the way they rolled in their sockets, unfocused and afraid. But it was the man's sclera that caught him off guard. Instead of being white, they had hemorrhaged and filled with blood, giving him a demonic look.

But Belchik's eyes settled and then turned toward Scott and focused. In the moment, Scott saw the same intensity and intelligence that had been there years before. Despite the man's ravaged body, he was still in there.

"Too late," Belchik said, his voice muffled by the oxygen mask. "To save the world, I'm afraid you have come too late."

CHAPTER 15

Belchik motioned weakly with a frail hand for Scott to remove his oxygen mask. He did so, glancing at the heart monitor to find where the pulse ox value was indicated. It was in the mid-90s with the mask. If it dropped too low without it, the resulting hypoxemia would render Belchik useless.

"What day is it?" Belchik said, his once powerful and commanding voice now thin and quavering.

"Thursday," Mara said.

"Thursday . . . Thursday . . ." Belchik mumbled, closing his eyes and groaning. "Why did it take you so long, Jim?"

Scott and Mara exchanged glances, both worried that after all their efforts, they were going to be speaking to a man without his full faculties.

"Jim Hawthorn's not here," Scott said. "This is Scott Roberts. Jim sent me to speak to you."

Belchik's eyes shot open. He slowly turned his head, lasered in on Scott, and said in a perfect, deadpan voice, "No shit."

Mara let out a laugh. Scott was relieved. Seemed the old spymaster still had some fight in him.

"Sir, you said in your letter to Director Hawthorn that you had information about Jacobslav Scarvan. Can you tell—"

Belchik held up a hand. "Wait . . . wait . . ." he said. "There had to be news yesterday. Where are my guards?" He shot a look at Mara. "You didn't kill them, did you? They are good men."

"No one was hurt," Mara said. "But they're out until morning. They might be good men, but they aren't very adept at their jobs."

Belchik grunted. "Guarding a corpse. Who can blame them?"

"The polonium," Scott said. "That was Scarvan?"

Belchik laughed. It created a deep, phlegmy sound and made the old man wince in pain. "The bastard always had a cruel streak in him. But this"—he made a motion toward his decaying body—"this was only part of his plan for me."

"What do you mean?" Mara asked.

Belchik pointed to a table against the wall. On it were framed photos of family members. Some old, a brother or sister perhaps. Others just youngsters, likely grandchildren. "After I was poisoned, my brother was in a terrible traffic accident in Saint Petersburg. Died instantly. Because of my ... condition ... I couldn't even go to his funeral. Two days later, my niece Liliya was alone in her apartment in Moscow where she choked on some food and died." Belchik paused, his lower lip trembling. "Two days after, it was my youngest grandchild. A drowning accident was the report this time. That boy was a fine swimmer. Strong. Healthy. How could he drown like that?"

"Scarvan?" Mara asked.

"Two days later, another. And another," Belchik said, the tremble in his voice still there, but now edged with incredible anger. "Another member of my family. Another so-called accident."

Scott looked at the full table with a rising sense of horror. There had to be over a dozen photos on the table. He looked back at Belchik's wrapped wrists, understanding the significance now. "You tried to end it," he said. "Thinking it'll stop when you're dead."

The old spymaster nodded. "My guards will not allow it. Some misguided sense of duty. Or orders from on high that the Kremlin does not want the story of Viktor Belchik taking his own life. That's why it was so important that you come."

"I don't understand," Mara said.

"I have information about Jacobslav Scarvan and in exchange"—he took a deep shuddering breath—"you must agree to kill me."

Scott and Mara exchanged a look. This wasn't part of their mission or anywhere on the table. Certainly, Moscow would piece together who had broken into the apartment for a clandestine meeting with their old spymaster. Maybe not them specifically, but that it was the United States would be their first guess. They wouldn't like it, but what would they be able to do about it?

But if they left Belchik dead, that would turn the tremors from Moscow into an earthquake.

Still, they needed to get the information from the old man.

"I'm not going to promise something I can't deliver," Scott said. "Tell me what you know, and then we will discuss it."

Belchik closed his eyes. "I understand this puts you in a terrible position. One Hawthorn would never have put you in if I'd indicated this was my purpose in the letter I sent."

"It can't be done," Mara said.

He opened his eyes and stared her down, fixating on the camera she held. "Then I will do it. You can film my last words as a record, removing all doubt that this was my own act. All I ask is that you leave me with the tools to finish what I started. Only then will Scarvan stop killing my family members. Don't you see? I have to do this. Look at them. Look at the photos."

Scott eyed the monitors next to Belchik's bed. The man's heart rate was pounding and erratic. His oxygen level down to eighty-two percent.

He placed a hand on the old man's forearm. It felt dry and scaly, like a reptile.

"Tell us about Scarvan and we will help you end this nightmare you're in," Scott said. "I swear it."

Belchik relaxed. He waved for Scott to put his oxygen mask back on. Once in place, he took long, phlegmy breaths and his oxygen level on the monitor slowly rose.

"Hawthorn always told me your word was one of the few

things in the world he trusted absolutely," Belchik said. "I hope he was correct."

"He was," Scott said. "Now, tell us what you learned about Scarvan that had you so concerned."

Mara stepped closer, making sure the audio was captured.

"I went to hospital for a scan. The kind where you drink barium fluids to coat your organs so the cancer flashes bright. Before he did this to me, I thought managing cancer was a terrible thing." He let out a derisive laugh. "It is nothing compared to this. Nothing."

"Is that where Scarvan came to you?" Mara said, trying to keep the old man on track.

"Yes, when I came out of the machine, the technician was gone. In front of me stood a ghost. He's an old man now, like I am, but worse. He wears a long beard, curly and wild. His face is like that of a farmer, beaten by decades in the sun. So wrinkled and creased that the younger man he once was is almost impossible to see. But his eyes, they are the same. Intelligent, cruel, burning with hate.

"He asked me if I knew who he was. His voice chilled me. But then, it always did. I called him by name, asking how in God's name he had survived. He smiled at the question, pointing upward. 'Yes, it was in God's name that I survived. And it is in God's name that I now live out my purpose.'"

Scott shifted uncomfortably. Nothing in Scarvan's dossier suggested the man was religious. If anything, he was the opposite. This reference to religion was troubling. Belchik must have picked up on Scott's expression.

"My face must have looked much like yours now," he said. "I've dealt with zealots before, we all have in our business. There's something in the eyes, like a fever, that burns inside the true believer. I saw this in Scarvan's eyes. And it scared me."

"He was there to kill you," Mara said.

"Yes, of that much I was certain," Belchik said. "But I'm an old man, already sick. That did not scare me. To be honest, I actually felt some relief at the idea. Before I knew how he would do it, of course."

"We need to know what he told you," Scott said. The longer they were in the apartment, the greater the likelihood something could go wrong. Another shift could arrive. There could be a check-in call they weren't aware existed that was missed. They needed to move things along.

"I will tell you," he said. "But first, I'll tell you that seeing him also gave me something I'd craved for twenty years. The chance to say I was sorry." He arched an eyebrow at Scott. "Like you, I've seen terrible things in the world. Done terrible things. But this . . . this betrayal, it never sat right with me. Has it with you?"

Scott swallowed hard, a dozen or more horrific images jumping to the front of his mind with terrifying intensity. The simple suggestion that he and Belchik were cut from the same cloth and carried the same skeletons was enough to dredge them up. He pushed them all away, a skill honed over a lifetime of practice. Operatives who never mastered the art ended up going crazy or ending it all once the burden became too heavy.

But he allowed the feeling about Scarvan to remain. He turned over the guilt he'd felt back then over participating in the man's execution. The conversation before the mission with Jim Hawthorn about whether he was confusing justice with revenge. How it felt to pull the trigger and watch the man stumble and then jump to his death over the railing of the ship.

Only not to his death. That part needed to be recalibrated in his mind. He had in fact not killed Jacobslav Scarvan in cold blood. Only wounded him.

Something told him that before it was all said and done, he would have another chance to finish the job. Unless Scarvan was still as good as he once was, and then the killing might go the other way.

"No," Scott lied. "I never felt guilt about what we did that night. What he did to that family was unacceptable. He deserved what he got."

Belchik looked him over, as if evaluating why Scott told the lie he had. Something told him the old spymaster could see right through him, better than any polygraph ever could.

"Then you are a stronger man than I," Belchik said. "I lived the with guilt for these last twenty years. I could have warned him off somehow. Could have appeased Hawthorn and my bosses above in some other way. Seeing him allowed me to say all this to him."

"Did he believe you?" Mara asked.

Belchik shrugged. "I don't know. Is that necessary?"

"I think it helps," she said. "If your goal is forgiveness."

"Forgiveness," Belchik whispered. "The thought hadn't crossed my mind."

Scott checked his watch. This was taking too long. "Sir, I appreciate this has to be very hard for you, but you understand more than most the position we're in right now. If you could just—"

"Of course," he said. "My apologies. You've been very patient with me. Scarvan's plan is to kill everyone involved with his betrayal. I'm certain your own intelligence services have already found links between Scarvan and recent deaths around the world." He glanced at Mara, reading her face. "Yes, of course they have. For some it was a fast death. For others, it's a deeper punishment." He raised a trembling hand at Scott. "I don't know what he plans for you and Hawthorn, but it will not be quick, I can assure you."

"I'll worry about that," Scott said. "But you said we were too late for the world. What did you mean by that?"

"His revenge is only a sideshow," Belchik said. "A personal battle while he prepares for war."

"What kind of war?" Mara asked.

"A holy war. Nothing less than the destruction of civilization, the decapitation of the world's power."

"He plans to assassinate the president?" Mara said.

"You Americans are always the same," Belchik said. "Always making yourselves the sun around which the rest of us spin." With great effort, he leaned up in bed, stabbing the air with his finger to make his point. "He means to assassinate all of them.

Every president. Every prime minister. Every king. And he won't stop until he does so."

"Why?" Scott said. "Has he gone mad?"

Belchik fell back into the bed. "I asked him the same thing, and his response left me no closer to the answer."

"What did he say?" Mara asked.

"That God willed it," Belchik said. "And that he was no longer just a man, but an instrument of God, fulfilling His promise as shown to the Prophet Spiros."

"I'd say that answers the question as to whether he's gone off the deep end or not," Mara said.

Scott seized on the new name. "The Prophet Spiros? Does that mean anything to you?"

Belchik gave him a look of approval, as if impressed he'd grasped the one salient fact. "Not then, but now, yes. There was a monk, a hermit really, named Father Spiros. He died recently. He had a reputation for curious visions and apocryphal writing."

"Where did he live?" Mara asked.

"Mount Athos," Belchik said. "Do you know it?"

Mara shook her head no, but Scott just stared at the old man. "We were at least twenty miles off the coast that night," Scott said. "He was shot four times. How could he have possibly survived long enough in the open ocean to make it there?"

"If you asked the old Scarvan, it's because he's the toughest son of a bitch to walk the planet. He's indestructible."

"And what did the new Scarvan say?" Mara asked.

Belkin pulled back his lips from yellow, stained teeth as if the next word were a curse. "God," he said. "He was saved for a divine purpose. And now he's the vehicle for that purpose."

"How could killing heads of state be part of a divine purpose?" Scott asked. "Toward what goal?"

Again, Belchik looked like he approved. "I would have liked to have you under my command back in the old days," he said.

"What was his answer?" Mara asked.

"Somehow over the last two decades, Scarvan has become

convinced that he is the instrument to bring about the end times." Belchik's voice grew soft. "He believes his mission will do nothing less than bring about the second coming of Christ. He believes he has become the wrath of God made manifest on Earth."

Belchik laid his head back against his pillow and closed his eyes.

"Is there anything else?" Mara asked. "Any indication who his first target will be?"

Belchik shook his head, keeping his eyes closed. "That is everything. I've thought through the conversation a thousand times, but there is nothing more I can give you." He finally opened his eyes and they were filled with tears. "Now, you must do your part. You must kill me so I can save my family."

Scott felt the dreadful weight of the decision he had to make. He glanced over at the table covered with the photos of Belchik's family, the ones killed by Scarvan. Would the murders stop once Belchik was dead? Scarvan seemed to be a man no longer in touch with reality. Perhaps his vengeance would continue even if the old man were dead. Leaving the spymaster dead after their visit would complicate matters with the powers above him. But that had never stopped Scott from doing the right thing before.

Nor had it ever stopped Mara.

"How do you want it done?" Mara asked, her voice flat, the way it was when she was on mission.

Belchik looked surprised that the offer had come from her, but he didn't hesitate.

"A pillow over my face will suffice," he said. "No need to leave a mess behind."

Mara stepped forward but Scott waved her off. "This is my task," he said. "I played a part in creating this on that boat twenty years ago. It should be me."

He carefully slid the pillow from behind the old man's head and gripped it tight with both hands.

Belchik looked around the room, taking stock one last time

at the world he was about to leave. Then his eyes settled on Scott. "Tell Hawthorn thank you. That I always respected him as an adversary."

"I will."

"And Scarvan," he said. "Don't underestimate him. Even at his age, I believe he remains the most dangerous human on the planet. You must stop him. No matter the cost."

Scott bit the inside of his lip. He'd killed dozens of men in his life. Men who'd begged for mercy. Bargained for their lives. Shown him photos of their families to try to get him to change his mind. All of them wanted that one last minute of life, to hang on, to hope for some way out. He saw this same thing in Belchik.

"Tell me when you're ready, sir," he said.

Belchik looked at the table with the photos of his family one last time, then nodded.

Scott placed the pillow over the man's face and pressed down hard. Belchik didn't react at first, but his body soon responded involuntarily as his oxygen ran out. His back arched. His legs kicked. His emaciated hands reached up to the pillow and clawed at Scott's forearms.

But only for a few seconds.

Then the old man's body went slack. Scott held the pillow in place, watching the straight line on the heart monitor next to him.

When he lifted the pillow, Belchik's dead eyes stared at the ceiling. Mara stepped forward and carefully closed them.

"I know that was hard to do," she whispered. "But it was the right thing."

Scott appreciated the words. And appreciated that it was only hard because he still valued human life, that he hadn't slipped into the cynical psychopathy that was dangerous for those who stayed in his profession for too long. At least that was what he liked to tell himself.

"Let's get the hell out of here," he said.

They pulled their masks back on in case there were pockets of the GX gas lingering outside the room. They went back through the apartment the way they'd come. Up to the roof, over the walls separating the units, back down through the travel agency. Mara did the kindness of giving the woman cuffed to the desk with her married lover a letter opener from one of the desks so they could cut themselves free once they left.

They didn't need to take apart the surveillance setup across the river. Hawthorn would send another team to clean up their tracks.

Once they were back on the street, heading to the train station, Mara finally broke the silence.

"We need to brief Hawthorn about what happened here," Mara said. "Do you want me to call it in?"

Scott wondered exactly how shaken up he looked for her to offer that. He set his jaw, digging deep to find the devil-may-care persona that had served him so well over the years.

"No, I'll make it."

"He would have done the same thing for Belchik," she said. "You know that."

Scott wasn't as certain. Hawthorn was a good man, one of the best he'd ever met. But nothing was more important to him than protecting the United States of America. Helping Belchik end his life was going to complicate things with the Russians right when cooperation was going to be essential to stop Scarvan.

"Hawthorn will get a message out to the protective details for the heads of state across the world. We need to find out what radicalized Scarvan," he said. "See if we can get a clue about the target he'll hit first."

"We need to go to Mount Athos," Mara said.

"That should be interesting," Scott said.

"Why's that?"

"Mount Athos is a rugged isthmus of land only accessible by boat. It's home to Greek Orthodox monasteries and hermitages."

"And?"

"And there hasn't been a woman allowed on that soil in over five hundred years."

Mara grinned. "Then it's about time there was one."

"I figured that would be your response. Like I said, it should be interesting. You make the arrangements, I'll call Hawthorn. Meet in ten minutes."

"If you survive the call," she said. "Good luck with that."

He watched her walk into the train station, by habit eyeing the surrounding area to see if she picked up a tail. Nothing.

Reluctantly, he pulled the encrypted sat phone from his jacket and powered it up. As he waited for the device to synch with the satellites overhead, he tried to organize his thoughts. No matter how he played out the conversation in his head, Hawthorn was going to be pissed.

But then again, he'd spent a career pissing the man off, so Scott had to figure he was used to it by now.

A minute into his phone call, it turned out he was wrong.

CHAPTER 16

"Damn it, Scott," Hawthorn mumbled to himself as he walked up to the guard gate facing the Treasury Building on East Executive Avenue. The area was lit up by floodlights in front of the guard shack. Staffers worked late at the White House, but ten at night was slow. A few people were leaving but he was the only one going in.

He showed his credentials and then passed through the metal detector like everyone else. The White House was one of the most secure locations in the world. Even someone with his history of service wasn't given a free pass.

The uniformed Secret Service manning the gate were polite to the point of being perfunctory. If they had seen him talking to himself on the way over, they knew better than to mention anything.

Nancy McKeen, the president's new chief of staff waiting for him on the other side of security, felt no need to be polite.

"What's stuck in your craw this late at night, Jim?" McKeen asked. Hawthorn grinned at the woman's dialed-up Alabama accent, a tool she used to get other people to underestimate her. It didn't fool Hawthorn. She was one of the toughest and most savvy operators in the Beltway.

"I need to see him," Hawthorn said. "Right away."

They turned and walked together. McKeen was twenty years younger and in good shape despite being a Southern politician. Politicking in the South included endless great BBQ and down-home food on the campaign trail. No self-respecting Southerner was going to vote for a man or woman who ate sushi and juiced veggies for breakfast.

"Why don't you tell me what's going on," McKeen said.

McKeen had been in Congress for six terms before Patterson had plucked her from the House to serve as his chief of staff. She'd sat on the Intelligence Committee and knew how the sausage was made. Still, Patterson had been clear that Alpha Team was not part of the regular chain of command and existed outside of the National Security Council apparatus.

But McKeen had the nose of a bloodhound and was no fool. She knew something was going on. Hawthorn imagined it bothered the woman not knowing. Or, in McKeen's own colorful language, it made her nuttier than a squirrel turd.

"I wouldn't ask if it wasn't important," Hawthorn said. "It's up to the president whether he wants you in the room. Not my call."

McKeen stiffened. "Hard for me to do my job if I don't know what the hell's going on, Jim."

"What can I say, the job sucks. But I told you that before you took it."

McKeen laughed. "That you did. I believe you told me only someone with their head full of stump water would take this job."

"And then you proved my point by taking it," Hawthorn said. He stopped walking, grabbing McKeen by the arm. "You know I like a good verbal sparring match more than anyone. But I'm serious. I need to talk to him, and I need to do it right away."

McKeen looked like she might ask more questions but stopped herself. She lifted her hand to look at her phone screen. "He's still in the Oval. He has the Secretary of the Interior on his way over to have a drink at the residence. Smoothing some ruffled

feathers over the pet programs we killed in the last budget negotiation."

Hawthorn had to hand it to the president. The man knew
how to work hard. One would think that would be true of every
occupant of the office, but that wasn't true.

"Cancel the secretary," Hawthorn said. "He'll need to have
his ego massaged some other night." McKeen started to object,
but Hawthorn held up a hand to stop her. "And get Mitch Dreslan over here." Hawthorn liked Dreslan, head of the president's
Secret Service protective detail. A bit of a rule-follower, but he
was a no-nonsense pro. The request had the desired effect on
McKeen.

"For shit's sake. You better tell me just what in the hell is
going on," McKeen said. "Is the president in danger?"

Hawthorn was surprised at the question. When wasn't the
president in danger? He knew Dreslan and his team gave the
president a daily assessment of the dozens of credible threats
against the president and the First Family, out of the hundreds
the Secret Service tracked each day. It came with the territory.

"Don't worry, you'll be in the room when we bring Dreslan
in," Hawthorn said. "Right now, I need to see him on my own
first. Do you want to escort me there? If not, I know the way."

McKeen pulled herself up, sniffed the air, and continued
toward the West Wing. "You don't have to be an asshole
about it."

Sometimes that's what it took in this town, Hawthorn thought.
He used the few minutes' walk to the Oval to organize his
thoughts, still unsure how to convey what Scott had shared with
him. It was his usual practice to lead any briefing with the worst
news, only he wasn't certain what it was in this case.

That Jacobslav Scarvan was now a religious zealot who believed himself to be on an apocryphal mission from God to execute heads of state around the world? Or that Scott and Mara
Roberts had performed a mercy killing of Russia's most famous
spymaster?

Either way, it wasn't going to go well.

*   *   *

"Is Roberts out of his goddamn mind?" Patterson shouted.

Hawthorn wanted to agree with the president, but adding fuel to the raging fire wasn't in anyone's interest. "I trust Scott and Mara took into consideration all the factors before—"

"Before creating an international incident?"

"With all due respect, sir, the Russians weren't going to like us breaking in just to chat with Belchik, either."

Patterson, who'd been behind his desk up to this point, came around it so fast that Hawthorn thought for a second that he might have to fend off a blow. It was a ridiculous notion, but that was the level of anger in the man's face.

"I knew that," he said. "I'd calculated that risk and the blowback and made my decision on that basis to give you the green light. How can I make a decision if I can't trust what will happen?"

It was Hawthorn's turn to feel his anger rise. Instead of raising his voice, he grew calm. Remaining silent for several seconds, the sound of his blood thumping in his temples.

"There is never certainty," Hawthorn said softly. "Not in this mission. Not in any mission. It's why we call the men and women that choose to go into the field to defend our country 'heroes.' Because they face incredible odds, and anything can happen at any time."

"Not this," Patterson said, his voice lower but his anger unabated. "This is a self-inflicted problem."

"Scarvan was killing his family," Hawthorn said. "A new family member every two days. Women. Children. Every two days. He begged Scott and Mara to help him end it. Not to end his own suffering, but to save his family."

Patterson took a step back. A look of horror flashed on his face as he turned away and walked to the fire at the far end of the room. He stared into the flames and pulled his hand through his hair. Hawthorn noticed that it appeared thinner and grayer since his inauguration. The office did that to all men, especially the ones who were good at the job.

"I'll need to speak to the Russian ambassador. Better they hear it from us than the media."

"I suggest against that, sir."

"And what do you suggest?" Patterson remained with his back turned.

"Admit nothing," Hawthorn said. "Scott and Mara were careful."

Patterson laughed, but there was no humor in it. "The Russians will know it was us."

"Of course they will," Hawthorn said. "But we never admit to it. Because once we do, they need to save face by taking action. Ignore it. Act surprised when the Russian ambassador comes tomorrow."

Patterson took a deep breath and let it out slowly. "There's more lying in this job than I imagined there would be. Did the other presidents you've worked for feel the same way?"

Hawthorn, feeling the presidential fury having passed, walked over to stand with him next to the fire. "They all discovered the same thing, but I wouldn't say they felt the same about it."

"What do you mean?"

"You hate the lie, sir," Hawthorn said, "but see the periodic need for it. Some who have sat behind the Resolute desk lied without compunction or qualm. Sometimes they lied so much they couldn't tell themselves what was true and what had come whole-cloth out of their ass."

Patterson laughed; this time it was real. A needed relief.

"We should tell Mitch Dreslan about this new threat in the morning," Patterson said. "I hate to see the kind of lockdown he's going to suggest. I'm not going to hide from this monster."

"But you do need to take precautions," Hawthorn said. "You and your family. There is nothing out of bounds for this man. You need to prepare yourself to make some changes until we resolve this threat."

The mention of his family had sobered him as Hawthorn knew it would.

"All right, we'll go over it in the morning."

"Sir, Mitch Dreslan is waiting outside the Oval," Hawthorn said. "As is Nancy McKeen. She's eager to know what's going on."

Patterson grimaced. "I'm sure she is. But I have a meeting in the residence with—"

"It's been cancelled," Hawthorn said.

"Become president, they said. Be the most powerful man in the world, they said." Patterson chuckled. "Look at all this power I wield."

"You do, sir. And that's why we have to ensure your protection."

"All right." Patterson crossed the Oval to pour himself two fingers of Johnny Walker Black. He indicated to Hawthorn, who shook his head. "Let's get this over with."

"One suggestion, if I may?"

"You say that like I could stop you from making it."

"The success of Alpha Team depends on its continued secrecy. We describe the new threat, but not the source of the information or the means of its procurement. On top of that, we cannot mention what Scott and Mara are doing next."

"At least that last part won't involve a lie," Patterson said, throwing back his whiskey. "Because as far as what the two of them are concerned with, I haven't got a goddamn clue what they're doing out there. And I'm starting to wonder whether they do, either."

As Hawthorn crossed the Oval to let Dreslan and McKeen in, he found himself wondering the same thing. Scott had been vague over the phone. Hawthorn hoped that had been a function of a lack of time instead of a lack of a plan. Wherever they were headed next, there was one thing of which he felt certain: Before this was all done, the body count was going to climb.

Hawthorn just hoped the good man standing in the Oval Office wasn't going to be one of them.

CHAPTER 17

"This is a terrible plan," Mara said.

They were in the train heading east toward Italy and then Greece. The tickets were purchased under an alias and they'd been careful to avoid the CCTV cameras, so they felt comfortable they'd gone unnoticed. The tickets were for Rome, but they would get off before that to rendezvous with a military helo to expedite the next part of their journey. Thessaloniki was the second largest city in Greece and, most importantly, the closest major city to Ouranoupoli, the small village where the ferry departed for Mt. Athos.

"You might be right, but I think it's also the only plan," Scott said. "There's no way you pass for a man, no matter how good the disguise."

Mara scrolled through the brief sent to her by Langley on her tablet. The more she read, the more she realized her dad might be right. Still, she hated the idea of sitting out a mission because of her gender.

Mt. Athos was a special polity within the Greek Republic, granted special sovereignty that was codified even in the admittance documents to the European Union. This sovereignty allowed the so-called Athonite State to restrict the flow of goods and people within its borders. Specifically, it allowed them to exclude any woman from touching their shores.

This was no small thing. According to the file from Langley, even female livestock were not permitted on the isthmus. In an uncharacteristic editorial comment, the writer of the brief opined that perhaps the purpose of this rule was to "keep the monks focused on their prayers instead of looking for love in all the wrong places." Mara laughed out loud at the comment, guessing the author was a woman who felt as chafed by the practice as she did.

Tradition or not, the gender politics of any church using their ancient texts to minimize the role of women in the world really pissed Mara off.

She'd seen the impact of entrenched misogyny all around the world. Saudi Arabia using the Quran to relegate women to the periphery of society. The Catholic Church for centuries had done the same, even though the first pope, St. Peter, had been a married man and women were important figures in the early church. When the Protestant faiths rebelled against the church's ways, they often chose to retain the misogynistic traits of the mother church, refusing female participation as clergy or in the church government. Many of the new churches over the last century had removed these restrictions, but the admonition in Colossians in the New Testament that said *wives, submit to your husbands* still found its way into even some of the more mainstream, progressive churches.

An entire part of a country in the twenty-first century that was off-limits to women didn't sit well with her.

The irony was that the entire setup was reportedly all due to one particular woman's request. According to tradition, St. John the Evangelist had been blown off course from Joppa to Cyprus to visit Lazarus. His traveling companion was a woman destined to become part of the very heart of the church, Mary, mother of Christ. They landed on the shores of Mt. Athos. When the Virgin Mary walked ashore, she was so taken with its beauty that she asked her Son in heaven to make it her garden. A voice came whispering on the breeze for all to hear, "Let this place be your inheritance and your garden, a paradise and haven of salvation for those seeking to be saved." That was enough to consecrate the ground as the garden of the mother of God. Since the rise of the monastic life over eighteen hundred years ago, no other females were allowed on the land.

"I say screw their traditions," Mara said. "They abetted and radicalized a terrorist. They can handle having a woman crash their party."

Scott looked up from his own reading tablet. He usually didn't read the brief but she suspected too he was a little short on his knowledge of the Eastern Orthodox faith. "Did you know that two popes excommunicated each other? The Catholic one and the Orthodox one? That's messed up. It was a thousand years ago, but it's still messed up."

"Are you listening to me?" she said.

"Not really," he said without looking up. "No need."

Mara felt her anger toward the traditions of the world's great religions shift to just focusing on the man in front on her. "No need?"

He kept reading. "Did you know the name Athos was one of the Gigantes in Greek mythology that challenged the gods? Athos threw a massive rock at Poseidon and it fell into the Aegean Sea where it became . . . wait for it . . . Mt. Athos."

"I'm about to throw a rock at your head," Mara said.

He finally lowered his tablet to his lap. "I said no need because we both know the right move here and that's for you to sit this one out. Trying to get these monks to open up to an outsider will be hard enough. If we start off by blowing one of the central tenets of their existence out of the water, they're not going to tell us a damn thing."

Mara knew he was right, but that didn't make it any less annoying.

"Whatever you say," she said, purposefully channeling her teenage self. It made Scott grin as he lifted the tablet back up.

She did the same, digging into the documents to try and parse out any clue that might help them.

The nameless CIA briefer had included the most colorful parts of the region's history. The mention of the mountain in the Iliad. The fact that Xerxes passed through the area on his way to invade Greece. And that after Alexander the Great died, the great architect Dinocrates had seriously suggested carving the entire face of the mountain into the image of the fallen king.

Beyond that were details of the political organization of the monastic state, the current leadership, a brief history of apocryphal prophecy coming from the community, as well as maps with both roads and ancient footpaths.

Mara felt the researchers at Langley were unheralded heroes. Only a few hours earlier, Mt. Athos hadn't been on anyone's radar as a potential destination. Now she had nearly two thousand years of history and a current database of every monk living there at her fingertips.

As she read, her mind wandered to Rick. She hadn't spoken to him for three days. He was likely back in DC now or would be soon. Certainly, after word of their interview with Belchik reached Rick's boss, all hell was going to break loose. Patterson wasn't a good listener, either. Early in his presidency, he'd overridden the Secret Service recommendations and warnings often enough to cause Mitch Dreslan to tender his resignation. Rick had been in the room for that meeting and had given her the play-by-play. Two ex-Marines going toe-to-toe right in the center of the great seal on the floor of the Oval Office.

Rick had told her the story as they lay in bed together, the sweat still cooling off their bodies from a sex session that'd left them both spent but satisfied. She traced her fingers over his chest and abdomen while he talked, loving the sound of his voice as he recounted what had happened.

Dreslan had brought Rick as a witness, just so that there was never any confusion about whether he resigned or was fired. He was pretty sure those were the only two outcomes the meeting might have. Dreslan presented the president with the facts, a one-page summary of the times in the last month that the president had directly ignored or reversed a decision by the Secret Service. Rick did a good Patterson impersonation and Mara laughed as he did a *Saturday Night Live* version of the president.

After he milked all the laughs he could get, Rick turned serious. The argument that got the president in the end was Dreslan saying he wasn't resigning because the president was putting his own life in jeopardy, but because he was putting his protective detail's lives at unnecessary risk. Dreslan had looked him in the eyes and said, "Sir, on any given day, any one of my agents will take a bullet for you. If it happens in the line of duty, I can live with that. But if it happens because of recklessness, whether it's yours or mine, I couldn't look at myself in the mirror. And if you think you could, then I can't work for you any longer."

The line worked. Patterson had backed down. Agreeing to listen more, take fewer unscheduled stops, work fewer rope lines. He wasn't perfect after that, but he was a lot better.

"You like him, don't you?" Mara had asked. "Dreslan."

"He's a pain in the ass," he'd said, his hands caressing her shoulder. "But yeah, he's a strong leader. Popular because he doesn't give a shit about being liked. He cares about the job getting done right." After Rick had told her that story, he'd turned quiet afterward, contemplative.

"I've never told anyone that story," he'd said. "There were only three of us in the room. It's the kind of thing that never gets out."

"And it never will," she'd said, kissing him softly, feeling the warmth from the trust he'd shown her as much as from his body pressing next to her. "I promise."

The train lurched to the side, hitting an old piece of track before smoothing out. It was just enough to shake her out of her thoughts and bring her back into the present. She felt a lingering desire for Rick and a worry.

If Scarvan intended to go after the president, then he would be in the line of fire.

The thought only pissed Mara off more that she couldn't go to Mt. Athos to question the monks there. At least she knew her dad wouldn't let them off easy. If anything, they might need to polish off their prayer books to get ready for what was about to happen to them.

CHAPTER 18

The teams transporting them across Italy and Greece were all business. Scott and Mara departed the train at the small town of Ventimiglia, Italy, where a beat-up pickup truck waited for them in the parking lot, driven by a man who looked like a farmer . . . if the farmer lifted every day and consumed a regimented diet to maximize his performance. That was the thing about some special operators: no matter the clothes they wore, it was impossible to disguise their bearing and their extreme fitness level.

This "farmer" greeted them and explained their ride was only twenty minutes out of town. He drove the truck in a circuitous route through the town's ancient streets, eyeing his mirrors for possible tails. Seeing nothing, they headed to the outskirts where a helo sat in an open field, all lights off.

Thanking their driver, they climbed into the AW139M helo with its signature elongated nose cone and strapped in. Scott liked the choice of aircraft. The AW139 had a max speed over 300km/h and, despite its high-performance design, was a rugged animal that could fly at twice the altitude of an Apache and land anywhere with its robust main and nose landing gears.

The helo was painted black and held no markings or insignia. Scott assumed there was a supply of decals stored on board so that that crew could change the helo's appearance and ownership in only a few minutes, depending on the needs of the situation.

There was a three-person crew: pilot, co-pilot, and one very nasty-looking man in the cabin with them who didn't take his eyes off them once. Langley may have told this crew to pick them up and give them a ride, but it didn't mean they necessarily trusted Scott and Mara.

"Good evening, gentlemen," Scott said, adjusting his headphones with directional mic so he could talk to the pilots.

"You mean good morning, sir," came back a female voice, clearly pleased to correct Scott.

Mara grinned. "Good morning, ma'am. Thanks for the ride."

"Our pleasure," she said. "ETA to Malaga airfield is less than thirty minutes. Hold on."

The pilot lifted off and the helo surged forward, accelerating into the night.

True to her word, they touched down twenty-five minutes later at a sleepy regional airport of the coastal town of Malaga. Once they disembarked, the helo wasted no time, ascending and streaking away. The Gulfstream G600 sitting on the tarmac with the steps extended was their next ride.

"What, the Citation X+ was being used?" Mara asked.

Either aircraft was overkill for their needs. Superluxe with beautiful interiors, these business aircraft had the added benefit of being the fastest in the market. Each of them went just under Mach 1. It wasn't subtle, but the good news was that neither were Europe's jet-setting crowd. The Gulfstream stood out in sleepy Malaga, but it would blend right in with the other jets in Thessaloniki.

As soon as they boarded the craft, the dual Pratt & Whitney engines spun up. A young man greeted them inside and directed them to their seats. "Sat phone connections are active. Director Hawthorn requests that you call once we're under way. If you need to reach us up front, you can call the cockpit on the phone on that wall," he said, pointing. "Or just knock on the door."

Scott and Mara thanked him and settled into the leather captain's chairs. Soon, they taxied off the runway and the jet soared into the lightening sky in the east.

"You call him," Scott said, meaning Hawthorn. "He likes you better."

"He should," she said. "You're the one usually causing all the problems."

She picked up the sat phone and dialed Hawthorn's secure number, which she had memorized. She put it on speaker.

"About damn time," Hawthorn said on answering.

"Hi Jim. It's Mara. We're both here."

"Any word from the Russians yet?" Scott asked.

"None," Hawthorn said. "We have eyes on the site and there hasn't been a new crew over yet."

Scott and Mara exchanged looks. "The men inside should have come around by now. No activity?" Scott asked.

"None yet," Hawthorn said. "Leave that to me. I'll navigate the absolute shitstorm you've stirred up with the Russians, or I'll at least manage our categorical denials that we had anything to do with it."

"I'm sure they'll buy that," Mara said.

"The timing's bad," Hawthorn said. "Cooperation with the FSB would be useful right now. We've gone through the list of other potential people Scarvan will go after. The list is actually shorter than you might think."

"That's surprising," Scott said.

"First, the operation to kill Scarvan twenty years ago was a closely held secret. There were too many people loyal to him inside the KGB, so Belchik didn't want to tip him off. But Scarvan is going after anyone even remotely associated with that night. Even the captain of the trawler was found dangling from the end of a rope."

"He's had twenty years to think about this revenge binge," Scott said. "He's making the most of it."

"You said that was the first reason the list was so short," Mara said. "What's the second?"

"The second reason is that most people on the list were already dead," Hawthorn said, pausing to let that fact sit in. "Scarvan's been busier than we thought at first. Just very careful. Nearly all appeared to be accidents, and no one put together the connections. Until now."

"How many people?" Mara asked.

"Thirteen that we know of," Hawthorn said. "Not counting Belchik's family members. Scarvan has proven the years haven't made him any less of a sick mind."

Mara thought of the table covered with the photos of Belchik's family. A few of his grandchildren had just been little kids. She felt a swelling desire to punish this man they were chasing.

"Who's left?"

"Three people. I just emailed you the files. Turn on the screen in the plane."

Scott grabbed the remote control and pointed it at the TV screen attached to the wall. Nothing happened. He pressed another button, shaking the controller as he did it.

Mara reached out a hand for him to hand it over.

He tried three other buttons before tossing it to her. She pressed a single button and the TV came to life.

"Smart-ass," he said.

"Old fuck," she replied.

"If you're all done over there, you should see Sergei Kolonov on the screen," Hawthorn said. An image of a young man in a Russian military uniform appeared.

"I know him," Scott said. "He was on the boat that night. One of Belchik's guns."

"Correct," Hawthorn said. Additional photos of the man flashed on the screen. He aged as the photos went on, turning into long-range surveillance pics by the end. There were shots taken in jungle settings, on airstrips that looked like Central or South America. "Last known photo was five years ago, working in Colombia for the Cali drug cartel. DEA thinks he's deceased but were working on dredging up confirmation."

"I recall he wasn't too happy with the duty he drew that night," Scott said. "After Scarvan went overboard, he hammered vodka shots the rest of the night, sending me looks. I thought he and I might get into it."

"It was only a year after that he followed the time-honored tradition of the disgruntled and disillusioned operator and became a mercenary," Hawthorn said. "If he's still alive, we'll find him." The screen changed to another man. This one lean and wiry, dressed in a tailored suit and wearing round spectacles. "Next we have Stefan Nochek."

"Don't know that name," Scott said.

"I do," Mara said. "Political operative. Works for the Russian oligarchs. Whichever one is paying the most."

"Right, back then he was a young KGB bureaucrat who acted as a liaison to the Kremlin. He would have counseled on the political side of the operation. Word was that he pushed hard for the operation, strategically using it to get concessions from the U.S. on banking issues facing the oligarchs at the time."

"And I assume we were willing to bend over and take their demands," Scott said.

"When there's a stench, follow the money and you'll find the source," Hawthorn said. "This guy is exactly the sort of man Scarvan would want to take out."

"Then why's he still alive?" Mara asked.

"Good question. It's either testament to the protection he has working for the oligarchs, or it could be that Scarvan simply had a long list to get through and Nochek's number simply hadn't come up yet."

"We should be on him," Mara said, seizing on the chance to have something to do. "We split up. I'll track Nochek while you visit the land of men wearing dresses and funny hats."

"Cassocks," Scott said. "Not dresses. And the hats are kamilavkas." He leaned toward the speaker phone, pretending to whisper to Hawthorn. "Mara isn't thrilled about the men-only policy on Mount Athos."

Mara ignored the comment. "Where is Nochek now?"

"That's the problem." A photo appeared of Nochek walking toward a private jet. He was surrounded by a protection detail of five bodyguards. "We don't know where he is. He was in Helsinki yesterday but left on a private jet. Flight plan said Brussels, but the plane never arrived."

"Can't Jordi track him down?" Scott said. "I thought he was the master of all things."

"He's trying," Hawthorn said. "And he's not very happy about not being able to find him."

Mara grinned, imagining Jordi cussing out his computer screens with his fake Cockney accent. "He'll find him eventually. When he does, I'll take the plane there and start surveillance."

"I agree," Hawthorn said. "And once you're done on Mount Athos, Scott, you'll tail the last person on the list. Anna Beliniski."

Mara knew the name, a former FSB operative well known to the CIA. Belinski had freelanced for a while before ending up working intelligence for the Czech Republic. Mara noted her dad's reaction. He straightened in his chair, his expression changing immediately. More interest. And something else.

"You know Anna?" Mara asked.

Scott, aware of his body language, slouched back into his chair, trying to recapture his practiced indifference. But it was too late, and he knew it. "We've met. A few times over the years."

Mara left it alone, but she was enjoying seeing him squirm. He never shared any details of his love life with her, except to insist he'd always been faithful to her mother while she'd been alive.

A new photo flashed on the screen. A woman in an evening gown, off the shoulder, her blond hair up, showing her perfect tan and sculpted arms. Her full lips were parted in a sly grin as if she knew the person taking the photograph was about to send it to the opposing intelligence service, and she couldn't care less.

"Wow, she was beautiful back in the day," Mara said.

"That's a recent photo," Scott said. "She's aged well."

Mara took a closer look at the screen. On closer inspection, they were a few wrinkles at the corners of her eyes, but they looked just part of her smile and not from time. She gave her dad a once-over. "You think she'd say the same of you?"

"Shut up, you twerp," he said.

"Regardless," Hawthorn said, "she's listed currently as a contractor for the Czech Republic. She was an assistant to Belchik when the order came down to eliminate Scarvan, so she would have known about it."

"And not warned him," Scott said. "So, he'll be after her. Has she been informed?"

Mara noted he hadn't asked the same question about Nochek.

"She and Nochek have been warned by FSB," Hawthorn said. "Ms. Beliniski was last seen in Prague. After you finish at Mount Athos, you're to find her and shadow her only. No contact. That will give you the best chance to catch Scarvan in the act."

Use her as bait, Mara thought. It was a practical plan, one she agreed with, but she watched her dad closely. He didn't say anything, but if she were to take a gamble, there was no way he was going to do as Hawthorn asked.

"Have the Russians given us anything new about Scarvan?" Scott asked. "They have to be actively looking for him, too, after what he's been doing."

"I don't think they are going to be in a sharing mood in the next hour or two after they find Belchik. His death complicates things. But then you already knew that, didn't you?"

"Speaking of moods, how did the president take it?" Mara asked.

"Great," Hawthorn said. "He was really excited. I think he's been saving up all those cuss words for a special occasion and the two of you really delivered. He told me to say thank you."

"It that why we got this fancy jet?" Scott asked. "A sign of his appreciation?"

"No, it's the fastest plane I could get on short notice so your asses can get where you need to get to so we can clean this mess up. With more time, I would have made you hitchhike your way there."

Mara grinned. This was Hawthorn at his best. It was when he lost his edgy sarcasm that you had to worry.

"What changes did Dreslan make after he heard the threat?" Mara asked.

"The president has developed a case of the flu. Public appearances canceled for the next few days to set a good example for the nation on how to slow its spread," Hawthorn said. "Rick Hallsey is back and Dreslan tasked him with running point on the Scarvan threat. He's a good man."

Mara appreciated Hawthorn not making her ask. Of course, the old man knew about her relationship with the Secret Service agent and that she'd be curious where he was in all of this. There wasn't much in DC that he didn't know about.

"I should probably call Agent Hallsey to brief him on the suspect," she said.

"Agreed," he said. "As for Mount Athos, Scott, you have a meeting set with Father Gregorio, the head of the Athonite State. He wasn't thrilled by the idea, tried to throw some roadblocks, but got onboard after a call from the Greek prime minister. Don't expect the red carpet, though. There's a reason these guys left the world to go live as monks. Not huge fans of outsiders banging on their door and asking questions."

"Got it. Any leads on someone that might know Scarvan?" Scott asked.

"Father Gregorio said he had no knowledge of a man named Scarvan and that he knows every monk personally by name and history. There's a printer on the plane. I'm sending you an image now for you to show him. I had our guys work it up based on the time passed and the description Belchik gave you."

Mara crossed to the back of the cabin as a paper scrolled out of the printer. It was a version of the image from the dossier she'd seen earlier, only this man had aged twenty years and now had a thick gray beard. The lines around his eyes were etched deep and the complexion was blotchy. A thick mane of curly gray hair framed his face. The man looked wild, more like a homeless man than a world-class assassin.

She handed the paper to Scott. "Shouldn't be hard to pick out in a crowd." He spoke back into the phone. "Did they do the age but with the hair different? Clean shaven? All the variations?"

"Already sent to your devices. You can print out the ones you think will be useful," Hawthorn said. "These have gone out to every intelligence agency we cooperate with and a few we don't. Everyone will be looking for him."

"Maybe we'll get lucky," Mara said.

"Not a chance," Scott said. "This guy's a ghost."

"He was. That was twenty years ago," she said. "He's bound to have lost more than a few steps over that time."

"Look at Jim," Scott said. "He can barely do anything anymore."

"I'm still here, smart-ass," Hawthorn's voice came from the phone.

Scott and Mara shared a laugh as Mara tossed him one of the bottles of water she'd discovered in the small fridge attached to her chair.

"Think how boring your life would be without me," Scott said.

"I'd be fly-fishing in Montana," he said. "Relaxing."

"Anything else, boss?" Mara asked.

"No, get some rest," he said. "I'll communicate updates as they come in."

They ended the connection. Scott leaned back in his chair. "You heard the man. We have an hour at most. I'm going to grab some sleep. Suggest you do the same."

"I'm fine," she said. "I'm going to go over this briefing again on Mount Athos."

"Overachiever." Scott sprawled out on the leather couch and closed his eyes.

"Someone has to be," she said.

"I heard that."

"Surprising with those old ears," she whispered.

"Heard that, too."

Mara smiled and dug back into the briefing document, hoping to find something useful within its pages.

CHAPTER 19

"I must leave this place!" Scarvan roared, throwing his bowl across the skete, shattering it against the stone wall. Two months of recovery had mended his wounds enough for him to walk tenderly down to the water and back. He still did not have the strength to fight.

His mind was another matter. That was ready to take the battle to his enemies.

Father Spiros didn't flinch. He gathered his hands together and closed his eyes in prayer.

"No, stop it," Scarvan said. "No more prayer. It does nothing. God is as useless as you are."

Father Spiros opened his eyes and Scarvan thought he saw a flash of anger in the old man. It was the first time he'd seen it, which was surprising. Scarvan had been less than an ideal patient.

Only one other monk knew he was there: a younger man named Misha, who Father Spiros had fetched to help drag Scarvan up from the beach to his skete. That was no mean task given that the old man's stone hut was perched some twenty feet up the face of a cliff.

There was a thin path carved along the rock that provided access. Less steps than a series of questionable footholds, more built for a mountain goat than a man. Still, it was possible to use if the ladder became damaged. Or if some mischievous brother moved it in the middle of the night.

Once he'd recovered enough to leave the bed, Scarvan had wondered how the two of them had hauled his bulk up the cliff. Brother Spiros had shown him the thick ropes and blocks of wood they used as pulleys to haul heavier items up. They'd wrapped him in a blanket, trussed him like a bird for the oven, and pulled him up.

That explained the how. Scarvan found getting the why out of the old man much more difficult.

He spent the first days of semiconsciousness certain that the door would be hammered in at any time, special operators with night-vision goggles and guns with laser sights spilling into the small space. He dreamed of it. Sometimes it was faceless tactical soldiers. Other times it was the faces of men he'd killed.

Many times, he'd opened his eyes to find Scott Roberts standing over his bed. Behind him, cast in shadow, watching in silence, were Jim Hawthorn and Viktor Belchik. Roberts raised his hand and pointed a Glock with a suppressor at his face. Scarvan cowered and whimpered, begging for his life the way so many weak fools had done in front of him over the years. Groveling in a way he'd sworn he never would. Then Belchik stepped forward, lips curled back in disgust. "Kill him," he said. Roberts pulled the trigger and Scarvan bolted awake in his bed. Drenched in sweat from fever. His wounds blazing with pain.

Each time it happened, the old monk had been at his bedside, reading from his Bible, ready to dab his patient's brow with a cool washcloth.

Once Scarvan was well enough to move, he knew he had to kill the men who'd saved him. Both the old man and the younger one who'd helped pull him up into the skete. If it was true that no one else knew he was there, then the two of them had to die. To ensure his presence remained a secret.

He waited until Misha arrived with new supplies. Just bread, vegetables, penicillin for the angry infections in Scarvan's wounds.

While the two of them busied themselves in the cramped quarters storing away the supplies, speaking of the gossip of their brother monks, Scarvan pulled himself out of bed on unsteady legs, gripping the knife he'd taken from his meal earlier in the day. It was not very sharp, but he'd killed with much less of a weapon before.

He staggered forward, fighting the dizziness. Focused on the younger monk's back.

But after only a few steps, he heard the old monk calmly say, "Misha, take the knife from our friend. I believe he means to kill us."

Misha turned, not in fear or shock, but with a look of annoyance and pity.

Scarvan gritted his teeth and tried to lunge forward, intending to permanently remove the man's expression from his face.

Instead, Misha easily sidestepped his advance, wrested the knife from his hand, and slapped him on the back of the head.

"Misha," Father Spiros chided, "unnecessary."

"Sorry, Father Spiros. Habit."

Father Spiros stepped forward and took Scarvan's forearm, guiding him back to his bed. "Like you, Misha has training. Served in the Greek army before finding his way back to God." He helped Scarvan lay down. "Just as you will do. In time. After you heal. After His plan for you has been revealed."

"And me," Misha added. "I've seen it, too."

Father Spiros reached out and patted the younger man on the arm. "Christ our Father came to Misha and showed him the same vision he showed me. A true miracle."

"Your asshole God better stay out of my head," Scarvan said. "I don't want him there."

Father Spiros didn't look offended or surprised. "In time, you will see. And then you will welcome Him in and wonder how you ever lived outside the warmth of his love."

"Not a fucking chance, old man," Scarvan said.

"In time," Father Spiros said.

Scarvan laid back into the bed, giving into the wave of fatigue from the short excursion across the room. He stared at the ceiling, not wanting to slip back into sleep, not wanting the nightmares to return.

But his body rebelled, and sleep did come.

As did the nightmares.

But something different came as well.

It wasn't complete the first time, only glimpses. Flashes of color. Howling wind. The smell of burning flesh. And there was a *presence*, something that towered over him, wrapped around him like darkness, but a physical thing.

There was a message in all the confusion. He could feel it and he fought to understand.

It wasn't until much later, with the help of Father Spiros, that he understood it was the first time he was exposed to the vision.

The first time he'd been before the power of God.

When he finally did understand, when he finally accepted the truth of it and surrendered himself to the path ahead, he thought back to that first night. How little he'd understood. How much he had yet to learn.

And that both he and the world would never be the same again.

CHAPTER 20

The ferry cut easily through the two-foot swell coming out of the southeast, its diesel engine leaving a thin line of smoke in the air behind them. The other passengers on the rectangular craft were a combination of religious men and workers. All men. The rules forbidding women on the isthmus were serious and strictly adhered to. When they'd been at the docks, Scott had seen women getting on a tour boat for Mt. Athos, but these cruised up and down the coast, never daring to dock lest they lose their license.

The monks on the ferry kept to themselves, casting suspicious looks in his direction. The workers, burly men in overalls and thick forearms, paid him no mind. They chain-smoked and snuck sips from flasks, lost in their own conversation that Scott's minimal Greek told him was about some soccer game on TV the night before.

The mountain loomed to Scott's left, its peak hidden by wisps of white cloud. The sight reminded him of the stories he'd learned as a child about the Greek Gods. He'd always wondered why the ancient Greeks chose a mountaintop as the location for their gods to congregate. But looking at it now, cloaked in mystery and beauty, he understood. And he imagined the actual Mt. Olympus was even more impressive.

He supposed it was fitting that the mountain overlooked an

isthmus entirely given over to monasteries and hermitages, a land filled with nearly two thousand souls who committed themselves to nearly constant prayer and reflection. Facts from the briefing book stayed with him about the particularities of Mt. Athos.

It wasn't unusual in the great religions of the world for men to segment themselves from society in an attempt to better understand and reach their god. But the extent of the rules forbidding any female presence seemed extreme by any measure. The monks did not raise livestock because of the necessity of having female animals. Even chickens were not allowed to be raised for eggs.

Mara had chafed at all these things, challenging the idea of a god or religion that pushed aside women in such a way. But she'd let it go quickly enough. They were here for a job and that job didn't include changing centuries of tradition.

Besides, she had plenty to keep her occupied. Once they landed in Thessaloniki, word from Hawthorn was that Nochek had turned up in Paris at the side of Oleg Manisky, an oligarch who'd made his billions through lucrative contracts bestowed on him by the Putin regime. She and Scott had said their goodbyes and she'd turned the plane around to pick up Nochek's trail.

He worried about her. Even though her training and her skill set made her one of the most lethal weapons in America's arsenal, she was still his daughter. It was his fatherly prerogative to worry. And it wasn't like she was heading off on a date or a cross-country ski trip like she had when she was in college. She was off to chase one of the greatest assassins in history. A little worry was justified.

As he watched the rocky shores of Mt. Athos rise in front of him, gulls circling overhead, the smell of the ocean air filling his lungs, he realized he was eager to get through this part of the mission as quickly as possible. He was hopeful that someone here could cast some light on the last twenty years of Scarvan's life.

Why had he stayed here for so long?

What worldview was coloring his actions?

How had Orthodox Christianity turned him into an end-of-the-world nutjob?

What was his plan to strike at the world's leaders?

Scott understood the man's quest for revenge. He didn't condone it, especially the deaths of his targets' family members that he used as punishments. But it was in character for what he knew about Scarvan.

Even his stated goal of assassinating heads of state could have made for some grotesque type of logic, a strike at the system that had aligned itself to try and kill him.

But his talk of the Second Coming and end of times was entirely different.

Something happened to Scarvan in his twenty years on Mt. Athos and discovering what it was might be the key to unlocking the man's next move.

There was a stirring among the other men on the ferry. Scott followed their gaze to the dock just ahead of them. On it was a cluster of monks or priests; even with the thorough brief he'd read he was unsure what to properly call them. They stood at the end of the dock, black cossacks whipping in the ocean breeze. An older man stood among them, clearly the center of gravity within the group. Next to him was a man in a black business suit.

"The protos and the governor here to meet us," one of the monks behind Scott whispered to his friends in Greek. "I told you to stay in your rooms. What did you fools do last night?"

Scott turned away to hide his grin. While he couldn't speak Greek except to order off a menu, he understood it well enough. They thought the reception party was for them. He decided not to say anything. Let the monks think through what they'd done during their visit to the mainland. Maybe eaten a lamb souvlaki, had too much wine, or maybe held hands with a girl. Or more. The presence of both the leader of the monastic state and its civil governor would be enough to test whether there were any guilty consciences on board.

The ferry docked in silence, the tension among the monks palpable.

When the governor raised his hand toward Scott and strode out to meet him, there were audible sighs of relief behind him. Whatever the monks had gotten themselves into was still a secret. They scurried past the dignitaries, heads bent low.

"Welcome to Mount Athos, Mr. Roberts. I am Nikkos Panagides, civil governor," the man in the suit said. "I've been instructed to help you in any way I can. May I introduce his Holiness, Father Gregorio, protos of Mount Athos."

Scott shook hands with Panagides. He knew from the briefing that the civil governor was a member of the Greek Foreign Service, a representative of the secular government. Even though Mt. Athos was a semiautonomous state, it was still Greek territory. While the position was largely ceremonial, it was a coveted spot in a rising career for a politician seeking the support of the Greek Orthodox Church. The key to that support was to leave the monks alone and not interfere with matters. Judging from the scowl that faced Scott from Father Gregorio, Panagides was failing that basic concept.

The twenty monasteries on Mt. Athos each had an abbot who exerted nearly complete control over the monks in his care. Each of the twenty was part of the Holy Community, a governing council of elders that created a legislative body with elected protos at its head. With only the Ecumenical Patriarch of Constantinople above him, the protos was not accustomed to being summoned, especially by the American government.

"Welcome to Mount Athos," Father Gregorio said, speaking English. "Please tell me how I can assist you during your short visit."

The man's cold tone wasn't lost on him. The men around him matched his attitude, none of them looking pleased to have him on their shore.

"There was a monk living here for the past twenty years," Scott said. "He would have left a few months ago. Gone back out into the world. Does anyone match that description?"

Father Gregorio turned to Panagides, speaking Greek. "I have already answered this question on the telephone. You brought me here so I can answer again to this idiot in person?"

Scott kept a blank expression, not wanting Father Gregorio to know he could understand. He turned to Panagides. "What did he say? Does he know someone?"

"He asks whether you have a particular name? There are many monks in Mount Athos," Panagides said.

"But you know every one of them," Scott said. "That's what you said over the phone."

"Then you already know my answer," Father Gregorio said, switching to English.

"I'd like to hear it from you, though."

The men around Father Gregorio looked outraged at Scott's tone, but the protos didn't flinch at it. He seemed a hard man, someone Scott wasn't going to underestimate.

"Mr. Panagides," Father Gregorio said. "Please ask the ferry to remain here. Mr. Roberts will need a ride home soon. Come, Mr. Roberts. Let's you and I walk alone."

Panagides looked like he might object, but a single raised eyebrow from the old man and he seemed to think better of it. He gave a half bow and jogged to the ferry that was already readying to go. In a hundred and thirty square miles of rugged landscape of only men, the protos was the alpha. And it was clear he wanted Scott to know it.

He motioned for his entourage to stay where they were and walked toward the land. Scott followed.

"Men come," Father Gregorio said. "Sometimes they go. At one time we numbered over seven thousand. Now we are just over two thousand. Men today are soft. They are weak."

"But one who stayed for twenty years and then leaves? Surely that is rare."

"Do you think the draw of the outside world grows less over time? That the devil relinquishes his hold on the hearts of men simply because of their age?"

Scott glanced over his shoulder. The father's men followed at a safe distance. There was one of them, younger than the others, his beard still jet black, who moved differently. His eyes scanned the area. His arms swung out a bit wider, telling Scott he carried a weapon.

A bodyguard.

Scott felt foolish for not spotting him sooner. He'd let the idea of a religious enclave lull him into complacency.

"You always travel with an armed guard," Scott asked, "or is that only since Scarvan showed his true colors to you?"

If he'd caught the old man off guard, he didn't show it. "I don't know a man named Scarvan. There has not been a man in Mount Athos under that name."

"But men change their names once they come here," Scott said. "Is that not true?"

Father Gregorio fingered the heavy silver cross hanging from his neck. "It is."

Scott stopped and put his hand on the old priest's arm. "I know the man I'm looking for lived here for the last twenty years." It was a lie. Scott knew nothing of the sort. It was all a guess. A damn good one, but still a guess. Still, certainty had an effect on most people. "There's no way you don't know who he is." Father Gregorio started to object but Scott raised his hand to stop him. "Jacobslav Scarvan is no ordinary man, Father. He's a weapon. A killer unlike any you could imagine."

"A killer like you, Mr. Roberts?" Father Gregorio asked.

Scott took a step away from the old man. "I don't know where you get your information, but—"

"Why is it that people are never surprised at the power and reach of the Catholic Church, but they are shocked to discover we have our own eyes around the world? The Orthodox Church has two hundred and sixty million faithful. It wasn't hard to find out who you really are."

"If you know who I am, then you know I'd only be here if the situation was serious."

"If you find this man you are looking for," Father Gregorio said, "what do you intend to do with him?"

"Do you want my honest answer?"

"I do."

"Twenty years ago, I shot him four times and watched him fall into the ocean in the middle of a storm," Scott said. "Next time I see him, I'm going to finish the job."

"So, you intend to kill him?"

"Yes," Scott said.

Father Gregorio looked hard into his eyes, sizing him up. He saw a strength and resolve there he liked. "Good. That was the answer I wanted," he said. "The answer I needed to hear. Come, there's someone you must speak to. The journey is not far. Thales Mitsopoulos, my 'armed guard' as you called him, will take you there. Alone."

"Who am I meeting with?" Scott said.

"The man who knows what this Scarvan has planned," Father Gregorio said.

"How do you know this?" Scott asked.

"Because, Mr. Roberts," the old monk said. "I believe he's the one who told him exactly what to do."

CHAPTER 21

Scarvan felt strong as he pulled his body through the warm ocean water. His daily swim had been no more than a few minutes of treading water when he'd started months ago. Back then, his gunshot wounds had healed on the surface, but the damage inside his body still left him in constant pain. The weeks spent in the old monk's bed had atrophied his muscles and sapped his stamina so badly that the first trip down from the skete had been sitting in a sling while he was lowered by rope to the ground below.

But now things were different.

His muscle definition had returned. His lungs returned to what they once were, powerful bellows that allowed him to exercise for hours. The diet that he thought might slow his recovery had seemed to aid it. He'd been unhappy to learn the monks abstained from meat, only eating fish on rare occasions, and then only when spelled out specifically on their religious calendars.

As a nod of deference to his savior, Father Spiros, Scarvan attempted to follow the structured lifestyle of the old monk. It was an odd existence, but one of discipline and rules, something familiar to Scarvan. He'd been in some sort of military role since the day his mother had been killed in Serbia when he was only a child. The streets of Belgrade had taught him how to scrape by and survive, giving him a mental toughness that had served him well through the years.

And he needed all that mental toughness now.

Betrayal.

The word endlessly rolled around in his head. Even when Father Spiros sat with him and talked of God and the punishments he had in store for the world, his mind wandered toward the question he couldn't let go.

How many people had known?

Who had been part of the plan to destroy him?

It wasn't about hurt feelings, although he allowed himself to feel sadness about the people he'd trusted that had let him down. Belchik being the worst of the lot.

No, the mental game of guessing the extent of the betrayal was all about creating the list of the people on who he needed to exact his revenge.

Once he healed.

After he killed the two monks who had saved him.

As he pulled his clothes back on, he felt a twinge of regret at the thought. Without Father Spiros, he would surely be dead. A decaying corpse on the beach, his eyes plucked and devoured by birds, his flesh consumed by crabs and insects.

Father Spiros and Misha, the young monk who helped carry his body to the skete on the first day. Couldn't forget about Misha.

The young monk didn't like him. Didn't like the way Father Spiros fawned over his new guest, especially when the old man spoke of him as if he were an answer to a prayer only he knew. Scarvan read it as jealousy, and that was an emotion that caused men to do foolish things. He didn't like that.

Whenever Scarvan left the skete, Misha was with him. On Father Spiros's instructions to help if needed, but clearly to watch him with the suspicion reserved for any predator invited into your home.

Scarvan wasn't certain what to do with the young monk. Certainly, he had to die along with the old man, but the question was how long could he afford to let him live.

He had his uses. It was Misha who had persuaded Father Spiros to adopt a cover story that explained the sudden appearance of his new guest. Scarvan was given the name Apostoli and it was quietly leaked that he'd arrived from the Petkovica monastery in Serbia on Father Spiros's invitation, to recuperate from poor health. The story had been necessary. It was a small community. Even though Father Spiros lived as an anchoritic hermit, far away from anyone else, he was still technically part of the cenobitic community of the Xenophontos monastery and under the jurisdiction of the abbot there.

Not only that, but Father Spiros had a following among many of the younger monks who sought him out, disturbing his solitude in a way other hermits would never allow. Some had moved to cells nearby, creating an informal skete, or collection of hermitages.

But Father Spiros enjoyed the visits. These were young men with deep-born dissatisfaction with the outside world. They'd come to Mt. Athos not so much because they'd turned toward God but because they'd turned away from the world. Father Spiros's brand of orthodoxy fit these men well. He promised them *theosis*, a union with God. His teachings were filled with absolutes and certainty. And the promise of radical change that would benefit only the most devout. It was how disciples were created.

These young men were not much different from those Scarvan had trained over the years, some as soldiers, others as agents. Many as nothing more than terrorists who served Moscow's cause of the day.

Disillusioned with the world, they were hungry to follow something. After the boredom of a monk's life settled on them, the violent prophecies of Father Spiros were like a beckoning call.

Still, even though he liked the old man and owed him his life, killing him was a necessity. He and Misha alone knew the truth of how he'd been discovered. It was a loose end that needed to be wrapped up.

"Apostoli," Misha called out from the rocks behind him, using his new cover name. "Come, it's time to return."

Scarvan shook the water from his head and squeezed the beard he'd grown since he'd come there. An orthodox priest without a beard was a problem. Fortunately, his Serbian heritage ensured growing a beard wasn't an issue. Wild curls hung far below his chin. The fact it was flecked with gray was another reminder to Scarvan that his best days were behind him.

This sense of mortality was new to him. He didn't find it surprising, given how close to death he'd come. But he'd flirted with that dark edge before and it hadn't affected him like it had this time. He found himself taking stock of his existence, overly self-conscious that there were more years behind him than ahead.

And then there were the dreams.

He'd chalked it up to the environment. The constant prayers by the two monks. The reading from the Bible by candle in the evenings. The Book of Revelations was the favorite.

Who wouldn't have nightmares hearing that every night?

In moments of weakness, he entertained the thought of staying on Mt. Athos. Becoming the man he pretended to be. Apostoli. An Orthodox man of God. Living his days in repentance.

But the idea would pass, replaced by rage against those who'd betrayed him.

Misha walked toward him, balancing on the jumble of boulders that made the shoreline. He wasn't the most graceful person, nor the most gifted mentally from what Scarvan could tell. But he was dutifully dedicated to Father Spiros.

"Father Spiros will wonder what's taking so long," he said. "You know how he worries about you."

Scarvan caught the man's disapproval in his voice. "You don't much care for me, do you, Misha?" he asked.

The monk didn't look taken off guard by the direct question. "No, I don't."

Scarvan laughed, not expecting such a direct answer. "Why is that? What have I done to earn your displeasure?"

Misha stepped closer. He appeared ready for this conversation, the thoughts lined up and ready to pour out. "We know nothing about you. Nothing besides the lies you've told us."

"What lies?"

The monk's face turned red, like he might explode. "You've said you don't know how you ended up on the beach. That you don't know how you were shot. Four times. That's no accident."

"Father Spiros believes I have amnesia," Scarvan said. "Brought on by trauma."

"Bullshit," Misha shouted.

Scarvan laughed out loud. If Misha had been a few steps closer he would have slapped the man on the back. "There, now you're talking like a man."

"You're a nonbeliever. A liar. And, for all we know . . . a murderer. Wanted by the police. Or someone else. Perhaps they are looking for you right now. Perhaps it would be better if you were found."

Scarvan closed his eyes and turned his face toward the sun, relishing the heat on his skin. He brought his left hand to the side of his neck and felt his pulse. Quicker than he wanted. All in expectation of what was about to happen.

He was out of practice.

A few calming breaths, and his heartbeat slowed.

When he opened his eyes, something must have changed in them because Misha blanched. He stumbled backward, twisting an ankle.

"I could be wrong," he said. "Probably wrong. What do I know?"

Scarvan stepped toward the young monk. Not quickly. Just the way a great cat crawls through the grass toward its prey.

"Father Spiros knows I'm here," Misha said. "He's expecting us. Both of us."

"Who did you tell about me?" Scarvan said.

"No one," Misha said, his voice cracking.

"There was someone," he said, jumping to the next boulder, closing the distance between them. "Tell me who."

"I swore an oath to Father Spiros!" Misha cried. "I told no one. I swear it."

"Do you swear to God?" Scarva asked. "On the damnation of your soul?"

Misha squared his shoulders, as if sensing how he answered the question had the gravest of consequences for him. "I swear to God that I've told no one about you."

Scarvan jumped one last time so that the two of them shared space on the same large rock.

He looked into Misha's eyes, searching, wondering.

"You know what?" he said. "I believe you."

Misha's blew out a sigh of relief, his shoulders dropping low as the tension released.

With explosive speed, Scarvan grabbed the young monk by the side of the head. He wrenched it sideways as he jumped, using the downslope to launch them both into the air.

Misha's skull hit the edge of the rock first, Scarvan adding his own weight to what gravity could have done alone.

A crack filled the air as Misha's head caved in.

Scarvan held the man's head firmly against the rock as his legs twitched and kicked from residual electrical impulses. The body didn't yet know what Scarvan had known the second Misha had given voice to the idea that people were searching for him.

The monk was already dead.

The act of smashing his head against the rocks was only a formality.

Blood blossomed around the wound, turning the rock dark and shiny.

He had to resist the impulse to raise the monk's head and smash it back down again. As satisfying as it would be, as much as he craved the release, he was smarter than that. A single injury and the explanation that poor, awkward Misha had tripped on his own feet and freakishly bashed his head on the rocks was plausible. But a person didn't repeatedly slam their heads against a rock until bone and brain spilled everywhere.

Scarvan stood, feeling the same satisfaction as after ejaculating. No, this was better than sex. It meant more. It brought him to life.

He turned his face back toward the sun and closed his eyes. He placed his hand to his neck and felt the steady pulse there, barely elevated despite the euphoria washing through him.

When he opened his eyes, he was surprised to see Father Spiros standing no more than twenty yards from him, in the shade of the rock cliff rising above. The old man walked toward him, steadier on his feet than Misha had ever been, looking like an ancient goat picking his way over the boulders.

Father Spiros stopped on a rock near Scarvan, choosing one that made him tower over him and Misha's dead body. He looked neither surprised nor disturbed by the sight.

"What did you see?" Scarvan asked.

Father Spiros slowly turned his eyes from Misha to his killer. "I saw the instrument of God's will do what had to be done," he said. "I knew it the moment I saw you on the beach. God has brought you here for a purpose. There is divine reason that you possess such power and skill. Don't you see? All of this pain inside you? All of this anger? It's from God, my son. And it serves His purpose."

Scarvan was shocked to find the world blur from the tears in his eyes. Something in what the old man said touched him. An entire lifetime that felt like a series of tragedy and misfortune suddenly put in the context of a greater calling.

"You've been having dreams, haven't you?" Father Spiros asked.

How did the old man know? Yes, he'd had dreams unlike anything he'd ever experienced. Vivid images. Sometimes of his past victims come back to torment him, but others as well. Even more disturbing. Filled with religious imagery. Angels descending from bloodred skies. Flesh torn from bone by violent winds. Blaring trumpets, announcing the end to all things on the Earth.

He simply nodded.

"I've heard you talk in your sleep," the old monk said. "The messiah has spoken to you as he has spoken to me. You can see it. I know you can. The only question is, what you will do about it? Will you strike me down here as you did with Misha? Will you run and deny the path God has chosen for you? Or will you stay and use God's gifts to do his will?"

A feeling tore through Scarvan unlike any he'd felt before. Perhaps it was the adrenaline of the kill at his feet. Or the festering betrayal by his country. Or the sense of mortality from his brush with death and his aging body. Whatever the cause, he felt something reach into his chest and take hold of him. Something strong, so powerful that it demanded his acquiescence. It demanded his fear.

Then Jacobslav Scarvan did something he'd never done in front of another man before.

He fell to his knees and sobbed.

CHAPTER 22

Mara checked her watch and did a quick calculation. Less than an hour before she landed in Paris. That meant her dad was on Mt. Athos by now, either getting information or getting kicked out. It could really go either way.

"How's Dreslan reacting to the threat?" Mara asked into the secure line.

"The president has been advised, but you know how that goes," Rick said.

She loved hearing his voice, especially when he was on duty. It took on a matter-of-fact, take-charge quality that she found appealing. It wasn't quite as good as the husky sound of his voice when they made love, but she guessed she wasn't going to hear that any time soon, secure line or not. His work voice would have to do.

"You guys know how real this is, though," she said.

There was a pause and for a second she thought that she'd lost the connection. When Rick spoke, he adopted a slow Southern drawl. "Ma'am, are you trying to tell this Secret Service agent how to do his job?"

This was Rick's reaction when he didn't like something. A joke. A different voice. It'd taken a while for her to pick up on it. She tried to imagine how she'd feel if Rick questioned whether she was taking a professional issue seriously enough. Not well. Still, this was too important not to press the point.

"I'm just saying, you guys deal with threats from nation-states, terrorist organizations with backing from oil-rich countries giving them nearly unlimited funds. I could see how a single man in his seventies might not press all the red panic buttons."

She heard Rick clear his throat on the other end of the line. Another tell when he was agitated. "We try not to ever panic," he said.

"You know what I mean."

"Jim Hawthorn came over and delivered a brief to the team," Rick said. "The message was received."

"He's a real threat, Rick."

"And what is it you think we face every day?" he said, his voice rising, his exasperation at the conversation now in the open.

"Nothing like this guy," Mara said. "I'm telling you."

"And I'm telling you that we're taking it seriously," he said. Then his voice softened. "I just hope you're following your same advice. I don't know where you are, but I expect it's somewhere you think Scarvan might be."

Mara glanced out of the window. The sprawl of suburban Paris stretched out in all directions beneath her as the plane descended. She had an urge to tell Rick where she was, what her target was, but she knew she couldn't. She was surprised to discover how much that bothered her.

"I'm taking all necessary precautions," she said.

"If you cross paths with this asshole, be smart," Rick said. "Choose your ground, only engage if you have an advantage. Heroes get memorial services, but they don't get to enjoy them."

"This coming from a guy whose job description literally includes blocking bullets with his body."

"Never said I was smart," Rick said. "Counting on you to carry that water in this relationship. Or as my pal, the master of soul, Freddie Scott, would say . . ."

"Oh no," Mara said.

"*Oh, baby, yoooou, you got what I neeeeed* . . ." he sang softly. "*You got everything I need . . . You're like medicine to me* . . ." She heard other male voices in the background chime in on the chorus and Rick stopped. Laughter broke out, men busting each other's chops. She heard Rick say he'd wrap up the call and be right with them and her heart sank.

"The guys don't like your singing?" she asked.

"They like the Biz Markie version," he said. "No class at all."

A pause. They both knew what came next.

"Be safe," she said.

"You do the same. And Mara."

"Yeah?" She expected he might have one more song for her, or at least a sweet parting thought. Instead, he was deadly serious.

"Remember what I said. If you face this guy, make sure everything's in your favor. If it's not, don't engage. You have a team behind you, including me. Trust that we have your back."

She heard someone call his name in the background.

"Have to go. Talk soon."

And then the phone went dead.

"Talk soon," she said to the empty plane.

She watched Paris get closer, allowing herself a little more time to think about Rick, about the last night she'd spent with him. About all the nights ahead that were possible.

She wasn't about to let Jacobslav Scarvan screw that up.

Opening her phone, she pulled up the file on Stefan Nochek. She had good intel on his location. A CIA advance team had him under surveillance. The images on her phone were less than thirty minutes old.

He was scheduled to meet with two men. One was unsurprising, Oleg Manisky, the most recent oligarch to pay Nochek handsomely for his services. The other caught Mara's attention as she was certain it had for the higher-ups at the Agency and in the financial crimes group at the Bureau.

Marcus Ryker, genius, playboy, billionaire, philanthropist. It was his own favorite description of himself as a real-world Tony Stark from Marvel's Iron Man series, albeit without the metal suit to turn himself into a superhero. Although there were rumors he'd spent millions of dollars on a secret project to rectify that situation.

For a man who'd been known to have his own PR people tip off the paparazzi about where he was going to be, his arrival into Paris had been low-key. Unless they'd been pulling out all the stops to track Nochek, she doubted Ryker's meeting with Manisky would have been noticed.

The shroud of secrecy intrigued Mara, but she suspected it would turn out to be just some business deal. Like most international business, much of it was done in varying degrees of gray when it came to legality.

The issue was that if Scarvan struck, he likely wouldn't care if one of the wealthiest and most well-known men in the world was collateral damage.

She rechecked her Glock and the other weapons she had stashed on her body. Something told her she'd come to the right place. Her intuition told her she was about to meet Scarvan for the first time. And her intuition was rarely wrong.

CHAPTER 23

Nochek knew he shouldn't be at the meeting.

He shouldn't be anywhere. His best course of action would have been to find the darkest hole in the middle of a jungle somewhere and bury himself in it until the Americans took care of Jacobslav Scarvan.

How the hell could the man be alive after all of these years?

He could have understood if he'd appeared a year after he was left for dead. If the kill was unsuccessful, it was unsuccessful.

But twenty years?

It made no sense.

Fortunately, those two decades had treated Nochek well. The rise of the political beast called *oligarch* had been perfect for a man with his mix of connections, abilities, and ruthlessness. Not quite well connected enough to be offered any of the sweetheart deals dispensed by Moscow directly, he'd facilitated the transfer of massive power and money from the State into the hands of his employers.

And he'd been rewarded handsomely in the process.

With a net worth approaching one hundred million dollars, stored safely in offshore accounts and in assets held in the United States, Nochek was wealthy by normal standards in the world.

But in the world in which he operated, he was a small fish surrounded by sharks. There was a saying that if you gave a man a hundred million dollars all you'd get is a frustrated would-be billionaire.

And that was why he had to be here.

Besides, Marcus Ryker had insisted. And so Nochek had no choice but to agree.

He wondered why Ryker needed the oligarch. Oleg Manisky had once been a respected military general but was now little more than a crime boss. When it came to reading people, weeding out those who were stealing from him or attempting to infiltrate his organization from law enforcement, he had almost preternatural instincts. Nochek had witnessed the man's legendary savagery firsthand when dealing with such things. In Russia, an oligarch was free to be judge, jury, and executioner among his own people. Manisky enjoyed the executioner role above all else.

Nochek hadn't told his boss about Scarvan. Didn't want to spook him. But he also wanted the man to increase his protection detail. Not that he worried about Manisky being a target, but if they were going to be together, Nochek wanted to benefit from the oligarch's muscle.

So, he'd manufactured a threat by one of the Chechnyan extremist groups who hated Manisky for his role in the brutal suppression of the country years before. This had been enough to get his boss to increase his personal guard and take extra precautions. Most of the men on the team had protected heads of state around the world. There was no honor in their new job, but Manisky paid a lot more.

"Do you think Ryker has the stomach for real business?" Manisky asked. They were in a bulletproof Range Rover with essentially the same armor and safety specifications as the limo used by the president of the United States. It could take an RPG round and keep on going.

"Don't let his public relations team fool you," Nochek said.

"That public persona is a character, purposefully cultivated as a distraction."

He watched Manisky pull at his collar. The man was fat, like a tick engorged with blood. His face was swollen and prone to flushing red with the barest of exertion. The doctor's warnings had done nothing to slow the man's rampant consumption of red meat, vodka, and women. Ryker was a health nut, exercising each day and eating only food carefully prepared by his nutritionist. Rumors were that he was part of all the latest hacks designed to prolong life: cryochambers, human growth hormone, stem cell injections, young blood transfusions. There was nothing Ryker wouldn't do to extend his life.

Intelligence he'd read indicated there was a secret lab where Ryker had sequestered some of the top minds in the field to work on a true elixir of life. Others postulated that it was a project designed to reach immortality in another way, by the downloading of the human mind into a computer, or even another body.

Whatever crazy thing Ryker was working on, it matched his public profile. Only someone with a world-size ego would think the universe so desperately needed him to survive death.

Nochek wondered if, like other aspects of the public Ryker, the lab was also part of the deception.

"You like him," Manisky said.

It wasn't a question, but a statement. Nochek had let his wandering mind lower his defenses. He noticed now that Manisky looked at him with one eyebrow cocked. The same look he gave even evaluating an enemy. Or someone he suspected of disloyalty.

"He's clever," Nochek said. "The people who think he's only hired brilliant scientists that make him look smart miss the point. He does hire the right people, but he steers their research. Breaks through when they have an impasse."

"Smarter than the dumbshit men you normally work for?" Manisky said.

Nochek didn't take the bait. Manisky was many things, but

vain wasn't one of them. He was trying to throw him off-balance. "Russia has some of the most brilliant minds in the world. How many do you see flying in private jets?"

Manisky laughed, deep and throaty. "This is true. There is the intelligence found in the classroom and then there is that found on the field of battle."

"Or on the streets," Nochek said.

"Does Ryker have this?" Manisky asked. "He appears soft to me. Unwilling to do the hard thing to get what he wants."

Nochek fought to keep his expression controlled. If Manisky had any idea at all of Ryker's reach and intention, he wouldn't doubt the man's ruthlessness. But it was not Nochek's place to impart this knowledge. That would be Ryker's. If he liked what he saw from the meeting. Nochek shrugged. "Is any billionaire a saint?"

"We'll see," Manisky said. "If this is a waste of time, I'll be very unhappy."

Nochek turned to look out of the window. The massive walls of the Louvre were on their left. Once a fortress, now the world's preeminent collection of art, it was a testament to how the world changed. He knew great change was coming, and in that change, wealth would matter greatly. He intended to ensure he was ready.

Minutes later the car came to a stop in front of a tall set of double doors set at a forty-five-degree angle to the street. A small sign indicated this was La Tour d'Argent, a restaurant that was to serve as the meeting spot for the two billionaires.

Ryker had chosen the spot over Nochek's objections. It fed Ryker's ego, a magnificent location to fit the magnitude of the conversation. But from a security standpoint, it wasn't ideal. The restaurant itself took up the entire top floor and all other access points except the main elevator, which had been secured by the advance team. Bomb-sniffing dogs had covered the place, as had the most sophisticated electronics sweep, performed to find any cameras or listening devices.

The problem with the location was the same thing that made

Ryker want it: the main room faced a wall of floor-to-ceiling windows with a world-class view of the Cathedral du Notre Dame, the Seine, and the rooftops of Paris. Even though the cathedral was still under a massive reconstruction project from a devastating fire that had nearly collapsed the entire structure, the bell towers still formed a beautiful view. The restaurant's windows were tempered glass, but that would do nothing to stop a sniper's bullet.

Nochek just made a mental note to stay out of the line of fire.

While there certainly were people who wanted Manisky dead, Nochek was only worried about Scarvan.

Two of Manisky's protective detail took positions next to the car door. It was a short distance to the front door to the restaurant and the bodyguards did a good job of blocking most potential shot angles. Still, Nochek knew Scarvan's reputation.

"Why don't you let me go first?" Nochek suggested.

Manisky already had his hand on the car door. He looked curious. "Are you nervous about this meeting?"

"Ryker chose the location," Nochek explained. "I didn't control who had the information that you would be here. The interior is secure. This is just a precaution."

Manisky removed his hand, hesitated, and then leaned back to let Nochek pass. He opened the door and climbed out, the first bodyguard looking surprised to see him. As he exited, he pretended to lose his balance and stumble forward, low to the ground. The bodyguard reached for him, just as Nochek hoped, effectively providing additional cover in case Scarvan had crosshairs on him. He made short work of the distance to the open door to Tour d'Argent and went inside.

Manisky followed behind, glaring at him. "You looked like a fool," he growled.

Better to look like one, than to be one, Nochek thought. He allowed the big man to enter the elevator first and then followed him in. He just hoped the meeting went well and that Scarvan didn't rear his ugly head.

CHAPTER 24

"Sky Two for Alpha," came the male voice over the com-link.

Her waiter was delivering another espresso to her table, so she didn't reply. The surveillance team should have picked up on that before contacting her.

She'd only met the husband-wife team briefly. They were in their mid-forties and all business. They introduced themselves as Bob and Nora Clemson, but it was understood those were not their real names. They spoke with Norwegian accents, but that, too, could have been something they adopted to further mask their identities. They were contractors, but highly trusted by both Langley and Jim Hawthorn himself.

They had set up in a perfect position on short notice. The fourth-story apartment had been rented on Airbnb the night before. It was nicely furnished, although the Clemsons' gear covered half the living room. On entering, Mara had immediately noticed the sniper rifle cases laid out next to the electronic gear.

The Clemsons were more than simply a surveillance team.

From their location, they had a perfect line of sight across the Seine and into the main dining room of La Tour d'Argent. If Scarvan appeared inside the restaurant, they had the approval to take the shot.

"Come in, Alpha," came the call again.

Mara smiled at the waiter and resisted the temptation to adjust her earpiece. If anyone was scanning for an operative, digging at her ear was a key giveaway.

Young recruits always adjusted their earpiece, especially on first transmission. She wasn't sure if it was some ingrained behavior from watching too many bad action movies or just natural instinct when a voice appeared from nowhere. Regardless, it was a good way to get caught.

The waiter returned her smile, but in a withering way reserved only for French waiters. He left to care for his other tables.

"Go Sky Two," she said.

"Targets have entered the building. Three tangos at entry. Heat signatures on four others on the top floor."

"Roger on seven tangos."

Mara sipped her espresso, her face turned toward the river and the hulking form of Notre Dame Cathedral. Just another tourist enjoying the time-honored tradition of whiling away time on the outdoor patio of a Parisian café. Her large dark sunglasses disguised the fact that her eyes were in constant motion, scanning each person who approached La Tour d'Argent. Scarvan had shown so far that he liked his kills to be personal. She didn't think a long-range sniper shot was his style.

But that was also before they had figured out what he was up to. Any operative worth their freight knew to adapt to changing circumstances. If Scarvan was aware he was being hunted now, then he might very well change his tactics.

"Sky Two," she whispered. "Do you have eyes on water traffic?"

"That's affirm," came the reply.

There was a faint indignation in the voice. As if insulted she'd think the surveillance team wouldn't think to scan the river for threats. But Mara didn't feel bad for asking. A river approach wouldn't give a shooter the solid platform needed for a distance shot through tempered glass into a darkened room. Mara would have ruled it out for that very reason and there was a good chance the surveillance team had done the same.

But none of them were Scarvan, so they needed to push their preconceived notions aside on what he might do.

"Possible new arrival," came the voice in her ear. Female this time. The other half of the Clemsons. "Approaching from the east."

Mara moved only her eyes to the left to catch the approach of two identical white Mercedes Benz SUVs.

"Let's see who's joining the party," Mara said, thinking it must be Ryker and his team.

The SUVs pulled up in front of La Tour d'Argent and parked. No one got out for a full thirty seconds. That didn't seem right.

"Someone having second thoughts?" she whispered.

Another thirty seconds.

"Sky Two," she said. "Any read on this?"

No reply.

Her eyes moved to the rented apartment across the river. Nothing looked out of the ordinary.

"Sky Two?" she said. "Sky One? Do you read?"

Something was wrong. Communications weren't infallible, but when this close and with perfect line of sight, there shouldn't have been any issue.

Just then, the doors of the front SUV opened. Three men in black suits exited, leaving the driver inside. Two took position by the rear right door and the third faced out to the street, scanning for threats.

The rear door opened and a man exited. Marcus Ryker was one of the most recognizable men in the world. "The billionaire with the great hair" is what the tabloids called him. A favorite Ryker line in interviews when asked about the sobriquet was that he preferred being called the billionaire with flair.

Beyond the tabloids and the playboy image he cultivated, Ryker had a genius mind and the business sense to use it. With him, his seemingly altruistic endeavors were always paired with a personal financial windfall.

It was well known he met with all manner of businessmen and world leaders, even the unsavory ones. When asked about it, he always had a pithy answer about how even the wicked needed redemption. In fact, he'd had some success transforming erstwhile arms dealers into legitimate businesspeople and convincing despots to open their markets and rejoin the world community. The State Department hated his meddling, but the man got results.

Still, it still felt odd that he would suddenly be in the middle of this.

And what had happened to her backup?

"Sky One, come in," she said.

This time, when no answer came, she followed her instincts and moved. If the Clemsons had been compromised, she wasn't going to sit there in the open.

She walked toward the restaurant and saw Ryker start to enter through the front doors, but then stop. He spun around, a phone to his ear.

Mara could have sworn his eyes locked directly on her. As if the person on the phone had told him what to look for.

A second later, he waved his hand in the air and everything happened in reverse.

He climbed back into the SUV. As he slammed the door shut, the three-man team jogged to the lead vehicle. Even before the last door was shut, the SUV roared forward, cutting into traffic. The rear vehicle followed fast behind. They turned right and were gone.

"Sky, Sky. Do you read, over?" Mara said, louder now that she was walking the street. "Did something happen upstairs?"

It was Nora Clemson's voice that came over the earpiece. She sounded far away, like her mic was across the room from her. "River," she said. "On the river."

Mara sprinted across the street and leaned over the low stone barrier. The Seine was twenty feet below, bordered by a wide walkway. In the middle of the river was a small speedboat with a single man on it.

Even from this distance, the man's wild beard and lanky frame were impossible to miss.

Scarvan.

Mara reached for her Glock, feeling like she was moving in slow motion as her brain registered what she was seeing.

Scarvan had a long cylinder on his shoulder. A targeting sight rested on top of it.

He didn't need his platform to be that steady.

This was no precision shot he was taking.

Mara had only grasped the butt of her gun when flames shot from the back end of the RPG.

The rocket-propelled grenade tore through the air, leaving a trail of smoke behind it.

Mara couldn't help but turn to follow its trajectory.

The RPG hit the bottom third of the window and disappeared inside. The window turned white as it cobwebbed in a million segments, but it held in place.

But not for long.

After a beat just long enough that Mara had thought the round could have been defective, the blast came.

Every window simultaneously exploded outward. Torrents of fire burst from the opening, curling to the sky. Black smoke poured out as debris rained down onto the street. Drivers swerved, smashing into one another.

Mara ripped her eyes away, swinging her gun back toward Scarvan.

But he was already back behind the wheel of the boat, gassing it forward.

Mara took aim and fired.

She knew it was a ridiculous shot at that range, but she had to try.

A few of the shots must have come close because he turned backward and looked in her direction. And then the son of a bitch waved.

She ran back to the street where a middle-aged man was standing next to his running car, filming the carnage from the bomb on his phone. She pushed him aside, showing her gun so he wouldn't try to stop her.

The street followed the Seine. If she hurried, she could catch up to Scarvan.

She surveyed the mess of stopped and crashed cars in front her. Impossible.

Twisting the wheel to the right, she jumped the car onto the sidewalk, smashing aside the empty café tables. She blared the horn and waved her hands for people to get out of her way.

She gathered speed, sending chairs flying.

Finally, she broke free.

She raced across the bridge. Glancing to her right, she saw smoke streaming from the Airbnb apartment where the Clemsons had been. She assumed they were dead.

A look to her left and she saw the speedboat in the distance, already past Notre Dame.

Mara looked up just in time to slam on her brakes and avoid ramming into the line of police cars on the opposite side of the bridge.

They were out of their vehicles, guns pointed in her direction.

She looked over her shoulder and saw police swarming there, too.

"Shit!" she said, hitting the steering wheel. She'd had her shot at stopping Scarvan and blown it.

She threw her gun out the window and extended her hands. The last thing she wanted was to give some young whelp a reason to shoot her by mistake. All they knew was that they'd stopped a car fleeing the scene of a terrorist bombing. There was a good chance there were more than a few itchy trigger fingers in the group.

As the Paris police approached her vehicle, shouting instructions, she thought through what she might have done differently.

The Clemsons' location had been too perfect, making it easy to find. If they'd been in place during the attack, Scarvan would be dead right now.

Instead, her team and the man she needed as bait had been eliminated.

But how? There wasn't time for Scarvan to kill them and then get to the boat and into position.

As Mara laid with her face to the asphalt street and allowed herself to be handcuffed and taken into custody, she realized how she'd underestimated Scarvan.

She'd been smart enough to recognize he might change his tactics, adopting a long-range shot instead of the close quarters of his other kills.

But she hadn't thought he might change the fundamental modus operandi.

Scarvan had acted as a lone wolf his entire career. But now he'd accepted help from the outside. Suddenly, he was even more dangerous.

And she hadn't thought that was possible.

CHAPTER 25

Scott clung to the armrest as the old Land Rover bounced over the rough road. The rocky terrain rose up on either side of them, covered in azaleas and scrub oak. They passed rows of well-tended grape vines. The monks may have given up on many of the amenities of modern life, but wine wasn't one of them. Certainly, wine was needed for Holy Communion, but judging from the extent of the vineyard, Scott doubted the wine's use stopped there.

Thales Mitsopoulos had proven to be a man of few words. Scott's questions during the first thirty minutes of their journey south had been met with single-word answers or a shrug of the shoulders. Either he was the most ill-informed man in the area, or he was under orders not to give him any information.

Scott had a pretty good guess which it was.

The Land Rover slammed into a pothole, bottoming out with a loud scrape of metal against rock. Fortunately, the vehicle was pretty near indestructible. Although it had its limits. Scott didn't like the idea of having a long delay in his schedule if the car broke down.

"Is your protective training better than your driving?" he asked.

At least the comment brought a wry smile from the younger man. "I'd be able to handle you, if that's what you're asking."

"Maybe if I was asleep," Scott said. "And you had an army with you."

Instead of being offended, Thales loosened up. "Father Spiros told me you were a vain man."

"Did he? I'm surprised he knew anything about me."

"The Church knows things," Thales said.

"And what is it that you know?" Scott asked, grunting as the front wheel smashed against a rock, knocking them a foot to the left. "Besides how to hit every obstacle in the road."

Thales cast a sidelong look at him. Partially from the comment, but also sizing him up. Scott knew that look. It was someone deciding what to share. Or how best to lie.

"I know they're scared," Thales said. "They fear this man, this shadow they talk about in whispers. Apostoli is what they call him."

"Apostoli?" Scott repeated. "Is that what they call Scarvan?"

Thales shrugged. "I don't know that name. Only Apostoli. They fear what he will do. That they will be blamed."

Scott understood. If it were true that Scarvan had used Mt. Athos as a base for over two decades, there would be a major investigation into how that happened once the dust settled. Right now, the havoc he'd wrought was limited to the inner circles of the intelligence community. If that extended to assassinations of world leaders, then the gloves would come off. There'd be Interpol, FBI, and Secret Service crawling all over Mt. Athos within hours. And there'd be hell to pay.

"Apostoli," Scott said. "That's Greek for apostle. If Scarvan was the apostle, then who was he following?"

"Who do you think I'm taking you to see?" Thales asked. "Enough talking. Besides, we're almost there."

Scott leaned forward to look out of the front windshield. Nothing in the landscape had changed to make him think they'd reached their destination. He'd expected to see one of the twenty monasteries located on the isthmus, but there was nothing but more rugged terrain.

Still, Thales pulled the Land Rover to the side of the barely discernible dirt road and turned off the engine.

Scott considered for a second that Thales was playing him for a fool, but he spotted a narrow trail leading through the rocks toward the sea cliff. He followed his guide's lead and climbed out of the car.

He was greeted with the smell of salt spray in the air along with the faint reek of fish and seaweed. Gulls cried out overhead, drifting on the updrafts coming off the cliffs. A quick scan in all directions confirmed what Scott suspected: not another sign of human activity anywhere nearby. A perfect place to be alone to talk to God. Or to hide from international intelligence agencies that wanted you dead.

Thales wasted no time with small talk. He removed his suit jacket and left it in the car. His shoulder holster holding his Glock on full display.

They picked their way along the path, walking in a slanted angle along the water's edge while slowly drawing closer to the cliff. It was ten minutes before Thales came to a stop.

"There," he said. "If there are answers to be had, this is where they will be."

Scott climbed up the small rise to stand by Thales. Their vantage point allowed them to see a half-moon bay made up of craggy cliffs and a stone beach being mercilessly beat by angry waves. Perched against the cliff face were four structures that varied from ten to twenty feet off the ground. Made of the same rock as the beach, they blended in as part of the landscape, their corrugated metal roofs the only thing that made them stick out.

"This is where Scarvan lived?" Scott asked.

"If Apostoli is the same man as this Scarvan you're talking about, then yes. That's what I'm told."

Scott tried to imagine the assassin in such a place. The hardship of such a life would mean nothing to the man, and the isolation would have been the perfect place to hide out. But for over twenty years? It made no sense.

"How many people live in these huts?" Scott asked.

"They're called sketes," Thales said, picking his way carefully down a stone path to the rocky beach below. "One man in each during the old days. A monk would live there in isolation, often for his entire life. In fact, some of them become so infirm they can't make the journey down the ladder, so they stay in the skete for years without leaving. The other monks tend to their needs until their death. Then there's a scramble for who will occupy the skete next. Especially if the prior occupant was a particularly holy man."

"Why is that?" Scott asked, slipping on a rock before regaining his balance.

"Once a monk dies, he often requests his bones to remain in the skete. These relics help guide the new occupant on their journey and search for God."

Scott grimaced but he knew better than to be surprised. After all, he'd been in churches throughout Europe where treasured relics were no more than a knuckle bone or a femur purported to be from one saint or another.

He didn't understand the draw of religion, but he was all too aware of the power it had on many. The greatest atrocities he'd seen had been done in the name of God. Then again, so had many of the greatest kindnesses and acts of self-sacrifice.

On balance, he thought the amount of evil far exceeded the good done, but that was just his bias. He'd seen more bloodshed than most, but perhaps been farther away from the good done as well.

"Stop," came a voice from above. "What do you want?"

Scott squinted, with the sun directly above them. They were completely exposed but there was no way to avoid it. If the voice belonged to someone working with Scarvan, they had a clear shot.

"Are you Urgo?" Thales asked.

"I am. What's it to you?"

"My name is Thales Mitsopoulos. This man is here to speak with Father Spiros."

"He's not to be disturbed today," the man named Urgo yelled. "Come back tomorrow."

Scott stepped forward but Thales held up a hand to let him handle it.

"We are here on the command of Father Gregorio. We will be respectful of Father Spiros's time."

The mention of Father Gregorio had an immediate effect. Urgo climbed across a rocky ledge that looked too narrow to support a mountain goat, let alone a person, then climbed onto a rickety wooden platform held up by fraying ropes. He flipped a lever and the platform descended, the rope clicking through a pulley suspended above. He jumped the last four feet and landed next to them.

He was an odd-looking man, squat and ugly with a rash covering half his face and neck. His hair grew in patches, making him look like a dog with mange. As bizarre as his appearance was, he looked Scott and Thales over like they were from a different world.

"How do I know you are who you say you are?" he finally said.

Thales reached into his front pocket and pulled out a leather wallet. He flipped it open to show an identification badge embossed with the seal of the orthodox cross. The odd man snatched it from his hands and held it up close to his face as if smelling it instead of reading. He snorted and threw it back to Thales.

"He knew you were coming, you know?" he said, licking his lips as if they were food promised him. "Prelates of the false gods, he called you. He knew. He knew."

"Did he tell you that I would smack you aside the head if you delay us any longer?" Thales asked.

The man's demeanor changed at the threat. He scowled, then turned and led them to the ladder, which went to the largest of the four sketes. "I will go up and announce you."

Thales pulled the man down off the ladder. "That won't be necessary. You said yourself, he knows we're coming."

Urgo wanted to complain but seemed to think better of it. He slunk to the side of the ladder and sat heavily on a rock with his arms crossed.

"Zealot," Thales whispered as he began the climb up.

Urgo spat at the bottom of the ladder, his eyes blazing with hate.

Scott decided the monk was a few cards short of a full deck but was likely harmless enough. He waited until Thales entered the skete before adding his weight to the ladder, then climbed up.

The inside of the skete was dark and smelled like disease and old age. He flashed back to the hospital where his daughter Lucy had spent her last weeks fighting cancer. On the run, he'd been forced to come to her undercover as one of the mainte-nance crew. Even there in a modern hospital with disinfectants, the smell of death had lingered. In this small, enclosed space, it was nearly overwhelming.

The skete was a long rectangle with one side carved directly into the cliff wall. Occupying one end was a bed surrounded by wide candles. In the flickering light, they saw a man sitting up-right, propped up by pillows, his head lolled to one side.

He was thin to the point of emaciation, his body not much more than tight skin stretched against bone, reminding Scott of Belchik. He was hairless, both his face and head. His hands rested one on top of the other on his lap. Whatever Urgo did to care for the old man, cutting his nails was not part of his rou-tine. Yellowed nails curled from the ends of his fingers, some of them cracked and torn. A bedpan rested against the wall next to the bed, but the stench coming from the bed meant either it hadn't been washed since its last use or Urgo had missed the old man's last movement.

Scott's heart sank. It seemed impossible the miserable figure in front of him would be able to give him anything of value.

Thales kneeled next to the bed and put an arm on the old man's shoulder. "Father Spiros. Wake up. Can you hear me?"

The old man's eyes fluttered and then bolted open. Scott was shocked to see that they glowed blue in the candlelight, glazed over with starbursts of cataracts.

"Apostoli," he croaked. "Is that you?"

Thales was about to answer when Scott held up his hand for him to stop. He moved closer.

"Yes," he said softly, doing his best to recall Scarvan's gruff Eastern European accent from years ago on the boat. "I am here."

Tears appeared in Father Spiros's eyes. His mouth opened and closed involuntarily, a faint smacking sound coming from his dry tongue. "Do you forgive me? Do you forgive my sin?"

"I do," Scott said. "Of course, I forgive you."

"You came back," the old man mumbled. "Does this mean it's done? You did as God showed us?"

"Yes," Scott answered, hoping to get something out of the old man. "I did what I had to do."

Father Spiros tried to lift his hands but could not. Under the covers, the man's thin legs moved. He snorted and grunted from the effort.

"Rest easy," Scott said. "The task is done. Just as you predicted it would be."

This seemed to calm the old man down. He closed his eyes and a wicked smile appeared on his lips. He whispered, "Every tree therefore that bringeth not forth good fruit is hewn down and cast into the fire." Father Spiros reached out and grasped Scott's arm. The old man's nails dug into his skin and his fingers were no more than claws of bone. "And what a fire it shall be, Apostoli. Because of you, my son." He released his grip and closed his eyes. "I want to hear it. Tell me how it was done."

Scott and Thales shared a look. They both felt on the edge of getting the man to say what they needed, but also on the edge of the subterfuge collapsing.

"I will tell you, but not now," Scott said. "I need to know what to do next. Your instructions from here forward were unclear."

The old man stopped breathing from several long seconds, his face slowly twisting into a grimace. Scott thought he might be having a heart attack or maybe a stroke.

What was actually happening was far worse.

When the old man's eyes opened, gone was the mad euphoria, replaced instead by fury. As he turned his head to bring Scott fully into his range of vision, he knew the old priest had figured it out.

"Where is Apostoli?" he said.

"Dead," Scott answered on impulse, following his instinct. "I killed him. Your plan failed."

The lie had an immediate effect. The old man groaned, lifting his hands to his face, seeming not to notice as his own curled nails scratched at his paper-thin skin. Scott misinterpreted the action, thinking it was despair. Instead, when Father Spiros lowered his hands, he was smiling, his rotting gums poking out from behind his thin lips.

"Last night in my sleep I saw thrones, and they sat on them, and judgment was given to them. And I saw the souls of those who had been beheaded." He stared at Scott from behind his gnarled fingers. "You're lying. You were too late, weren't you?"

"Who was beheaded, Father?" Thales said, stepping forward for the first time. "The men who tried to kill him?"

The priest turned to him as if seeing his other visitor for the first time. "The men who have tried to kill God's world. As I saw in my vision, this shall herald the end of times. Have you seen it? Has He come?"

"Has who come?" Thales asked.

For the first time, the old man had a frightened, panicked look. "And then they will see the Son of man coming in a cloud with power and great splendor." He reached out to Scott, a look of confusion in his eyes. "Apostoli, I'm sorry I lied to you. I wanted to see the Messiah too much to wait. Please forgive the weakness of an old man. Forgive my lie."

Scott kneeled on the floor next to the bed. Maybe they'd catch a break after all. With the old man fading in and out, it was just a matter of time for them to pull the information out of him.

He adopted the deep Eastern European accent once again. "Tell me," he said. "Explain your vision and how I'm supposed to deliver God's plan."

Slowly, his voice weakening, Father Spiros began to speak.

CHAPTER 26

Scarvan had been on Mt. Athos for six months. He would never have believed it had someone told him that was to be the case the day he woke up in the old man's skete. A few days. A week at the most. The minimal amount of time for his body to heal enough for him to travel. That's what he expected.

But there he was.

Six months.

While his enemies still roamed free. Enjoying their lives. Filled with pride that they had been able to kill him. The bastards.

But something had happened to him in this place. Something unexpected.

For the first time since he'd been a child at his mother's knee, he was actually contemplating the existence of a power greater than himself. There had been no place for religion in his life. The only god he swore fealty to was that of the gun, of punishment, of power.

Father Spiros had opened his eyes to the idea that perhaps he'd been serving God all along. That His infinite wisdom caused him to know the evil in the hearts of men and also gave Him reason to hand-select those to do His work.

Whether they were aware or not.

The idea had seemed ridiculous to him, the mutterings of an

old fool who had lived alone too long eating wild berries and drinking rainwater.

But there were the dreams.

At first, he thought them no more than his fever talking to him. A parade of ghosts from his past coming to berate and scream at him for taking their lives. This he could handle. It was no different from when they'd begged him to spare them the first time. Anger now, instead of pathetic groveling, but the heart of it was the same.

But then things changed.

He'd been on Mt. Athos a month when the dream became something different.

That night, he found himself in the ruins of a soccer stadium. The edifice to man's leisure transformed by a few bomb runs into a symbol of mankind's true pastime, waging war. The once-lush green grass was brown and burned by the blistering sun. Shredded refuge shelters blew in the hot wind. The burned husk of a Red Cross ambulance lay on its side where there had once been a goal. The stadium seats were pockmarked with black spots where campfires had burned on cold nights.

Scarvan recognized the place, but only as it had been in his youth. Rajko Mitić Stadium. In Dedinje, just outside Belgrade. He and his friends used to sneak in when they were teenagers, watch the match, drink too much, sometimes get into a fight with fans from the other team when they were in the mood.

But he'd never seen it like this.

Now he stood in the center of the field, a spot where his heroes once stood at the beginning of the game, all promise and potential no matter the season's record. Kickoff was always a fresh start.

But standing there didn't feel like a new beginning. Far from it.

He spun in a circle, feeling his heart pound. A ringing noise filled his ears. He searched for a way out, but every exit was piled up with rubble.

No.

Not rubble.

There were stacks of bodies.

Charred. Twisted in unnatural poses. But still stacked like firewood. Barricading the outside world.

Or perhaps locking him in.

"What is this place?" he shouted.

Feeling eyes on him, he spun around. At the far end of the field, down by the ambulance, stood a little girl in a white nightgown. She had blond hair that lay flat, reaching down to the middle of her back. She walked toward him, and he felt the most incredible mixture of awe and fear he'd ever experienced in his life.

As she approached, he saw that both her nightgown and her pale, white skin were perfectly unblemished. In a world of dust and ash and debris, she was untouched.

Scarvan reached for his gun. A knife. Anything.

But in a moment of terror, he realized he carried none of these.

Worse, he wore no clothes at all. He was stark naked.

A wave of embarrassment and shame came over him. He covered his genitals with both hands. He looked for something with which to cover himself, but there was nothing. He was exposed.

The little girl stopped fifteen feet from him, regarding him curiously.

"Do you not know who you are to me?" she asked.

Her voice was both the sound of water in a stream and the roll of thunder in a night sky. Somehow both peace and terror at the same time.

"I don't," he said. "I don't know this place."

The little girl smiled but Scarvan shrank away from her. Inside the girl's mouth was nothing but incalculable darkness. No tongue or teeth, just an endless void that pulled at him with its own gravity.

"This is a place you made," she said.

"It's horrible."

The girl looked sad at the comment, as if he were making a

statement about her. "It's necessary. This you did for me. And I honor you for it."

In a moment of perfect clarity, Scarvan realized what was happening. He straightened and pulled his shoulders back, feeling his confidence come rushing back. "This isn't real," he stated firmly. "All of this is a dream. Or a hallucin—"

The girl rushed at him, no more than a blur from the speed. She smashed her fist into his chest, and he flew backward through the air. He landed hard, gasping for air. He held his chest, coughing.

A shadow blocked the noon sun and he looked up.

The girl stood over him. "I saved you for a reason. Spiros knows it. But do you? Can you ever accept it?" She turned her head to one side, studying him. "I think you can. In time. But now . . . wake up."

Scarvan had bolted up in bed. Father Spiros was sitting in his usual chair next to him, Bible in hand. Scarvan grabbed his chest, rubbing at the burning pain there.

Heart attack?

He didn't think so, but he wasn't sure.

He swung his legs over the edge of the bed and tried to get his bearings in the small hut. He pulled open his shirt and, even in the candlelight, could see the deep red mark on his skin from the impact. Within a day, it would be a nasty purple bruise that radiated across his chest.

Father Spiros closed his book. "He came to you," he whispered.

"What are you talking about? It was a dream. A little girl. Just a dream." He heard the desperation in his own voice and hated the sound of it.

Father Spiros smiled and nodded at his chest. "A dream? I think not. And do you not think the Lord Father can come in any way he sees fit? Man, woman, child, creature. Don't dare to believe you can understand His ways." He leaned forward. "Did He tell you what must happen? Did He show you the path He's chosen?"

Scarvan pulled his shirt closed. He wanted nothing to do with this. With any of it. He scrambled to his feet and shoved the old man to the side. He sprinted to the door and burst through it, gasping for air as if he'd been underwater on the edge of drowning. He lunged for the ladder, grasped it, and swung his legs around.

But his foot missed the first rung and he slipped.

The moment of weightlessness as he fell the fifteen feet seemed to stretch out seconds longer than could be possible.

He twisted in midair, his training taking over to protect his head and spine.

His right foot hit first, hammering into the ground with shattering impact.

It disappeared into a crevice between two rocks, the flesh on his shin scraped clean. Then the mass of his body carried to his right, snapping his tibia with a crack that sounded like gunfire. He screamed as he reached down. The bone jutted out from where its jagged edge had broken the skin. It felt like his entire leg was on fire.

When he closed his eyes fight back the pain, it was the child's face from his dream that he saw. And a sense of peace came over him just before he passed out.

By the time Scarvan had come around, he was being hoisted back up to the skete in the rope-and-pulley system. A young boy named Urgo pulled hard on the rope as he moved slowly higher. His body turned and his leg slammed into the rock face, sending a round of agony shooting through him.

He next woke back in the same bed where he'd recuperated from his injuries on the boat. Only this time his leg was wrapped in a heavy plaster cast that encompassed his foot and extended up to the middle of his thigh. It was another month before he left the skete again.

A month of radical dreams, visits from dark memories, and a recurring vision of the young girl in the stadium. Each time he awoke, Father Spiros was there, often reading, sometimes whispering near to his ear, describing the very same things that he'd shared with the old man. As if he could see inside his head.

To pass the time, Scarvan read the Bible as well. He'd known many of the stories from when he was a child, but there was so much in the pages that surprised him. God was not the benevolent figure his mother had prayed to. Within the pages he read, he found a God he understood. Angry and vengeful. Filled with violence and aggression. A God intent on punishment for those creatures who failed to follow the divine rules.

Finally, he asked Father Spiros the question that had been gnawing at him. "This girl. She's already told you what she wants me to do, hasn't she?"

The old man grew very quiet. It was a long time before he answered. When he did, it was in a steady, clear voice. "God appears to everyone differently. I do not see a young girl as you describe. He comes to me as a voice inside of a brilliant light."

"You didn't answer the question," Scarvan said.

Father Spiros templed his hands together and leaned forward. "Yes, I know what will be asked of you. But I've also been told you must learn the truth for yourself."

"So, you will not tell me?"

"I cannot tell you," he said. "I cannot choose to go against God any more than I could choose to fly or choose to swim under the ocean."

"I don't believe this is God speaking to me," Scarvan said. "These are dreams. Delusions. Nothing more."

The old man gave him a pitying look. Scarvan felt the emptiness in his own words, but he didn't care. It was better than admitting that he believed. That admission came with consequences he didn't want to imagine.

It was another three months before he asked Father Spiros to baptize him.

Shortly after that, he killed for the first time for his new God.

CHAPTER 27

Scott felt a chill climb up his spine. He realized that until that moment he'd let himself believe that Scarvan had been out of the game for the last twenty years. That his complete absence was the only way to explain why he'd managed not to turn up back on the grid again to raise suspicion.

Now his mind went to the dozens of covert missions carried out by unknown operators over the years. He knew most of his own work left the intelligence agencies around the world scratching their heads, poring over data trying to determine who had been inside their borders.

Perhaps Scarvan had been more active than he'd thought. The idea of Scarvan killing for God made him uneasy, but he wasn't sure why. After all, Scott killed for his own country. Was the idea of a nation any less ephemeral than religion? All based on an idea, on faith in a system, on the idea of allegiance to a greater cause.

But in the end, Scott knew that while he fought for his country, he really had always gone into harm's way for his family. For his friends. For the men and women walking down any street in America. There was an old saying that there were no atheists in foxholes. But whoever had come up with that saying likely hadn't spent much time in the trenches. At the end of the day, soldiers might pray to God when they faced the enemy, but they stood and fought because of their buddies on either side of them.

"Who was it?" Thales asked next to him. "Who did he kill?"

Father Spiros turned to him as if just realizing the younger man was in the room. His eyes cleared, fully lucid.

"Brother Misha," he said. "He was the only other person on Mount Athos who knew for sure where Apostoli came from. He helped me nurse him back to life."

"Then why would he kill him?" Thales asked.

Scott already knew the answer. "He was a loose end."

Father Spiros let his head roll to the side, so he once again looked at Scott. "Poor Misha suffered the sin of jealousy. He knew Apostoli had been chosen to change the world and he hated him for it. One day he threatened to tell others of how we'd found him washed up on the beach. That was his last day on earth."

"But he didn't stop there," Scott said. "He's killed others for you."

"Killed . . . killed . . ." the old man muttered, his lips curled as if there was a foul taste in his mouth. "He fulfilled his purpose. As God instructed."

"Or was it as you instructed?" Thales said. "I know your politics, Father. I know you did not choose this stone hut for yourself. The patriarch himself remediated you here decades ago. To isolate you. To stop the poison you leaked into the young minds in the monasteries."

This got Scott's attention. Something the analysts at Langley had missed in his brief. They'd warned of missing pockets of information. The world on Mt. Athos was insular and hard to penetrate. And who was kidding whom? Greek Orthodoxy wasn't exactly a known hotbed of fundamental terrorism.

The old man clucked his tongue in annoyance. The sound was thick and sticky.

"A week with me and you would have been one of my disciples," he said. "I can see the fire in your eye. God needs soldiers like you. Just like he needed Apostoli. Orthodoxy or die."

Scott recognized the saying from his briefing book. Years earlier, the monks at the Esphigmenou monastery on Mt. Athos had rebelled at the idea of the patriarch's outreach to Catholicism to create a dialog. In a show of disobedience, they had refused to include ranking members of the church hierarchy in their daily prayers. Finally, the Church had had enough and went to court to label them as schismatics and therefore squatters on the monastery property. What followed was a multiyear standoff with monks inside the high walls of Esphigmenou surrounded by police. It was during that time that their slogan, *Orthodoxy or Die,* was made popular as the media hovered nearby, hoping the whole thing would turn violent. Instead, the monks waited out the authorities and eventually formed their own Order of Esphigmenou.

"I'm supposed to believe that Jacobslav Scarvan came here and found religion?" Scott said.

"Not religion," the old man said. "He achieved theosis, a direct connection to God. First through catharsis, the purification of body and thought. Then, theoria, a personal vision sent to him alone. In this place, the Lord speaks to those prepared to listen."

"And what did God tell you to do?" Scott asked. "What did He tell Scarvan?"

"To defend the one, true faith from those who would subvert its purity." Father Spiros's speech was slow and labored, each word a challenge to get out. "Orthodoxy has been plagued by false leaders. Those who would compete with Catholicism by diluting what is holy and just. By joining those who have bastardized our faith. These people had to be stopped. Apostoli, the man you call Scarvan, was the vehicle God sent to me. And he fulfilled his duty."

Scott noticed Thales rear back in horror. He understood something he did not.

"What is it?" he asked, checking the door and windows in case a threat had appeared there without him seeing it.

"Petros," Thales whispered. "You're talking about Petros."

Father Spiros looked away from the younger man. "I did as God commanded me to do."

The name was familiar to Scott, but he couldn't place it. He looked to Thales to tell him.

"In 2004, Petros VII, the patriarch of Alexandria, died in a helicopter crash on his way to Mount Athos. Twelve people died when his Chinook went down over the Aegean. No cause was ever determined. Not publicly anyway."

"Scarvan," Scott said.

Father Spiros shrugged his shoulders. "Was it? Or was it the hand of God?" He turned his head so that his eyes looked directly into Scott's. "From my point of view, there is no difference."

"You crazy old shit," Thales said. "You'll pay for what you've done."

At this, Father Spiros wheezed and coughed, the sound a deep rattle in his chest. It took Scott a second to realize the old man was laughing. But the phlegm in his throat caused him trouble and his cough turned worse.

Scott reached out and propped the old man up, cringing from feeling the bones protruding under his robe. The man was not much more than a breathing skeleton.

"Get some water," Scott told Thales as the old man gasped for air between ragged coughs.

"Better to just let him die," he said. But he crossed the skete and brought back a mug filled with water he found there.

Scott poured some carefully into the old man's mouth. He sputtered on the first attempt, but on the second he was able to swallow and get back control of his breathing.

When he lay back down, tears had trekked down his cheeks and his face was flushed from the exertion. He groaned and held his stomach.

"I'm sorry, Apostoli," he mumbled. His eyes closed, his voice drifting, losing grip again on reality. "I should not have lied to you. But no matter how much I whispered in your ear while you slept, you would not change your belief."

"How did you lie to me?" Scott said, playing along.

"You did this. It's your fault," Father Spiros said. "You misunderstood what God told you. I'm certain of it. I wanted to see the coming of the Lord you would bring about. I needed to see it with my own eyes. But you wouldn't leave my side while I still lived. So I had to make you believe I was dead. To free you. To set you on your path. Don't you see? Don't . . . you . . ."

Scott grabbed the old man by the shoulder and shook him. Not too hard, fearing the fragility of his bones and that his skin might tear.

Father Spiros opened his eyes but they were focused on a distant spot, seeing a landscape only he could see.

" 'Behold, he cometh with clouds; and every eye shall see him. All kindreds of the earth shall wail because of Him. His head and his hairs are white like wool, as white as snow; and his eyes are as a flame of fire.' "

"What is Scarvan planning?" Scott said, raising his voice. "Tell me."

" 'His voice is the sound of many waters. And he has in his right hand seven stars; and out of his mouth comes a sharp two-edged sword.' "

Scott didn't care about the man's brittle bones any longer. He sensed he was losing him. The chance to understand Scarvan's plan was slipping through his fingers. He pulled the man up from the bed, using one of his hands to support his head as if he were a newborn baby.

"Where is he going?" Scott shouted.

In a moment of clarity, the old man's eyes turned to Scott. "The Lord demands the world be on its knees when he arrives. Sometimes the body is so diseased, the only mercy is to remove the head. Apostoli will cleanse the world in a rush of fire. This is the Lord's will as it was shown to me. It is how it shall be. There is nothing you can do to stop it. And I will not tell you another thing." Father Spiro looked past Scott and smiled, his thin, dry lips cracking open as he did. "Now, Urgo. Do what you must."

Scott spun around to see the odd caretaker monk standing inside of the door to the skete.

A shotgun in his hands.

"Wait!" Scott shouted.

But it was too late.

CHAPTER 28

Mara was pissed.

But she knew her anger needed to be directed at Scarvan. He had executed his plan right under her nose, killed her surveillance team, and then gotten clean away. The easy thing to do was to lash out at the French police for apprehending her instead of pursuing Scarvan as she'd told them to do.

As frustrating as it was, they'd only done their job.

She'd sat silently in the squad car that had transported her to the station and then ignored the carousel of inquisitors who'd come in to question her. Their tactics had varied from screaming at her to offering her food and drink to put her at ease. Through it all, she'd stared at the clock on the wall, lost in her own thoughts of where she'd screwed up the mission.

She knew Hawthorn would work his channels within the DGSE, the *Direction Générale de la Sécurité Extérieure*, the French intelligence arm. They'd be mad that an asset had been operating on their soil without permission. A formal complaint would be filed, and it would go into the circular bin at Langley with all the other complaints from nations around the world.

Funny thing was they never complained when a U.S. counter-intelligence operation tipped them off about an imminent threat. Or even stopped one, handing over the bad guys in a nice bundle.

That was what she was supposed to have done.

Instead, two operatives were dead. Not to mention however many people were in La Tour d'Argent or who had been injured from the debris.

A rocket-propelled grenade. Launched from a goddamn boat. She still couldn't believe it.

It was a full hour before three men in suits from the American Embassy arrived to escort her out of French custody. Men dressed in black body armor glared at her as she walked through the station. These were GIGN, part of the French National Gendarmerie. She'd worked with them before and knew they were hardened professionals. While they could accept that she wasn't the perpetrator, she understood the stares.

She had information about the attack. And she wasn't sharing.

Mara had been on the other end of that particular equation before and she'd hated it. But it was Hawthorn's call on what to share. She knew the protective details had been put on alert about Scarvan, but that was when the targets had been heads of state.

An explosion in the middle of historic Paris was something else.

Once they were out of the police station and into the waiting Mercedes SUV, she was handed a satellite phone.

"Mara," Hawthorn said, "thank God you're all right."

His reaction surprised her. Gruff disappointment was more his style when a mission was botched. He was getting a little more sentimental in his old age. "Sorry, boss. I blew the chance."

"I already have footage," Hawthorn said. "With the approach he took, he should have been an easy target for the surveillance team. The plan was sound."

Except for the part where I didn't take into account he might not be working alone, Mara thought. "Any leads on who took them out?"

She almost called them the Clemsons, but it felt awkward using their fake names. Especially now that they were dead. Somehow it seemed disrespectful.

"The building security cam was wiped, but that wasn't unexpected. The ATM camera across the street from the main entrance gives us a good look, though."

"And?"

"Nothing yet," Hawthorn said. "On first pass, all foot traffic entered multiple times. Residents or other renters. Some have their faces obscured but even those are IDed by their clothes worn earlier in the day."

Mara closed her eyes, thinking it through. Imagining how she would do it. The fact that the lobby video was gone meant the operative knew they would be on it, otherwise why bother taking it? That meant they came in through the main entrance.

"He took someone's clothes," she said.

There was silence on the other end of the line. She didn't have to explain. Hawthorn had been at the game longer than she had. He'd played more permutations that she could even imagine. He knew she was right. She imagined he was processing how he'd missed it.

"We'll dig in and send you the image once we sort out which one it was," he said. "We both know it likely won't tell us much."

"Paris has more cameras per square mile than Moscow. We might get lucky," she said, not really thinking they would. "But there's something else I need you to get Jordi working on."

"Name it."

"Someone tipped off Marcus Ryker that the hit was about to happen," Mara said, remembering the way the man had frozen and then turned and looked right at her. "And whoever did it knew I was on site, too."

That Ryker had stopped in front of La Tour d'Argent and done an about-face was something Hawthorn already would have known from video analysis. The idea that whoever had called with the warning also knew about their operation meant one of two things: either Mara had been followed or there was someone on the inside.

If their operation to pursue Scarvan wasn't small and compartmentalized already, Mara knew how Hawthorn operated. The circle of trust was about to get a lot smaller.

A nagging thought occurred to her, just on the periphery of everything else she was processing. *Was it possible that was exactly the reaction Scarvan wanted?*

"Can you tell these suit monkeys to take me to the apartment where the Clemsons were killed? They seem to think I'm getting on an airplane."

"That's on my order, Mara," Hawthorn said. "There's nothing to see at the apartment. French police removed two bodies. They're playing nice with our team, so if there's anything useful, we'll get it."

"I want to—"

"Sergei Kolonov turned up," Hawthorn said.

Mara felt a surge of excitement. There were only two people left of any consequence for Scarvan to target, outside of Hawthorn and her dad, of course. The question was whether Scarvan would continue on his quest now that they'd tipped their hand they were on to him.

Given the chance, Mara would have bet good money that he would.

"Where is he?"

"Prague."

The excitement from a few seconds earlier was replaced by a splash of cold water. The beautiful city was forever carved into her mind as the site of her mother's death. She'd read the CIA report a hundred times, always ending on the photo of the Charles Bridge where it'd happened.

Terrible memories that all came flooding back at her with that one word.

Prague.

"Are you there?" Hawthorn said.

Mara shook her head as if that simple act were enough to push that kind of psychological trauma away. It worked enough for her to find her voice. "Got it. I assume the details will be on the plane?"

"They will. And Scott will meet you there once he's done on Mount Athos."

"Any word?"

"No, but he left with a single man and drove out into a remote area of the isthmus. Hopefully it's not a dead end."

Mara at least felt relieved that Scarvan's presence in Paris had meant her dad had been relatively safe. She wasn't looking forward to debriefing him about the missed opportunity to catch their target.

Someone else spoke near Hawthorn and she heard only muffled sounds as he covered the phone and talked to them. When he got back on the line, he sounded pleased. "It appears you have one thing to do before you leave Paris."

"What's that?"

"Thanks to Jordi's good work here, our French friends have detained Marcus Ryker at Le Bourget. He was about to leave on his private jet. He's agreed to an interview before he departs. I want it to be you."

Mara grinned. "Usually you only have bad news. I hope this is the start of a new habit."

"Don't get your hopes up," he said. Then he turned serious. "Be careful, Mara. He puts up a front, but Ryker is as clever as they come."

"The question is whether he's also dangerous," she said. "I expect I'm about to find out."

CHAPTER 29

Paris-Le Bourget was the busiest general aviation airport in Europe. While the smaller aircraft that typically made up the fleet for general aviation enthusiasts had a place there, the airport was really designed for one specific purpose: to cater to the massively affluent jet-setters from around the world when they wanted to visit the City of Light.

Alpha Team's Gulfstream was also parked there, fueled up and ready to take her to Prague. While the G5 was top of the line, it still paled in comparison to some of the private rides of the rich and famous.

There were two styles on display on the tarmac. First were the small, sleek, and sophisticated planes, tricked out so they looked like something from a sci-fi thriller. These tended to be for short hops and to get into small airports, often just a landing strip cut out of the forest near someone's Loire Valley chateau or German castle.

Then there were the larger aircraft: Boeing 737s, DC10s, Airbus 319s, with interiors that made them more flying luxury hotels than aircraft. Mara had been on some that made Air Force One look like a worn-out motel by comparison. Then again, most of these aircraft didn't have countermeasures to fend off surface-to-air missiles or the communication infrastructure to fight a protracted war without ever having to land.

Then again, maybe some did.

Of particular interest to her was the Boeing 787 she saw on the tarmac, elegant stairs rolled up to the closed door. The tail and fuselage were covered with the distinctive RYKER logo that was part of every brand Marcus Ryker owned. Subtlety was not the man's strength.

There were only a handful of private 787s in the world and most of them were outfitted by Westral Aviation Management. The CIA had attempted to infiltrate the company. Private buyers of three-hundred-million-dollar jets tended to be the kind of people who had information the CIA would find helpful. A few listening devices here and there on the planes could have yielded valuable information. It was the kind of initiative privacy groups loved to find out about and lodge complaints against. But regular Americans expected their government to do whatever was necessary to keep them safe.

Unfortunately, those who could afford to buy such an aircraft could also afford the best counterintelligence measures on the open market as well. There was no shortage of professionals available for contract work to make sure the Agency—or any other intelligence service, for that matter—didn't slide in during the construction process to plant a device or two.

Even so, they'd been successful on some of the planes destined for Middle Eastern destinations. Dormant listening devices buried into component parts manufactured further down the supply chain were nearly impossible to detect until they were activated. And if it was done in short bursts, then they would only be discovered if there was a scan happening at the precise moments they were turned on.

Yet somehow, Ryker had avoided any technology getting onto his plane. The fact that it was Ryker Labs that served as the contractor to develop the eavesdropping devices likely had something to do with it.

That and Ryker had experimental tech that far exceeded what he shared with the rest of the world. He likely had counterintelligence measures that would make the hardware guys at Langley salivate.

But she had a few tricks up her own sleeve. She opened her bag and removed the Skittle, a microdot listening device that was only as big as the candy it was named after. It was record-only, no transmission. That meant it needed to be retrieved at some later time, but it also made it nearly impossible to find. She intended to find a way to install it on Ryker's plane.

Until her driver delivered the bad news.

"Ryker is waiting in the Vendome Lounge," her driver said.

"Hawthorn said he agreed to do the interview on the plane," she said.

"Changed his mind, I guess."

They stopped in front of an airplane hangar. A short red carpet led to a double set of glass doors manned by two men in suits. A metallic sign that said ADVANCED AIR SUPPORT was posted next to the door.

Mara had been here before. Hangar H5 had been completely transformed on the interior as a super-luxe waiting area. There were four different VIP lounges, showers, nap rooms, and even a private prayer room. The fact that the prayer room was equipped with a washbasin, rug, and an ornate compass so the faithful could align themselves with Mecca gave an indication of the normal clientele.

"Want company?" her driver asked.

"No, I'm good. Shouldn't be long. Can you confirm my plane is ready to roll?"

"Already done, ma'am. Your pilot says engines are warm and he's ready when you are."

Mara appreciated the man's efficiency. Her people skills had been lacking on the ride over, her frustration at the events of the day overriding her first principle:

Try not to be a jackass to people.

"Thank you," she said. "I appreciate it."

The driver looked up in the rearview, a little surprised. He gave her a short nod in acknowledgement. "Ryker. He's like a real live Tony Stark. My nine-year-old son wants to grow up and be him when he gets older." He paused for a second. "I hope he's not an asshole."

"Me too," she said. She took a deep breath and opened the door. She slipped the Skittle into her pocket, doubtful it would be of any use now. But she was never one to close off an option.

One of the suits opened the door for her. As he did, he spoke into a wrist mic announcing her arrival. Another man met her inside and walked her past the other VIP lounges. They reached the end of the hallway and the man knocked on the door.

"Come," came a voice from the inside.

The man opened the door but then stepped aside to allow her to pass him. Once she stepped in, he closed the door behind her.

The room was decorated in a modern fashion, with a collection of white leather furniture arranged into a U shape around a brushed metal and glass table. There were two floor lamps made of stacked shiny metallic balls capped with square white shades. On the wall was a black and white photo of a woman posing in front of a creatively lit aircraft.

On the couch sat Marcus Ryker, unmistakable from the thousands of photos Mara had seen of the man. He wore different clothes from when she'd seen him about to enter La Tour d'Argent only hours earlier. A fresh shirt, some kind of luxurious fabric with a slight sheen to it that highlighted his athletic physique. He was handsome, with a square jaw covered in a fashionable level of scruff, hair worn wild in a *I-don't-give-a-shit* kind of way. There was a reason he was often on inane lists ranking the sexiest men alive. It was his eyes that gave Mara pause. They were ice blue, nearly luminous under the interior lights. But she expected that.

What she hadn't expected was the chill she'd feel from them. She knew the look in those eyes.

They were the eyes of a killer.

This was going to be more interesting than she imagined.

CHAPTER 30

Shit.

Marcus Ryker didn't do surprises. He spent sizeable amounts of money to ensure he never had to have the uncomfortable sensation of playing catch-up. Ever.

This was the second surprise in one day. And that made him unhappy.

The phone call outside La Tour d'Argent had tipped him off to get the hell out of there. The man on the phone had even directed his eyes to the operative watching him from the café across the street. From that distance, he hadn't been able to identify who it was.

But he knew the woman standing in front of him all too well. *Mara Roberts.*

It took every bit of his self-control to keep the emotion from flickering across his face.

"Hello," he said standing. "I'm Marcus Ryker. Nice to meet you."

"Mara Roberts."

He waited as if she might include which agency she represented. He was interested in reading her when she lied to him for the first time. But she offered nothing. The choice said even more.

"Please." He motioned toward the leather chair next to the sofa. "Can I get you something? Water, coffee?"

"No, thank you," she said, taking the offered seat. "This shouldn't take long."

"I'm always more than happy to be interviewed by sophisti-cated women," he said, playing the part of his public persona. He would have said *beautiful* or *attractive*, but he knew this would have offended her. Maybe he'd save that for later.

"I saw your plane is ready," she said. "Where are you heading?"

He appreciated her smooth, conversational delivery. He de-cided a more direct approach was better.

"You're here about my meeting with Oleg Manisky at Tour d'Argent earlier today," he said.

If she was surprised by his frankness, it didn't show. "Yes. Only there isn't a Tour d'Argent anymore."

"I saw on the news. Terrible incident. Unbelievable really. Any suspects?"

Mara pursed her lips and let a few beats of silence fill the air. Her eyes didn't leave his. He felt his skin prickle. It was the same cold look her mother had been able to deliver.

"I can't comment on ongoing investigations," she finally said.

Ryker gave her a thin smile. "And what investigative arm do you belong to, Ms. Roberts?"

"The one that hates bad guys," she said.

"And you think I'm one of those bad guys?" he said.

"Right before you walked into Tour d'Argent, you received a call that warned you of the attack. Who was it?"

Ryker crossed his legs and leaned back. He wasn't accus-tomed to people being rude to him. His was a life surrounded by those who catered to his every whim and impulse. Some did so because they were paid extravagant sums of money. Others be-cause they believed in his vision for the Omega. The end of times.

But none of them spoke to him with anything less than com-plete deference.

He didn't allow it.

"As I'm certain you know, I also work for the U.S. government from time to time," he said. "In my role as global business innovator, I have the occasion to meet with a variety of people your intelligence services are eager to learn more about—governments, sovereign equity funds, industrialists, and yes, Russian oligarchs. Some of these men"—he stopped and cast her an amused look—"and women, although they are mostly men, are unsavory."

"Like the newly departed Oleg Manisky," Mara said.

"Exactly," he said. "My business with Mr. Manisky was to get his assistance with TASS."

Mara didn't rise to the bait. Of course, she would know that TASS was the Russian Space Agency, but she saw zero need to say so to prove it. Ryker found the self-confidence appealing.

"My own foray into space exploration has hit a few bumps in the road." Bumps being massive explosions of his supposedly reusable launch vehicles. "While the scientific community likes to posture that they are above competition and intent on cooperation in order to advance humanity, you'll never meet a more suspicious and insular group."

"So, Manisky was going to help you build rocket ships?" Mara said. "Was he planning on using the sex workers he human traffics in to build the parts? Or maybe lend you his paramilitary force he maintains in Ukraine . . . just in case you needed it?"

Ryker spread his hands wide. "If I only met with angels, I'd meet with no one at all."

"That still doesn't answer the central question."

"And what's that, Ms. Roberts? You've dragged things on a little here." He unfolded his legs and leaned in toward her. He allowed his voice to show just the edge of the building rage he felt for being detained by this pettiness. "What is the central question, according to you?"

She didn't react at all to his tone. Her voice inflection didn't change. "Who was on the phone? Who warned you an attack was coming?"

Ryker sat back. This woman was not about to be intimidated. "That's a good question," he finally said. "Would it surprise you if I said I didn't know?"

That question got a smile from his questioner. But it was thin. Not a sign she was amused. "How about, it wouldn't surprise me that you would say you didn't know who it was."

Ryker let out a barking laugh and pointed at her. "I see why they sent you. You're good. You don't fluster easily and you're on point. Ever thought of leaving government work and joining the private sector? Ryker Industries is always looking for talent."

"Maybe I can get your card," she deadpanned. "Who was on the phone?"

Ryker stood, smoothing out his suit jacket. Mara remained seated, which infuriated him.

"I received the call on my private cell phone. Only a few people know that number. Your boss is one of them."

"You don't know who my boss is."

"I mean your ultimate boss. The one who sits in the Oval Office," he said. "But there was no sign who this call came from."

"But you still picked it up?" she asked.

"Like I said, the few people that have this phone number are the kind of people who get their call answered."

"What exactly did the voice say?"

Ryker smiled. He appreciated her directness. "It was a modulated voice, put through some kind of device, so I can't even tell you if it was a man or woman. This person simply said, 'If you go in the building, you will die along with the Russians.'" Ryker shrugged. "Seemed like a good time to leave."

"Was that all this person said? Video shows you looking around the area, as if you were searching for something very specific."

There was more, but Ryker didn't feel like sharing it. Not that it was anything damning, but he'd had just about enough of being interrogated. "I'm afraid that's it," he said. "And, I might add, exactly what I already told the French authorities who asked me to wait for you."

"The ones who detained you?" she asked.

Ryker didn't like the sound of that. He knew that was exactly why she'd chosen the words. Just to get a rise out of him. Even a small one. "They were very polite," he said.

"Money has that effect on some people," she said.

"But not on you," he said. Ryker crossed the room to the small bar and selected a bottle of Glenfiddich. He held it up to offer some to her, but she just stared back at him. He poured two fingers into a glass and swirled it, smelling its fragrant notes.

"I read somewhere that you were a teetotaler," she said. "Is that just part of the cover story?"

"I don't drink," he said. "I'd love to, but when I was younger, it was a problem. So I stopped. But I do love the smell of it."

"Doesn't having it in your hand prove too tempting?"

"Only for someone lacking self-discipline," he said.

Mara stood. As she did, he admired her body. Athletic but feminine. Her face beautiful without all the makeup that the women in his life typically wore. He admitted that he found her all the more attractive after her display of self-control and toughness in the interview.

It was too bad she was at the center of her government's hunt for Omega.

That meant at some point he would need to have her killed.

A pity.

"Funny choice of words, self-control," she said. "Coming from someone who cultivates his brand on the idea of excess. Seems to be a direct contradiction."

"Nothing exceeds like excess," Ryker said, reciting the tagline he used in many of his interviews. "Just marketing. In fact, if you look closely at my work, you'll see it stands in defiance of the reckless excesses of the human race. My labs search for sustainable fuels, methods to eradicate the microplastics now pervasive in the world's food supply, ways to engineer our way out of the inevitable freshwater crisis which will be the greatest calamity in human history if we don't prepare."

"All Ryker Industries profit centers," Mara said. "You're quite the humanitarian."

"And you are quite the cynic, Ms. Roberts," he said. "I find that to be an unattractive quality in a woman."

"Then I expect we won't be dating. Thank you for your time, Mr. Ryker," she said. "And I think I will take you up on your offer."

He was confused. "The drink?" he asked. "Or the opportunity to come work for Ryker Industries?"

"Neither," she said. "But be assured I'll be taking a closer look at all your work. Have a good flight."

She turned and walked out. After she left, he had the unsettling sense that she'd gotten more out of the interview than he'd meant to divulge. Nothing terrible, but enough to raise her suspicion of him.

Damn Stefan Nochek. Before today, Ryker had left no wake from his Omega actions. Slowly and carefully rebuilding after the disaster in DC. And now it appeared he was on the radar of the person he least wanted tracking him down.

Strangely enough, he found it exhilarating.

CHAPTER 31

The shotgun blast was deafening in the enclosed space of the skete.

Scott jumped to his right, toward the nearest wall. But as he did, he braced himself for the searing pain of shot tearing through him.

How could he have been so careless? At the minimum he ought to have positioned his Greek escort at the door. Or locked it.

Instead, he was about to die at the hands of an amateur.

A split second later he was able to register that the first blast hadn't hit him.

Instinct took over.

He rushed forward, staying low.

As he hoped, the monk's first shot had pushed him backward and sent the barrel of the gun up toward the ceiling.

The barrel was just starting to come back down as Scott's shoulder slammed into the monk's chest.

They flew backward together but the monk was not the amateur Scott had thought him to be. The man struck downward with the butt of the shotgun, making contact with the base of Scott's neck. Pain blasted down his back, but it didn't buckle his legs. Luckily it wasn't a clean hit, or it might have put him out of commission.

It was time to stop underestimating his opponent.

Scott twisted his body, pushing his right arm under the man's elbow. Using his weight, he leveraged the joint with merciless force, dislocating it. The monk yowled in pain, dropping the shotgun. Scott snatched it out of the air, turned it in one smooth motion, and jabbed the butt into the man's throat.

The monk sagged to the floor, both hands on his throat, gagging.

Scott opened the breach and pumped the remaining shells out of the gun. Then he tossed it to the side.

"Do you have any more weapons?" he yelled. His ears were still ringing from the first shot. He could barely hear his own voice.

The monk shook his head no, but Scott wasn't going to take his word for it. He roughly conducted a quick search of the man's body. Finding nothing, he shoved him toward the back of the hut. "Stay," he said, using the same voice he'd use for a disobedient dog.

When he turned, he was shocked at the sight.

Blood was everywhere.

Splattered over the bed. Soaked through the bedsheets.

Scott had fully expected it to be Thales's dead body he would find, but that wasn't the case.

Instead, the monk had shot Father Spiros in the chest.

Thales was holding the old man's hand and leaning over him.

Scott ran to the other side of the bed. Unbelievably, Father Spiros was still alive. Blood flecked his pale face. His mouth was drawn back in an agonizing grimace. His eyes stared up at the ceiling, blinking hard.

"What is Scarvan going to do?" Scott said, willing the old man to speak. "Does he have a nuclear weapon? Something biological? What is it?"

Father Spiros's head lolled to one side until he was looking at Scott. His lips pulled back further, the grimace taking on the look of a sneer.

"He will cut the heads from every snake," he said. "In the chaos that follows, the Lord shall come. I know this to be true."

"What does that mean?" Scott asked. "Tell me."

"I know this . . . to be true . . ." the old man said, the last word fading into a sigh.

And then his body went rigid and his eyes went wide, as if he'd seen something terrifying.

Then he went still.

Dead.

Thales marched across the hut and grabbed the odd little monk who cowered there.

"Why?" he roared. "Tell me why you did this thing?"

The monk cried out, pushed past Thales, and rushed to the bed. There he crouched down, kissing the man's feet over and over. He buried his head in his one good hand. The other arm hung limply at his side.

Scott watched dumbfounded. Could it be possible the man had shot Father Spiros by accident? One look at how perfectly centered the shot was dispelled that idea. But the remorse seemed real.

"I was his friend, his only friend," the monk said. "I cared for him when no one else would."

Scott nodded to the old man's now destroyed chest. "Hate to see what you do to your enemies. Why did you do it?"

The monk lowered his head onto the mattress and sobbed.

"You'd better start talking, asshole," Scott said, "or I'm going to bury you up to your chin in the sand out there and see how the crabs like the taste of you."

Whether due to a guilty conscience or the fear of Scott's threat, the monk started to talk.

"He made me swear," he cried. "If he ever became delirious, if he ever lost his faculties and seemed ready to give up the secret of what Apostoli planned, then I was to do what I just did." He turned to the old man. "This is what you swore me to do, Father. Forgive me."

Thales grabbed the monk roughly. "You know what the plan is, then? Tell us."

"He never told me, I swear it," he said. "Only that Apostoli was on a mission from God to change the world. Father Spiros and I were to be together to watch the coming of our Lord and Savior."

"When?" Scott growled. When the monk hesitated, he grabbed him by the arm that he'd already dislocated. The man whimpered in pain. "I said when?"

"Soon," the monk said. "Sometime next week is what he told me." He began to sob uncontrollably again. "He was so close to making it. So close."

Next week. It was Friday now. The fuse on the situation just became a lot shorter than what Scott had expected.

"You have to know more," Scott growled. "You're going to tell us everything."

"No . . . I've told too much . . ." Urgo wept as he spoke. A line of spittle hung from his mouth. "I didn't want this . . ."

"You're part of it now," Scott said. "You better hope you have something to help us."

Urgo trembled, sobs racking his body. "This isn't what's supposed to be . . . Father, I'm sorry . . . I'm sorry . . ."

Without warning, the man lurched up from the edge of the bed, throwing his shoulder into Thales and running for the door of the skete.

"Wait!" Scott shouted.

But it was too late. Urgo screamed as ran through the open door. And then silence.

There was a split second in which Scott's mind didn't process what he'd just seen. The initial annoyance of the man running when there was clearly no escape was replaced by a realization of what had just happened.

He and Thales glanced at each other and walked to the door, leaning out.

Urgo lay sprawled on the rocks below where he'd hit headfirst. Judging from the odd angle of his neck and the halo of blood spreading around him, it was clear they no longer had someone to question.

Scott held out his hand to Thales. "I'm taking your car."

Thales, shaken by monk's suicide, looked incredulous. "We

should search the skete. There could be things here that can help us."

Scott didn't think so. He had a sense that he'd learned as much here as he was able. Father Spiros was unlikely to have trusted the fool who'd just shot him with any intelligence of value. But with the man dead, he really didn't expect there to be much in the way of evidence. The fact that the old man had put such a dramatic fail-safe into place made him believe there wouldn't be anything of value lying around the stone dwelling, either.

No, there was a sense of operational purity about it. The one man who knew what Scarvan was about to do had just bled out in front of him.

He would need to figure out what it was from the clues he had.

Cut off all the snake heads at once.

Send the world into chaos.

Scott had no idea what to make of it. Thankfully there was a great team back in DC that just might. Hawthorn had assembled some truly great minds under the Alpha Team banner. He just hoped the inactivity over the last six months hadn't dulled their senses.

"The keys," Scott said, hand outstretched. "I'll send in reinforcements, but just in case you're right and there is something here—"

"—we need to ensure there are no other crazies like this one over here that will clean the place out. I get it." He tossed Scott the keys. "You know how to get out of here?"

"The second goat track on the left," Scott said. "Straight on 'til morning." Thales gave him a confused expression. Scott didn't have time to explain the reference. "Call me directly if you uncover anything."

"Is this real?" Thales asked as Scott headed to the door. "Does this single man have the ability to carry out an attack that will change the world?"

"A handful of men on airplanes brought the world nearly

two decades of war after 9/11," Scott said. "Whatever Scarvan has planned, it will be far worse."

As he left the skete and climbed down the ladder to the rocky ground below, it occurred to Scott what that plan might be. He immediately dialed his sat phone, his heart pounding in his chest. He needed to tell Hawthorn and have the team check on his idea.

If he was right, Scarvan was even more of a madman than he'd thought.

CHAPTER 32

Mara didn't like Marcus Ryker, but she couldn't put her finger on the reason why.

She'd spent the flight from Paris to Prague replaying her interaction with him in her head. As an expert interrogator, she'd spent her share of time with sociopaths. The wannabes who'd watched too many movies twirled their mustaches and made broad pronouncements about their distaste for society. It was people like Ryker who were harder to read.

Her instincts told her there was something off with him, but she had to admit he was a unique case.

A man with a higher net worth than most small countries and a brilliant scientific mind who had literally changed the world.

Was it a delusion of grandeur if, in fact, your impact on the world was undeniable?

Certainly, there was a massive ego there, but that was expected. Ryker had used that persona to his advantage, cultivating it at every turn. She didn't doubt for a second that he had some idea who had called him to warn him of the attack. Or at least a few guesses. Anyone with the extent of his wealth and with business interests spread through so many countries was bound to have friends in high places. And more than a few enemies.

But the data collection team back at Alpha headquarters hadn't been able to find anything either. Through an agreement with NSA, they had access to the most powerful surveillance tools in the world, especially outside America's borders. The call into Ryker's phone had been located and isolated, but whoever had been on the other end had covered their tracks well, bouncing the signal all over the world in a way that made it impossible to track. Even that precaution was likely a red herring designed to keep them occupied. Chances were that the caller had used a burner phone, discarded after one call.

None of that really bothered her. Someone who knew what was about to go down had been able to reach out and avoid additional collateral damage of one of the most-liked and respected businessmen on the planet.

Maybe she should be thankful someone had decided Ryker had been worth saving.

But there were two problems.

First, all of this only reaffirmed that Scarvan had an accomplice. Or perhaps many. Someone had killed the Clemsons. And certainly, Scarvan hadn't made the call himself. What did he care of collateral damage? Why would he have risked Ryker warning Nochek of the attack? What were the chances that Scarvan's accomplice would have Ryker's personal phone number? Unless they'd known well in advance that it was Ryker who was going to meet Nochek.

If that were the case, perhaps there was a connection somehow between Scarvan's group and Ryker.

The second issue was the mania she'd seen in Ryker's eyes when he'd talked about his work. It'd been like the curtains were pulled back for just a few seconds, revealing the real man behind the carefully crafted facade.

. . . *in defiance of the reckless excesses of the human race.*

Those were the words he'd used.

And with them came a flash of rage and righteousness that she'd only seen in the eyes of fanatics.

Perhaps she'd misread it. Maybe she wasn't impervious to the man's famed charisma after all.

Or maybe there was something wrong about Marcus Ryker.

Her aircraft taxied to a remote maintenance hangar in Vaclav Havel International Airport where a representative of the *Bezpecnostni Informacni Sluzba*, BIS for short, would ensure her visit to their country went unreported. Nikolas Koudelka, the head of this intelligence service, was an old friend of Hawthorn's and so she was told to expect full cooperation.

She liked the BIS motto, *Audi, Vide, Tace*: Hear, See, Be Silent.

She hoped Koudelka's men had heard and seen something useful since learning of Sergei Kolonov's presence in the city.

Scarvan had already slipped through her fingers once. If he came after Kolonov, she didn't intend to let it happen again.

The BIS assistance was welcome. The person waiting for her when she walked down the stairs from the jet wasn't.

The woman was in her late forties, maybe early fifties. She was fit, carrying herself with the perfect relaxed posture of someone who was once a competitive athlete. She wore designer clothes, Gucci by the look of it, a cream-colored suit with a white scarf flecked with the same blue of her eyes. Her blond hair was pulled back, giving her an efficient look, like she was there to work. Her face was as beautiful as it was inquisitive. There was something about it, perhaps the placement of her eyes, or maybe the slight narrowness of her cheekbones, that made her look ready to question everything she saw. She looked as incredible for her age as she'd looked in the photograph Mara had been shown on the plane.

As she closed the gap between them, she studied Anna Beliniski's eyes. She was surprised by what she saw there.

Recognition and pure delight.

"Welcome to the Czech Republic, Mara," she said. "So good to meet you."

She was taken aback by the enthusiasm in the woman's handshake. "Mara Roberts. And you are?" Mara didn't want to show she already knew who the woman was.

"Anna Beliniski, I'm with BIS, here to support you in any way you need."

Anna was the other person on Scarvan's list. The woman her father apparently had some prior relationship with. She remembered Hawthorn telling them that she was working for the Czech intelligence service now, but there had been no indication that she would be joining the mission. She wondered if Hawthorn had any idea.

"Nice to meet you. How briefed in are you?" Mara asked, following Anna to a waiting sedan parked inside the hangar. The sedan had tinted windows, making it difficult for any curious eyes to determine who had just arrived and been given the special treatment through immigration and customs.

"Director Hawthorn walked me through some of the pieces in motion," she said. "I believe you know of my past involvement here."

Mara caught that there was perhaps a double meaning here—both her relationship to Scarvan, but perhaps fishing for whether Mara knew anything about her and Scott. She was surprised Hawthorn had briefed her himself and not let her know before arrival. But she liked how the woman had phrased her answer. Whenever another intelligence officer told her they were fully briefed on a mission, it made her think them foolish. As field agents, they were all told what the powers-that-be thought they needed to know, nothing more. It was supposed to be different with Alpha Team, but she wondered how many secrets Hawthorn still kept.

"Do we have a location for Kolonov?" Mara asked, impressed as the sedan was waved through a variety of checkpoints leading out of the airport.

"We have a location. We're going there now. Also, every major transport station has been sent photos of Jacobslav Scarvan. The CCTV system AI has been programmed to prioritize a facial recognition for him both with and without his beard."

Mara was familiar with the sophisticated artificial intelligence now being used in European capitals. In the trade-off between safety and security, Europe had stepped more strongly to the security side of the equation than America. At least as far as the American public knew. Cameras covered nearly every inch of the streets in every European capital and AI software produced surprisingly accurate facial recognition results out of the terabytes of data it gathered.

"I assume nothing yet. If you'd spotted him, that would have been the headline."

"Nothing," Anna said. "But if something turns up, we'll be notified immediately."

Mara sensed the woman wanted to say more but was having trouble finding the words.

"What is it?" she asked, fearing bad news.

"It's just a pleasure to meet you," Anna said. "I . . . know your father. He speaks very highly of you."

Mara was surprised at the admission.

"Was this recently?" Mara asked. Her father had always insisted he'd never cheated on her mother, even for a field assignment.

"We met a lifetime ago," she said. "Then worked together again two years ago. When he was in Prague looking for answers to your mother's death."

The implication wasn't lost on her.

"You were helping him when he was persona non grata to the U.S. intelligence community?"

"Like I said, I knew him from many years earlier. When we were both young agents, we worked on a mission together here in Prague. And we'd see each other periodically over the years." She paused as if relishing the memory.

Mara felt her face heat. She'd always wondered about her dad's early days in the Agency. She'd seen some of the files, heard a few stories from some of the old saws who were riding desks at Langley now, but it was always just snippets. Always the heroics.

She'd once stung him with an accusation of being the philandering playboy that was part of the Scott Roberts mythos. He'd been livid, saying he'd never once cheated on her mother.

Now she was sitting in front of a beautiful woman who she imagined as nearly irresistible two decades earlier.

A hand on her leg startled her.

"I can see I've given the wrong impression. Nothing happened between us, not back in the old days. If I'm being honest, I wanted there to be. I wanted it very much."

"Attracted to married men?" Mara asked.

"Not at all. You know how it is. We didn't share personal details until later in the mission, until after I'd grown to . . . know him. But in the end, he told me about his wife and two daughters back home and he refused to betray them."

"Why are you telling me all this?"

Anna shrugged. "I felt you deserved to know that your father was an honorable man. I didn't know it at the time, but it's a rare commodity among men in this world."

"See where that got him," Mara said.

"It got him you," Anna said. "And your sister. He told me wonderful stories about Lucy as well. I'm so sorry for your loss."

The sentiment was nice, but it immediately put her back in Lucy's hospital room, watching as the cancer destroyed her. And that final afternoon, when she'd laid down on the bed to comfort her, falling asleep next to her as she'd done hundreds of times when they were little girls. Only this time when Mara woke up, her sister was cold and silent. Gone. Leaving behind her son for Mara to care for.

"I'm sorry . . . I didn't mean to . . ."

"No, it's fine," Mara said, snapping herself back to the present. "This all just . . . just caught me off guard."

Anna leaned back in her seat. "I take it Scott never told you about me, then?"

"You know how he is."

Anna laughed. "What's the expression? 'Stubborn like a moose'?"

"Usually we say mule, but moose works for him, too," Mara said, warming to this woman. She seemed like a perfect match for her dad. Someone who could bring a little joy into his life. "My dad's on his way here," she said, enjoying how the woman tried to hide her reaction to this news. "Only a couple hours behind me."

"Really? I hadn't heard that. Was his trip to Mount Athos fruitful?"

An alarm went off in her head. Everything slowed down as she reevaluated her surroundings. The driver glancing back too often in a rearview mirror angled to watch her, not the road behind them. The front passenger angled in his chair at nearly forty-five degrees, even though he twisted his torso to make it seem like he was facing forward.

Anna. Her right hand inside the designer purse discreetly placed between her leg and the door.

She'd not told her about Mt. Athos.

And she was pretty damn sure Hawthorn wouldn't have given up an operational detail like that to someone outside of Alpha Team.

She did her best not to let her face betray any emotion.

"A dead end," she said. "Kolonov is our last real chance to catch Scarvan. That's why we're here."

Mara thought she'd pulled it off, but this woman was good. Her expression changed as she looked down at her purse. Slowly, she removed the Sig Sauer handgun and shrugged.

"These are interesting times," Anna said, as if that explained everything. "One can never be too careful in a world of shifting alliances."

Mara felt her stomach drop. She cursed herself for not being more careful. For being lulled to sleep with the conversation about her dad.

"And what side are you on, Anna?" she asked.

She smiled and pointed the gun at Mara. "I'm on the side most likely to win."

CHAPTER 33

Jim Hawthorn put down the phone and reached a hand to his desk to steady himself. He'd faced all manner of threats in his career, including the existential nuclear threats of the Cold War.

It'd been a while since he'd felt the immediacy of a threat this size.

Or felt like his adversary had the ability to pull it off regardless of his efforts to stop him.

Even having divined Scarvan's intentions, assuming Scott's conclusion was right, the whole thing was starting to remind Hawthorn of watching a talented street magician. One who explains his trick, even urging his audience to watch closely, and then still pulling it off right in front of their noses.

Only the trick Scarvan had planned wasn't to entertain.

It was to bring chaos to the world.

Hawthorn picked up his secure phone and punched in a number from memory.

"'Mornin', Jim, what can I do you for?" came the answer on the second ring. As chief of staff, Nancy McKeen was never away from her phone. Her Alabama drawl made Hawthorn feel like she'd perhaps taken the call on her front porch back home, maybe whiling away time on a rocking chair, just hoping someone would stop by to visit for a spell. He knew in reality she was hunkered down in her office only feet away from the Oval Office. McKeen was a brilliant DC operator. Most importantly, she was someone President Patterson listened to.

"Nancy, I'm coming over. I need time immediately."

"If I ask, I suppose, once again, you're not going to tell me what's going on over the phone," she said.

"Is Mitch Dreslan over there?" Hawthorn asked.

"Goddammit, Jim. If—"

"It's no more immediate than it was twelve hours ago," Jim said. "We have every reason to believe that Jacobslav Scarvan is not in the United States. Not yet."

A long pause, then a heavy sigh. "Shit, anyone else I'd threaten to stripe their hide for not telling me what's going on right goddamn now, but I don't suppose that's going to work here."

"I don't suppose it is," he said. "My people are working on a few things first. I want to give everyone a clear picture when I go over it."

"All right, I'll clear the deck. Make up some excuse for messin' up the official calendar. Again."

"And get Dreslan. He needs to hear this."

Hawthorn hung up the phone and checked his watch. Greece was seven hours ahead of DC. Scott would gain an hour flying to Prague. He just hoped he arrived on time to help Mara face Scarvan.

If Scarvan even showed up.

It was a fortunate coincidence that Kolonov showed his head when he did, giving Scarvan a chance to settle that one more score from the boat.

Hawthorn believed in coincidence, just not the kind that favored him. He'd seen it go the other way too many times. An operative on a mission running into a long-lost schoolmate in a foreign country. A phone intercept plucked at random for review to throw a wrench in the works of a covert job. One of his agents selected for additional random screening that led to their cover being blown.

He believed in bad luck, but he was suspicious when it went his team's way.

No, Kolonov's reappearance had to be more than coincidence. He was sure of it.

Hawthorn walked over to the small office located as far away as possible from everyone else in the Alpha Team headquarters. Jordi Pines liked his privacy and other people liked the distance between themselves and the odd smells that came out of the computer genius's room.

Hawthorn knocked on the TOXIC CHEMICALS sign covering most of the door. He didn't want to walk in catching the man doing something he couldn't unsee.

"Entrée," Jordi bellowed theatrically.

Hawthorn opened the door, wrinkling his nose at the smell of old pizza, incense, and body odor. Jordi looked up from his bank of computer screens, his hand deep inside a family-sized bag of Cheetos.

"The king graces my door with his presence," he said, his mock-English accent especially strong today.

Hawthorn took stock of the room, a hoarder's lair of garbage and pop culture. He'd made the effort to connect with Jordi, he'd prided himself through his career on being able to form a strong personal connection with all of his people. The way in had been their mutual appreciation first for *Downton Abbey*, and then for Spider-Man. Hawthorn was a fan of the original comics, and Jordi of every reference, in every medium since the superhero had been a flash of inspiration in Stan Lee's and Steve Ditko's brains. Like everything Jordi Pines, the Spidey fascination bordered on obsession.

"Busy?" Hawthorn asked.

Jordi shrugged. "Just breaking into sovereign government mainframes, burrowing into social media platforms, and using every camera in Europe to try to find this Scarvan bastard. You?"

"About the same," he said. "Spoke with Scott. We think we know Scarvan's plan."

"Is it something dastardly and diabolical?" Jordi asked.

Hawthorn explained Scott's theory. It seemed impossible given the man rarely saw the light of day, but Hawthorn could have sworn that Jordi actually turned pale as he described it to him.

"That's grade-A evil mastermind shit, right there," he said when Hawthorn was done. "At least we have a possible timeline for his main attack. What do you need me to do?"

"Kolonov showed up just in time for Scarvan to have a crack at him before his final act. That's too much of a coincidence. I need you to find out why. Who pulled him out of hiding? Who set up the meet in Prague?"

"Find that out, we find out who is helping Scarvan," Jordi said. "You think it's our good friends at Omega?"

"I wouldn't be surprised that, once you find out who it is, we trace them back into Omega. This whole thing feels like them."

Jordi looked doubtful. "You think they planted Scarvan for twenty years and just now brought him out of retirement for this?"

"No, I think Scarvan's decision to disappear was his own doing. And so was his reappearance. But since he's been out in the open, my suspicion is that Omega hitched itself to him. Providing assistance when they can."

"To keep us busy and off their trail," Jordi said. "Not that we were honestly doing that great of a job of it to begin with."

"Maybe this is the opportunity we've been looking for. Helping Scarvan might turn out to be a mistake on their end. It could expose them and give us the way in we're looking for."

"Or, if we screw this up, they could send the world into chaos and leave us and every other intelligence agency in the world scrambling for years trying to sort out the aftermath."

"That's why we can't screw this up," Hawthorn said. "I suggest you start working your magic on those things," he said, waving at the massive computing power in the room.

"On it," Jordi said. As Hawthorn turned to leave, Jordi called out, "Are you making sure my girl has the support she needs out there?"

Jordi was Mara's connection and the man was fiercely loyal to her. He had no doubt his priorities were Mara first, the rest of the world a distant second.

"I wouldn't worry about Mara," Hawthorn said. "I'd just worry about the person stupid enough to go up against her."

Jordi was no fool. He knew the dangers of the world. He knew that a sniper bullet from a half mile away didn't care how talented the person was at the end of its flight path. He tossed the bag of Cheetos to the side and wiped his orange fingers on his shirt.

"Unfortunately, the world is full of stupid people. Let me get to work finding them for you."

Hawthorn closed the door behind him as the clacking of the keyboard filled the air. He knew Jordi wouldn't stop until he found an answer or was given some other task to pull him off of it.

He called and asked his driver to bring the car around. It was only ten minutes to the White House, but he was looking forward to that time to collect his thoughts.

He had to convince the president to cancel one of the most important public appearances of his administration, all on circumstantial evidence collected in a monk's stone hut in the middle of nowhere.

His argument wasn't going to be well-received: a lone-wolf assassin everyone had thought dead for over twenty years was going to infiltrate into the U.S. when every law enforcement officer would be looking for him, procure the materials he needed to create a powerful bomb, then somehow deliver the device into the center of what for four hours would be one of the most heavily guarded rooms in the world.

If it were anyone but Jacobslav Scarvan, he would have thought it all impossible. Especially now that they knew what to expect.

But Scarvan specialized in the impossible. Hawthorn had seen it many times.

To make it worse, based on what had happened in Paris, Mara had concluded Scarvan was not acting alone. If Omega was helping him, then things just got much worse.

Scott had pieced it together. Scarvan intended to remove the head from the diseased body of the world, sending it into chaos.

At first, they thought perhaps a round of assassinations. Taking out heads of state one by one. Not unlike the revenge he was taking on those involved with his own betrayal.

But Scott had realized it was something bigger than that.

What if every head of state could be killed at one moment? One explosion?

Every country in the world left leaderless in an instant? *Cleansed in a rush of fire*, was how Scott said the old monk described it.

The chaos that followed would be incredible. Many countries had succession plans. Fewer had a history of following those plans.

Not only that, but with the world already teetering on the edge of multiple regional wars—the South China Sea, Kashmir, Yemen, North Korea, Ukraine, the list growing longer each day—the leadership vacuum was bound to lead some country to miscalculate and try to press an advantage.

If Omega was behind this, then there would be other levers applied once the world's leaders were killed. Nudging the system toward collapse.

Scott had pieced it together. A quick search revealed his greatest fear.

Every world leader was scheduled to be in New York in three days.

Every single one. Most with an entourage of dignitaries, past leaders, royal family members, head diplomats.

It was the perfect target. During the remarks of the U.S. president commemorating the event, they would all be sitting in a single room.

In one explosion, all world government would be decimated. The chaos following would be incredible. The type of thing that would keep every intelligence agency tied up for years. Effectively keeping all attention away from Omega.

Hawthorn wasn't a religious man, but he said a short prayer nonetheless.

He asked that Mara and Scott would find the son of a bitch and kill him where he stood.

Otherwise, in three days, the seventy-fifth anniversary of the United Nations was going to be the scene of the greatest terrorist attack in world history.

CHAPTER 34

"What the hell is this?" Mara asked. She had a distaste for having guns pointed in her direction.

"Mr. Kolonov would like to meet with you," Anna said. "These gentlemen work for him. They asked me to make the arrangement."

Mara considered the ways she could disarm the woman in front of her. In all scenarios, she won the struggle, but didn't cover the man in the front passenger seat.

"Are you working for him, too?"

"No, but I am a pragmatist as much as I am a patriot. Hawthorn, like always, wouldn't tell us exactly what's going on. The U.S. always treats us like a pawn in their games. I thought it best to make the decision to meet Kolonov as linear as possible."

"By linear you mean me doing what you tell me to do?"

"If that's how you want to phrase it, yes."

"So, you thought you'd get some info out of me with this whole 'let's be best friends' schtick first?"

Anna didn't seem offended. "It was worth a try. But now we'll meet Kolonov together and I will see what's really happening."

"You're not a very trusting person, are you?" Mara asked.

"Belchik turned up dead after you and your father visited him. Curious, isn't it?"

Mara had known the word would get out eventually. Belchik was a legend in the intelligence community. But she was surprised the news that it was she and her dad who'd done the mission was out, too.

"Not sure what you're talking about," Mara said, assuming the interaction was being filmed. She wasn't going to admit to anything. "Besides, I've heard that Belchik had received lethal doses of radiation courtesy of an old friend. Perhaps someone put him out of his misery."

"Perhaps. But then there was that explosion in Paris. You were on the scene there as well. This has my bosses wondering whether there's something larger going on here. Maybe there's something else the United States doesn't want getting out. Whether this story about Jacobslav Scarvan is a convenient cover for some larger operation to clean up a mess."

"You pulled a gun on a U.S. operative to make your point?"

Anna looked at the gun as if surprised Mara would make an issue of it. "This? I'm just a very careful person. I didn't know how you were going to react to being told we're going to see Kolonov and that I'm going with you. I also don't know if Kolonov has an issue with you. This insurance policy is also here in case one of these fine gentlemen in the front has orders to kill you. And me along in the process."

The men in the front both glanced back as if for the first time considering their passenger could put a bullet in the back of their heads at any second. The man in the passenger seat slid his right arm up to show the snub-nosed shotgun he had pressed against the seat pointed their way.

"See, now we all know where we stand," Anna said. "Less prone to miscalculations, I find."

"You think all this is a cover of some kind?"

Anna gave a dismissive shrug. "My bosses think so."

"Not sure resurrecting a KBI agent from the dead would be

my go-to for a cover story," Mara said. "Besides, I thought you trusted my dad."

"If you think having sex with a man is the same as trusting him, you and I need to have a talk," Anna said. "He's terrific in bed, by the way."

The reference was meant to shock her. She didn't give the woman the pleasure of seeing her react. "A lot of women say that, so maybe it's true."

The comment hit the mark and Anna frowned. Mara filed the look away, not sure if she'd meant for her to see or if this woman did harbor some true feelings for her dad.

"Okay, let's go see Kolonov," Mara said. "I just hope Scarvan doesn't try to take him out during the meet. That would be inconvenient, for all of us."

Mara took some pleasure in seeing the two men in the front exchange worried glances. It seemed Scarvan's legend was alive and well, even among Kolonov's thugs.

The sedan snaked its way through the streets of Prague, seeming to travel back in time as it did. Utilitarian office buildings and sleek new retail outlets gave way to increasingly narrow streets and older architecture. They crossed the Legion Bridge over the Vtlava. As they did, Mara caught a glimpse of the Charles Bridge just to the north. It was pedestrian only, a fact she appreciated since she didn't want to be any closer than she had to be. The memory of her mother crowded in on her, threatening to overwhelm.

Mara pushed these thoughts away, angry with herself for letting them intrude when she ought to be focused on the matter at hand.

A glance over to Anna confirmed the woman was studying her closely, gauging her reaction.

Surprisingly, she saw compassion in the eyes staring back at her. She wondered if that was just part of the woman's act, or whether at the heart of it she was sincere.

While she had a gun trained on her, Mara really didn't give a damn.

Although she did note that the gun now pointed more at the man in the front passenger seat than at her.

The sedan continued deeper into the labyrinthine roads of the Mala Strana, or Lesser Quarter, the area under the Prague Castle. This area had been formed in 1257 but rebuilt in the sixteenth century after fire decimated the early architecture. While the rebuilding had changed the architecture to a more baroque look, the curving, narrow streets had remained the same. It was useful for ensuring they weren't being followed. Not so useful for avoiding an ambush from the windows above. The image of Scarvan balancing the RPG on his shoulder in Paris came to her and she shuddered.

"We are here," the man in the front seat said.

The driver pressed a button and a wide arched wooden door facing the street rumbled open, revealing a short passageway the led into an interior courtyard.

A metal security post blocked their way in the center of the cobblestone entry. A man walked out, checked with the driver, and then signaled to someone hidden inside. The post lowered into the ground and they rolled forward through the arch.

Mara took notice of the cameras on both sides of the car and the slits cut into the stone. Perhaps once meant for crossbows to protect the entrance she was certain that they were just as useful for guns.

The car pulled into the stone courtyard. It was beautiful inside. The sixteenth-century walls had a well-earned rose-colored patina. Plant boxes lined the walls and were on every balcony and window. These were filled with flowering plants, the most abundant being jasmine, which filled the air with its sweet scent. A fountain burbled in the corner, a stone statue of a young boy playing a flute.

Hardly what she expected as the meeting place with a hardened criminal like Kolonov.

"I'll take that," the man in the passenger seat said to Anna, holding his hand out for her gun.

"Like hell you will," she said. "Hardly worth protecting myself up to this point just to hand over my gun after you bring us behind closed doors."

The man stared her down, a menacing look that likely made most people on the other end of it cower. It had no effect on Anna.

"Wait here," the driver grumbled.

The man in the passenger seat continued to glare at them, his body turned to better cover them with the shotgun he'd shown them earlier.

Mara knew the status quo in the car wouldn't change until the driver returned with some kind of verdict from Kolonov. She watched as he entered the house, leaving the door open. It was less than a minute before Kolonov himself appeared. He looked more like a banker than the head of security for a Central American drug cartel—tailored designer suit that he wore open collar, slicked back hair, gold jewelry, skin a dark tan.

"What does your father say? 'Showtime'?" Anna said.

He did say that. She found herself wondering about when he would join them and what he would find when he got to Prague. She just hoped he wouldn't be searching for her body to bring back home.

"Showtime," she agreed, opening the door.

Kolonov stood in front of the still-open door. A casual glance around the courtyard showed at least three men in the windows standing guard. No wonder he'd allowed them to keep their weapons. Any move against him would be suicide. He must have felt confident enough that neither she nor Anna was willing to trade their lives for his.

Perhaps he possessed an accurate sense of his relative importance to the world's intelligence agencies. He was a bad actor, but not one worth too much effort or sacrifice to bring to heel. If he were killed, someone else just as ruthless would just fill his spot.

"Ladies," Kolonov said, opening his arms wide as if he were welcoming longtime friends. His English was very good, but had an odd accent to it, all at once Spanish and Russian. "Thank you for agreeing to see me."

Two men appeared from inside the house carrying chairs. They set them around a stone table near the fountain. Kolonov motioned them to the table and waited for them both to sit.

"Water? Tea?" he asked. "Something stronger?"

"Have you had any contact with Jacobslav Scarvan?" Mara asked.

Kolonov grimaced but gave a short nod. They would get down to business. "How can you be sure Scarvan is alive?"

"I spoke directly to Viktor Belchik," Mara said. "He told me Scarvan visited him. After he poisoned him with radiation, he systematically killed a member of Belchik's family every other day. Does that sound like Scarvan to you?"

Mara felt Anna's eyes on her but kept hers on Kolonov.

"This is why you killed Belchik," Kolonov said. "A mercy."

"I heard he passed away after we left him. It was someone's mercy. Not mine."

"Your father's, then?" Kolonov asked.

"What does it matter?" Anna said, injecting herself into the conversation. "Belchik is dead. You know what happened in Paris. Nochek is dead. Many others who have crossed Scarvan are dead. You're still alive."

"For now," Mara said.

If Kolonov was rattled, he didn't show it. The only tell he had was a slow tapping on the table in front of him with a single finger.

"I wronged Scarvan, this is true. But only because it was my duty to follow orders from my superiors."

"Scarvan launched an RPG into Tour d'Argent in broad daylight to kill another man who was just following orders," Mara said.

"Seems like he doesn't accept that as an excuse," Anna said.

Kolonov added a second finger to his tapping.

"If you are correct, then why wouldn't I just get back on my plane and go back to Central America? Disappear into the jungle until this blows over? Let you Americans deal with this shit?"

Mara leaned forward, whispering as if Scarvan might be just around the corner listening to them. "You left the jungle and came to Prague just when it was your turn on Scarvan's list. Do you think that's a coincidence? Because I don't. Whoever you trusted that brought you here is someone whose trust I would rethink."

For the first time, Kolonov looked rattled. He scanned the four walls around them in the courtyard as if seeing it as a trap rather than a protective cocoon.

This time it was Anna who leaned forward. "Why did you come to Prague? Who sent for you? Because whoever it was threw you right in front of a train hurtling toward you. And we all know there's only one way to stop a train like that."

Kolonov pushed himself away from the table and stood. The waters on the table sloshed in their glasses, spilling onto the stone. "I'm going to make a few calls."

As he turned to walk into the house, Mara called out, "Don't take too long. Scarvan could be a day away from attacking or minutes." She spoke loudly so her voice carried up to Kolonov's men in the windows above them. "The sooner you can wrap your head around the idea that you need our help, the better chance all of us have of not dying simply because we were too close to you."

Kolonov looked as if he might say something more but thought better of it. He pulled a phone from his jacket pocket and went inside.

"Clever," Anna whispered. "Puts a bit of pressure on him and makes him paranoid about who in his organization set him up."

"Not that clever," Mara said, pouring herself another glass of water. "Just true. If Scarvan's going to blow this place up with another RPG or drop a payload from a drone into this courtyard while we're here chatting, I'll be pissed off if I die trying to talk sense into that idiot."

"Who do you think set him up?"

"Don't know," Mara said. "But I'm thinking more and more that some old friends might be behind the scenes pulling the strings on this one. If I know Hawthorn and my dad, they are already working on that angle."

CHAPTER 35

Scott felt his stomach turn as he rode through the streets of Prague.

When he was a younger man, he'd prided himself on being able to compartmentalize his emotions during an operation. His world became the mission and nothing else. Every second boiled down to a calculation of risk and reward.

Consequences be damned.

But over time, the consequences had added up. A teetering pile of memories, regrets, even guilt.

He understood those three things were inextricably linked. Not from the CIA shrink he was required to attend periodically to check up on his mental well-being. That process was a farce, and everyone involved knew it. The questions in those sessions were basic and the answers came from agents professionally trained to lie convincingly.

The only breakthroughs in those sessions were when an agent wanted to be done with the field. The fastest way to wash out was to answer the questions truthfully. To admit to the dark demons, the blood lust to avenge fallen comrades, the cynicism about America and her leaders. The conversations were "privileged," but it wasn't hard to understand how far that privilege extended. Basically, to whoever in the chain of command wanted to read the transcript or view the session video.

But Scott was self-aware enough to know he had issues to re-solve. The tough-guy persona worked as the outward-facing version of himself, but that did nothing to make the sleepless nights go away.

Quietly, he'd read up on the subject. Treating his own mental health as just another problem to solve. From that, he'd come to at least intellectually understand the power of traumatic memories. How they even have a physiological component, etching into the brain like the wood-burning tools he'd used as a kid. Those traumatic memories hovered on the edge of conscious-ness, ready to crash through with little or no trigger. They were layered with regret, the desire to rethink the event, always ask-ing what could have been done differently.

There were religious adherents who practiced self-flagellation, whipping themselves with knotted cords until their backs turned slick with blood. There were no scars on Scott's back, but he was a master at whatever the mental equivalent was of slashing open his skin daily.

He curled both of his hands into fists, allowing the rage and sense of betrayal to fill him. Then, with a flick of his wrists, he opened his hands, fingers splayed.

Release.

It was a cheap trick, the kind he used to roll his eyes at. But damn if it didn't make him feel better.

If nothing else, it signaled his brain to focus back on the mat-ter at hand. The nightmares and recrimination would be there waiting for him later; they didn't need his constant attention.

He pulled out his phone. Hawthorn answered on the first ring.

"We have a recording of Kolonov being told to come to Prague," he said. The call was piped through the car's speakers, so Hawthorn sounded like the voice of God.

"Tell him who found it," came Jordi's voice from somewhere in the same room as Hawthorn.

"Send the information to Scott's phone."

"Did you tell him?"

Scott grinned. Hawthorn and Jordi had become Alpha Team's odd couple. Their interaction felt like it might be penance for something Hawthorn had done earlier in his life.

"Here, you're on speaker," Hawthorn said.

"Scott, Jordi here. Can you believe the conditions I'm working under?"

Scott made the turn to parallel the river and go down to the Legion Bridge. He'd already received the coordinates of the building where Anna Beliniski had taken Mara to meet with Kolonov.

Anna. That was another complicating factor. He wondered how she and Mara had hit it off. Either as fast friends or not at all. He doubted there would be any middle ground with their two personalities.

"What'd you find out, Jordi?"

"I isolated the call traffic between Prague and Medellin, Kolonov's last known whereabouts. Came up empty. So, I broadened the search, expanding out in hundred-kilometer sets from Prague, until I—"

"*What* did you find, not *how* did you find. Let's skip to the end where you have information for me," Scott said. He'd been on the receiving end of Jordi's lectures on his brilliant craftwork before, and they were never short.

"If you want to take all the fun out of it."

"I do."

A heavy sigh on the other end of the phone. "All right, I just sent you an audio file. The guys here haven't been able to place it yet. A couple of low-probability hits, but I don't think they have it yet."

Scott's phone pinged with a message. He opened it and played the audio file, turning up the car speakers. The recording had some static, a residue Scott knew was the result of decryption technology. The criminals of the world thought their encrypted calls were risk-free. What they didn't know is that most encryption technology had the CIA's hands all over them, ensuring they were built with backdoor access whenever Uncle Sam's interests were deemed to be at stake. The privacy groups would have a field day with that one if they ever found out, but they liked not being blown up by terrorists as well.

"My benefactor will guarantee your safety and double your fee," came the voice over the speakers. Scott turned the volume down just a little, finding the balance between maximum volume and minimal distortion. *"Prague. Tomorrow. We'll contact you once you land."*

He knew the voice. The last time he'd heard it, the man had bested him in a fight in the middle of the National Mall. As sirens closed in on their position, the man could have finished him off, but instead chose to let him go. Not out of mercy, but because Scott had been injured before their fight, and the man wanted Scott's best. Wanted to prove he was better.

It was another moment that had been haunting him. Scott had faced down death more times than he could recall, but this one had been different. He'd been totally exposed, at the mercy of the assassin in front of him. This time he'd felt the potential to lose his new connection with Mara, with his grandson, Joey. And it shook him.

And now here he was.

"Asset," Scott said. "That's the Omega operative from the National Mall."

Another voice was in the car now; this one had an odd Russian accent. Kolonov. *". . . not a good time for me right now. Perhaps in two weeks."*

Asset returned. *"My benefactor does not like to be told no and he does not like to wait."*

"I have responsibilities here. My employer would not—"

"You will find your current employer has no more need for you this week. If you refuse to come to Prague, no further employment will be available to you from this point forward. Perhaps this doesn't matter to you. Perhaps you are ready to retire to a house on the beach and live out the rest of your days in obscurity. If that's the way you think things will end."

"This call is over," Kolonov said.

"I suggest you call your current employer and see if I'm right. I'll see you in Prague tomorrow."

The recording ended.

"He must not have liked what he heard when he spoke to his employer because six hours after this call he was on an airplane for Prague," Hawthorn said. "This was the same operative that was activated in DC. He's good. Very good. In Paris, a team was taken out right before Scarvan's RPG attack. They're working together."

Scott tried to think through the new information. Driving the busy street actually helped him, occupying part of his brain so the other could work through all the iterations of what could be going on.

"After what he's been through, do you think Scarvan would join another organization? Subject himself to another hierarchy?"

"Sounds like you don't think so," Hawthorn said.

"No, I'm convinced he found God on Mount Athos. And not the charitable, forgiving God of the New Testament, either. His God is filled with vengeance and retribution. He believes his actions will bring about Armageddon. I don't think this guy joins a new team."

Jordi jumped in. "Omega's helping him without being asked."

"Or, at the minimum, soft coordination," Scott said. "I don't think Omega is pulling the strings."

"But they are making sure no one gets in Scarvan's way," Hawthorn said.

Scott agreed. "That gives him access to funds, materials, transportation, even men if he needs them. As if it were possible, he just got a lot more dangerous. Does Mara know?"

"She suspected after Paris," Hawthorn said. "But we just got this intercept. Once Mara made contact with Anna Beliniski, she's been dark."

"This puts Omega right in the middle of this," Scott said. "We have to stop Scarvan when he comes for Kolonov, or we're in for a world of hurt."

His phone vibrated and he glanced at the screen. "Putting you on hold," he said, not waiting for them to acknowledge. He switched to the incoming call. "Nice of you to finally call your old man."

"Nice of you to wrap up your vacation in the Greek Islands," Mara said.

"Now we can vacation together. Anything fun planned?" he asked.

"Actually, I'm here with Kolonov. He's decided he would like to join us. Maybe together we can catch a bad guy."

Scott fist pumped the air, enjoying both the good news and his pride in Mara getting the job done.

"I'm only five minutes out from your location. Do you already have a plan how we're going to lure Scarvan in?"

"Just a second," Mara said.

There were muffled sounds. Men shouting. Mara said something, but not to him.

He turned up the volume, so the sounds filled the car.

Pfutt pfutt pfutt.

Small-arms fire.

An explosion.

A man screaming.

"Mara? What's happening?"

"Shit," Mara said. "Scarvan's here."

CHAPTER 36

Mara ran to the nearest doorway, her Glock in her hand. She ducked inside, back to the wall.

Anna appeared in the same doorway, taking position on the opposite side. Gun also pulled.

"How many did you see?" Anna asked. All business. Not a trace of panic in her voice.

"None," Mara said. "You?"

"Saw two men down. Didn't see how many shooters."

"There might only be one."

Anna's expression turned incredulous. "Scarvan wouldn't do a one-man assault on this location, would he? Makes no sense."

"We didn't think he'd do it, so maybe that's why it make perfect sense," Mara said. "My dad's a few minutes out, but this might all be done by the time he gets here. We need Kolonov. Where is he?"

Anna pointed across the courtyard to the opposite site of the U-shaped building. "He went through that door. Come on."

They fell into a two-person room-clearing movement, working their way through the building. Mara felt in her gut that Scarvan was attacking on his own, but that didn't mean he was the only danger. Kolonov's men were likely to shoot at anyone who wasn't one of their own. For all she knew, Kolonov might have thought he'd been betrayed and given an order for her and Anna to be shot on sight.

Gunfire raged on the floor above them but also from the third story on the other side of the courtyard.

Either she'd been wrong and there was more than one attacker or Kolonov's men were panicking. Firing at shadows and any movement.

Anna took position beside the door leading to the next room while Mara covered their rear. She risked a quick look and pulled back just as the wooden frame splintered in a hail of bullets.

"Found him," she said to Mara.

"How many?"

Anna held up two fingers. Then, loud enough to get his attention but hopefully not give away their position if Scarvan was close by she said, "Kolonov, let's help each other."

"You bitches set me up," he snapped.

"You really think we had a tactical team come charging in, guns blazing, while we were still here?" Mara said. "Think about it. It's Scarvan. Either alone or with a team. And he's not here to get me."

A man from the courtyard screamed and a shadow passed by the window, falling from above. He landed with a heavy thud.

"Let's work together on this," Anna said. "We all want the same thing here. I'm coming in."

Mara shook her head. "Are you crazy?"

Anna gave her a wink. "A little bit."

As she turned the corner and walked into the room, Mara fell in behind her, ready to react if Kolonov's men fired.

"Hold," Kolonov said.

Mara sighted Kolonov's thug, a younger man who looked completely out of his depth. His eyes flitted between the two women entering the room and his boss, fear and uncertainty painted on his face. A combination that could easily lead to a mistake.

"How about you tell your man to lower his weapon?" Mara said. "He looks a little nervous."

Kolonov seemed to agree. He pushed on the man's shoulder, turning him toward the windows.

"Did you see him?" Kolonov asked. "Did you see Scarvan?"

Anna answered. "He has to be upstairs. But that gives him visibility down into the courtyard. Makes getting to the car a risk. What egress points do we have available?"

Kolonov's thug leaned forward in the window, craning his neck to look up into the courtyard. Suddenly, a stream of bullets strafed the room from the outside, blowing out two of the windows.

The man fell back, his own gun going off as his hand spasmed. The bullet took out a chunk of plaster directly over Kolonov's head.

They all took cover from the flying shards of glass. Kolonov crouched to the ground.

"Fucking amateurs," he said.

Mara was thinking the same thing. No way Scarvan was indiscriminately shooting up the place. He was a surgeon, not a carpet bomber. Kolonov's own men were shooting at anything that moved.

"We need to get the hell out of here," he said. "You two are going to help me."

Mara grinned. Men always wanted to feel like things were their idea. Whatever. She turned to Anna and spoke to her in a low voice for her ears only. "You get him out of here. Keep him in pocket in case Scarvan gets away."

Anna wrinkled her brow, not happy with the plan. "Scarvan's here. That's what we wanted. We need to take him out. This was the plan all along."

What they wanted was to surprise Scarvan in a trap of their own making, at a time of their choosing. Playing defense to an onslaught hadn't been the plan at all. She left that alone. It didn't matter now. "If he aborts, if he decides it's too hot and slips away, he'll come for Kolonov again later. We need Kolonov alive and in hand in case that happens. Scarvan could already be gone for all we know."

"What's going on?" Kolonov said. "What are you two talking about?"

Anna locked eyes with Mara for a long beat, a silent battle of wills. Finally, she turned and strode toward Kolonov. "Come on, we're getting out of here."

Mara's phone chirped. She dug an Airpod out of her pocket and put it in her ear. The Apple engineer who'd designed it likely never thought his tech would be used to coordinate firepower in a shootout.

"Go," she said.

"Coming in hot," he said. "Where do you want me?"

"Through the main arch." She peered out through the window, confirming that the metal security post was still down, careful not to show too much of herself. "The gate is closed, but it's just decorative. The inner metal barrier is open."

"Roger that."

"We're straight across from the gate, floor level. We have Kolonov."

"Do you have eyes on Scarvan?"

"Negative," she said. "Multiple hostiles on site with itchy fingers."

"Sounds great, be right there."

Outside, she heard a horn, imagining her dad careening down the street outside as pedestrians scrambled to get out of his way.

Anna slid to the window next to her.

"Cover," Mara said.

They both raised their guns.

A second later the front gate leading into the courtyard blew off its hinges and a black Mercedes SUV roared through it.

Both Mara and Anna laid down a barrage of gunfire at the second-floor areas. Indiscriminately at first, but then the muzzle flashes gave away positions of the few men Kolonov had left in the building.

Mara adjusted her fire and one of the men dropped when her slug tore through his shoulder.

Anna ran to the nearest door and pulled it open.

The vehicle reacted, swinging out wide to the right, then heaving back left. The rear tires slid out on the cobblestones and the entire vehicle slammed sideways into the side of the building. Driver's door lined up with the opening to their room.

Scott opened the door and spilled out of the car as bullets pinged off the roof and hood. He dove and barrel-rolled into the room.

He ended up at Anna's feet.

"Hey there," he said, grinning.

Anna shook her head, doing her best to look annoyed. "Dinner. A play. These are the normal things people do."

Scott turned to Mara. "Isn't she great?"

Before Mara could respond, Kolonov got all of their attention.

"I see him," Kolonov said, on the floor, carefully glancing up through a window at an angle. "I see Scarvan."

Sirens wailed from the street outside, getting closer. The gunfire and Scott's SUV slamming through the gate hadn't gone unnoticed.

Scott, Anna, and Mara all turned deadly serious.

"Where?" Mara said.

"Second floor, west wing of the building. Third window in," he said. "He's just standing there in full view."

Anna was in position first, next to Kolonov. "I see him," Anna said, raising her gun.

"Take him," Scott said.

Mara leaned out from the doorway, only needing a split second to acquire the target.

Scarvan stood at three-quarters angle at a tall window that exposed him from knees to head. The wild beard Mara had seen on the boat in Paris was gone, trimmed back into a goatee, but it was him.

He stared back at them, unafraid, shoulders relaxed, head cocked as if curious what they would do next.

Like he was in a zoo watching animals interact.

"Do you have the shot?" Scott asked.

"Something's wrong," Anna said.

Mara felt it, too. But she couldn't put her finger on what it was.

Scarvan held up his right hand, purposefully showing them what he held.

It was a detonator. But for what?

Anna fired. Three quick shots.

Instead of buckling over, Scarvan first splintered and then shattered into a thousand pieces.

A full-length mirror.

"Oh shit," Mara said.

A concussive blast *thump*ed from the opposite end of the courtyard. The archway leading to the outside road lit up and then crumbled inward. Three stories of sixteenth-century brick and plaster collapsed and blocked the only way out.

Scarvan had waited until Scott had gotten there to lock them in. And keep out any chance for backup.

This wasn't only a trap for Kolonov.

It was a cage designed for her and her dad, too.

She spun around to formulate a plan and her stomach dropped.

Only her dad and Anna were there.

Kolonov was gone.

CHAPTER 37

"Where the hell did he go?" Mara asked.

Anna looked to Scott. There were two interior doors and a spiral staircase to the upper and lower floors. Scott shrugged, with no idea which one Kolonov had taken.

Anna launched into action first. "I'm going this way." She pointed to the door in front of her. "You two figure out the rest." Without waiting for an answer, she ran out of the room.

"I like her," Mara said.

He gave her a smirk, but he spoke quickly, all business. "Scarvan's not leaving here until he settles this score with Kolonov. If you find him first, let the bait sit. Be patient. If you don't have a sure thing on Scarvan, don't force it."

"I got it," she said.

Scott grabbed her arm. "I'm serious, Mara. Be careful."

She nodded, wondering at the last time she'd seen her dad actually scared of another operative. She put the Airpod back in her ear. Their regular gear would have been better, but this would have to do. "Check check."

Scott nodded. "Com-check good. Let's go get this asshole."

Mara jogged to the spiral staircase, looking both up and down for any movement, straining for any tell of which way Kolonov had gone. Scott brushed past her and took the stairs up.

"I guess I'll take down," she said.

While the stairs up were decorative wrought iron, the ones going down were solid stone, like in a castle going down to the cellar.

She moved quickly, crouching low in the hopes that anyone sitting in wait around a corner would have their weapon trained on where they expected her head to be.

The temperature dropped with each step and the air tasted musty and damp. The lower level was far deeper than she expected, perhaps going to the original ancient foundation of the home.

"Status?" came her dad's voice in her ear. It crackled as the stone around her disrupted the reception.

"Nothing but spiders and ghosts down here," she whispered. "I'm going to . . . wait a minute."

The corners of the staircase this far down were covered with spiderwebs, but not a single one crossed the stairs. Mara didn't think that was from the spiders being polite. Someone had been down these stairs not long before. Didn't mean it was Kolonov, but it meant she needed to keep going.

"What . . . it?" her dad said, breaking up.

"Someone came down here recently," she said. "He might be down here. Copy?"

". . . ara . . . come in . . ." And then the signal was gone completely.

She allowed herself to feel the frustration, but only for a second. She hated the idea that her dad and Anna might engage Scarvan at any minute and she'd be crawling around a cellar, far away from the action.

A noise came from below.

She stopped, wondering whether or not her footsteps had been too loud. Or if her whispered voice might have carried.

The noise came again.

A dragging sound. A grunt of exertion.

Definitely human.

Crouching even lower, Mara eased herself down the last few

steps until she saw a landing on the bottom. The corridor ran both ways and she imagined it traced the outline of the villa above. Stacks of chairs lined the wall in front of her, protected against dust with cloth coverings.

One of the coverings had a swath of blood smeared across it.

Mara's heart sank. Kolonov had not been injured. She was likely following one of his goons hiding out from the firefight above. If so, the man was not only worthless to her, but dangerous as well. A brutal combination.

Still, she had to be sure.

"Kolonov," she called out. "Is that you?"

Shots erupted, deafening in the enclosed space of the cellar.

There were several lights strung overhead in the corridor and three switches at the base of the stairs. She put her hand on them.

"I'm just looking for Kolonov," she said. "I'm trying to help him. I can help you. You're injured. Let me assist you."

"Kolonov not here," came a voice, deep and edged with pain.

Mara wanted to believe the man, but that just wasn't how things worked.

She clicked the lights off, sending the entire corridor into darkness. Staying low, she glanced around the corner and put the lights back on.

As she expected there to be, there was a man at the far end of the corridor, about thirty feet away. He slouched against the wall, left hand to his stomach, right hand hanging at his side, holding a gun.

Disoriented by the lights turning off and on, he was slow to react.

With great effort, he tried to raise his gun toward her, but without much success.

The man gave up and leaned harder into the wall.

"I said Kolonov not here."

Mara caught movement behind the man. Her first thought was that it was Kolonov and the man had been covering for his employer. That split-second hesitation cost her.

Instead, someone else materialized from the shadows behind the man. Face covered by night-vision goggles, it didn't register at first who she was looking at.

But as one hand reached out to the light switch at the far end of the hallway and the other raised a gun at the injured man before him, the alarm bells rang in her head.

Scarvan.

The lights went out and gunfire tore through the darkness.

Mara threw herself left, finding the opposite wall with her shoulder. Crouching down, she lifted her gun, recreating the scene from seconds before in her head.

Then she sprayed the corridor with an entire mag, thirteen shots sent downrange with a hope and a prayer, given that she couldn't see a thing.

He had night vision.

The thought screamed at her and her body immediately reacted.

She barrel-rolled to her right, misjudging where the wall opened to the stairs, slamming her knee into the stone. She found the opening and scrambled into the stairwell. Her hands moved automatically, ejecting the magazine and slamming a new one home.

She considered trying the phone but decided against it. If the stone had cut off service halfway down, then it certainly wasn't going to work now.

Scarvan was looking for Kolonov, just like she was. There was a chance he'd already found and killed the man. If that was the case, then he might pursue her. Kolonov was certainly still his primary target so, not finding him here, he would continue the search instead of tangling with her.

He was either already gone or creeping up the corridor toward her.

Playing it safe wasn't in her blood, so she put a hand on the light switch. If Scarvan still had the night-vision gear on, the lights should blind him momentarily, giving her the advantage.

If she was lucky, she could get off a disabling shot before he recovered.

She took a deep breath, tensed her legs to propel herself forward, and then flipped on the lights.

Going from dark to light even disoriented her, but only for a split second. She covered the hall, staring down the end of her Glock's sights, every nerve raw and ready.

Empty.

He'd taken option two and run the other direction, away from Mara. Which likely meant Kolonov was still alive.

She was about to run after him, hoping to at least track him through the footsteps in the fine coat of dust that covered everything, when she felt her hair stand on end.

Just thinking about tracking the footsteps made her look to the floor.

A single track was there, leading from the stairs down the corridor. Kolonov's injured henchman.

But along the far wall, spaced far apart from someone running, was another set of prints.

Coming toward her. And past her.

She spun around, knowing her mistake was going to cost her. She just didn't realize how much.

CHAPTER 38

Scott wasn't happy.

He'd lost coms with Mara not long after they'd separated. She was a big girl and could take care of herself, but that didn't mean he had to like it.

As he worked his way room-by-room on the second floor, he tried to tell himself he'd feel the same way if he was paired with any operative, that good coms were a requirement on a search-and-destroy mission through a building to be effective. But he knew that was only partly true. Yes, the lack of coms made the job harder and more dangerous. But as much as he tried to compartmentalize their professional roles, Mara was still his daughter. The anxiety over her safety was just a different level.

Scarvan had wreaked carnage throughout the villa. The rooms were staged with museum-quality furnishings, ornate wood furniture resting on finely woven rugs. Oil paintings and tapestries depicting pastoral scenes. Even the ceilings were showcases of art, covered with plaster medallions and painted frescoes.

Only now, these rooms contained periodic tableaus of violent death. A splash of red blood against a wall. A toppled table, its contents now piled onto a hulking dead body with a halo of blood around it. Another room with a dead man sitting on a settee as if waiting for an audience with an important dignitary, except that his head was lolled back, exposing a knife slash across his throat deep enough to show his vertebrae.

Scott knew the stories about Jacobslav Scarvan and, unlike most tales told about his adversaries, he actually believed them.

It was why he believed that if the man's intention was to bring massive devastation to the world order, Scott took it seriously.

The intensity with which he was settling his old scores first showed the man's mania and his ruthlessness. But it also exposed a weakness. Each of the missions to exact his revenge put his larger mission at risk. That meant it was too personal with him. And Scott knew he had to find a way to use that to his advantage.

But he couldn't do anything if he couldn't find the man.

He reached the northwest corner of the villa. The turn to the right here brought him parallel to the street below and directly in line with the section destroyed by Scarvan's explosive device. From here, the sirens on the street were distinct. They were close. The rubble that filled the courtyard entrance would keep them at bay for a while, but not for too long. Time was running out.

Scott cleared a bedroom, moving his gun from corner to corner, seeking out any sign of his target. He wanted Scarvan, but Kolonov would do for now. He just hoped to avoid some low-level henchman with an itchy trigger finger hiding under a bed or in a closet.

The next room was only half there. The other half lay in a pile of brick, plaster, and red roof tiles one floor below. A gap nearly twenty feet across opened between one side of the villa and the other. Somehow, the wall on the street side had remained mostly intact, but the roof was gone, exposing the open sky above.

Some of the most flammable materials had either burned or were still smoldering, filling the air on both sides with a heavy smoke that swirled in the slight breeze coming from above.

As Scott strained to make out what was in the room beyond the gap, his worst fear materialized in front of him. A ghostly image, like something from one of the nightmares he had every night.

Scarvan stepped forward. Holding Mara in front of him as a hostage.

CHAPTER 39

Scott's mind went blank. Not from lack of thought, or from emotional reaction. It was complete hyper-awareness. Observe. React. Pure instinct. He was in the zone.

But there was one thought that penetrated through. An unhelpful thought that wouldn't go away no matter how hard he resisted.

Unless I'm perfect in the next thirty seconds, Mara's going to die.

"I came for Kolonov," Scarvan said. "Where is he?"

Scott raised his gun, taking aim at the small part of Scarvan's head just to the right of Mara. She was conscious but appeared groggy. Blood trickled down the right side of her face. She had her hands bound behind her back and a thick rope around her neck tied into a noose. The sight tore into Scott, exactly as Scarvan would have predicted it would.

"Let her go and we'll go find him."

Scarvan pressed his gun harder under Mara's chin. He lifted up on her wrists behind her back, forcing her up on the balls of her feet to keep her arms from being torn from their sockets. The noose around her neck tightened, turning her face red.

"I thought your daughter would be harder to kill," Scarvan said. "Disappointing."

"She has nothing to do with this. It's me you want. Let her go and I'm all yours."

Scarvan laughed, a thick, phlegmy sound. "You're all mine anyway," he said. "But not yet. I have plans for you."

"You mean New York?" Scott said, desperate to buy time. The gambit seemed to work. Even from a distance he saw a flash of anger on Scarvan's face. No one liked to be predictable.

"We know all about it. Courtesy of your friends on Mount Athos. Seems they don't like you much, either."

"Kolonov," Scarvan growled. "Tell me in the next ten seconds where he is."

"New York will never happen. You're too damn old to pull something like that off."

"You may think you're clever," Scarvan said, "but the end will come. About what day or hour no one knows, not even the angels in heaven, nor the Son, but only the Father."

"I'd heard you'd found religion," Scott said, stalling for time. Anna was the unknown variable. He had to give her time to see this standoff and decide how to intervene. "Never had much use for it myself. You really think God will forgive you for all the things you've done?"

" 'Though your sins are like scarlet, they shall be as white as snow; though they are red as crimson, they shall be like wool.' " Scarvan yanked hard on the rope around Mara's neck.

"What about all those ideas about love and mercy? Doesn't seem like you're living up to that side of the deal very well." Scott said.

"Death can also be mercy," Scarvan said, forcing Mara to her knees at the edge of the gap. The fall was at least fifteen feet. The area beneath was a tangle of wood support beams, plaster, and red tile from the roof. She would survive the fall, but not if he hung her by the noose from her neck before she reached the bottom. "Let me show you."

"No, wait!" Scott yelled, lowering his gun. He sank to his knees, the mirror image of Mara on the opposite side of the gap. "Please, I'm begging you."

Mara's head rose a few inches, her eyes more aware now.

They darted back and forth, as if sizing up the situation for the first time. When she finally made contact with his, he recognized the look. He knew Mara's rage when he saw it.

He shook his head, a sudden premonition sweeping him that he was looking at his daughter alive for the last few seconds.

But before Mara did anything, another voice filled the air.

"Scarvan, is this the piece of shit you're looking for?" Anna called out.

They all turned to the courtyard. Anna stood with Kolonov in front of her, her gun trained on his back.

For a second, everything froze. The sirens outside seemed to drift away. The smoke hung in the air. Each killer did the mental calculation of every permutation of how the three-way standoff might end.

Scarvan moved first.

He shoved Mara forward, holding on to the rope to keep her from falling off the ledge. The rope was tied off behind him, so if Mara went over, Scott would be watching his daughter's hanging like in an old Western.

He snatched up his gun and took aim. Scarvan was exposed, but if he was shot, he'd let go of the rope. If that happened, Mara died.

In the second it took him to realize this, he tried to calculate whether Anna would reach the same conclusion. Or if she did, whether that would be enough to stop her from killing Scarvan.

Feeling like the world moved in slow motion, he turned to Anna just as she raised her gun from pointing at Kolonov to taking aim at Scarvan.

Scott swiveled on his right knee. Reflexes from a lifetime of fieldwork kicking everything into a heightened sense of reality. He saw everything. Doubted nothing.

Before Anna could fire at Scarvan, Scott pulled the trigger, sending a single bullet down range.

It hit its mark perfect, slamming into Anna's right shoulder. Spinning her around and to the ground, sending her own shot toward Scarvan off in a wild direction.

Kolonov broke into a run, seeking cover in the villa. He didn't get far.

Scarvan shot him in the leg first, sending Kolonov to the ground. The next shot was the other leg. Purposeful. The intent to injure. To draw it out.

Another shot, this one in the arm. Then the other arm.

Kolonov writhed on the ground, pitifully trying to pull himself toward one of the cars in the courtyard for cover. He left a trail of blood behind him.

Scott watched helplessly. If he shot Scarvan, Mara would go over. Then he realized Anna was reaching for her gun from the ground. "No!" he called out. He shot at the gun on the ground, hoping to hammer it hard enough to blast it out of her reach.

The rock on either side of the gun splintered with the first two shots. A micro-adjustment and the third shot hit the gun and skittered it across the ground.

By time he swung back around, he saw Kolonov drag himself up onto his knees. He faced Scarvan directly, lips pulled back in a bloody grimace.

"Fuck you," he said. A split second later, his face caved in and the back of his skull exploded, leaving a fine red mist in the air.

Then came the uncertainty. With that piece of work done, what would Scarvan do?

Scott jerked back toward Scarvan, bringing his gun to bear on him.

By the time he did, he was looking down the barrel of the gun pointed at him.

Both men froze.

Scarvan had the advantage and they both knew it.

Scott couldn't fire first. It would mean Scarvan letting go of the rope and Mara hanging.

But if Scarvan fired, would Scott be quick enough to get a shot off?

The two old pros held the stalemate for only seconds, but it felt like time itself had stopped.

A wicked grin spread across Scarvan's face. He mouthed two words and Scott read the man's lips.

Not yet.

With a twist of the rope around a piece of debris from the caved-in roof, Scarvan shoved Mara forward.

She didn't go over the edge. Her feet balanced on the edge of the drop-off as she leaned out at more than a forty-five-degree angle over the space below. Too far forward to pull back. The tension on the rope around her neck the only thing keeping her from falling.

"No!" Scott shouted.

When he looked back past Mara, Scarvan had already disappeared into the smoke-filled room behind him.

Scott surveyed the drop below, picked the best landing spot and jumped.

The pile of tiles collapsed when he landed, burying him up to his thighs in the debris.

"Hold on!" he shouted, climbing out and across the wreckage of the collapsed building.

Mara's face was a dark red, almost purple. Her eyes bulged from their sockets. It was only a matter of time before she passed out.

If she fell, the drop would snap her neck.

Worse, she was shifting her feet as the edge of the floor bent and crumpled beneath her.

He fell and scrambled back to his feet, almost under her now.

Then gunfire erupted from the courtyard. Shot after shot.

A quick glance told him it was Anna.

Shooting at Mara.

What the hell?

As he turned back, the floor gave way beneath Mara.

Scott reached up, hoping to somehow be high enough to break her fall. But it wasn't going to be enough. He wasn't going to be able to reach her. Her neck would snap when the rope snapped tight. He was going to lose his daughter. His little girl.

"NO!"

Mara fell. As she did, the rope broke. Anna had been shooting at the rope and had at least nicked it.

Mara's body twisted in midair. Scott caught her lengthways, absorbing the impact of the fall. They tumbled together down the pile of debris.

The second they came to rest, Scott pulled Mara to him, fighting the hangman's knot still choking her.

He finally got it loose and Mara sucked in a full breath, coughing and sputtering.

But alive.

He held her to his chest, rocking her the same as he'd done when she was a little girl. And she let him, clutching on as she fought to get her breath back.

Scott looked over at Anna. She held her gun to her side, a red blotch of blood covering her shoulder where he'd shot her.

He was surprised by what he saw in her face. He'd expected anger, rage even. They both knew Scarvan would be long gone now. They'd missed their chance. Scott had chosen to save his daughter over eradicating an international threat.

Not only that, but he'd shot Anna. On purpose.

But there was no anger in Anna's expression as she stared at him holding his daughter. Only acceptance. Even a small nod that could be interpreted as approval.

Scott hugged Mara tight, realizing the cost for his decision could be immense. If Scarvan had his way, hundreds were going to die. And if Scarvan's plan worked, those deaths would lead to chaos that would destroy the lives of countless others.

Because of the choice he made, those deaths would be on Scott's head.

"Scarvan . . ." Mara croaked. "Did you . . . was he . . . ?"

"He got away," Scott said. "But we'll get him. I swear we will."

CHAPTER 40

Chaos reigned outside the villa. Smoke billowed from inside. Debris from the caved-in roof spilled out into the street from what had been the archway entrance into the courtyard. The entire area in front crawled with police hastily setting up a containment area, pushing the civilian bystanders away.

Asset watched carefully from the first-floor window across the street. He was angry at himself for not choosing a higher floor or even the rooftop. That would have given him an angle to see into the courtyard once the explosion had collapsed the upper stories into the entrance.

But who would have guessed Scarvan would blow the place up?

He marveled at the man's audacity. A solo assault against an unknown number of gunmen. Most of which had been hired goons, but others, like Mara Roberts, Anna Beliniski, and even Kolonov himself, were highly trained operatives. Without the element of surprise, any one of them posed significant risk as an adversary. And then the addition of Scott Roberts. The timing of when Scarvan blew the charges in the archway seemed to indicate Scarvan had planned on Scott joining the melee the entire time.

Either brilliant and audacious, or stupid and arrogant.

Fine lines.

Asset had called his employer during the battle for instructions. His orders had been to observe only, unless his help was needed in the most extreme circumstances to keep Scarvan alive. Once the crazy old assassin had purposefully locked himself up in the villa with high odds stacked against him, Asset didn't see a clear path for the man to extricate himself.

On the phone, his employer had shared his exasperation, but his orders didn't change. Observe and report.

Then the last series of rapid-fire shots happened. With that, Asset imagined the old man had miscalculated and was laying somewhere instead in a pool of his own blood.

Until he caught the barest glimpse of a figure jumping from the roof of the villa to the next building. Even though it was fast, the man's figure was unmistakable. Scarvan. Escaping to fight another day.

To execute his plan in New York City. A plan that matched perfectly with his employer's goals. Scarvan owed him now. It was his employer who'd arranged the meeting between Nochek and Manisky in Paris. Who'd insisted on Kolonov meeting in Prague. Without that assist, Scarvan would still be hunting.

He picked up the encrypted satellite phone and pressed a stored number. As it rang, Asset wondered whether Scott and Mara both survived the ordeal.

One thing was certain: If Scarvan was leaving the scene, Kolonov was dead. That was a guarantee.

Marcus Ryker answered the phone. "Report."

"Our friend has finished his task."

"And our favorite family?"

Asset smiled at the perfect timing. Down below, enough debris had been hauled aside to allow passage out of the villa. Scott Roberts, helping Anna Beliniski, came out first. Mara was right behind them.

"They both survived," Asset said. "Are you placing them on the target list?" He hoped the answer was yes. Asset owed them both. The last time he'd met Mara, she'd bested him in one-on-one combat. As for Scott, his reputation as one of the best in the business made Asset want to add him as a notch in his belt. And they had unfinished business with each other.

"No, they have a role to play," Ryker said. "Let them lead the charge trying to rally the bureaucracy against Scarvan. Head to New York and await further instructions."

Before Asset could reply, the line went dead.

He slid the phone back into his pocket and watched the scene in the street below. As he did, he raised his hand, holding his thumb and fingers out like a kid pretending to hold a gun. He took aim at first Scott and then Mara, pulling the trigger as he made soft, whispered sounds of gunfire.

With a last, longing look at the two of them, he left the room and followed his egress route to the back of the building and out into the street. Within a few hours he was on a flight under a different identity on his way to New York City, ready for the next phase of the operation.

Ready to play his part to set fire to the world.

CHAPTER 41

The flight back to the United States was quiet and tense. Mara's throat ached, both from friction burns on her skin from the rope, and internally from the savage pressure the noose had exerted on her. Her voice came out sounding like a frog's, so she avoided speaking to give it a chance to heal.

That worked out since she also had nothing to say to her father. She couldn't deny that she was thankful he'd sacrificed the mission to save her hide. Just as equally she fumed that she'd cost them the chance to stop Scarvan. It'd been her carelessness in the basement that allowed her to become a hostage. Without that, Scarvan couldn't have leveraged her dad's emotional attachment to get what he wanted.

Typically, it was a net positive when she and her dad worked together. Hell, they were nearly unstoppable. But Prague had showed the weak spot the Alpha Team performance psychologist had warned them about. In their world, sometimes casualties were unavoidable to achieve an objective. Would either of them be willing to sacrifice the other, even to save dozens or even hundreds? They'd argued they would, that they wouldn't give each other any more or any less consideration than another teammate. The psychologist's report had disagreed, citing a conflict of interest that could put the group's objectives at risk.

Scott had chosen to save Mara and had shot one of their

teammates in the shoulder to make it happen. Looked like the psychologist was going to be a happy man to be proven right.

In stark contrast, the teammate who'd been shot wasn't happy at all.

Anna sat in the last seat of the Citation X, her arm in a sling. The doctor had forbidden her from making the journey until she'd undergone twenty-four hours of rest and observation, but she'd only laughed at the suggestion. With a phone call to Hawthorn from her boss, the head of counterintelligence for the BIS, she was quickly discharged and given clearance to accompany them on the flight back to the U.S. to assist in the continued operation, temporarily on loan to the Alpha Team.

Mara had to admit it: the woman was tough.

What she loved the most was that she appeared to scare the hell out of her dad.

Her dad had been on the phone with Hawthorn three times during the first half of the flight. Overhearing his side of the conversation, she didn't need to be debriefed as to what was going on back home. The Secret Service was taking the threat seriously, as they did any truly credible plot against the president's life. But they refused to cancel any upcoming event.

The last phone call had been a three-way conversation with Hawthorn and Mitch Dreslan, the head of the Secret Service. It didn't take long before her dad was shouting into the phone, calling Dreslan a goddamn idiot. For some reason, that didn't go over well, and the call ended early.

They had their work to do once they landed. It was why Hawthorn had redirected their flight from New York back to Washington, DC. He wanted them to make their case directly to President Patterson and his national security team. The fact that Hawthorn hadn't been able to convince them on his own showed the size of the obstacle in front of them.

Like Hawthorn, she knew Patterson liked intel from the source closest to the information. He distrusted the bureaucracy and the chain of command, knowing both turned even sensitive matters of national security into a high-level game of telephone. Only in this version of the child's game, when the message morphed, whether due to interpretation or hidden agenda, wars could start, and people died. All presidents since Bush were haunted by the specter of the intelligence community's report on Saddam Hussein's weapons-of-mass-destruction program used in the decision-making process that launched two decades of war in Iraq.

After the last call, her dad had grown sullen and then finally dozed off in his chair. She wondered when was the last time he'd slept.

She was surprised when she sensed Anna walk up next to her seat. She held a steaming cup in her hand. "I found chamomile and honey in the galley back there. Good for your throat."

Mara took the offered cup and sipped. It felt wonderful. "Thanks."

"May I?" she asked, pointing to the chair next to her.

Mara nodded. As Anna took her seat, she smiled at her dad. "The ability to sleep anywhere is a gift," she said.

Mara agreed. On mission, sometimes sleep came in ten-minute increments. "How's the shoulder?"

"I've had worse," she said. "For all his imperfections, your father is a damn fine shot. He stopped me without causing any permanent damage."

Mara appreciated the sentiment. But they both knew that at the distance her dad had taken the shot, there was a huge amount of luck that had gone into the type of wound she'd received. An inch either direction and the bullet would have smashed through bone or pierced a lung. Her dad was a good shot, but not that good. No, she'd been damn lucky, and they both knew it.

"I'm sorry he did that," Mara said.

Anna scrutinized her. "Are you? If I'd gotten the shot off, you would have gone over that edge. I knew that was the case. But I still was going to shoot."

Mara felt an odd blend of emotions. Respect for Anna's truthfulness, but still unsettled at the cold manner she described how she'd nearly sacrificed her to achieve her goal.

"I would have done the same thing."

"Maybe," Anna said, not sounding convinced. "If I was on the ledge, maybe. But what if it was him?" She pointed over to her dad. "Would you have taken the shot then? Or if you'd been in his place, would you have let me take the shot, knowing we'd get Scarvan, but your father's neck would be snapped in the hangman's noose?"

Mara had played the scenario out a million times since the villa, trying to determine not only what she could have done differently—starting with not getting caught—but what her dad could have done differently to resolve the standoff. Each version, though, netted the same result: she and Scarvan both dead.

"I don't know," Mara said. The answer frustrated her, but it was honest.

Anna seemed to appreciate the response. She put a hand on Mara's arm and leaned in. "I wouldn't be hard on your father, then," she said. "I'll forgive him if you will."

"Just like that?" she asked.

"He was saving what he loved most in the world," Anna said. "Isn't that why we all do this job?"

"What is it that you love?" Mara asked.

Anna turned looking forward, struck by the question. "I love the world, I suppose. People." She turned back to face Mara. "The promise of more."

Mara accepted that. She had her dad, but she also had Joey. And now Rick, too. He wasn't just a fling, at least not for her. Maybe there was something long-term there. The promise of more.

"I know what you mean," Mara said.

"But we will meet Scarvan again, hopefully in time to stop his mad plan. When that happens, you very well could be in the same position I was in at the villa. The same position your father was in. Only this time it might not be just that Scarvan escapes, but that he kills hundreds, maybe thousands. You have to be ready for that. You have to know what you'll do."

Mara sipped her tea. There was no response she wanted to give.

Anna stood, nodding to Mara's cup of tea. "Need a refill?"

Mara shook her head. "No, this is just the right amount." She was talking about both the tea and Anna's odd version of a pep talk. "Thank you."

"My pleasure," Anna said, her kind tone and smile somehow coming across like a discordant musical note. This was a complicated woman. Mara hoped her dad knew what he was doing with her.

Anna walked over to where Scott was asleep against the window. She sat next to him and leaned over, placing her head on his chest. He stirred and, careful to avoid her bandaged injury, pulled her closer to him. Mara heard them speak in low voices and then they kissed. She turned away, suddenly feeling like she was intruding on their privacy.

As the jet soared over the Atlantic, she tried to get some sleep of her own. But each time she tried to fade away, Scarvan's grinning face appeared in front of her. The bastard had not only gotten the best of her, he'd gotten into her head, too. She stayed awake for the hour, thinking through her conversation with Anna. What would she sacrifice to stop Scarvan? Who would she sacrifice?

After spinning on the question for far too long, she reached the simple conclusion: stop the son of a bitch before it ever got to that point.

She called that Plan A and decided to go with it. After that, she shut her eyes and slept like a baby the balance of the trip into DC.

CHAPTER 42

Hawthorn never shrank from a fight, even with the president of the United States. Not when it was warranted. And not when the president was being an obstinate pain in the ass.

For as many fatal flaws the previous occupant of the Oval Office had, and Preston Townsend had enough of those to go around, at least Hawthorn had been plugged directly into the man's psyche. He'd been best friends with Townsend's father and had known the president since he'd been a child. That gave him the ability and the right to call him out on his bullshit when he saw it.

President Patterson had no such connection to Hawthorn. They did have a relationship, more professional than friendly, but one built on mutual respect. The idea for Alpha Team had been the president's own and he'd considered no one except Hawthorn to be its leader.

Still, in the coming confrontation, he knew he could only push so far.

That was why Scott and Mara could prove helpful. He knew full well they would speak their minds, no matter the consequences. Sometimes that served a very direct purpose, even it was likely to rattle a few cages.

He'd met his team at Joint Base Andrews when the Citation

X landed. He'd spoken to Scott by phone during their flight but wanted a full briefing from his team on the drive to the White House, hoping he could glean something new from his questions. But by the time they arrived at the White House and made their way to the Oval Office, not much of the landscape had changed. They were dealing with a highly trained, motivated operative willing to die to accomplish his goal.

The Secret Service's nightmare scenario.

"Hello Mr. President," Hawthorn said, stepping in first. "Thank you for seeing us."

Patterson sat behind the Resolute desk, jacket off, his reading glasses perched at the end of his nose as he read the documents in his hand. He didn't look happy. "You'd think my own intelligence services would have been able to know the Russians and the Chinese were meeting last night. Or that maybe they'd have some idea what they were talking about about? Nothing. First time I saw it was on CNN this morning."

Hawthorn took stock of the people in the room. Mitch Dreslan, director of the Secret Service, tall, lanky in a cheap suit and a wide tie. Nancy McKeen, Patterson's chief of staff, a no-nonsense, take-no-prisoners practitioner in the dark art of bureaucratic war, stood on the back wall like a gunfighter not wanting anyone to get behind her. Rick Hallsey, Dreslan's rising star, assigned to the president's protective detail for the upcoming trip to New York. He glanced at Mara and caught the look between them. He tried to give his team some semblance of privacy, but he still knew full well that the two of them were in a serious relationship. He wondered if Dreslan knew about the connection. It certainly added an interesting dynamic to the room.

"I'm doing the UN speech in New York, Jim," President Patterson said. "There's no discussion about that." He threw the document on the desk and stood. "Even if I don't know what the Russians and Chinese are up to."

Hawthorn watched as the man pulled his suit coat on. He knew Patterson to be a creature of habit. While he'd work behind his desk with his coat off and sleeves rolled, he always donned the jacket when he got up.

"Sir, with all due respect—"

"Whenever I hear that phrase, I know something's coming I'm really not going to like." He motioned for his guests to sit on the sofas in front of the fireplace. He took one of the chairs for himself while Hawthorn sat on one couch and Scott and Mara sat on the other. Dreslan, Rick, and Nancy McKeen remained standing where they were.

"Sir, Jacobslav Scarvan is an imminent threat to your safety. Precautions need to be made."

"Precautions are always taken," Dreslan said. He sounded testy and Hawthorn recognized the tone of someone mad that someone was playing univited in their sandbox.

"Mitch, you and your team are the very best in the world," Hawthorn said. "But it's not going to be good enough. Not this time."

Dreslan's face betrayed none of the annoyance Hawthorn was certain he felt. The Secret Service head hadn't climbed the ladder as far as he had by wearing his emotions on his sleeve.

President Patterson turned to Scott. "Jim here tells me you have a theory of what the guy plans to do."

Scott cleared his throat. "Yes sir. I think it's more than a theory. I'd give it a ninety-five percent likelihood. In this business, that's as good as it gets."

"Tell me your thinking," the president said, sitting back in his chair as if ready for a long story.

"After Scarvan was shot and left for dead, he somehow made it alive to the shores of Mount Athos. It's a remote isthmus, part of Greece but governed as a semiautonomous state. The entire area is dedicated to monastic life, whether in the monasteries or in smaller living units all the way down to tiny, one-man huts called sketes."

The president made a motion with his hand, indicating Scott needed to speed things up.

"Scarvan was found and cared for by an old monk named Father Spiros in one of these tiny, remote huts. Which is how he evaded notice. Unexpectedly, during his recovery, it appears Scarvan found religion."

"Eastern Orthodox?" the president asked.

"A variation of it," Scott said. "Monks choose to live in the isolation of the sketes for many different reasons, mostly having to so with their desire to be closer to God. For Father Spiros, the skete was the Church's desire to have him farther away from the other monks."

"A troublemaker," the president said. "Something you can relate to."

The president's attempt to lighten the mood fell flat. Scott continued. "Yes sir. Only I don't subscribe to a religious dogma of such orthodoxy that I'm willing to set the world on fire to punish it for its failings."

Scott paused. The president shifted uncomfortably in his chair, his eyes moving to Hawthorn.

"Keep going, Scott," Hawthorn said. "I think you have the president's attention."

"Father Spiros believed in an apocryphal interpretation of the Bible, with intense focus on the Book of Revelations. Moreover, he operated under the belief that God had shared with him the path to the end times. In a series of visions, God showed him how the world must be cleansed with fire in order to usher in a new world."

"How is this any different than the typical doomsdayer, whackadoodle bullshit we hear all the time?" Nancy McKeen asked.

"Father Spiros's apocryphal vision came with a role for Scarvan to play. The world's descent into chaos was a necessary predicate for the second coming. You're right, doomsday cults around the world share the same idea. You see it every time there's a war in the Middle East, or back during the Cold War face-off between the U.S. and the USSR, there's someone pointing to the signs of the end times. Only Father Spiros wasn't content to watch the world crumble. His vision was that man had a necessary role to play in helping the world's descent and, being an obedient instrument of God, the task fell to him."

"And he convinced Scarvan to believe these same things?" McKeen said. "Seems a little farfetched, doesn't it?"

The president looked as if he agreed with her. Hawthorn jumped in. "The details are unclear on how it happened, but the results speak for themselves. In 2004, Africa's senior Greek Orthodox leader, Patriarch Petros VII of Alexandria, Egypt, flew to Mount Athos, intent on silencing an elderly monk there who was creating a following among several young priests across the world. This subversive movement called not only for an extreme orthodoxy, but a punitive form of it. There are always zealots in any religion, but in this case, it was taking on real-world implications."

"Like what?" Nancy asked.

"Followers of Father Spiros took over a monastery on Mount Athos and barricaded themselves in with enough guns and ammo to fight off an army. The Church threatened excommunication, but they denied the Church's authority. The standoff went on for years."

"That's it?" Nancy asked, looking incredulous.

"When Patriarch Petros, the third most senior person in the Orthodox leadership, flew to Mount Athos to confront Father Spiros, his helicopter crashed minutes from landing, killing him and all twelve people on board. Only small bits of wreckage were found."

"That was so long ago," Rick said, speaking up for the first time. "Scarvan was dumped into the ocean twenty years ago. Why now? Why would he wait?"

"That was my question, too," Scott said. "I went to Mount Athos to find the answer."

"And?" the president asked.

"Somehow along the way, Scarvan pledged not to leave Father Spiros's side while he was alive. Apparently, he had visions of his own and was working on a different set of divine instructions."

"Someone ought to check what kind of mushrooms the monks are growing," McKeen said.

Rick followed up on the questioning. Hawthorn noticed Dreslan's disapproving look at his subordinate. "So, he waited until Father Spiros died before he left?" Rick asked.

"Only Father Spiros finally grew tired of waiting," Scott said. "He not only wanted to set fire to the world, he wanted to watch the flames. After years of trying to convince Scarvan to leave Mount Athos and bring about their plan, he instead faked his death so Scarvan would launch into action."

"Nice," McKeen said. "Sounds like a real charmer. I assume we have this Father Spiros in custody for questioning?"

"No, one of Spiros's followers, following the old man's orders to kill him if it seemed like he might endanger the operation, shot him in front of me."

"Then we have that person to interrogate," the president said.

Scott shook his head. "That man is not available to be questioned. When we made it clear he would answer to us, he threw himself off a cliff and broke his neck."

"Jesus," the president said under his breath.

"That's who Scarvan thinks he's helping," Mara said, taking over the narrative. "But before he executes that plan, he had other executions on his mind." She went through the litany of the Russian operatives Scarvan had killed and detailed their interaction with Belchik. Finally, she described Scarvan appearing on a boat in the middle of the Seine shouldering an RPG. Everyone in the room had seen the footage and been briefed, but they were all ears hearing a firsthand account of the event.

Mara left out her interview with Marcus Ryker. When she'd glanced over to Hawthorn when she got to that part of her story, he gave her the barest of signals for her to stop.

"This man should not be underestimated," Mara said. "Even with us guessing at his target, he still poses a threat."

"Prague is a good example," Hawthorn said. "Scarvan raided a secure location, him against how many men?"

"At least ten, maybe more," Mara said. "Not to mention me, a Czech counterterrorism operative, and Scott toward the end of the engagement."

"And killed Kolonov and then just got away?" McKeen said. "How is that possible?"

Scott spoke up. "Because, even at his age, we're dealing with one of the most dangerous operatives there's ever been. That's what we're here trying to explain."

"And now he's coming for me in New York?" the president said.

"No, he's coming for the world," Hawthorn said. "Motive, means, and opportunity."

"Motive," Scott said. "His religious zealotry and his twenty-year festering anger over what happened to him at the hands of his own country take care of that. Means: even at his age, he's demonstrated that his craft and abilities are incredibly danger-ous. And, as you've already been briefed, we believe Omega is supporting his efforts, giving him access to funds and whatever weapons he needs. We don't know how he'll deliver his blow, but we know he's capable of making it happen."

"And opportunity?" the president asked. "He's going to hunt down heads of state one by one. I suppose he'd be starting with me?"

"No sir," Scott said. "When you deliver your speech to the United Nations General Assembly to all the gathered heads of state, Scarvan will be there. And he plans to kill every last one of you."

CHAPTER 43

Mara eyed the president, gauging the man's reaction. She saw the moment he made the connection.

"The United Nations," the president said, almost sounding impressed with the audacity of the whole thing. "Son of a bitch."

Most of the room was silent as he said the words. The exception was Nancy McKeen, who gave a derisive snort at the suggestion.

"Impossible," she said. She looked at Dreslan. "That's impossible, right?"

Mara jumped in. "In two days, there's a General Assembly meeting in New York to celebrate the seventy-fifth anniversary. This will not be a normal general assembly meeting. Nearly every country plans to have their head of state or government attend to act as the ambassador for the meeting. Each delegation will include past leaders and dignitaries."

"A hell of a gathering to take out if your goal is to destabilize the world order," Rick said.

The comment earned him a glaring look from his boss. Dreslan shook his head. "Because of the attendees, the level of security for the event is incredible. We've been working on it for a year, in earnest for the last six months. There's zero chance Scarvan penetrates more than one layer of hard security."

"I wouldn't underestimate him," Mara said.

Dreslan's face reddened. "Getting into the General Assembly hall would require him to penetrate nine levels of security. For that session, it will be the most secure building on the planet, even compared to this one."

"Besides," Nancy said, "we're not having the president of the United States skip out on the largest gathering of heads of state on U.S. soil, for Christ's sake."

The president held up a hand. "Nancy, please." He turned to Hawthorn. "Look, Jim, I'm taking this seriously. I know you're not an alarmist and you and your team wouldn't be in here if you weren't legitimately worried. But this Scarvan. He is human, isn't he?"

"Yes sir," Hawthorn said. "But he's a master at thinking of solutions to problems no one imagined. Accessing areas thought impenetrable is what this man does. If you could just—"

"The gala," Rick said, cutting Hawthorn off.

The room turned toward him.

"That evening, there's a gala reception at the New York Public Library," he continued. "The Rose Reading Room is being transformed into a sit-down dinner for the heads of state. We'll have it locked down, but there are more vulnerabilities there than at the UN. That's where he might go for it."

"We have an iron-tight plan to secure the building," Dreslan said, again looking frustrated with his subordinate. "We will protect the attendees at both events using every means at our disposal."

"But Special Agent Hallsey is correct. It is less secure than the UN building," Hawthorn said.

Rick, as if sensing he'd already gone too far, remained silent. Reluctantly, Dreslan agreed. "The UN was built with the intention of heads of state safely coming and going. The New York Public Library presents more issues. Especially this year."

"You're talking about the protests," Patterson said. "We've had this discussion. Several times. I don't want to change that decision."

"What's the issue with the protestors?" Mara asked, sensing she was wading into the middle of an argument.

Patterson gave a dismissive wave of his hand, as if giving approval for Dreslan to share with the group.

Dreslan answered, but he didn't look happy about it. "We're following standard protocol with the UN arrivals, blocking streets in the area to create a secure zone. The UN has a say in security arrangements there. There won't be a protestor within blocks of the building."

"World's greatest democracy," Patterson mumbled, "and we're telling people they don't have a say."

"But the gala, that's under our control," Dreslan continued. "Protests will be allowed closer to the event location."

"How much closer?" Mara asked.

"Bryant Park is being designated," Dreslan said. "And another area blocked off at Forty-second and Fifth all the way to Grand Central Station."

"How can we lecture all these totalitarian regimes about allowing dissent and then cordon off half of Manhattan just so they can arrive comfortably to a dinner party?" Patterson said. "I want them to hear the voices in Bryant Park. I want American democracy on show as they arrive."

"I'm not qualified to say whether the protestors are a good idea or not," Scott said. "But seems to me that Scarvan's stated intention to take out the entire gathering of world leaders will not be helped or hurt by their addition, except perhaps to tie up more resources to control the crowd."

Dreslan bristled. "Thank you for your analysis. I would never have agreed to the protest areas unless I was confident we can provide adequate security."

"The best protection is still not to attend," Mara said. "Mr. President, would you consider doing the UN address and then skip the library event that evening?"

"He can't skip the dinner," Nancy said. "The optics on that would be terrible. And what if there was an attack? All the leaders killed except the president, who decided at the last minute not to attend? How would that look?"

The room grew quiet as what she'd said sank in. The president spoke first. "Are you suggesting that if the room of world leaders gets blown up, you think it'd be better for me to be in the room because of the optics?"

Nancy backtracked, sputtering her words. "It's not what I meant. We're just spitballing here anyway. Jesus."

The president stood. When he did, everyone followed suit.

"I've made my decision," he said. "I'll attend the UN General Assembly and represent the United States of America with honor as her delegate that day. If Scarvan is still in the open after that, I'll develop an illness, or some kind of crisis, and we'll cancel the gala event that evening for everyone. If it's not safe enough for me to go, I'll not allow others to risk it." He pointed to Dreslan. "Secure both locations to the best of your ability. It's not just me you're protecting. If something happens to this group of world leaders, not only will it bring dishonor on America, but the world will spin into chaos."

He walked around his desk, looking out the window, his voice changing.

"Imagine the turmoil if this madman pulled it off. Wiping out every head of state in one blow. The financial markets will crash. Hardliners across the world would use the opportunity to exploit any weakness to grab power. Every hotspot in the world will explode during the resulting leadership fights."

He turned back to face the room.

"We can't let this thing happen." He pointed to Scott and Mara. "You two need to catch Scarvan. And when you do, you put him down."

CHAPTER 44

After the meeting was over, Mara was able to talk briefly with Rick. They'd shaken hands like colleagues instead of lovers, even though everyone around them knew they were in a relationship. No public displays of affection while on the job. That was their rule. It was especially true in the White House.

Still, touching his hand sent a shudder through her body. She couldn't wait to get him alone. Especially after his performance in the Oval Office. Watching his mind work and seeing him stand strong against Dreslan turned her on more than candles and champagne ever could have. He'd texted her that they had a chance to meet, but only for an hour, between three and four. She decided to make it work, intending to make the most of the hour.

At 2:45, she made her way over to the newly refurbished W Hotel, a reimagining of the historic Washington Hotel just across the street from the Treasury Building. Hawthorn had insisted on the short break to give them time to grab a shower and a change of clothes. She secretly wondered if he'd done so knowing it would give her a chance to see Rick, but she didn't ask. She decided to just assume he did and allowed herself to feel thankful toward her boss.

Her first order of business had been to place a call to Joey.

Marie answered the phone, Lucy's mother-in-law. The older woman made things easy. There was never any undertone to her voice, only genuine happiness at hearing her voice. She shouted for Joey, who was apparently outside with some of the neighbor boys from the next farm over.

While they waited, Marie updated her on Joey's activities over the last two weeks. Even though Mara had called every day since she'd been gone, she'd only connected a handful of times. She appreciated Marie's effort to share what a great time Joey was having—fishing, riding bikes, overnight campouts with his new buddies. The best summer a young boy could have. When Joey got on the phone, Mara had him share all the same stories, careful to sound surprised and amazed as if hearing everything for the first time.

Then she heard some other kids in the room calling his name and Joey politely asked if he could go back outside and play. Mara of course told him he should do exactly that and said her goodbyes. Once Marie was back on the phone, she didn't ask once when Mara would come get Joey. Mara knew she desperately wanted to keep him there. And, not for the first time, Mara wondered whether she was being selfish not letting Joey have that normal life.

Lucy had asked Mara to take care of Joey, to protect him and keep him safe. She took that mission to be her most important. But what was the use of protecting him from stubbing his toe or from breaking his arm climbing a tree if the world collapsed around him?

Her dad used to say his missions were never about saving the world. It was about protecting his family, who lived in that world.

She'd never truly understood that until now.

Still, she wasn't about to make any decision on that. Not right in the middle of a mission. If anything happened to her, the paperwork was already set up to have Marie and Ted take guardianship over Joey. And they'd expressed that they'd be more than happy to take on that responsibility at any time.

It was something she needed to consider.

But not today.

Mara said her goodbyes and promised to call again when she could. Marie told her to be safe and not to worry about Joey. Mara hung up the phone feeling only a short pang of guilt for not being there for the boy, but mostly gratitude for his terrific grandparents. Joey's other set of grandparents were a devil-may-care international assassin and a dead woman. The kid was batting .500 on stable role models in his grandparents. That was pretty good in baseball, and maybe it wasn't a bad average in a family, either.

Mara entered the hotel off of Fifteenth Street and made her way through the new lobby, taking in the new hipster vibe of the place. The check-in area had been transformed from marble and pillars filled with old-world charm into a sleek, glistening area with a shining black-and-white color scheme. Each of the three check-in desks was fronted by backlit white panels covered with caricatures of political figures and businesspeople. A soft, funky beat filled the room from hidden speakers.

She bypassed the front desk and headed to the bank of elevators. Rick had already texted her their room number.

As the elevator rose to the eighth floor, she felt the sexual tension building. The attraction to Rick was his mind, his dedication to his country, his character that she'd seen on display over and over in both his work and out in the world.

But he was also an incredible lover.

And that was all she was thinking about.

She caught her reflection in one of the mirrors in the hallway and stopped. She looked like hell. She'd been in her clothes since the day before, an off-the-rack suit purchased in Prague by Anna's aide, who had guessed her size and taste. She'd showered in Prague, washing her own blood out of her hair from where Scarvan knocked her unconscious. But her neck had turned a dark purple and was laced with scratches. It wasn't her sexiest look.

But based on the way Rick had looked at her when they'd been together in the Oval, that wasn't going to matter.

She undid her hair, allowing it to spill across her shoulders, sweeping it in front of her neck. It hid some of the damage from nearly being hanged less than twenty-four hours ago, but just barely. She shrugged. It was going to have to do.

She found their room, double-checking the number on the text she'd received. She knocked in a playful cadence, expecting the door to open right away.

No answer.

She checked the room number again. It was correct.

She knocked again, a sinking feeling in her chest that maybe he'd been delayed.

But he would have contacted her if he was going to be late or had to cancel.

She was about to knock a third time when she heard a noise come from inside the room. She smiled, thinking through the next ninety seconds, imagining how fast she could get Rick's clothes off him.

The door opened. A gun pointed at her face.

There was no time to react. Nothing to do.

She shifted her eyes from the gun to the face of the man holding it.

It was a face she knew. A man she'd fought and bested the last time they'd met.

She knew him only as Asset.

"Hello, Mara," he said. "It's time we had a talk. Please come in."

CHAPTER 45

Scott opened the door to Alpha Team headquarters for Anna. He figured it was the least he could do since he was the reason for her arm being in a sling. Surprisingly, she'd seemed to have already gotten over him shooting her. In Scott's prior experience, people tended to hold a grudge for a while after they'd been shot. Jacobslav Scarvan being the perfect example.

But Anna was a pro. Not only that, but she understood better than most his attachment to Mara. It was left unsaid, but if the circumstances had required a fatal shot instead of just a flesh wound, there was no doubt between them what would have happened.

And Anna was fine with that.

Which was one of the reasons Scott found her to be such an amazing woman.

"So, this is where the magic happens?" Anna said, looking around at the command center at the heart of Alpha.

Scott grinned. It was the same line she's used the first time they'd gone into his bedroom together. He would rather have been there than in the middle of Alpha, but he knew that was pressing his luck. Anna may have got why he did what he did, and she may have been a pro, but he wasn't so far out of the doghouse to expect any love right now.

"This is it," Scott said.

The room appeared like a mini command center for a space launch. Rows of lightning-fast computers manned by young, tech-savvy analysts. Screens covered the far wall, capable of working both individually and together to create larger images. Photos of the United Nations building and the New York Public Library appeared on the screen, along with schematics, architectural drawings, security layouts, and other information the team was using.

Jim Hawthorn walked from his office and extended his hand. "Good to see you, Anna. Thank you for agreeing to help. Sorry to hear what happened."

Anna reached out awkwardly with her left hand. "It's what happens when you spend time with the wrong people. Happy to help any way I can."

Hawthorn directed their attention back to the screens. "We have two teams working. Blue team has the UN building and red team on the NYPL."

"NYPL?" Anna asked.

"New York Public Library," Scott said. "Its main branch on Fifth Avenue is the location for the gala after the General Assembly session. Not only will it be the greatest collection of heads of state but add to that a who's who list of dignitaries and celebrities that want to mix with the power brokers of the world."

"Our thinking is that one of these two locations is Scarvan's target," Hawthorn said. "Of the two, the NYPL has the easier security to breach."

"I'm not certain that's the case," Anna said.

That got the two men's attention.

Anna walked to the screen showing an aerial view of the UN building. "Everything about this place screams security. Hardened perimeter. Controlled entry points. Underground arrivals. The place looks like a bunker."

"But?" Scott asked.

"Its apparent strength is the weakness. Leads to complacency. Even you two assumed Scarvan would hit the library."

Hawthorn was all ears. "How does he do it?"

"Diplomatic immunity protocols are the way I'd go in," Anna said. "For all these safeguards and controls, diplomats require secrecy to ply their trade. The norms allow for diplomatic pouches to go unchecked. This can be an entry point for toxins, bomb parts, etcetera that can then be reassembled inside. We've all done it ourselves."

Hawthorn and Scott shared a look. They actually had not. Anna gave them a disapproving look.

"Well, you didn't hear it from me."

"Let's say he's used the diplomatic pouches. You'd need people on the inside to pull all this off," Scott said. "Take possession. Stash the contraband someplace."

"Each country submits documents for members of their delegation. Background checks are conducted, but it's not hard to submit the bio of a look-alike to get clearance. If it's some lower-level person, a simple bribe works to smuggle something in. If it's someone in authority, like a delegate, then they are shown a great deal of deference once inside. The whole idea of egalitarianism in the institution means the smallest country has equal access as the heavyweights."

"So, you think Scarvan has what he needs already in place?" Hawthorn said.

Anna shrugged. "I'm not saying that. I'm just saying we need to take care not to let the perception of security blind us. But if he does have the means to carry out the attack already inside, the question becomes, how does he get in?"

"His face is plugged in to every facial recognition software imaginable," Hawthorn said. "He steps foot in Manhattan, and we'll pick him up. Or we'll pick up anyone walking around with a full-face mask on."

"Unfortunately, you won't know he's wearing a mask," came a man's voice with a British accent. Jordi Pines walked out from a back room wearing board shorts and an enormous T-shirt with the face of Jeff Bridges as the Dude from *The Big Lebowski* on it. The analysts at their desks watched him warily as if a new species of animal had just entered their cage.

"Anna, this is Jordi Pines," Hawthorn said. "He's our secret weapon."

Anna reached out to shake Jordi's hand. Jordi held up his hand to show it was covered with orange dust. Doritos or Cheetos, Scott couldn't tell which. Perhaps both.

"Not too secret," Anna said. "I'm familiar with Mr. Pines. Or at least his reputation."

Jordi looked around the room as if making sure everyone had heard. "Whatever you've heard is only the stuff I let people know." He lowered his voice. "The real goodies I keep secret."

"You are wicked, aren't you?" Anna said. "Truly wicked."

Jordi giggled like a child. Scott enjoyed the way she'd effortlessly gained the large man's affection. Damn, she was good.

"Jordi," Hawthorn said. "What did you mean we wouldn't know he's wearing a mask?"

"Come on, I'll show you," he said.

He turned and walked back out of the room the way he'd come in. As they followed, Scott noticed a palatable sense of relief in the room. Jordi was a bull in whatever shop he wandered into; apparently the headquarters for Alpha Team was no exception.

They followed him back through a long hallway, then entered Jordi's den. A long room with a computer workspace at one end and what looked like a mad scientist's lab at the other.

Jordi pulled up a chair that looked like a captain's chair in a science-fiction movie and rolled in front of a bank of computer screens. His rather thick fingers danced nimbly over the keyboard as the screens lit up. A series of faces appeared sequentially on the screen, each time covered with small green dots connected by geometric lines.

"Facial recognition, like everything else, is just math," Jordi said. "These geometric shapes are processed by advanced algorithms in a deep learning protocol."

"English, please," Scott said.

"The system learns over time, getting better, needing less information to formulate a match," he said. "Scott, walk across the room there."

Scott did so, noticing a camera set up in the corner of the room. He appeared on the screen, a green square framing his face and the dots and lines moving as he walked.

"Good," Jordi said. "Now come back."

Scott obliged. "Now, to fool the system you could use a prosthetic mask. Not a bad option. There are some really great fakes out there designed just for this purpose. There's a guy in Europe who sells them at cost just because he hates the idea of the police state watching everyone all the time." An image on his screen of a man in a hoodie popped up. It took Scott a few seconds to recognize the man was wearing a mask. It was good enough to fool a casual observer but wouldn't hold up to any kind of scrutiny. Jordi handed Scott a pair of glasses. The frames were heavy and thick. When he put them on, he saw the glass was clear.

"Go on, give us another walk," Jordi said, laying his fake British accent on thick.

Scott did so. On the screen, his face was blurred out in a white circle of light.

"Whoa, what's that?" he asked.

"The glasses are transmitting, right?" Anna asked.

"Look at the big brain on Anna," Jordi said. "Yes, a broad-spectrum output designed to confuse any camera."

"But what good would that do?" Hawthorn asked. "Anyone with white light overriding the system just gets flagged for intercept."

Jordi picked up another set of glasses and handed them to Scott. "Last time, I promise."

Scott put on the glasses and walked across the floor. From where he was, he could see that there were no bright lights on the computer screen this time. It looked like there was no difference, except that Hawthorn and Anna leaned closer to the screen, audibly gasping at what they saw.

"What is it?" Scott said.

He walked back and looked at the frozen image on the screen. It was his body, but Jordi's face.

"Now there's a handsome devil," Jordi said.

Scott took off the glasses and looked at them closely. "How does it work?"

"Same idea," Jordi said. "Except instead of the light trying to wipe out the camera sensors, it's forming its own invisible hologram that hovers over the actual face."

"Like wearing a mask except no one else sees it," Hawthorn said.

"What makes you think Scarvan has this technology?" Anna said. "He's been on Mount Athos for twenty years. I imagine he barely knows how to search on Google."

"Mara's report from Paris was that Scarvan had help," Scott pointed out. "The surveillance team was taken out by someone else as Scarvan rode up on the boat in the Seine."

"If it's Omega helping him," Jordi said, pointing to his lab at the other end of the room, "then I imagine he had access to everything here and more. Well, except some of my newest things, which are probably more advanced."

Scott grinned, always amused by Jordi's fathomless ego in his work. He wasn't sure if it was charming because of the fake accent, or because it was typically true.

"The point is, whether it's this particular piece of tech or not, our facial recognition system is Swiss cheese," Jordi said. "Holes all over it."

"Let's brief Dreslan on this," Hawthorn said. "Better yet, get Rick Hallsey over here. He seems to have a good head on his shoulders and open to ideas. Let's get him on board first. Any idea where he's at?"

Scott checked his watch. Just after three p.m. "I have a pretty good idea. I'll call him."

Anna arched an eyebrow and he caught the look.

"What?" he said.

She didn't say anything, but her stare was unrelenting. Scott threw up his hands. "All right, I'll call in fifteen minutes," he said. "They're young and haven't seen each other for a while. It'd be a miracle if it took that long."

CHAPTER 46

Mara's first instinct at the door was to strike. That first split second of facing down a gun was the best opportunity to change the dynamics of the situation. But against an adversary like the one she faced, it was high risk. Likely deadly.

Like a professional baseball player with a third of a second to decide whether to swing at a pitch or not, Mara did a series of nearly instant calculations.

Asset was no normal assailant.

If he meant to kill her, he could have performed a long-range sniper shot. No need for the close quarters and the cloak-and-dagger of intercepting her here.

And if Rick was still alive inside, then she needed to get the lay of the land before deciding how to proceed.

All of this happened with the electric speed of instinct. And she held herself in check.

Asset gave her a short nod as if he knew exactly the calculus that had occurred in her mind. He stepped back and invited her in.

"How's your leg?" she murmured as she walked past him. The last time they'd met, she'd stabbed him in the leg with a knife stuck through her own hand.

If the comment got any kind of rise out of him, he didn't show it.

Mara breathed a sigh of relief as the short foyer opened to a suite. Rick sat, bound and gagged, on a chair in the center of the room. He stared at her with longing eyes. His entire body language an apology for not preventing all of this from happening.

"All right, asshole," Mara said, turning to Asset. "You have my attention. What do you want?"

"Let's start with your weapons," he said, indicating toward the bed.

She appreciated the professional courtesy of the man not spelling out exactly how she should do it. They both knew how to disarm in a way that wasn't perceived as a possible threat. As she removed her Glock and tossed it on the bed, she noticed for the first time some of the things Rick had prepared for her.

Champagne on ice. Chocolate-covered strawberries. Fresh roses in a vase.

All a little cliché. All of it perfect.

Asset seemed to notice the same thing. "Looks like I interrupted your fun."

"Not too late to leave," Mara said. "That would probably be best for all of us."

Asset checked his watch. Mara wondered if he was expecting additional help, or just timing how long before he needed to hit his egress plan.

"You're hunting Jacobslav Scarvan," Asset said. "I know how to catch him."

Mara felt her heart beat faster. She tried not to give away any tells. "What do you know about Scarvan?"

"I know his plan is aggressive. Very aggressive," Asset said. "People I work for believe it is too much. They want it stopped."

Mara thought through the implications. This might be a breakthrough. Or a trap. "These people you say want it stopped. You mean Omega?"

Asset smiled thinly. "Never heard that name. What is it? One of your American conspiracy theories?"

"Funny, you were working for Omega last time we met," Mara said, circling the room to make her way over to Rick. "Or did you forget?"

A dark cloud passed over Asset's face. Mara imagined many men had seen that look as one of the last things they'd seen in their lives. She was fascinated to see the man raise two fingers to his neck, as if checking a corpse for a pulse. He held it there for five seconds of silence. When he removed it, the cloud had passed.

"I remember well," Asset said. "I've been looking forward to reminiscing with both you and your father at some point. Unfortunately, this other matter gets in the way of that right now. You need my help if you want to stop Scarvan."

"And we're just going to trust you?" Mara asked.

Asset pointed toward Rick. "If she removes your gag, are you going to behave?"

Rick glared at him as if trying to drive a projectile through the man's eye socket through sheer force of will alone.

Mara put a hand on Rick's shoulder. "He'll be fine," she said. "Won't you?"

He nodded. She looked to Asset, who indicated for her to proceed. She pulled the gag from Rick's mouth and he inhaled sharply once it was out.

Rick fixed Asset with another death stare. "You're an asshole."

Asset looked to Mara as if in protest. *See what I mean?*

"Let's leave the who and why alone for now," Mara said. "How can you help us stop Scarvan?"

"I know his plan for the United Nations building. I can tell you exactly what's going to happen. My employers just need a couple of assurances."

"Your assurance is that I'm going to come find you when all this is over," Rick said.

Asset turned to Mara and waited. Her curiosity was piqued. "What assurances?"

"They would prefer that you kill Scarvan but understand your odd Western ideas about due process. If you capture him instead, he must never learn that we provided any assistance."

"So, if he gets away, he doesn't come looking for you," Mara said. "That's fine."

"Secondly, my employer wants any mention of assistance left out of any report filed, confidential or otherwise. The press and media obviously cannot know."

"Okay," Mara said. "What's his plan?"

"Third assurance," Asset said. "You can share the information I give you, but you can't reveal your source. Not to anyone." He pointed first to Rick. "Not Mitch Dreslan." Then he turned to Mara. "Not Jim Hawthorn. Not your father. No one."

"This is ridiculous," Rick said. "You want our help in stopping him? Then just tell us."

"I could stop Scarvan if I wanted," Asset said. "He's an old man. Wouldn't be hard. But my employer wants zero culpability."

"Sounds to me like your employer thinks you'll miss and then Scarvan will come after him," Mara said. "How does that make you feel?"

The dark cloud reappeared, and Mara thought she might have pushed the man too far. It was all good intel, though. Knowing Asset's ego could get the best of him so easily might come in useful at some point.

"Do I have your assurances?" Asset asked.

"What's the recourse?" Rick asked. "Suppose we violate one of these assurances?"

"Then my employer has tasked me with killing your president as a penalty," Asset said. "I will take my time. It could be weeks. Perhaps months. But with my skill, I will accomplish my task. I think you know this is not a boast."

She put her hand on Rick's shoulder, anticipating he would lash out at the comment. But he didn't. Perhaps he sensed the same authority and certainty in Asset's voice as she did. When she looked down, they made eye contact. He shook his head and mouthed the word *no*.

Mara turned to Asset. "I accept the conditions. Now talk."

Asset indicated to Rick. "I need to hear it from him, too."

Rick hesitated, but with a look from Mara, he nodded.

"It's a bomb," Asset said. "Already inside."

Mara felt the world tip sideways as she heard the words. "How strong is it?"

"Powerful. But it's also dirty," Asset said. "Using polonium."

"A dirty bomb going off in the middle of New York City?" Rick said. "Jesus."

Asset nodded. "The blast will be powerful enough to kill everyone in the General Assembly. Any who survive by some miracle will likely die later from radiation poisoning. I think you've recently seen what that looks like."

Mara caught the implication that Asset had watched her and her father in Seville. All without their knowing. She wondered whether Scarvan had been there as well.

Rick spoke first. "The UN is filled with radioactive sniffers. They would have turned up a bomb on site."

"Not if it was stored properly," Mara said. "A heavy lead box would block all the gamma radiation. That's what the detection systems are all keyed on. Where is the bomb stored? How does Scarvan plan to detonate?"

Asset strolled to the window. Outside was a perfect view of the National Mall, the Washington Monument framed as if on a tourist's postcard. He was clearly enjoying having his audience's full attention.

"When I was growing up, I was trained to despise America by men who had good reason to hate her. Still, even those men spoke of George Washington with respect. Not a great general, but a leader who held his army together through sheer will. Americans think it was because of his charisma, and I'm sure it was part of that. But he also shot deserters and used the lash to secure order. This is the lesson America has forgotten. Principles require the use of power to enforce them. Otherwise . . . chaos."

"How about we debate American history over coffee some other time?" Mara said. "The bomb. Where is it hidden?"

Asset continued to stare out the window. "I don't know for certain. I know what it was transported in, but where it is now is unknown."

"Lot of help you are, then," Rick said. "Don't you think we were already going to tear the building apart to secure it?"

"I doubt you'll find it," Asset said. "It will be made to look like a container. A suitcase. A planter. Part of a desk. Who knows?"

Mara tried to suppress her rising impatience. "Can we cut the dance and get to what you really have to help us?"

Asset turned from the window, a look of professional appreciation on his face. "The detonator is wireless, set to a cell phone but with a specific long-wave radio frequency as a backup in case cell reception is blocked in the room. Designed to circumvent your jamming devices." He pulled out a piece of paper and placed it on the bed. "This is the frequency. If you block that frequency, you block the ability to detonate the device."

"We want Scarvan," Rick said. "Otherwise he's still the same threat."

Asset pulled a set of handcuffs from his back pocket and tossed them to Mara. "Wrist to wrist will be fine. The key is on the bed here. I just need a small head start when we part ways."

Mara knew there was no negotiation here. Both she and Rick were getting out of this alive, which was more than she could have ever hoped for when Asset had first opened the door. She handcuffed herself to one of Rick's wrists tied behind the chair. She considered faking the connection, but she knew Asset was too good for that, so she did it correctly.

"You didn't answer about Scarvan," Mara said. "Sounds like your employers want him out of the field. Help us get him."

"I'll know more the day of the event." Asset tossed a phone on the bed. "I'll reach you on this. Most importantly, don't let them cancel the event. If they do, Scarvan may not ask for my employer's help next time and we won't be able to assist you."

He walked over to have Mara show him that the cuffs were properly engaged. Satisfied, he walked to the door. Before he reached the hallway, he said, "We still have unfinished business, you and I. This doesn't change that."

"Look forward to seeing you again," Mara replied. "Train up a bit so it's more fun."

Asset's expression didn't darken this time. Instead, he smiled. And if Mara didn't know better, she would have thought he actually found the comment funny. He let her have the last word and left the room.

Rick leaned back. "I'm so sorry I put you in this position. He was already in the room when I got here. I don't know—"

She shut him up by kissing him hard on the mouth. After, she used her free hand to untie the rope around his legs tying him to the chair.

"How about we hobble over to the bed together and get that key. I don't mind the handcuffs, but this isn't how I'd use them."

"Agreed," Rick said, awkwardly standing with the chair still attached to himself once the rope loosened. "Then we need to discuss how we proceed from here. Who we tell about this? Who we don't?"

Mara tugged on the cuffs, causing Rick to lose his balance and thump back down to the floor, hitting the chair hard with his ass.

"We can't tell anyone," she said. "This guy is the real thing. That was no idle threat."

"What do you think I do for a living?" Rick said. "Guard the president against pie-throwing environmentalists? We have threats like this guy every day."

"Not like this guy," Mara said. "Besides, we can act on the information without revealing the source."

"You think Dreslan will accept that?"

"We'll say the intel came from Alpha Team. Blame me for not giving up the source. We never mention this interaction. Even if asked directly about it." Mara leaned in. "But we need you to push Dreslan. He's dragging his feet on this, and I'm not sure why."

Rick nodded. "All right. We'll do it your way."

Mara saw there was more he wanted to say but was holding back. She was tempted to just ignore it and move on, but that was her weakness in relationships. And she wanted this one to work out. More than anything.

"What is it?" she asked. "What's wrong?"

He looked away, deciding whether to engage. Finally, he said, "Lies. They come to you a little too easily sometimes. That worries me. With us, I mean."

Mara was taken aback. Emotionally, the implication hurt. The timing for a comment like that was pretty shitty, too. Her instinct was to lash out, mount a defense, throw gas on the fire.

Instead, she took a deep breath and pushed that instinct away.

"I've never lied to you," Mara said, thinking mostly it was because he knew which questions not to ask. When he did wander into questionable territory, she preferred just not to respond at all. It was their shorthand for *I can't tell you that.*

"Then we don't lie through all of this," he said. "We don't tell the others, but you and me, we tell each other everything about this mission. All right?"

Her training immediately gave her the green light to agree. If that was what he needed her to say to feel better, then sure. A cost-free statement.

But she hesitated. This was different. She actually intended to keep this promise.

"The thing is," she said softly, "sometimes the truth can get you killed."

"We take that risk," he said. "This is too important."

She assumed he meant the mission, but he could have easily meant what they had together. She didn't ask for clarification.

"No lies," she said.

They kissed. And as they did, she couldn't help but wonder which of them would be the first to break the vow they'd just made.

CHAPTER 47

"That was Mara," Scott said, hanging up the phone. "She and Rick will meet us there."

Hawthorn and Anna nodded at the news. They were all in a black SUV being driven to Secret Service Headquarters at 950 H Street, just blocks away from the more famous address of 1600 Pennsylvania Avenue, home to the agency's most famous protectee.

While presidential protection was almost entirely how the public saw the Secret Service, it was actually a small part of its mission. In fact, the agency was first formed to combat widespread currency counterfeiting in the second half of the nineteenth century. It was why the agency had been under the jurisdiction of the U.S. Treasury Department until the reorganization of the entire intelligence community in 2003. After that, it was brought under the umbrella of the newly formed Department of Homeland Security.

With 136 field offices and offices around the world, the Secret Service's mandate was broken into two missions: investigation and protection. The investigation mandate was rarely seen or acknowledged by the public. Responsibilities extended into financial crimes, electronic investigations, and intellectual property crimes. But the Secret Service was also a valued partner in the Joint Terrorism Task Force (JTTF) and assisted with the National Center for Missing & Exploited Children (NCMEC).

But nothing captured the public's imagination like the Secret Service agent standing watch over an American president.

Even the protection mission is more complicated than the public appreciates. Protectees include the president and immediate family, the vice president, past presidents, and foreign dignitaries on American soil. They are responsible for the physical security of the White House and Treasury and all foreign diplomatic missions. They review and investigate all credible threats and take the lead on National Special Security Events (NSSEs), which in the current situation gave them jurisdiction and responsibility for the events in New York.

While a failure in the investigation mission was a hard pill to swallow, failures in the protection arena were the nightmare scenario for any agent.

Dealey Plaza still haunted the organization. Reagan's near miss did, too, but at least it'd been years before the public understood just how close Hinckley had come to killing the man.

So, while Dreslan was the director of an agency spanning the globe with over 7,000 employees engaged in hundreds of types of missions, threats against the president always came first.

The Secret Service headquarters never made the tour for out-of-town guests to DC. From the street, it looked like any other office building in town. Fronted by a five-story building with the original brick look, the building rose to ten stories to fill the rest of the block. An old three-story building of row houses was attached to the left side of the building, but each window was covered by thick wood like it was an abandoned building. In reality, the windows were sealed to better protect the men and women inside from prying eyes. And because nothing said government job better than a windowless room.

Scott, Hawthorn, and Anna passed the checkpoint to park in the underground garage beneath the building. If the Secret Service had their way, it was how every dignitary would arrive at every location. A controlled setting. No sightlines for a shooter. Perfect.

While politicians liked not being killed, they liked being in power even more. That meant being elected, so that meant appearing in public. That battle between the mission to keep those they protected alive while constantly getting pushback on the needs of those same people to work rope lines, attend public events and make outdoor speeches was what drove every Secret Service protection detail crazy. The stress was also why the Secret Service had one of the highest rates of alcoholism and divorce in the intelligence services.

As they parked the car, Scott saw Mara's vehicle at the security check-in behind them. They waited and joined up together. As she and Rick walked up, he'd expected her to have at least some glow of satisfaction about her. Or maybe Rick might have the smallest bit of self-consciousness. He was Mara's father, after all, and it didn't take a brain surgeon to guess how the two of them had spent their hour break from this madness together.

But there was none of that. They both looked focused and intense. On the job. He wondered whether that was just a mark of their professionalism, or a sign that there was trouble in paradise. Maybe the last hour hadn't been as fun as they'd expected.

"We have new information," Mara said as they walked up. "It's a dirty bomb. Already in the UN but Scarvan needs to get in to assemble it."

Scott blinked hard. "How do you know this?"

Rick stepped forward. "There's a cell phone trigger, but an RF backup if that fails."

The elevator behind them opened and a young agent who could have appeared in the recruiting manual for the Secret Service stepped out. "Director Dreslan is waiting for you," he said.

Hawthorn whispered to Mara. "How certain?"

Mara glanced at Rick. "Single source," she said. "Someone in position to have the information. Could be misinformation, but my gut tells me it isn't."

"Who's the source?" Scott asked.

Mara shook her head. "Can't say."

Scott froze in place, not quite believing the answer. Anna,

standing next to them, picked up on the sudden tension. "I'm going to let the four of you discuss this," she said. "I'll occupy our very handsome, young Secret Service minder." She walked toward the elevator, giving them space.

Scott waited until she was out of earshot. He didn't hold Mara's secretiveness against her. It was good procedure. But he wasn't prepared for the stonewall look on her face even with Anna gone. He knew that look well enough. Hell, he'd been on the receiving end of it off and on since Mara had become a teenager.

"In the last hour, a source approached the two of you with this information?" Hawthorn asked. "But it was delivered on the condition that the source not be revealed."

Mara nodded.

Scott pointed to himself and Hawthorn. "This is us. I understand not telling Anna because you don't know her, but . . ."

"I'm sorry," Mara said. "Not this time. Trust me on this."

Scott felt the word *trust* cut into him. He wondered whether this was all a show for Rick. Proof that she wouldn't reveal the source to her inner circle so he wouldn't, either. That had to be it. Why else would she keep it from him?

Hawthorn may have reached the same conclusion, because he didn't pursue it. "Okay, we take this to Dreslan as high-confidence. We don't rule out other scenarios. The good news is that if Scarvan still needs to assemble the bomb, we have a chance to intercept him."

"Let me go over this with Dreslan," Rick said. "No offense, but he doesn't much care for you."

Scott couldn't suppress a grin. Hawthorn didn't flinch. He hadn't survived as long as he had in the jungles of DC without ruffling feathers. Scott just appreciated the young agent's frankness. Maybe he was a good fit for his daughter.

"Agreed," was all Hawthorn said.

"We look for the bomb inside," Rick said. "The building was going to be swept as a matter of protocol anyway. Now we can adjust search methods to a specific radiological signature."

"But here's the hard part," Mara said. "If we find it, we leave it."

Scott got it immediately. "Bait for the trap."

Hawthorn agreed. "We get Dreslan to go harder on the physical search on all entries into the building," Scott said. "Jordi just demonstrated how the facial recognition systems are basically useless. We're going to need more manpower."

"We'll get it," Rick said. "In a budget pinch, the Counterfeit guys get screwed. There's always money to protect the president."

"In case both of those fail, we need to ensure our jamming tech is ready to stop the detonation signal," Mara said.

"The Secret Service SOP is to shut area cell towers and jam RF channels whenever there is a credible threat," Rick said.

"That's what worries me. That protocol is in every TV show and thriller novel. Omega has been ahead of us when it comes to tech. Jordi's RF blockers need to be on-site as well. We need to be on-site to see if there's something we can do better here."

"What about this meeting?" Scott asked, nodding down the hallway where Anna was keeping the young Secret Service agent on a holding pattern while they spoke.

Hawthorn was decisive. "Rick and I will meet with Dreslan, the rest of you can get to work." He glanced at Rick. "Don't worry, I'll let you do all the talking. Use Mara as the obstacle to revealing the source. Leave yourself out of it. Are we good?"

They all nodded. Scott called out to Anna. As she walked back to them, he noticed a quick exchange between Mara and Rick. It was discreet, a brush of the hands and a glance, but it was enough. He knew that look. A terrible combination of trust and doubt. They had a secret between them. The question was whether they were going to keep it.

CHAPTER 48

Asset watched the car leave the underground garage. He was surprised to see them leave so quickly. The SUV had tinted windows that prevented him from seeing inside, but the plates told him it was Mara and Rick's vehicle. That meant the old man, Hawthorn, was likely meeting with Dreslan now. He wondered whether they'd already violated their vow to keep the source of their information a secret.

He'd find out soon enough.

He dialed the encrypted satellite phone.

Marcus Ryker picked up on the first ring.

"Is it done?" Ryker asked.

Asset appreciated that the man always got to the point.

"Yes."

"And you warned them about the consequences of revealing who gave them the information?"

"I did," Asset said. "Not sure what difference it will make. Scarvan will figure it out once he gets wind of the Secret Service searching for radiological signatures."

There was a long pause on the line. Asset wondered whether he'd crossed a line. He was paid to execute directives, not challenge his employer's strategy.

"Perhaps," Ryker said. "Scarvan used polonium with Belchik. It's a reasonable precaution to take." Another pause. Asset didn't know whether the man was thinking or just multitasking. "Or perhaps it doesn't really matter whether they share the source or not."

Asset shook his head. He should have seen it from the start. He'd been a pawn in a larger game and hadn't realized it. "That was just a play to drive a wedge in the group."

"Who do I trust? Who don't I trust?" Ryker said. "It occupies a considerable amount of my energy these days. Why not have them wrestle with it, too?"

"And the president?"

"What about him?"

"If they break the promise, you want me to follow through on the threat?" Asset asked.

Ryker's voice took on a detached tone. Slower. An octave lower than before.

"Civilization is in a deep dive. My objective is a controlled emergency landing. The slightest miscalculation and it'll crash into the side of a mountain. If that happens, then instead of the right people dying, we all will."

Asset waited for clarification. When nothing came, he weighed whether to ask more directly for instructions. Ryker had already made his intentions clear when he'd told him the threat to deliver. He'd treat it as a standing order until otherwise instructed.

"I'll go to New York as support," Asset said. "Is there anything else you want done here in DC?"

"No, go to New York," Ryker said, his usual clipped tone suddenly back. "Ensure our plan is executed. I want updates along the way."

The line went dead. Ryker wasn't much on goodbyes.

Asset imagined Omega had eyes on the ground watching his every move. He doubted Ryker had any lack of intel. Then again, Asset was in a silo on his own. Thanks to Scarvan, he possessed information no one could access.

The night Scarvan had showed up in his hotel room in Seville still had him rattled. Every precaution he'd taken to hide his location and secure the room had been thwarted. Returning from watching Scott and Mara case Belchik's villa, he'd intended to grab a quick shower and two hours of rest.

Instead, there'd been a shadow standing in the corner of his hotel room, gun in hand. The man seemed to absorb light. Draw in the oxygen from the room that made the atmosphere thick and stifling. Once, as a teen, without a weapon, Asset had been stalked by a wolf in the Bosnian forest. He'd never forgotten the naked vulnerability he'd felt in the presence of a pure predator with superior innate skills. Jacobslav Scarvan's presence had exactly the same effect.

Asset's limbic brain had screamed at the danger in front of him. His training allowed him to avoid the mistake of pulling his weapon. He knew if he had, it would have been the last thing he did.

Lucky for him, the man had come to talk.

And Scarvan hadn't wasted words. He'd laid out his plan and his demands of Omega. Asset had been amazed by what Scarvan knew of the organization. There were some details he had wrong, indicating the man had pieced together incomplete information to draw conclusions. But he knew enough to be dangerous to Omega in general. And to Marcus Ryker in particular.

But Scarvan didn't care about Omega. Not really. He only wanted the means to achieve his end.

The interaction lasted only a few minutes. A litany of demands followed by a test of whether Asset had committed everything to memory. He'd passed and earned a begrudging grunt of approval from the much older man. And then he'd walked out of the room.

Asset remembered feeling as if he could suddenly breathe again. Out of character for him, he'd laughed. An unusual outlet of nervous energy.

Inside, he seethed at the reaction. Disappointed he'd been unable to control his emotional response. Certain Scarvan had been able to see his discomfort. His fear.

As Asset packed his gear for the trek to New York, he wondered whether he'd have a second chance to prove himself. Perhaps he would suggest to Ryker that Scarvan knew too much. The idea of hunting the man excited him, just the way hunting Scott Roberts did.

He hoped in the next two days to have the opportunity to do both.

CHAPTER 49

Mara watched the video footage of Air Force One taking off from Andrews Air Force Base on its way to LaGuardia. The UN address was only hours away.

She rubbed her eyes and downed the last of her coffee. The last two days in New York had been filled with many things, but sleep wasn't one of them.

Scott stepped up next to her, cradling his own cup of coffee like it was a precious artifact. "You okay?" he asked.

"Yeah, just great," she answered. "You?"

He took a drink of his coffee. "Love New York. Great city. Nice restaurants. Terrific shows."

She laughed. The United Nations security center where they stood had been their home for the last two days. The regular UN protection team had resisted their operation being taken over, but a personal call from the president to the UN secretary general had worked things out. Not long after, the building had literally crawled with every manner of law enforcement and intelligence personnel to engage in the search for Scarvan's bomb. K-9 teams were flown in from around the country. The most sophisticated equipment to sniff out radioactivity arrived from military research labs; every inch of red tape was cut by executive order.

Since hitting the ground, neither of them had left the UN building. Rick had been back and forth between the UN and the New York Public Library where the General Assembly reception would be held later that night. As long as they stopped Scarvan from blowing the largest collection of world leaders into smithereens, that is.

Based on their complete lack of results over the last forty-eight hours, she had a growing sense of dread that their efforts were going to prove fruitless.

"Hawthorn is on the flight up," Scott said. "He's going to pitch Patterson again on cancelling the UN address."

"Brave man," she said. The president hadn't been shy sharing his feelings about their inability to find any trace of either Scarvan or the bomb supposedly already hidden within the UN building. Hawthorn's stonewalling about Alpha Team's source of this information hadn't helped, either. He and Dreslan were barely on speaking terms. The president's frustration was no secret.

Rick walked into the room, surveying the busy staff until his eyes landed on her. Even given the circumstances, she felt a surge of comfort seeing him. Even in the world of shit they were in, he was a reminder there was still good to be had in the world.

As if to provide a balance to that feeling, Dreslan walked in behind him.

"Here comes some bullshit," Scott whispered. "Guaranteed."

Rick walked toward them, stopping to ask a question here and there from agents along the way. Dreslan looked impatient.

"Good morning," Rick said when he reached them. "Can we grab some time in the boardroom?"

"Sure, Rick," Scott said, "we've got nothing else going on."

"Looks to me like you're watching TV and having your morning coffee," Dreslan said. "I think you can spare a few minutes."

Mara nudged her dad, glaring at him to behave. The four of

them went into the conference room in the back corner of the command center. No one sat down.

"Who was your source about the bomb?" Dreslan asked.

"What, no foreplay?" Scott said.

Dreslan looked as worn out as Mara felt. Hell, she probably looked just as bad, too. They were all on edge, all too aware that they could be on the cusp of one of the greatest intelligence failures of the century. If they had advance warning and Scarvan still managed to pull off his attack, their names would be in the history books. At least Dreslan's would.

"I'm not fucking around here, Roberts." He pointed an angry finger at both her and Scott. "Both of you. Your holier-than-thou, cowboy bullshit routine is getting old. You have information that could assist this investigation and you're withholding it. If this thing happens, you're going down. Both of you."

Rick's eyes were focused on the floor. They'd decided over the last two days to let Dreslan believe that only Alpha Team knew the source. It gave Rick cover to do his job. But the pressure had been constant and intense. Each time, Mara saw the anguish on his face as she took the beating meant for both of them.

"Knowing the source wouldn't change our response," Mara said. "It would just blow out an important source of information for later use."

"Or give my people a chance to review the information this source provided. Dissect it to determine if there was something the two of you missed." Dreslan sneered. "That's assuming there even was a source."

"What's that supposed to mean?" Scott said.

"I know about you two. And Hawthorn. Chasing after Omega, this ghost organization you've convinced the president is such a threat." He snorted, the noise reserved for people who believe in UFOs and Bigfoot. "A year of chasing shadows. Not a damn thing to show for it."

"Sir, why don't we—" Rick tried to inject, but Dreslan was on a roll.

"Then this Scarvan reappears on the scene. Your team hasn't proven to be of any value to the president recently. You know what they say, never look a gift horse in the mouth."

"Why don't you just spit out what you're trying to say," Mara said. "Stop dancing around it."

Dreslan glared at her. "I think there is no source. That you made the whole damn thing up to reassert yourself into the chain of command. Or worse, maybe there's some other reason you don't want the president to be at the UN for his address."

"Careful, Dreslan," Scott growled.

"Maybe there's some other nation who wants him to stay away so the U.S. loses face," Dreslan said. "Maybe that nation found someone willing to assist them."

"What you're describing is an act of treason," Mara said.

Dreslan shrugged. "If it fits."

For a few seconds, no one moved. It was as if time had frozen.

Then all hell broke loose.

Scott pushed the chair next to him out of his way and clambered around the conference room table toward Dreslan. Rick stepped in front of his boss, his large bulk and years of protective detail training taking over.

"You son of a bitch," Scott said.

"Dad, stop," Mara said.

"I'm not the one holding secrets here, assholes," Dreslan said. "I'm the one doing my job."

Scott pushed against Rick but met a brick wall.

"Back down!" Rick yelled at Scott. "Right now!"

But Dreslan, maybe feeling protected, wasn't done. He pointed to the door to the conference room. "There are uniformed Secret Service outside this room. You two will go with them into custody."

"This is insane," Mara said. "On what charge?"

"Obstruction of justice. Impeding a federal investigation. Being assholes," Dreslan said. "Take your pick."

"The president will never allow this," Mara said.

"The president signed off on this," Dreslan said. "He's as tired of this game as I am."

Rick shook his head. Slowly, he turned so he faced Dreslan.

"Rick, no," Mara said.

"You'll have to arrest me, too," Rick said. "I know the source. I was there when he made contact."

Dreslan turned a new shade of red. Thick veins stood out from the man's neck. Mara considered the real possibility the man could have a coronary right in front of them. She gave Rick a look that she hoped showed her disappointment in his decision to come clean. It was hard to pull off because she secretly loved that fact he'd stood up to his boss, even if it was tactically wrong-footed.

"What in the hell are you talking about?" Dreslan said.

"I was in the room when the source made contact with Agent Roberts. I witnessed the entire interaction and can say the information she reported from the exchange was full and accurate."

Dreslan looked from one of them to the other, his anger contorting his body. "I can't believe this. You're right, I should lock all three of you up."

"Mara and I are the only ones who know the source's identity. Scott and Hawthorn have no idea. Our silence was a condition of us receiving the information."

"A single, uncorroborated source?" Dreslan raged. "Are you all out of your minds?"

Mara spoke in soft tones, trying to deescalate the tension. "Let's say for a second we were played by this source. That it was misinformation. Every precaution you've taken here at the UN building were things you already would have done. The only difference is that you received unlimited budget to execute your mission. Where's the harm?"

Dreslan fell quiet. He took several deep breaths, regaining his composure. When he spoke, his professional demeanor had returned. "The harm is that if a bomb goes off in the General Assembly, killing every person in the room including the president of the United States, we're all going to spend the rest of our lives wondering what we could have done differently to stop it. I'll have doubt. You two," he said, pointing to Rick and Mara, "will have certainty that you made a bad decision."

A loud knock on the door, then it opened.

It was Anna.

She read the room easily enough but didn't seem thrown by the tension.

"We found the bomb," she said. "And I'm not sure what's more incredible, where it was or who found it."

CHAPTER 50

Mara gave Jordi Pines a huge hug. He smelled like pizza and Axe body spray, but she didn't care.

"Easy, Mara," he said. "You'll wrinkle my shirt."

She clapped him on the shoulder. It was hard to find a section of his shirt that wasn't covered with wrinkles. He was as smart as they came, but you'd never guess it by looking at him. In fact, Dreslan had balked when they'd insisted Jordi come up and aid the search. The FBI presence on the task force really didn't want him. He'd once worked for them and there was widespread fear in the leadership that he'd left with more than just his ergonomic chair and keyboard. Jordi had hinted that he might have slipped a few insurance cards out of the FBI's deck. Just in case.

"Tell us," Scott said, speaking for everyone in the room.

Jordi looked to Anna, who pursed her mouth shut and motioned him forward. She wasn't going to do any of the talking for him.

"It was nothing, really," Jordi said. "Just tried to think like a diabolical nut cruncher myself. How would I do it? How would I get a bomb in the building without anyone knowing?"

Dreslan shifted his weight, impatient. But the headline that they'd found the bomb had him holding his tongue.

"We knew from Mara's source that it was in pieces, requiring Scarvan or some minion of his to assemble on-site. The fact that it had polonium was another piece of the puzzle. Which is why we have all these sniffers here. Easy to fool if the nuclear material is encased in lead. Wouldn't even need to remove it from the lead casing at all prior to the explosion, assuming whatever compartment it was in would get shattered."

"Let's get to it," Scott said. "The short version."

Jordi looked annoyed. There were few things he liked more than describing his brilliance to an audience.

"The piece no one else was looking for was the detonator," Jordi said. "There was a chance Scarvan was going to bring it in with him when he assembled today, but I didn't think so. It's gonna be hard enough for him to sneak in already." Jordi cast a nervous glance over at Dreslan and Rick. "But we all think he's going to find a way to pull it off. Still, why add carrying a detonator on your person when trying to do the impossible? No, I decided the denotator had to be in the building already."

"You found an unbuilt bomb by tracking a detonator that wasn't activated yet?" Rick asked.

Jordi beamed. "When you say it that way, sounds bloody brilliant, doesn't it?"

"Jordi," Mara said, growing impatient herself. She thought Dreslan might come across the table any second and choke the rest of the information out of her friend if he didn't get on with it.

"Another point of info from Mara's source. A cell phone trigger. Pretty typical among assholes trying to blow shit up. It's in all the movies. Simple. Effective. Elegant, even. But we have the technology to block cell phone reception in any given area. Once he knew Scott and Mara were on his trail, he had to think they would figure out what his plan might be and take the precaution to shut down cell phone use in the UN building. If they could convince the twats in charge of the thing to do it, that is."

"We better be getting to the goddamn point here," Dreslan said.

"Jordi, please," Mara said.

Jordi nodded. Even he had the emotional intelligence to see Dreslan was on the razor's edge. "Mara's source said long-wave radio-frequency trigger. But, if it's me, I want a two-way exchange. I want the ability to perform a system check. So, I did two things. One, created portable RF blockers." He pulled out a small metal disc from his pocket. "RF for radio frequency for the slowpokes in the room. A ten-time improvement over the jammers typically used, covering a much broader spectrum, especially ultra–long wave, which typically isn't even a consideration. Has to be within seventy-five feet of the bomb to work, so you need a lot of them. But I figured we could use them to create a shield inside the General Assembly room. We turn off cell phone and block all RF, no detonation."

"But you said you found the bomb," Rick said. "Did you, or did you just figure out a way to block the detonation?"

Jordi sniffed. "You say that like it's no big deal. But you're right. I said I did two things. And this is where I really outdid myself," Jordi said. "I wired into all the nuke sniffers you lot have in the building. They update through long-wave radio frequency. So, I piggybacked on their sys-admin protocols to measure their RF inputs, then created an algorithm to search for unexpected spikes or aberrant broadcasts. Found quite a few, so had to refine the search routine a few times, then work out a triangulation—"

"It was located in the offices of the Greek mission to the UN," Anna said. "Seems like Father Spiros's influence spread farther than Mount Athos."

Jordi slumped his shoulders. "Yeah, we found the bomb in the Greeks' office," he mumbled. "Thanks, Anna."

Anna rubbed his shoulder. "Sorry, dear. But you were carrying on."

Mara took in the new information. In retrospect, it seemed an obvious choice. Then again, Scarvan's career had created contacts throughout the world. Especially in the roughest corners of the globe. All of whom held offices at the United Nations. But the Greek delegation would have members committed to the Church. Perhaps Father Spiros had plotted for years to get his acolytes into positions of authority for just such a moment. But it would have taken someone like Scarvan to not only source and provision a bomb like this, but to execute the final infiltration into the General Assembly.

Dreslan pulled his phone from his jacket.

"Who are you calling?" Scott asked.

"Coordinating the FBI bomb squad and the evacuation of the building until we secure the bomb," Dreslan said.

"Wait," Scott said. He turned to Jordi and Anna. "Who else knows we found it?"

"The offices were empty for the security sweep," Anna said. "So just the two FBI bomb squad guys that went with us. They confirm it's in two sections, so it has basic assembly still required. I told them not to report it up the chain of command until Dreslan gave them authority to do so."

"Did they listen to you?" Mara asked, not sure how well the FBI was going to listen to a Czech operative on loan to Alpha Team.

"I took their radios," she said. "And sat their asses outside this door."

Mara made eye contact with Rick. She wanted him to be the one to suggest it.

"Sir," he said, turning to Dreslan. "We have the bait. Let's use it to catch a fish."

CHAPTER 51

Jacobslav Scarvan completed his prayers close to three a.m. He felt the true presence of God flowing through him, pure rage and vengeance for the insults suffered at the hands of His own creation. The world had ignored the rules as had been clearly laid out.

From the beginning, obedience had been the only requirement.

And humanity had failed on every level imaginable.

Scarvan's thoughts turned to the story of the man tasked with guarding the Ark of the Covenant back in the time of Moses leading the Jews to the promised land. After days of marching in procession, the ark holding the sacred Ten Commandments began to slide from the litter on which it was being carried. This man, seeing the ark about to fall, ran to it, hefting his shoulder against it to prop it up. The second he touched the ark, God struck him down. It wasn't that the ark held any particular inherent power; instead it was God meting out His justice into the world. Man had been told not to touch the ark, told that God did not need their protection. The man's action had been an insult, one that God would not suffer.

He and Father Spiros had debated this story many times. If it were true that God's point was that He needed no assistance from mere mortals, then why had so many wars been fought for

His glory? Why were they being called to drive His plan forward? If God wanted to strike down the world, why not simply send another great flood? Or burn humanity to the ground as He had done to the Sodomites?

Father Spiros had told him to search his heart for the answer. To ask of himself whether he felt the calling to be a vessel for God's work. To wonder at the honor of being an instrument of a divine plan.

In the end, the visions were clear. God willed his actions. That had pleased Father Spiros.

What hadn't pleased him was God's directive to care for Father Spiros until his death. Then and only then was he to return to the world.

He wondered whether a similar vision had driven his friend and mentor to end his life in order to pave the way for Scarvan to complete his task.

He'd found the old man's robe and shoes on the cliff's edge. A search in the raging waters below had not turned up the body. A strong rip current meant the old man's body could have ended up a mile off the shore, eaten by sharks, never to be found.

The loss had been hard to take. Not only to lose his spiritual guide, but the evidence showed that Father Spiros had done the unthinkable. Suicide. An abomination in God's eyes. Eternal condemnation.

This ultimate sacrifice riddled Scarvan with guilt. Had he misinterpreted God's commandment that he not embark on his mission of vengeance until Father Spiros had gone to the Lord's embrace? The General Assembly gathering was too perfect an opportunity to let pass, Father Spiros had argued. In his own way, the old man had cleared the one obstacle blocking Scarvan. But at such a cost.

He prayed each day for his mentor's soul, even though he knew for certain that Father Spiros would burn in hell for what he'd done.

Perhaps Scarvan completing his mission would earn him

enough of God's favor to earn a special dispensation for his friend.

The knock on the door startled him even though it was expected.

He viewed the hallway through the peephole, then opened the door.

Alexis Papadopoulos, cultural attaché to the Greek delegation to the United Nations, walked in, bowing his head reverently as he did.

Alexis was in his early sixties but had lived the first half of his life working the family olive tree farm. His face carried the wrinkles of a much older man. He was lean and almost exactly Scarvan's height.

The other thing they'd shared in their life was a devotion to Father Spiros.

That, matched with Scarvan's teaching of basic tradecraft, had made Alexis a vital way to get the bomb into the UN building. Even the man's last name, the most common in Greece, lent itself to the mission. Such a common name made background checks more difficult, turning up duplicates and false positives that complicated records.

Another example of God sending the perfect vessel at the perfect time.

Nearly perfect, that was. Early on, Father Spiros had recognized Alexis's potential value to them. On Father Spiros's instruction, he'd entered the bureaucracy and worked his way up the ladder in the foreign service. Father Spiros had directed the man's career for the last five years, using his political clout to get him the spot on the UN delegation.

Alexis dumped a small bag onto the table that served as a desk in the small hotel room.

"Here," he said. "I've brought you everything. ID cards. My briefcase. A detailed log of every conversation I've had over the last three days. Who it was with, what was discussed."

"You kept your interactions to the minimum?" Scarvan asked.

"Yes, I told them I was ill as you suggested," he said. "That I wanted to be in the meetings to not miss anything, but not really participate. I even pretended to forget things already said, blaming my cough medicine and lack of sleep."

"I hope you didn't overdo it," Scarvan said. "Don't want them telling you to stay home."

"I'm part of the bureaucracy, but I might as well be a political appointee. Everyone knows the Church favors me," he said. "Even the prime minister knows to leave me alone."

"Good," Scarvan said. "Remove your clothes."

Alexis hesitated. "I brought clothes for you. They are mine, but clean."

"I want the smell of them," Scarvan said, his voice making it clear that there was no discussion to be had.

Alexis pushed off his shoes and began to undress. "The bomb is positioned as you requested."

"And the security sweep?"

"They have been through several times. With machines. With dogs. With people. Nothing."

Scarvan shifted through the pile on the desk, placing everything into an orderly fashion. He tried to think of any other questions to ask the man, but he'd already done his homework. He waited until the man was standing in his underwear.

"I will remain here until it is done," Alexis said. "In God's name."

"In God's name," Scarvan agreed.

Then he raised his hand, pointed a suppressed Glock at the man's forehead, and pulled the trigger.

The back of Alexis's skull blew out. A spray of blood and brain coated the wall behind him.

In the upcoming mission, there could be zero loose ends. Having the man he was going to meticulously impersonate to gain entry into the UN Building potentially getting cold feet was an unacceptable risk. Besides, once the mission was complete, there was no use for Alexis Papadopoulos in the world.

Scarvan said a short prayer for the man's martyred soul.

Then he got to work. He had eight hours to become Alexis Papadopoulos. And then it was time to finally set that last part of his plan in motion.

As he prepared, he wondered whether Scott and Mara Roberts would play their parts as he planned. As much as they wanted to think they were unpredictable, he felt like he knew them.

It would be one of the great pleasures of his life to see them suffer.

CHAPTER 52

"Positive ID."

It was a tech manning one of the computer stations in the command center. Mara scanned the room and spotted the young woman with her hand raised in the air. It wasn't necessary. Every head in the room had pivoted to look directly at her.

Mara jogged over to her station along with Rick, Scott, and Anna.

"Scarvan?" Rick asked.

"Yes, sir."

"Where?" Scott asked.

The tech pointed to the screen. On it was a tangle of different colored lines. It took Mara a second to figure out what she was looking at. A subway system.

The bastard was taking the subway on his way to commit his atrocity.

Only something was wrong.

"That's not New York," Rick said, confused.

"No sir," the tech said. "It's BART. San Francisco."

Mara caught her dad's eye. This was an unexpected wrench in the works.

"Do you have video?" Mara asked.

The tech punched away on her keyboard. The public transit

areas in major U.S. cities were a surveillance professional's playground. Cameras everywhere. Face-recognition software. Air samplers. The works.

"Here," she said.

They all leaned in toward the screen. The video played through once, then rewound and played again on a loop. It showed a busy platform filled with commuters. The AI program running in the background showed each face it evaluated by a small green square appearing on each person, tracking movement until a lock was created.

In the center of the track, dressed in a long black trench coat, was a man staring at the platform camera. He bore some resemblance to Scarvan. Tall, lean, a wild shock of hair.

"Zoom in, please," Rick said.

The tech froze the frame and zoomed in. The resolution turned grainy, but the program compensated, and it slowly turned into a crisp photo.

It wasn't Scarvan. It was a man wearing glasses with thick black frames. Similar to what Jordi had shown them only two days before.

"I don't understand," the tech said. She pointed to the upper right-hand corner of her screen. It displayed a score of ninety-five percent match to Jacobslav Scarvan.

"Positive ID," called out another tech in the room. "I have Scarvan in the subway system in Rome."

"I have him in Tokyo," another called out.

Anna pointed to the screen and the desk next to them. "Positive ID. Antwerp."

"Jesus," Rick said. "So much for the lone-wolf theory. This guy's getting an assist all around the globe."

"New York!" a tech in the far corner of the room called out.

They all jogged to that desk. The video was already up. This one looked more like Scarvan, but it was hard to tell. He kept his face down and stayed in crowds as he moved to his train. It was the 7 train, heading to Grand Central Station. The nearest subway station to the UN building.

Rick put a hand on the tech's shoulder. "Contact NYPD liaison officer. Need a takedown in Grand Central. Seven train arriving in . . ."

"Six minutes," the tech said. "On it."

As the tech conveyed the information to the NYPD contact, Mara leaned in. "Misinformation campaign. He'll have us chasing our tails all day. This is Omega. Has to be."

Rick glanced around at the others. He took her by the arm and pulled her aside. "Why would they do that? Our source, this . . . this . . . Asset, he said Omega wanted to stop Scarvan."

"What if that was misdirection, too?" Mara said. "What if he was playing us the whole time?"

Scott stepped into their space. "Or Asset was telling the truth and Omega is running the plan so Scarvan isn't scared off."

Mara glared at her father. The pact to not tell anyone Asset was the source hadn't lasted with him. She'd told him the truth early on. The stakes were too high. Still, she hadn't planned on Rick finding out this way.

Rick stared openmouthed, first at Scott, then at Mara. Betrayal written all over his face. Mara hated seeing him look that way at her.

Scott saw the look, too. "There's no time for that," he said. "I've shared this intel with no one else. Not even Hawthorn. Bottom line, our best opportunity is to let this play out and intercept him when he tries to access the bomb."

Mara did her best to stay professional. The look on Rick's face was killing her. "Run down these Scarvan sightings," Mara said. "So Scarvan doesn't get spooked. Just don't use any of your resources here."

Rick pursed his lips. Mara had seen him angry before, but always at someone else. The anger she could live with, that would pass. It was the disappointment in his eyes that ate at her. She'd seen that look before from men in her life. Always at the end of relationships.

Anna walked up to them. "The takedown team is assembled. Is there a problem?"

"No, no problem," Rick said, never taking his eyes off Mara. "Things are perfectly clear now."

Scott stabbed a finger in the man's chest. "Son, you need to get your head in the game."

"And you need to get out of my face," Rick said.

The two men stood toe-to-toe, neither willing to budge. It was Anna who broke the tension.

"Should I get a ruler?" she asked. "We're measuring dicks, right?"

"Enough," Mara said. "We'll come back to this. The three of us will join the intercept team. There could be eyes anywhere in this room that report back to Scarvan, so be careful."

Rick gave the barest shake of his head, but he stepped away. Mara knew giving him advice right now on keeping a secret wasn't her best move. But this was business.

She just hoped he saw it the same way in the end.

"Come on, Mara. Let's go," Scott said.

Rick had already turned away and was marching back to the first terminal that had the positive ID on Scarvan.

As she, Scott, and Anna left the room, she took a look back over her shoulder. Rick was watching them leave, his eyes boring into her.

"He'll get over it," Anna said, surprising her. "And if he doesn't, then he's the wrong man. Just remember that."

As they left the room together, Mara pondered the wisdom of accepting relationship advice from a single, fifty-year-old woman whose idea of a good catch was her father.

Like the rest of her private life, she pushed it aside for the job at hand. Rick would have to wait. Right now, there was another man she had to worry about.

They assembled with the enhanced FBI Special Weapons and Tactics Team. These were hard men, disciplined and well trained on everything from hostage rescue and stronghold assaults to counterterrorism and high-risk arrests. Weapons ranged on display included both MP5s and Remington 870 shotguns.

There were ten of them.

Mara wondered whether that would be enough to face Scarvan.

CHAPTER 53

Scarvan barely recognized his own face as he passed the mirror in the hallway. He'd gained access into the Consulate General of the Hellenic Republic with ease, waved through by security who called him by his name, Alexis. Using a napkin to cover his mouth as he coughed, he avoided speaking as much as possible. He had a good sense of Alexis's voice, but conversation was the weakest link in his disguise.

A single question or reference to something only the real Alexis would know could give him away. The greatest part of his disguise was in the room ahead of him.

"Good morning, Alexis," Petro Angelides said as he walked into the reception room. There was a cluster of men in suits holding steaming cups of coffee. "I heard you aren't feeling well today."

"Good morning, Prime Minister," Scarvan said with a slight bow. "Just a cold is all." He coughed into his napkin for effect. "Wouldn't miss today, though."

"Everyone keep their distance from Alexis today," the prime minister said, laughing. "It wouldn't do to have the entire Greek delegation miss the gala tonight because we were all ill!"

The men around him laughed as men kissing up to power do, with deep, knowing chuckles recognizing their own sycophancy.

Scarvan waved a hand and gave his own chuckle in order to fit in with what was expected. Then he excused himself to the restroom, where he stayed until the delegation was ready to leave.

The car ride from the consulate on Seventy-ninth Street and Fifth Avenue down to the UN building on Forty-sixth Street and First Avenue was uneventful. Scarvan was in the prime minister's vehicle but mumbled something about not getting everyone sick and climbed into the front passenger seat. The prime minister's protective detail didn't like the arrangement, but a single word from the prime minister and Scarvan was given the seat.

Everything was going precisely as planned.

The security to enter the United Nations complex was more orderly than he expected. Keeping a line of vehicles with heads of state in them exposed in a slow-moving line wasn't optimal. Not all of them had the equivalent of the Beast, the armored vehicle used to transport the president of the United States. A machine capable of withstanding a direct hit from an RPG, let alone a sniper's bullet. Most countries had bulletproof versions of a Mercedes Benz sedan or some kind of hardened SUV. Security details knew the term *bulletproof* was only meant to make their protectees feel safe. It was more like bullet-resistant.

Instead, the security teams had been given specific times to arrive at the entrance, staggering when the heads of state would make their appearance. In the diplomatic world where status was always on display, the nations were given times to arrive by a nameless protocol officer. The UN prided itself on evenhandedness, so the arrivals were in alphabetical order to avoid the appearance of preferential treatment. Regardless, on this day, with increased security, the decision had been made for the Security Council members to arrive last, with President Patterson arriving just before his speech to the General Assembly.

Based on that criteria, Greece was scheduled to arrive in the middle of the list. Scarvan would have preferred to arrive even earlier, but he could make it work.

The first layer of security was only a flash of the driver's badge, a quick visual inspection inside the vehicle and the trunk, a 360 with the K-9 unit, and a cursory look under the hood and undercarriage with a mirror at the end of long pole. The team operated like a pit crew at a race, each with a job to do as quickly and efficiently as possible.

Once inside the complex, the cars with the principals in them were directed to the underground entrance. This ensured added security on exiting the vehicle. The other cars in the motorcade peeled off to a secondary parking area where the occupants who were to enter the building went through more extensive screening. The entourage attending the head of state was assumed to be well-known parts of the inner circle, which is why Alexis had served such an important role in the plan.

"This is unusual," the prime minister said in the backseat.

Scarvan leaned forward. As the car inched along, he saw what the prime minister was looking at.

There were lines at the second level of security that entered the building from the garage. Metal detectors complemented by men with additional wands. Cameras covered the area, certainly employing the most advanced facial recognition software available. Each person was having their hands swabbed for traces of any bomb-making material. Scarvan knew he would pass such a test, he'd made sure of it, but the security level so soon concerned him. He couldn't get caught here.

"Let me find out where you go," the head of the prime minister's security detail said, opening the door and climbing out.

"Like hell I'll stand in that line," the prime minister muttered.

Scarvan watched with interest as the head of security made his inquiries. The person he spoke with pointed to a much shorter line to the right. The head of security gesticulated wildly, pointing back to the car and then to the door. The man he spoke with shook his head. The message was clear: Everyone went through security.

When the car rolled to a stop, the security man was there to open the door.

"Sir, your entrance is this way," he said.

Scarvan exited the car, coughing violently.

"Alexis, come with me," the prime minister said. "You don't need to stand in this longer line."

Scarvan knew empathy wasn't Angelides's motivation. He, more than anyone, knew that Alexis Papadopoulos was the Church's man. And what politician didn't want the Church in their corner?

"Thank you," Scarvan said.

"Alexis is coming with me," the prime minister said to the others. "I'll see the rest of you inside."

The security man walked Scarvan and Angelides to the VIP line, introduced them to the UN protocol officer there, and then took his leave.

The protocol officer apologized for the inconvenience of the added security, adding that in the interest of fairness, all entrants had pass through security. The implication was clear. Some countries, even their leaders, were not to be trusted. Greece, the protocol officer's tone suggested, was not one of those countries, but the game had to be played.

Scarvan wanted to ask whether they would make the American president go through a metal detector, but kept his mouth shut. He already knew the answer.

Even with all of his precautions, he felt his heart rate elevate as he approached the entry-point. The facial recognition software likely wasn't a problem. The prosthetics and makeup would see to that. The prime minister was asked to pass through the metal detector, but the officer with hand swabs waved him past. Scarvan extended his hands and allowed them to be swabbed. He'd tested for residue in his apartment, but what if the unit here had a higher sensitivity? How long before the questioning turned first awkward and then aggressive?

"Thank you, sir. Enjoy the day," the officer said.

Scarvan nodded, coughing again into his napkin.

He followed Angelides into the building, both of them being led by the protocol officer assigned to them.

"Prime Minster, there is a reception of world leaders. I will take you there now," the protocol officer said. "The rest of your party will be informed of where to go and when to meet you next."

Alexis coughed again. "Sir, I must find a restroom. I will see you inside."

The prime minister stopped and turned, looking at him curiously. Scarvan froze, trying to think if he'd forgotten to modulate his voice properly. Angelides knew Alexis from meetings, but they didn't know each other socially. Scarvan had counted on him not knowing the man's mannerisms that well.

"Are you sure you should be here?" the prime minister said. "Your eyes. They look terrible."

Scarvan waved him away. "Go, please. I'll be fine."

Whether the prime minister was satisfied with the answer or simply reached the limits of his fake sympathy, he turned and followed the protocol officer to mingle with the other heads of state.

All of who would soon be dead.

CHAPTER 54

Scarvan found his way to a restroom. He relieved himself, washed his hands, preparing himself mentally for the next step.

Walking out of the restroom, he followed the mental map he'd committed to memory in his planning. The thirty-nine-story Secretariat Building was to the south, connected to the Conference Building that housed the General Assembly where he now stood. This was the first part of the plan where he anticipated something might go wrong. If the Secret Service had taken over site security as he expected, then they might have cordoned off the Secretariat Building entirely. Condensed the secured area to the smallest possible square footage.

But as he walked toward the connector, he saw traffic going both ways in the hallway. Uniformed police were checking IDs on the way toward the other building. A bank of metal detectors blocked return entry.

He'd anticipated that. Wouldn't be a problem.

He flashed his ID to the policeman, striding confidently past him. It didn't take long to cross into the Secretariat Building. There was actually a fair amount of activity here. The seventy-fifth anniversary had created a great deal of interest and many of those who wanted to participate but who lacked the credentials or connections to be on the other side of the complex were being entertained here. Large-screen TVs were set up so people could watch the upcoming speeches.

Scarvan waded through the crowd, knowing facial recognition software was analyzing him each step of the way.

He went into the restroom at the far end of the lobby. He counted the stalls and grimaced when he saw the one he needed was occupied.

He washed his hands, buying time. The man in the stall let out a grunt as he pushed. Scarvan felt the ridiculousness of the situation. The destruction of the world order in a flash of radioactive explosive was being held up by a man taking a shit.

Perhaps there was poetry in there somewhere.

Finally, the man rose, flushed not once but twice, and then exited. Scarvan didn't make eye contact. He continued to wash his hands, knowing it would raise suspicion if he entered the stall immediately, given there were several others open.

Once he heard the front door open and close, he walked into the stall, wrinkling his nose from the man's stench. He closed the stall door and got to work. One of the coins he carried in his pocket had an edge filed down. This edge worked perfectly as a screwdriver. The toilet paper holder was one with a metal box that held an extra roll above the one being used. Using the coin, Scarvan removed the four screws holding the entire box onto the stall wall. Once he removed it, the extra weight confirmed Omega's man had delivered as promised. Using the coin again, he removed the single screw on the back and opened the secret compartment above the second roll.

Scarvan removed a Glock 43 and an extra magazine. The small size was necessary to smuggle in, but the cost was only six rounds in the magazine and one in the chamber. A total of thirteen rounds. It was an insurance policy only. And it made a statement that he'd been able to circumvent security this far.

Scarvan secured the toilet paper holder back onto the stall wall, hid the gun in the small of his back, then straightened his tie and walked out.

Three uniformed police were waiting for him.

He froze, fighting back a surge of anxiety. Where had he made a mistake? How had they caught on to him so soon?

"All done in there, buddy?" the nearest cop asked.

Scarvan reassessed their posture and body language. These men weren't here to arrest him. They were waiting their turn for the stalls.

"Yes, sorry," Scarvan said, holding his stomach. "Ate at a street cart last night."

The three cops didn't bother to acknowledge the comment. As Scarvan washed his hands, he wondered if the three of them would later uncover how close they had come to stopping him. A story they could tell their grandkids.

It would be a vastly different world by then. But it would still have old men who told stories of their adventures. Perhaps around campfires instead of in lit rooms with air conditioning, but there would still be stories.

Scarvan left the bathroom, feeling more confident with the gun.

He walked with the flow of the crowd so as not to draw attention to the eyes invariably watching the area in whatever command center they'd set up.

The elevator bank was operational, allowing people to go up to their offices as needed on the big day. There were no more metal detectors—anyone someone would want to kill was in the General Assembly building—but he needed to swipe his ID card to access the elevator area.

Once here, he waited for an elevator he could ride alone. He passed on two that had occupants, pretending to be waiting for someone. On the third attempt, he was able to get an empty one. He swiped his card again and punched in the seventh floor. This was where the Hellenic Republic had a small office. Hidden in the wall safe of that office was the next step in the destiny God had revealed to him back on Mt. Athos.

The elevator reached the seventh floor and stopped.

But the elevator door didn't open.

He felt his heart rate accelerate. Perhaps they had shut down the office floors after all. That wasn't protocol, but he knew his threat had thrown protocol out the window.

Or maybe it was just that the elevator was stuck.

He pressed the OPEN DOOR button. Once. Twice. Then over and over.

Nothing.

He eyed the emergency button. That wasn't optimal. Pressing an alarm wasn't the best way to stay under the radar.

The floor indicator said 7.

He was so close.

Then he heard a noise.

Metal on metal.

Then a wrenching sound.

Mechanical parts being forced to move.

The door shuddered.

Then it split open, a half inch.

An inch.

He pulled his gun and took aim. *So soon?*

Perhaps his adversaries had been better than he'd given them credit for.

He shot at the one-inch opening, knowing it wouldn't do much good unless some idiot was dumb enough to stand right in front of it.

A small tube was fed into the crack and a second later, smoke billowed from it.

Not smoke, gas.

His impulse was to block the tube, yank it toward him to cinch it off.

But it was no use.

They had him trapped. Resistance was futile.

As he inhaled the gas, feeling it enter his bloodstream, his vision blurred.

A shock of pain in his knees was his only warning that he'd fallen to the floor.

He ended up with his back against the wall, chin to his chest, barely able to keep his eyes open.

The elevator door split open wider and bright lights lit up everything around him. Men in gas masks barked orders but he was beyond being able to answer them.

It was all he could do to stay conscious. He wanted to see them. He wanted to see everything.

Then he was there. Scott Roberts. Hovering in front of his face.

"Hello, Jacob," Scott said, his voice muffled behind his mask. "Sorry to ruin your big plans."

As Scarvan finally allowed his eyes to close and his mind to drift off, he consoled himself with Scripture.

To all things there is a purpose under heaven.

Even this.

Especially this.

CHAPTER 55

Hawthorn got off the phone, relishing the sense that the weight of the world had lifted from his shoulders.

There would be some other weight out there to replace it, there always was. Omega was still a threat. The men who'd helped Scarvan smuggle a bomb and gun into the United Nations were still at large. Whether they were Omega or not remained to be determined.

But for a few minutes, Hawthorn allowed himself to feel the win.

He looked across the large sitting area of the Lotte New York Palace suite, a five-thousand-square-foot space on three levels. The Lotte had replaced the traditional Waldorf Astoria favored by presidents for decades. Once the Waldorf had been purchased by a Chinese conglomerate in 2014, the change had been made for both optics and national security reasons.

Hawthorn had been in both locations with presidents and found the sleek, dark wood and the towering floor-to-ceiling windows an improvement over the Waldorf. And the large outdoor terrace with sweeping views of the city was incredible.

He realized that before he'd gotten the news that Scarvan had been captured, he hadn't even noticed the view. Now, suddenly, he found himself looking from window to window, soaking in the unique beauty of the sun reflecting off the New York sky-line.

Mitch Dreslan stepped in from the terrace, ending a phone call. He caught Hawthorn's eye. They had both received the news. Dreslan pumped his fist in the air. The action was a bit theatrical for Hawthorn's taste, but what the hell. He returned the gesture, even coupling it with a wide smile.

The two men strode across the room and met in the middle for a handshake.

"No injuries. Not a single shot fired," Dreslan said. "Bomb squad has secured the bomb segments."

"I heard," Hawthorn said. "A fine result. Your men are to be congratulated."

Dreslan sniffed. "Your team did well, too," he said, pulling his hand back. "But I'm still not happy how the whole thing panned out."

Hawthorn shifted his position so that he was side by side with Dreslan, their shoulders nearly touching. He leaned in, a conspirator telling a secret. "Mitch, take the win. Hell, we both know they don't come that often. Not like this. The credit for this is all yours."

Dreslan hesitated, but he didn't move away, which was a good sign. "I suppose you're right. I should brief the president. He's on the third floor."

"I don't think you need me for that, do you?" Hawthorn said. He lifted his phone. "Just reach out if there's anything in the debrief you need from me or any of my team."

Dreslan looked at him suspiciously. When there was favor to be curried with the commander-in-chief, it was unfathomable that any member of the government bureaucracy would miss the chance to claim at least some of the credit. Unless there was some other angle.

Hawthorn almost felt sorry for the man as Dreslan's face showed him trying his best to work out why Hawthorn was lay-ing the plum at his feet.

"Before you go, can I ask for a favor?" Hawthorn said. Dreslan looked immediately relieved. Quid pro quo. That was something every DC operator understood.

"What's that?"

"Rick Hallsey," Hawthorn said. "Go easy on the kid. I know he's in the shithouse for not coming clean with you about the source, but he's a good agent."

"Is this about giving the kid a break, or about his relationship with your agent, Mara Roberts?"

Hawthorn gave him a nod. Maybe he'd underestimated Dreslan. He made a mental adjustment for the future.

"How about we say it's a little bit of both?"

"I have to punish him a little," Dreslan said. "He kept a material fact hidden from me. He ought to be running counterfeit cases out of the Oklahoma office for what he pulled."

"That would be a waste of talent, don't you think?"

Dreslan glanced at the twisting staircase that led to the suite's upper floors. Hawthorn knew he was eager to deliver the good news to the president before he heard it from someone else.

"I'll put him in the doghouse for a week or two. Starting with the gala tonight at the library."

"Nothing in his permanent file," Hawthorn said. It was a statement, not a question.

Dreslan didn't like it, but he agreed. "You're burning up quite a few chits to help this kid. You have a weakness for your people, Jim. Almost makes me like you."

"Let's not get carried away," Hawthorn said, turning toward the exit.

"That's it?" Dreslan asked.

"That's it," Hawthorn said. He held up his phone again. "Reach out if you need anything."

Hawthorn left the suite, passing a phalanx of Secret Service agents in the hallway. He grinned as he imagined Dreslan bounding up the stairs to tell the president the threat had been neutralized and that the UN anniversary agenda would be going on as planned.

As he rode the elevator down, he marveled at the sense of relief he felt. Not only for his country, but for his family. Scarvan's revenge against Belchik's family members had shaken him more than he'd let on. He was an old man. He loved life and wanted as much of it as the good Lord would give him, but he had no misconceptions that his time wasn't nearing its end. But his kids. His grandkids. He could not have borne having anything happen to them.

But as he breathed easier and allowed himself to relax, he felt a nagging impulse worm its way up from his gut.

Instinct had served him well over the years. And he'd learned to listen to it.

If he was loosening his grip, was the entire security apparatus doing the same thing? Were they being set up? Was Scarvan the weapon or the distraction?

By the time the elevator hit the ground floor, Hawthorn's natural paranoia had returned in full force. He pulled out his phone and called Scott.

"Is he awake?" he asked.

"Still pretty out of it," Scott said. "It'll be a bit before I start the interrogation."

"Good, I'm coming down. The site under Grand Central?"

"That's the one. Everything okay?" Scott asked.

"Is everything ever okay?" Hawthorn replied.

"You're a real pick-me-up, you know that?" Scott said, then he turned serious. "You feeling what I'm feeling?"

"Like maybe this was a little too easy? That we might be getting set up?"

"Yeah, those two things."

"That's why I'm coming down," Hawthorn said. "Where's Mara?"

"She felt the same way. We decided she'd stay on-site at the UN and then the gala tonight. We need to stay forward on this."

"Agreed. I'll come down."

He ended the call as a member of his own protective detail signaled to him that his car was waiting outside. He considered that he might be overreacting, that maybe he ought to just take the win earned by the hard work of his team and the professional men and women of the Secret Service and the FBI.

But resting easy wasn't in his nature.

Especially because he knew failure wasn't part of Jacobslav Scarvan's.

CHAPTER 56

Mara heard the applause from inside the General Assembly, signaling that the president had finished his remarks. As the host country, the United States had been afforded the honor of addressing the collected world leaders last. From what Mara had heard through the speakers outside the room, Patterson had mostly stayed on script, largely delivering platitudes about global cooperation and the indispensable role of collective security.

The exception was a moment when Patterson issued a warning that the age of great wars could be forever in the past, or still just on the horizon. That great nations could afford to disagree but could not afford the cost when those disagreements solidified into red lines on which there could be no compromise.

The line that caught Mara's attention was a surprising warning from the leader of the free world. "If such disagreement without compromise as we have seen from some of the great members of this body continue—and I put my own country in this category," the president said, "then I believe we could see another great war within this decade. And the cost of that war would be more than the world could afford to bear."

That section of the speech had been delivered with a sternness not on display in the rest of Patterson's talk. He paused after saying the words, lending them even more significance.

Then he returned to the prepared remarks on the teleprompter in front of him. The difference was impossible not to notice and Mara knew the punditry would be analyzing that section more than any other. There were many nations the words could apply to, not to mention Patterson's domestic rivals in Congress. But having an American president openly warn of a global war within a few years would make news. Mara was certain of it.

Mara returned to the command center as the heads of state left the General Assembly and joined either small receptions in the building or headed to their transportation to get ready for that night's gala.

If anything happened, she wanted to be in the central hub.

And she hoped to steal a few minutes with Rick.

Capturing Scarvan had been a huge national security win. Selfishly, it was also good for her chances to patch things up with Rick. If that was even possible. The way he'd looked at her after learning she'd violated his trust and told her dad about Asset after they'd agreed not to share that with anyone gave her some doubt. He'd put his career on the line by not telling Dreslan what he knew. And Dreslan wasn't the kind of guy to forget such a thing. There was a chance Rick could lose his job over this. And how did it look that she safely had hers because she shared the information?

The irony was she didn't want the job. Not really. She wanted a life. And, faced with the prospect of losing Rick, she was surer than ever that she wanted a life with him. If she hadn't screwed things up beyond repair.

Advice on the issue came from an unlikely source. As she stood in the command center, watching a bank of monitors showing the surveillance feeds from around the property, Anna walked up and stood next to her.

"Quite a day," she said.

Mara nodded. "Quite a week."

Anna shrugged her bandaged shoulder. "At least the man you love didn't shoot you."

Mara cocked her head to the side and gave her a look.

"I do love your father," Anna said. "Does that surprise you?"

"I didn't know the two of you saw that much of each other," Mara said. She knew her dad's whereabouts on most days. Weekend trysts in Prague weren't typically on his schedule.

"I love him in my own way. And I think, in his way, he loves me," she said, staring at the screens in front of them, doing the job even during the conversation. "We live in a different world from most people. We see things others never will see. Exposed to threats and near misses that the world doesn't need to know about."

Like today, Mara thought. There would be no headline about the work done to avert disaster. The world would continue to spin as if nothing had happened. But the men and women involved knew how close they'd come. And that knowledge took a toll.

"What we do can create a bond," Anna said. "Or it can create walls if you have the wrong expectation. If you're looking for a normal relationship, regular Wednesday date nights, coffee together every morning before work, pillow talk about the events of the day, and all that, then you're going to be disappointed."

"What if that's what I want?" Mara asked.

"Then I'd say I know you better than you know yourself," Anna said. "Or at least I know I thought the same thing more than once. Even tried it more than once."

"And?"

"I'm standing here with you, aren't I?" she said. "Having played my part in saving the world from itself once again. The rush is intoxicating. And it's addictive."

"And it's never-ending," Mara pointed out.

"That's true. You might even say that world-saving is a growth business. Men with ill intent will always rise up to do evil. And people like us will meet them on the field and do battle."

"Do you ever feel like it's not worth it?" Mara said. "That it's just inevitable that one day the bad guys are going to win? Whether that's a mushroom cloud over New York City, or a global pandemic of a man-made weaponized virus, with technology, isn't it just a matter of time? And if it is, shouldn't we try to have an actual life until it happens?"

Anna finally took her eyes off the monitors and looked at her. "Maybe you're right. But if there is a mushroom cloud over New York or Paris or Prague, I need to look at myself in the mirror and know I did everything I could to prevent it. Knowing there are evil men planning the destruction of society, and knowing I possess some unique skills and experience to help stop them, I don't think a regular life is possible. For me, anyway. Everyone must make their own path."

She nodded at Rick walking toward them.

"But you also must choose carefully the people to walk that path with," she said.

Rick slowed his approach a few feet from them. "Am I interrupting?"

"No," Anna said. "I was about go to the Czech embassy. I'm attending the gala tonight. I'm told there's a dress waiting for me that will make me look ravishing. Will I see you both there?"

"Hawthorn asked me to attend," Mara said. "Another set of eyes. We may have stopped Scarvan, but a congregation of world leaders is still a plum target for any one of dozens of terrorist groups in the world."

Anna looked to Rick. "How about you, young man? Will I see you there?"

"I'll be there," Rick said. "But I doubt you'll see me. Dreslan's on the warpath. Last I heard, I'll be patrolling the stacks under Bryant Park during the event."

"That's a shame," Anna said, sliding past him. "I would have loved to see you in a tuxedo. I'll leave you two to chat."

Rick feigned interest in the wall of video monitors. Most heads of state had left the building, so there wasn't much to see.

"Is it bad?" Mara asked.

"It isn't good," Rick said. "The fact it all ended well helps. Maybe a demotion instead of jail time."

"I don't think it would have come to that," Mara said.

"There was a credible threat to the president if you shared the information. You didn't want it to leak and put the president at risk."

"Which, to my boss, implies he couldn't be trusted with the information," Rick said. Some staffers for the security team walked past and Rick paused until they were gone. "But you told your dad after we agreed to tell no one."

"Which implies you can't trust me?" Mara said.

Rick glanced around, checking that they were alone. "Yeah, if you want the truth. That thought had crossed my mind. I'm not even saying it was the wrong move to tell him. But why hide it from me?"

"Because this was bigger than us," Mara said. "You know that."

"See, that's the problem," Rick said. "The direction we were headed, where I thought we were going, there wasn't anything bigger than us."

"Guess you were wrong about that," Mara said, hating the words as they came out of her mouth. God, she didn't feel that way. She wanted to be with him. She wanted to share everything with him. But she was too damn stubborn, and she knew it.

Rick maintained his composure, either because of the other people in the room with them, or because he'd expected as much from her. He made a show of looking at his watch. "I've got to go. Let's get through the gala tonight and the Scarvan debrief over the next couple of days. Professional only. Some time apart would be good, I think."

She wanted to say she was sorry, but the words stuck in her throat. This was the part of relationships she always sucked at. Offense was her best defense, and the vulnerability she felt kicked that instinct into high gear. It took everything she had to not make some smart-ass remark. Instead, she swallowed hard and said, "I agree."

Rick seemed put off-balance by the response. He hesitated, checked his watch again, then turned and left.

Mara blew out a deep breath. She ought to go after him.

Grab a room and talk things out. Time apart could defuse the situation, but most likely just deepen the divide she felt gaping between them.

But when she moved, it was in the opposite direction. As she walked away, she had a gnawing sense she was also walking away from her best chance to fix her relationship.

She had a job to do. And if she was going to be undercover at a gala of world leaders, she had to look the part. As she left the command center, she caught sight of her reflection in a window. Three days of little sleep and maybe one shower in between had her looking a mess. Maybe postponing the talk with Rick wasn't the worst thing. A shower, a little makeup, maybe even a brush through her hair would make a world of difference. The dress that had been purchased for her wouldn't hurt, either.

Mara decided she'd give Rick some space. Right until the gala was over and the security team stood down. Then she'd get over her asshole ways, find him, and have a real conversation about how she felt about him. She'd done her part to save the world. It was time for her to spend a little time saving herself.

As she left the command center, she felt a surge of confidence she could actually pull it off. Not because of her ability to manipulate people, but because she was ready to come clean and have an honest conversation. If it wasn't enough, then nothing would be. But the relationship wouldn't end because she wrapped herself in a hard shell like she normally did. She was going to get out of her own way and see where the path took her.

It was a giddy feeling and she found herself smiling like a fool as she walked the halls of the United Nations building. She just had to get through the gala dinner at the New York Public Library first. How hard could that be?

CHAPTER 57

Scott couldn't remember the last time another man intimidated him. Could have been his drill instructor at Quantico. Or maybe the Navy SEAL commander who hadn't wanted a CIA puke in his unit on his first deployment overseas.

Those men hadn't wanted to kill him, but they both could have done so without breaking a sweat or even breathing hard.

Scarvan not only had those same skills, but his eyes burned with an unmistakable desire.

Given a few seconds with his wrists unbound from the metal ring embedded into the table in front of him, with his legs unshackled from the irons that were attached to the floor, Scott knew Scarvan would try to do the worst imaginable things to him.

And, even in his old age, Scott wondered whether he'd survive such an attack.

Hawthorn stood next to him at the one-way mirror, watching their prisoner. Scarvan sat with his head tilted back, eyes open, staring at the fluorescent lights strung above him. His mouth moved, minutely, almost impossible to see.

"What do you think he's doing?" Hawthorn asked.

"Praying," Scott said. "He's been doing it since he regained consciousness."

"Jacobslav Scarvan the Penitent. I never would have imagined it."

Scott looked around them. There was a room built up around them, but a few windows showed the unique location. Deep under Grand Central Station were a series of unused areas: storage yards for subway cars that hadn't been used in decades, old offices for the maintenance teams that were left to rust and gather dust when they'd been moved above ground. Even an old subway platform with shiny tiles and archways leading to stairs that were bricked up.

After 9/11, the CIA had sought out black sites to have "conversations" with people of interest in terrorist plots. Sometimes those conversations had an urgency to them given the information required was about an active attack in progress or something imminent.

The subterranean tunnels right under Grand Central Station had served that purpose well over the years. It was accessible via a specialized train or a heavily guarded service elevator in the basement of an office building right above them. From this spot, after interrogations were done, prisoners could be transported anywhere in the country by train.

It was a perfect spot for Scarvan. If the man was going to talk, Scott thought it might be in the sudden aftermath of his plan being thwarted. Once Scarvan was locked up, he guessed the old man would clam up and just wither away in his old age.

"Are you ready?" Hawthorn asked him.

"Sure. What kind of question is that?"

"You look a little on edge is all," Hawthorn said.

"I'm fine."

"Good," Hawthorn said, slapping him on the back. "Because the guy scares the piss out of me. Have fun."

Scott crossed over to the door and let himself in.

Scarvan didn't shift his eyes. He continued to stare at the light above, lips moving in near silent prayer. A soft whisper came from the old man, unintelligible.

Scott pulled out the chair opposite him and sat down heavily.

He leaned back, consciously working to appear in control. He waited in silence as Scarvan continued to pray.

"We found the bomb," Scott finally said. Scarvan stopped his prayer and slowly lowered his gaze until he met Scott's eyes. "Crude work, but the bomb guys tell me it would have done the job."

In fact, the FBI's bomb unit had been impressed with the sophistication of the device. As Jordi had predicted, there were two pathways to detonation, cellular and long-wave radio frequency.

"Smart encasing the device in a lead framework to avoid detection," Scott said. "Would have been easy enough to set off in the middle of Times Square. But you had a more specific group you wanted to kill today, didn't you?"

"I was like you once," Scarvan said, startling Scott with his clear English. "Dedicated to my country. Sacrificing for her. Giving my life." Scarvan leaned his head to his left, indicating the shoulder where Scott had shot him on the boat so many years before. "You saw the thanks men like us get once our usefulness is gone. That will be your fate one day. You'll see."

"Maybe," Scott said. "I don't think I'll become a mass murderer, though, and hide behind God when I do it."

Scarvan said nothing at first. He shook his head as if he were dealing with a child. Finally, he leaned forward, his voice a low, husky whisper.

"You are a murderer, Scott Roberts. The gods you hide behind take the form of an eagle and the stars and stripes of your flag. Tell me, do the dead come to you at night? Do they demand things of you? Answers? Penance? Do they offer forgiveness? Or only damnation?"

The dead did come for Scott, ready to insert themselves into a dream, or even a waking thought.

"That's how we're different. My conscience is clean," Scott said. "But you're right, I do hear the dead. The ones who were killed by bombs in public places. The kids torn apart by shrapnel for some political purpose. If there's any guilt, it's that I didn't do enough to save them. For you, I expect you get pleasure from the screams. The more terror, the more you enjoyed it."

Scarvan let out a deep laugh.

"You think that's funny?" Scott asked.

"No," the old man said. "I think you're full of shit."

"Really? How's that?"

Scarvan looked like he might not take the bait, but it was too much for him to pass up.

"You and your government like to drape ideals around you like a cape, like it will be an invisibility cloak masking your own evil. How many innocents have been killed in the name of freedom? In Iraq? In Afghanistan? Your CIA runs operations the same as everyone else. Don't tell me about the innocent. There are no innocents. Only sinners who deserve punishment."

"Punished by who? You?" Scott said. "Is that from that brain of yours getting a little scrambled from your swim in the Aegean? Too many weird mushrooms with the Greek monks?"

"Joking. That's the way it is with you," Scarvan said. "It's your defense. It shows great weakness. I didn't know that about you before."

"There you go casting judgment again. But that's your new gig, right? Deciding what's right and wrong. Who lives and dies?"

"Not me," Scarvan said. "Judgment. Retribution. And, yes, punishment, all will come from a God displeased with His creation."

"Where did all this God stuff come from?" Scott said. "Is that what you were doing for all those years you were missing? Going to Sunday school? Reading your Bible? Mostly Old Testament by the sound of it. Angry, vengeful God and all that."

Scarvan leaned back in his chair as far as his chains would allow. Perhaps he'd caught something in Scott's voice, sensed a confidence that Scott knew he had a card to play. And he did. A good one.

The old man suddenly grew cautious.

"You know where I spent those years," he said.

"That's right, I do," Scott said, like they were two friends having a beer and discussing their summer travel. Scott pulled his phone out of his pocket, idly scrolling through his photos as he spoke. "Beautiful place. The bars aren't very good, but you can't have everything." He looked up suddenly. "Want to see some pictures from my trip?"

Scarvan glared at him. He didn't like the direction things were going.

"No need, I'm aware of what it looks like," Scarvan said.

Scott smiled as he turned the phone toward the old man. He was enjoying this probably more than he ought to. But there was a point to it. He needed Scarvan off-balance. Needed to shake him from this smug confidence. If he could do that, then he just might make a mistake. Give him something, anything, to help lead him to who helped him get inside the UN.

He had just the thing that might do the trick.

He forced the phone into Scarvan's line of sight. "You're going to want to see this." He put a finger on the screen. "Or maybe you don't. But you know what?" He flicked to the next image. "That's too fucking bad."

CHAPTER 58

The Stephen A. Schwarzman Building, the main branch of the New York Public Library that stretched from Fortieth to Forty-second Streets on Fifth Avenue, always left Mara in awe. She'd come to New York with her mom and Lucy when she was thirteen. A girls' weekend that made her and her sister feel like adults. Nice dinners, two Broadway shows, a carriage ride through Central Park, and a stay at the Plaza Hotel. But it was the trip to the NYPL that left the greatest impression of the trip.

As much as Mara spent her early years as a tomboy ready to take on any boy in any sport, or in any playground fight for that matter, she was also a full-on book worm. She'd blown through the books deemed age-appropriate for her, Nancy Drew and the like, before discovering Neil Gaiman's book *Coraline*. From there she'd jumped into his books for adults, hiding them once she discovered there were words in them that she wasn't supposed to say in good company. Once, her dad had found her well past her bedtime with a copy of *American Gods*. He'd read it before and knew exactly what was in it. He left the room and came back with a pen flashlight, suggesting she read under the covers so she wouldn't get caught.

From there she consumed everything. She discovered Tolkien and C. S. Lewis, Frank Herbert's Dune series, the horror of

Stephen King, the lyrical voice of Michael Chabon, the beauty of Toni Morrison, the boldness of Hemingway.

So, when New York was still in the planning stages, she'd begged her mom to add the library to their schedule. Lucy complained and called her a big nerdo, but she didn't care. And neither did her mom. Not only did she put it on the schedule, but she signed them up for a tour of the building. This addition cut into their free shopping time, which made Lucy pout for two days, but she got over it.

The visit was everything she'd hoped for, but in a surprising way.

The architecture of the building was awe-inspiring. From the massive stone lions standing guard at the stairs leading to the front entrance, to the edifice of the majestic Beaux-Arts building—a term she'd learned in her research before the trip—everything signaled that literature was something special. Something to be revered, honored, treasured.

Walking inside felt the same as any one of the cathedrals she'd been to around the world. Astor Hall, named after John Astor, the original benefactor of the library, was a soaring space of marble archways, grand staircases, and elaborate lighting fixtures. A temple to books. A solemn space designed to make clear that what lay within was something worth protecting, worth wrapping with the most beautiful and permanent building that could be imagined. Even Lucy stood openmouthed in that entrance lobby, amazed by the scale of the building.

They'd joined the tour in the lobby and spent the next hour walking through the hallowed halls, up and down wide stone staircases that look like they ought to be in a royal palace instead of on the corner of Forty-second Street and Fifth Avenue.

They were about twenty minutes into the tour when Mara asked the question most of the adults had thought but were too afraid of looking stupid to ask:

Where were all the books?

The docent of the tour gave her a high five and pulled a lollipop from her pocket, saying she always rewarded the first person to ask that question. Lucy glared at her as she stuck the lollipop in her mouth. The docent explained that while tens of thousands of books were on display, over 3.5 million additional items were stored away from the public, accessible on request. These were stored in the seven floors under them in a massive steel bookcase that, if laid out end-to-end, would stretch over eighty miles long. Then she walked them to a window and pointed outside. They crowded around and looked out to an enormous rectangle of open grass, lined on each side by towering trees.

Bryant Park.

"And another million books are out there, only six feet under the grass." the docent said. "In the eighties, the area under Bryant Park was excavated and massive new bookstacks were installed. Completely climate controlled, moisture controlled, and connected to the main library through a one-hundred-twenty-foot-long tunnel with a conveyor belt system that sends a book from the stacks to any of the distribution points in the library."

Mara remembered the sense of awe she felt on that tour, at the idea of there being so many books in the world. That awe was given an electric boost when they came to the Rose Main Reading Room, a space that had become one of Mara's favorite places in the world. After passing through a marble archway, they faced a dark wood structure that served to divide visitors either left or right into the enormous space. The wood structure continued, bisecting the hall, creating a workspace for librarians and giving both sides of the hall a bank of stations where patrons could request books.

This room once again filled Mara with the same reverence as any church she'd been in. Perhaps even more so. She didn't believe in a God, not the one described by man anyway, but even at the age of thirteen, she did believe in the power of knowledge and books. This space, nearly three hundred feet long with fifty-foot-high ceilings, totally unencumbered by any support pillars, was a marvel just with its size. Add to that gorgeous arched windows allowing natural light into the space, the grand, tiered chandeliers, rows of wooden work desks filled with writers and readers and poets and researchers, and Mara found it hard to breathe as she took it all in.

When she looked to her mom, she saw she was watching her, not looking at the room at all. She slid an arm around her and pointed up. The ceiling was ornately carved wood with enormous central panels painted to look like blue sky with soft billowing clouds, giving everything an ethereal feel.

As Mara stood in the Rose Reading Room as an adult, she felt the echoes of the awe felt by her thirteen-year-old self. A recent renovation had transformed the room into its former glory after years of deferred maintenance. But she couldn't separate her feelings from the memory of her mother. A clear and pure love from that moment with her mother's loving hand sliding around her back to hold her as they looked at the beauty in front of them. It created complicated emotions that she didn't have time for.

"Excuse me, ma'am," a young Secret Service agent said. "We're about to open the room."

Mara shook herself from her memory and nodded to the agent. She took another look around. The Reading Room had been transformed into a dining space, the long worktables covered with white linens, fine china, and silver befitting a formal state dinner at the White House. Staff scurried among the settings, pouring waters and lighting candles. She'd wanted to review the layout before everything started. It all looked in order, but she couldn't shake the feeling that she was missing something.

"Just getting the lay of the land," she said.

"Yes, of course. If you could step this way, please."

She left the Rose Reading Room and displayed her credentials to get a look at the room where the world leaders would gather just prior to the event. She was wearing a black dress that was tighter than she would have chosen for herself, and shoes with heels that frustrated her with their damn awkwardness.

She carried a small purse with her ID, but no gun. She was eyes and ears tonight. The ears part included a sophisticated earpiece connected to Jordi Pines.

"What do you think, Jordi?" she asked. The agent looked confused, so she pointed to her ear to indicate she was talking to someone else.

"I think he's a bit young for you," Jordi said, enjoying being able to speak without the agent hearing him.

The agent stepped closer. "I think we have things buttoned down," he said. "Unless you think we forgot anything." The tone was playful but with an edge to it. Clearly, he didn't think the Secret Service needed a second look, regardless of who the person was in front of him.

"Saucy," Jordi chirped in her ear.

"Just two minutes," she said, turning away from him. "The room, Jordi," she said. She assumed Jordi had tapped into every surveillance camera in the library and was watching her. "Talking about the room."

"Your beautiful Boy Scout there is right about protection," Jordi said. "Looks buttoned up. Would have preferred to install the same RF blockers we had set up at the UN. Just in case. But that's just me."

"But then I wouldn't be able to hear your beautiful voice," Mara said. The agent pointed to his watch and literally tapped it. Subtle. She held up a finger. One minute.

"Needn't have worried, selected a specific band for this radio that wouldn't have been impacted. I'm smart that way," Jordi said. "Do you at least have one of the portable RF blockers with you?"

"No, I don't." She looked for a camera, found one, and walked up to it so she was looking right at Jordi. "Spit it out," she said. "You have a bad feeling about this place?"

"I don't know. It's just put all these big-shot a-holes in the same place twice in one day, feels like tempting things, don't you think?"

"Ma'am, I have to insist," the young agent said.

Mara nodded and walked to the exit. "Everyone at Alpha watching this place?"

"The whole team is on it," Jordi said.

She put a hand over her mouth. "Do you have eyes on Rick Hallsey?"

"Are you using government resources for you own personal benefit, Agent Roberts?"

"Only if you get off your ass and tell me where he is," Mara replied.

As she exited the Rose Reading Room into the antechamber that once held the card catalog, she spotted the heads of state with their dates waiting for admission into the room. These were from smaller nations. While protocol suggested all states were treated equally, there was certainly a recognized pecking order. Just as at the UN building, the members of the Security Council would be the last to arrive to the room.

"Ohhh," Jordi said. "He must really be in the doghouse with his boss."

"Why?"

"He's holding down the fort in the bookstacks under Bryant Park," he said. "If there was a Siberia for this event, that'd be it. Even bathroom duty in the main building would be closer to the action. Looks like you've done wonders for his career."

"Shut up. Can you patch me into his coms?"

A long pause. "You know when you're out with a friend and that friend is going to text their deepest feelings to their boyfriend at one in the morning? The responsible thing to do is take the phone away."

"This is different," she said.

"This is for national security," Jordi deadpanned.

"No, you're right," she said, making her way down the long, marble hallway to the staircase. "Forget it. I'll talk to him after."

"Trouble in paradise?" Jordi said. "Want to talk to Uncle Jordi about it?"

"Maybe another time," she said. One of the attendees caught

her eye across the room. A man in a tailored suit surrounded by a small crowd over which he was holding court.

Jordi must have used his camera angles to determine where she was looking, because he said, "Is that our new friend?"

"It is," Mara said. "I didn't expect to see him here. I think I'll go and say hi."

"Can I listen in?"

"If I said no, would you still listen?"

"Probably."

"Thought so. Come on, this might be fun."

Mara walked across the room toward the small crowd and prepared for round two of her conversation with Marcus Ryker.

CHAPTER 59

Asset appreciated the temperature-controlled environment in the stacks. In his career, he'd had to burrow into places with horrendous conditions to lay in wait for his time to act. Caves filled with insects. Barns with rodents mistaking his fingers or cheeks for an easy meal in the middle of the night. Drainage culverts with leeches and snakes.

Compared to those missions, hiding for the past forty-eight hours in the lower level of stacks in an obscure section holding research materials on eighteenth-century public works projects had been a vacation.

Still, that long in the dark, holding as still as possible, forced the mind to wander. The magnitude of what he had been tasked to do hadn't been lost on him. The long hours in the dark had given him time, maybe too much time, to imagine what the consequences of his actions would be.

He held no affection for the world leaders that were about to die. They were all corrupt, vile manipulators. The self-described elite who played gods with the billions of human lives on the planet. And with the planet itself.

If anything, he held more in common with the massive protest expected to fill Bryant Park thirty feet over his head. The transformation of the open lawn into a sanctioned protest site had not been in the original plan. He'd expected the park to be empty, part of the cordoned security zone that would extend two blocks in each direction around the library. But the decision to allow the protest had proven to be great politics. The American press was giving high marks to President Patterson for allowing dissent to be heard by the attendees. He imagined the park was already at capacity, protestors shoulder to shoulder to speak out against the oppressors. Little did they realize that they were about to have a front-row seat to the destruction of the world order.

Asset knew his role. There was a vast plan that extended far beyond what he'd been allowed to see. He was to execute his part of it and trust that Omega understood how to manage the chaos that was sure to follow.

And chaos was exactly what it would be.

The people gathered in the library were just that, people. No special powers. No divine rights. Just politicians who'd survived their cutthroat occupation long enough to rise to the top of the dung heap. Each of them had competitors waiting in the wings who would like nothing more than the chance to take their place.

In some countries, the transfer of power would be orderly.

In others, there would be brutal, bloody contests. The military in many places would assume control. Perhaps using the confusion to launch strikes, acquire territory, destroy their rivals.

The economic impact alone would spin the world off its axis. Markets would crumble. Shock waves through the banking system would be akin to what happened after 9/11. But then the world's governments at least had leaders to help govern through the quagmire.

No, if the goal was to dissolve the glue holding the world together, this was a masterful place to start.

The genius of Jacobslav Scarvan.

Omega had only attached itself to his plan. Added support where needed. Obviously, the most important function was acquiring not one, but two tactical nuclear devices.

But once the plan changed to make the UN a red herring,

Omega had ordered Asset to perform the final stroke of Scarvan's plan. The old master had known that allowing his own capture was required to sell the ruse and lull the security apparatus into a false sense of confidence.

Brilliant.

The meeting with Mara Roberts and Rick Hallsey had all been orchestrated by Scarvan. By helping Alpha Team stop his attack at the UN, Scarvan had managed to make it seem like Omega wanted no part in destroying a gathering of the world's leaders.

It was just the opposite.

But with Scarvan's capture, supposedly with Omega's help, the threat would appear to be diminished. Security would still be tight, there was an endless list of bad actors in the world, but the president would still attend the event.

There had never been a way to get the bomb into the General Assembly. But the Secret Service didn't need to know that. The goal had always been to get just as far as it did before he was caught.

Scott and Mara had played along beautifully. Manipulated like puppets on strings. Strings that had been attached to Scarvan's fingers.

The bomb was here with him.

The delivery system into the Rose Reading Room was as simple as it was perfect.

Only minutes left before it was go time.

Just then, the lights flickered on. Someone entering the stacks area.

He didn't worry at first, his hiding spot was good enough.

But then he heard a new sound. Heavy breathing. Soft scraping on the linoleum floor.

A dog.

If they came close, that was a problem.

Asset pulled his suppressed Glock from his side and readied himself. He loved dogs and would shoot the owner first to see if he needed to shoot the dog as well. He wanted to avoid it, but a well-trained dog would rip him to shreds if given the chance.

He craned his neck to get a look down the row of book-shelves.

Two men passed the opening with a German shepherd on leash. One in uniform, the other in a suit. They passed his row, but he was certain they would pass back by his direction.

Even as he readied himself, he wondered about the cosmic forces in the universe and whether coincidence or fate played a hand.

One of the men was Rick Hallsey.

CHAPTER 60

"You have nothing I want to see," Scarvan said, looking away.

But Scott reached out and grabbed the man by the chin. He stuck his phone in front of his face. "Don't be rude," he said.

There was a shot of him arriving at the port on Mt. Athos. A photo that included the newspaper from that day. It was old-fashioned, but it worked as a time stamp.

Scarvan didn't struggle. He watched the screen as Scott flipped through the images. A shot of the countryside from his trip. A photo of the sketes built up against the rock face.

"Man, this looks like a tough place to spend a few decades," Scott said. "Can't say I blame you for going a little soft in the head. All of this *I'm an instrument of God*. Where'd that even come from?"

Scarvan stared at the screen and then at Scott. The muscles in the man's jawline twitched and bulged even as he otherwise held his composure.

"Father Spiros," Scott said, as if just remembering. "That's right. He took you under his wing. He found you with a few holes in your body, but the real hole was where your country used to be. When Belchik ripped that out, you were lost. Until Father Spiros gave you something new to worship, right? You were a little old to find a new father figure, weren't you? But it must have been nice. Having someone who believed in you. Gave you a higher purpose? Someone you could trust completely. It had to devastate you when he died."

"It was his time," Scarvan said. "God called him home."

"That chestnut is right up there with *Everything happens for a reason.*"

"It does," Scarvan said. "You will come to believe that one day. Maybe today."

"Still, I understand you wouldn't start your crusade while he was still alive," Scott said. "That must have been hard. On both of you."

Scott flipped to the next photo. Father Spiros in bed. Scarvan pulled in a sharp breath.

He tapped the screen to start a short video of the old man, arm feebly raised in front of him. "I'm sorry, Apostoli," he mumbled. His eyes were closed, his voice drifting. "I should not have lied to you. I'm sorry. Do what they say. Help me. Please."

The lab techs in Alpha Team had done an amazing job changing the old man's words just enough to make them an appeal for help. Scott was counting on Scarvan's emotional reaction to rattle the man. Get him to make a mistake.

The next part of the video was where Father Spiros was shot and killed. The clip ended before that happened.

Scarvan lifted his face back to the light above the table and closed his eyes.

"That has to hurt. Have someone you trust fake his death, just to get you off your ass and do what he told you to do. Ouch."

Scarvan said nothing. Scott had hoped for a bigger reaction.

"We have Father Spiros in custody," Scott said, pushing the gambit.

"I don't believe you," Scarvan said, without looking down.

"Really, I can let you see him. Would you like that? Have one more conversation with your mentor? What's that worth to you?"

Scarvan shook his head slowly. "How did you expect this to go? You offer me to see Father Spiros and I—what? Give you the names of my accomplices?" Scarvan's voice grew louder, the emotion finally showing up. "Tell you how I was able to get a gun and a massive bomb into the United Nations building? Did you really think it would be that easy? Did you really think any of this would be easy at all?"

"Tell me who helped you and I can set up a video line to Father Spiros. You could be talking to him ten minutes from now. I know you want that."

Scarvan's expression changed. The emotion on display only seconds earlier was gone. Replaced by a smugness that came from knowing something no one else knew.

"Perhaps you're not the adversary I thought you'd be," Scarvan said. "Pity."

Scott shifted his position in his chair. He clicked through everything that had happened in the last minute, trying to pinpoint why Scarvan's attitude had suddenly changed. He went over the words. The man's actions. Staring at the light. Meeting Scott eye to eye.

But just before that.

Right before the change in behavior.

Scarvan had glanced down at the table.

No, not the table. Scott's hands.

His watch.

There were no clocks in the room, purposefully done to disorient the person being questioned.

But Scott hadn't removed his watch.

Why would Scarvan care what time it was? He was caught. The bomb secured.

Unless . . . unless . . .

Scott bolted up from his chair. He saw a flicker of alarm cross Scarvan's face.

"You son of a bitch," Scott said.

Scarvan smiled. "Is your beautiful daughter attending the gala?" he said. "I understand anyone who's anyone was planning to be there."

Scott's right hook connected with Scarvan's face. It wasn't his strongest punch; he wanted the man conscious. But it was enough to unleash the sudden fury he felt. With a satisfying crunch, he heard the man's nose break.

Scarvan. Father Spiros. Asset. Omega.

They'd all played him.

The attack was never going to be at the UN. There was no way they were ever going to get the bomb into the General Assembly hall. Getting it as far as they did, farther than anyone thought possible, made them all think they'd stopped the plot.

They'd only stopped the distraction.

Scott ran to the door. He had to call Mara.

"It's too late!" Scarvan yelled. "It's all over!"

"I set my watch fifteen minutes fast, asshole," Scott said. "You haven't won yet."

As he left the room, he heard Scarvan laughing. "Doesn't matter. You're still too late. It's just like you said: everything happens for a reason. Do you believe me now? DO YOU BE-LIEVE ME?"

Scott sprinted from the room, pulling out his phone and dialing.

"Jesus, Mara. Pick up. Pick up your phone."

The call didn't go through. Instead it ended in a recorded message: "I'm sorry, but your call cannot go through at this time."

They jammed the cell phones.

Holy shit.

Maybe the world was going to burn after all.

CHAPTER 61

"Mr. Ryker," Mara said, holding out her hand. "We met in Paris."

Ryker turned from the two men he was speaking with, his expression blank for a second as he tried to place how he knew her. When he finally made the connection, it came with a satisfying grimace.

"Ms. Roberts," he said, accepting her hand. "Nice to see you again. Under better circumstances."

The two men he had been talking with took the hint and excused themselves. Mara smiled, wondering if Jordi could hear the conversation with her earpiece in her lipstick purse. She turned to look over the crowd. "Quite a gathering," she said. "So many powerful people."

"Some of them are powerful," he said. "Some of them just like to imagine they are." He stepped in front of her so that she was looking right at him. "Which one of those are you?"

Mara knew she shouldn't enjoy getting a rise out of the man as much as she did, but she couldn't help herself. Part of her still wanted to know who had tipped him off in France. Another part enjoyed the exhilaration of talking to one of the most influential people on the globe.

"Under the right circumstances, I have the right kind of power," she said. "Arresting people who've committed crimes, for example."

"I'll keep that in mind if I ever commit one," he said.

"Is any billionaire really innocent?" she asked, knowing Jordi was going to like that line.

Ryker waved at someone across the room, but his attention was on her. "You don't really like me, do you?" he asked.

She shrugged, enjoying the game. "I don't think I've thought about you enough to form an opinion."

He pretended the comment stabbed him in the chest. "Ouch," he said. "Playing on my ego like that. Do they teach you that at the Farm? Is that what they still call the school at the CIA?"

Mara wasn't surprised he'd pieced together who she was after her conversation with him in Paris. "You must have me confused with someone else. I never said I was with the CIA," she said.

"I have resources," he said. "I think I can find out who shakes me down at my own airport."

Mara laughed. "Shake you down? If I ever shake you down, you'll know it."

"Threat or promise?" Ryker asked. His phone rang in his pocket. His expression changed; all the playfulness gone. "I'm sorry, I have to take this." He took the call and listened, nodding his head. Finally, he said, "Yes, I'll come right away." He hung up the phone and turned back to Mara. "My mother is ill. She was to come with me tonight, she loves this sort of thing."

"I hope it's not serious," she said.

Ryker checked his watch. "I had hoped to see the president's speech tonight. Looks like I'll be watching it with my mother instead of with an attractive CIA agent. Some other time?" he said, extending his hand to her.

"Of course," Mara said, shaking it. "Give your mother my best."

Ryker slid past her, two bodyguards falling into step behind him. She reached into her pocket and reaffixed her earpiece.

" 'Give your mother my best'?" Jordi said. "Did you just get run over by the Marcus Ryker charisma express?"

"Shut up, Jordi," she said. "I was playing it up for you."

"Sure you were. Just cozying up with a roguishly handsome billionaire. Nothing to see here."

"I'm going to take you out of my ear if you're not careful."

"And he loves his poor, sick mother," Jordi said. "What's not to love?"

Mara worked her way through the crowd as Jordi chirped in her ear, going on about Ryker's good looks. She ignored him, knowing any response would just keep him going.

Finally, he fell silent. "Are you done?" she asked.

"For now."

"Good, then find Hawthorn for me," she said. "As much fun as that was, I have a bad feeling about tonight."

"You have Scarvan in custody. Can't we just enjoy the party?"

"We're working. Find Hawthorn. Please."

With Jordi guiding her, Mara found her boss in the exotic book collection, a space that had been turned into a VIP holding area. The president was inside so the cordon of security made it impossible for her to get in, even with her credentials. Fortunately, she knew one of the Secret Service agents and he agreed to go inside and pull Hawthorn for her.

It was less than a minute before he came striding out.

"What's wrong?" Hawthorn asked.

"Nothing yet," Mara said. "I just have a feeling . . ."

Hawthorn took her by the elbow and led her away from the agent that had retrieved him. "I feel it, too," he said. "I can't reach Scott."

"What do you mean?" she asked. "How long?"

"Checking now," Jordi said in her ear.

"Only the last couple of minutes," Hawthorn said. "But it's not just him. I can't reach anyone at the GCS site. Do you have Jordi online?"

"He's checking now."

"Confirmed," Jordi's voice said. "All coms are out at the GCS site. Nothing's coming in or out. It's a black hole."

She relayed the information to Hawthorn.

"Let's take a pause," he said. "The com system at GCS is designed to restrict access. Prevent outside surveillance. A glitch would make the whole place dark."

"A glitch just when Scarvan is being questioned? Right before this thing starts?"

Hawthorn bit his lower lip. She'd seen the distant look in his eyes before, thinking through permutations, playing red team offense against his own position, weighing odds, distributing resources a hundred different ways. All in a matter of seconds.

"We're going to talk to the president," he said. "With me."

She followed, pausing only as the Secret Service detail briefly challenged his ability to wave her through. A more senior agent stepped in quickly and let them pass.

In the room, Mara's step faltered. The scene in front of her was surreal as the heads of state from many of the most powerful nations of the world milled around sipping either coffees or glasses of wine. She wasn't one to get starstruck, but the assembled political power in front of her was unlike anything she'd seen before.

"Mara," Hawthorn said.

She refocused and nodded that she was with him. As she turned, she saw Dreslan making a line toward them.

"Can I help you two?" he asked.

"I need to talk to the president," Hawthorn said.

Dreslan turned serious. "Is there a new threat?"

"The communications are out where we're holding Scarvan," Mara said.

"Shit," Dreslan said. "What else?"

"It's too much coincidence, Mitch," Hawthorn said. "I don't like it."

"That's all you have?" he said. "You can't get in touch with whatever black site you guys are using for Scarvan, and you want to pull the president?" He pointed over to where President Patterson was speaking through a translator with the Russian president. "Christ, Jim. He's a little busy right now."

"This doesn't feel right," Hawthorn said. "And I think you know it."

"Feel isn't enough," Dreslan said. "If there's something even close to concrete, I'll be the first person to get him the hell out. You know that. But now that we're here, we can't pull him without setting off a cascade effect to every protection detail in the building."

"We should at least let the president know our concern," Mara said.

"Your concern has been noted," Dreslan said. "Thank you. Now if you'll excuse me."

He turned and walked back to the president. Mara took a step forward to follow him, but Hawthorn put a hand on her arm to hold her back.

"No," he said. "He might be right. It's not enough. Keep working. Where's Rick?"

"Dreslan put him in the stacks under Bryant Park," she said. "Punishment for not sharing his source."

Hawthorn shook his head. "Could have picked a better time to make his point. Okay," he said. "Let's keep in touch."

Mara pulled out an additional earpiece from her purse and handed it to him.

"I hate these things," he said, putting it in. "Giving Jordi a direct line to my ear always has a downside."

"I heard that, Grandpa Jim," Jordi said. "Mic's working."

"Let's go. Keep your eyes open. If something's off, I'd rather err on the side of caution. If we're wrong and cry wolf, we might get fired. But if it is a wolf . . ."

". . . we'll be damn lucky it doesn't kill us along with the rest of the sheep," Mara finished.

CHAPTER 62

The dog smelled him from twenty feet away. Maybe it was because the stacks were hermetically sealed, specially designed to keep any mold or mildew from growing on the millions of pieces of paper stored there. That design, combined with a 360-degree air transfer system, scrubbed by the highest-end filters in existence, ensured the only smells in the massive area were that of paper, glue from the bindings, and leather from some of the older tomes.

The smell of a man hiding in place for forty-eight hours, sweating, pissing into bottles, defecating into sealed bags, eating food, belching and passing gas, must have seemed like a fire alarm to the well-trained dog.

The German shepherd's handler was caught off guard. Either he was lazy, or he had zero percent expectations of finding anything on his routine search. Regardless, he did the thing that a K-9 professional never allowed and lost control of his animal.

The dog tore down the narrow aisle between the bookcases, snarling and barking as his nails scraped on the linoleum floor. It stopped under Asset's hiding spot, the top shelf of the stack, seven feet off the floor, in the space between the books facing opposite directions on different aisles.

A quick look down the aisle confirmed his assumption: the

K-9 handler and Rick were running toward his position, guns pulled.

He had the option of climbing down the opposite side, landing in the next aisle over from his pursuers. The move would have bought him some extra time if he'd been discovered by the humans, but the dog made it trickier.

Besides, he found it easy to kill men who were trying to capture him. He liked dogs a lot more. If there was a path that didn't include killing the dog, even if it was as a little riskier, he'd take it.

"Jesus, someone's up there!" the K-9 handler shouted. "Hands up, motherfucker! Right now!"

"Call off the dog," Asset said, putting on a strong New York accent. "I aint hurtin' no one here."

The German shepherd went ballistic on hearing the voice. A smell could mean someone used to be in a place, leaving behind odors even after they'd moved on. But a *voice*. Now that was the jackpot.

"Hands where we can see them!" Rick shouted.

"Easy, easy," Asset said, working the accent. "I'm jus' a guy lookin' for a place to sleep is all. Not hurtin' no one. Promise."

"Then get the hell down here," the cop said, sounding a little less menacing now. Asset smiled. Could this asshole actually be buying his story?

"I ain't doin' nothin' 'til you call off your dog," Asset said. "I ain't stupid."

Asset watched the cop look to Rick for validation. Rick trained his gun on Asset's location and nodded.

"Texas. Return," the cop said.

Texas the German shepherd instantly obeyed, running back to his master, who retook control of the animal by grabbing its lead.

"Now, get your ass down," the cop said. "Slowly, no sudden moves. Let's see your hands the entire time or Texas here will bite your nuts off. You got that?"

"Yeah, man," Asset said, knocking books off the shelf in

front of him to clear the way to jump down. "I'm not gonna get arrested for this, am I? Not hurtin' anyone. Jus' finding a place to sleep is all."

His Glock was safely stashed into the waistband of his pants. The cop would discover it the second he started his pat-down. He was never going to get that far.

"Hands!" Rick shouted as Asset turned to slide off the top rack on his stomach. As he fell the last few feet, he kept his hands high, palms toward them.

Texas growled and barked at him, but the cop corrected him, and the dog fell silent. He licked his chops, no doubt thinking of the salty taste of blood that would be his with only one small command from his master.

"Turn around!" the cop yelled. "Hands behind your head, fingers together. Now."

Asset didn't like the idea of having his back turned on the dog. All it took was for the cop to have a bad attitude and a mean streak to send the dog at him like a missile just for a little sport. If he did that, Asset wouldn't have time to react.

Instead, he slumped his shoulders forward and held his hands out toward the cop. "If you're gonna arrest me, I guess jus' put the cuffs on me now. I got bad knees, you know."

"Don't make me sic this dog on you," the cop said. "Turn around."

"Take it easy," Rick said. "This guy looks harmless enough. Here, let me hold Texas and you go cuff him." The cop started to object. "My radio and cell phone aren't working down here. Neither are yours. We need to get this guy into custody and get to where we can communicate with central command. This guy in here means there was a breakdown somewhere. We need to figure out where. Figure out how bad it is."

"I gotta take a piss," Asset said. "Can we jus' get on with things? Or do you want me to just go here?"

The cop hesitated, but he handed Texas's lead to Rick and then carefully stepped forward, gun still pulled. With his free hand, he pulled out his handcuffs.

"Okay, let's just take this nice and slow," the cop said.

Asset watched Rick tie the dog's lead to the metal bookcase. Apparently, he was a dog-lover as well. It was nice to meet a kindred spirit.

Kindred in more ways than one.

"Officer," Rick said. "I'm sorry, I don't remember your name."

Asset found the confused look on the man's face amusing.

"Brody. Matt Brody," he said. "Why? Are the radios working? You calling this in?"

"No," Rick said. "I just find it disrespectful not to know the name of the man you're working with."

He shifted his outstretched hand six inches to the right, lining up precisely with the back of Officer Brody's head.

He pulled the trigger.

There was an explosion of blood and brain that filled the air where the cop's face had been only a split second earlier. The body remained upright longer than Asset would have thought, some trick of physics and anatomy. A wide flap of skin and tissue hung loose, attached just above the eyebrows, but flapping over a crater beneath that.

After a full three seconds, Officer Brody fell forward. Texas yanked and pulled on his lead, barking and snarling. Everything about his training directed him to come to his partner's aid. But it wasn't meant to be.

Asset nodded to Rick. "Saved the dog." His tone and look conveyed that he appreciated the move as opposed to seeing it as some kind of weakness.

"No such luck for Officer Brody," Rick said. "Is everything in place?"

Asset checked his watch. One minute ahead of schedule.

"You were instructed not to ask for this duty in the stacks," Asset said. "It could raise suspicion."

"Relax," Rick said. "It was all Dreslan's idea." Then, as if considering something for the first time, "He's not . . . you know . . ."

Part of Omega, too? Asset thought. *How the hell would I know?*

"I'm not allowed to share that information with you," Asset said. "Other assets are not revealed unless they are told in advance. You should like that rule, it protects you as much as it protects me." He pointed to the top shelf. "Since you're here, you can help me get the bomb down."

Rick stepped back. "Not a chance. I can't afford to have any potential for residue on me. Especially traces of radiation."

Asset didn't bother arguing. Rick wasn't under his chain of command, so he couldn't order him to help. And the man was so close to the Alpha Team inner circle that he was just about as important to Marcus Ryker as Asset himself.

As he pulled the compact bomb from the shelf, he decided that relative value between him and the Secret Service agent could prove to be a problem in the future. But that was a problem for another day.

"That's it?" Rick said. "I thought it'd be larger."

"Miniaturized nuclear device," Asset said. "The Americans were always warning about a nuke the size of a suitcase. Here it is."

"A nuke? I thought it was a dirty bomb. The polonium piggybacking on a conventional explosive. No one ever said it would be a nuclear device."

Asset grew quiet, analyzing Rick's stance, his voice, his body language. If he had to kill this man, his employer was going to be very upset. But he'd be even more upset if Rick got cold feet and torpedoed the operation they'd all worked so hard to bring to fruition.

"Is that a problem?" Asset asked, ice cold.

Rick pursed his lips, eyeing the device. Finally, he shrugged. "Fuck it, what's the difference?"

Explosive power of about one thousand tons of TNT, thought Asset. But he didn't say it.

"Is the delivery vehicle online?" Asset asked.

"Ready to go," Rick said. "System access cut off from the outside to prevent any interference."

"The radio frequency blockers they had on-site at the UN? They didn't bring them here, correct?"

"Correct," Rick said. "Anything else?"

"If you're here, might as well get some value from you. Is the egress up into Bryant Park still secure?"

When the stacks had been built, there'd been a concern about a fire blocking the single exit from the area under Bryant Park back into the main library. An escape hatch had been dug out, exiting at the far end of the lawn area right in front of the Josephine Shaw Lowell Memorial Fountain. The six-foot-by-twelve-foot metal door was disguised as a plaque honoring the committee who had restored Bryant Park in some past renovation. Thousands of people, tourists and New Yorkers alike, passed the spot every day, not knowing the metal sheet was on a hinge and covered stairs leading down into the stacks.

It was their way out.

"Yes, nothing's changed."

"All right," Asset said, hefting the nuclear device onto his shoulder. "Let's finish the job."

CHAPTER 63

It only took a couple minutes to make their way to the book train.

Asset had retrieved a bag of dog treats from Officer Brody's corpse. Whether it was because of the treats, or because Rick had been with the cop before he was killed, the dog settled. When they'd first led the dog away from its handler's corpse, it continued to look behind it, whimpering. Each time it did, Asset fed it a treat. Soon, it was walking next to Asset as if they were on patrol together.

He knew the dog was a soft spot, but he rationalized that the animal might come in useful before the night was through.

They worked their way through the stacks to the book train.

For years, the stacks had been connected to the main library through a conveyor belt system. A request for a book would be sent from one of the research rooms, originally through pneumatic tubes and later online, then a worker would pluck the book from the shelves and place it on the correct conveyor belt. In all the research rooms, the belts would run continuously as a book approached, sometimes taking five to ten minutes.

The last renovation of the library had replaced this antiquated system that was prone to breakdowns with a state-of-the-art system that was the envy of librarians around the world.

Powder-coated steel tracks replaced the conveyor belts

throughout the library. Individual book trains, single-serve carriages that were two feet long and a foot wide, crawled along the tracks on their own power, carrying up to thirty pounds of books. A latching system meant the trains could transition from horizontal to vertical without a problem as the train rose up inside the building as if on an elevator. The container holding the books turned on a swivel to reorient as the train trudged toward its destination.

The best part was that there was no conveyor belt to run and disturb the librarians in the research rooms. Or to break down, causing delays for requests. If a single train went offline, it was simply removed from the system for repair.

And, most importantly for the purposes of people who might want to utilize the system to transport a nuclear bomb into the middle of a gathering of world leaders, unless there was someone with an eye on the computer screen tracking the locations of the trains in the building, no one at the receiving end of the train would know it was approaching until it arrived.

It was the perfect bomb delivery system.

And as the Rose Reading Room filled with world leaders, including the president of the United States, no one was watching the system.

Asset loaded the bomb, designed to fit perfectly into the book train. He patted it like it was a small child, Moses set to drift on the Nile.

"Do you want to press the button to change the world?" he asked Rick. "Or do you want me to?"

He already knew the answer, but he wanted to see the man squirm.

"No, you do it," Rick said. "It's your job."

"Suit yourself."

Asset located the button to start the bomb on its ninety-second journey to the Rose Reading Room. They would be safe if they stayed underground in the stacks. Over six feet of dirt over them, followed by a thick concrete encasement designed to block all moisture, a bunker that could have been designed to survive a nuclear blast.

The problem with that scenario was they wouldn't be able to leave for a few decades without walking through a radioactive wasteland outside.

Asset double-checked the RF transmitter and receiver. He would detonate the bomb from a safe distance once he was above-ground. A detonator instead of a timer had been at Ryker's insistence. He wanted to ensure the bomb struck during the U.S. president's speech when every leader was in the room. These functions were prone to delays. He wanted to be sure that the devastation was absolute.

Everything was going according to plan.

"What in the hell do you two think you're doing?" a new voice said behind them.

Instinctively, Asset stepped away from Rick. If there was one shooter, no reason to give them an easy way to cover them both.

As he turned, he saw a uniformed NYPD cop. A young kid. Acne on his face. His jacket a size too big for him.

He had his gun pulled.

Texas didn't react. This was a cop, after all. Probably someone he knew better than Asset and Rick.

"Where's Brody?" the kid asked.

"Easy does it," Rick said. "I'm Secret Service. My badge is in my jacket pocket. I'm reaching for it now."

"Stop right there!" the cop shouted. His eyes kept flitting to the device in the book train. Nothing about this was normal. "I don't want to see you even tr—"

A red circle the side of a quarter appeared in the center of the kid's head. As Asset's bullet tore through his brain, the cop's nervous system sent out one final message. In that message, the kid's hand clenched tight, pulling the trigger on his service revolver.

The weapon discharged and Rick doubled over, clutching his stomach.

Texas barked and pulled at his leash but responded to Asset's commands and calmed down quickly.

Asset stepped over a groaning Rick Hallsey, pulling back his hands to examine his wound. His shirt was already drenched in blood. And it smelled foul.

"Asshole," Rick said through gritted teeth.

"Asset," he corrected. "Something you no longer are for our employer."

He smashed a right fist into Rick's face, knocking the man out. If his employer grew curious and even subjected him to a lie detector test, he wanted to be able to say he didn't kill Rick. But he was happy with how things worked out. He wondered if Scarvan would be pleased.

He supposed not until the bomb went off. He checked his watch.

Two minutes until he was to start the train on its ninety-second journey.

He used the time to make the best of a bad situation and began to remove the young cop's uniform. It was just his size.

Maybe Scarvan's belief that God had ordained them to do this was right.

Asset just hoped that whatever divine protection might be left would extend to him safely getting away. He'd know soon enough.

CHAPTER 64

Scott tore up the metal staircase. He hadn't been able to reach anyone outside the black site. All systems were down. Anna stayed to keep watch on Scarvan, in case the coms blackout was a precursor to some kind of assault to free him. It would be madness, but it was shaping up to be a day for surprises.

By coming up from the subterranean levels of Grand Central at the right spot, the New York Public Library would only be a block away. At a full sprint, he could get there in less than a minute once he got to street level.

His leg muscles screamed as he churned up the stairs, taking two at a time. He'd lost count at five floors. He just pushed it out of his mind and willed himself to go faster.

Mara was there.

World leaders be damned, all he cared about was Mara.

As he got closer to the surface, he repeatedly pressed his earpiece, trying to contact Jordi.

"Come in! Come in, Jordi!"

Nothing.

After Scarvan had made his mistake with the time, he'd clammed up. Scott knew no amount of pain would make him talk. Still, the three extra seconds he'd taken to break the man's nose had been time well spent.

As he charged up the stairs, he tried to generate a plan.

He didn't know what Scarvan had in place, but whatever it was he'd thought it would have already been done. That meant it could happen any second. Or could have already occurred.

Mara could already be dead.

The thought pushed him even harder, finding a reservoir of energy he hadn't tapped into yet. He had to be getting close.

"Jordi! Can you hear me?!"

Still nothing.

This transmission issue could be from being in the ancient metal and concrete staircase rising from the bowels of the original subway construction. But the black site coms, that was a different matter. That was a sophisticated, coordinated attack.

Omega.

And he expected the same at the library.

The remaining hope he had was that Jordi's logic about the detonation remained true.

That whatever device they'd been able to get into the library wasn't on a timed countdown, but cellular and radio frequency.

They could shut down the cellular in the area.

The portable RF blocker in his right hand was their chance to stop the detonation. But it had to be within seventy-five feet of the device to work. That was a problem.

He reached the top of the stairwell and punched in a code on the lock to get it open.

The door opened into an alley filled with dumpsters and New York's most permanent residents, massive rats that regarded him with only mild interest.

He got his bearings and sprinted toward Forty-second Street. "Jordi!"

"I'm here," came the voice his earpiece, distant and crackling. "Scott?"

"Is Mara okay?" he asked.

Static.

What did that mean? Had Jordi been attacked too?

Mara.

Oh shit.

"... here ... hacked our ... can't even talk to ..."

"Jordi, I can't hear you. Scarvan has a bomb. In the library. You have to warn them. Jordi!"

Nothing but static.

Scott ran faster, a sense of foreboding that when he turned the corner on Fifth Avenue, he might see billowing smoke, fire, and chaos.

The crowd was thicker here, people attracted to the immensity of the event, encouraged by the area being designated an official protest area. Scott pushed his way through, breathing a sigh of relief when he saw the building.

No smoke or fire.

Not yet anyway.

They still had a chance.

CHAPTER 65

Jordi Pines hated everything he saw.

Every system he looked at was compromised. And it had happened all at once. Every audio feed, surveillance camera, satellite transmission. All of it. Gone.

His brain tried to quantify the size of the attack, the necessary power to circumvent his private security settings and firewalls. He couldn't fathom it.

Because if he could have, then he would have built the defenses stronger.

The only outlet to the outside world was the single-band radio feed he'd established with Mara. And that was wonky at best. When Scott had come online, it'd thrown him off.

"Scott, I can hear you!" he shouted into his mic. "Status?"

The feed was back to static.

He toggled to Mara, multitasking as his fingers flew on the keyboards in front of him, fighting to bring his prized systems back online.

"Mara, your dad just made contact," he said.

"Status?"

Great goddamn question.

He pressed a final button and at least one system was back up. He had geo-location on the earpieces. Three dots on the screen showed the relative locations of Scott, Mara, and Hawthorn.

He pressed another button and combined the three devices into one open system.

"En route to the library. Front entrance," he said.

"Is there a threat?" Hawthorn said, his voice sounding distant, like he was in a well. "I have eyes on the president across the room from me."

A squelching sound erupted on the line and Hawthorn was gone.

"What just happened?" Mara asked.

Jordi hit the table his fist. He was failing his team.

"I was trying to increase his power. I think I just fried his earpiece. Dammit."

"Stay focused, Jordi," Mara said. "I need you. Can you reach my dad?"

"No, nothing but static."

"But you can still see where he is?"

Jordi rechecked his screen. The dot continued to move, edging closer to the main entrance. "Yeah, I've got him."

"That'll have to do."

CHAPTER 66

Scott shoved his way violently through the crowd. He picked a line with no women or children in it and relived his old running back days from college, lowering his shoulder and bellowing, "Police, get out of the way!"

It was New York, so many in the crowd were unimpressed and didn't do much to move. Those who didn't got a feel of what 210 pounds of muscle felt like when Scott was on a mission. He ignored the creative slurs hurled his way as he pushed on.

He spotted a uniformed motorcycle NYPD cop, leaning against his bike. He weighed the pros and cons.

It all depended on what kind of cop the guy was.

Scott decided to risk it.

He ran to the cop, pulling his CIA credentials out. "I need you to clear a path for me through this crowd. Right now."

The cop hesitated, reaching for Scott's credentials like they were written in a foreign language. He was older, late forties, the kind of guy who'd been passed over for promotion and was running out the clock for his pension. He didn't look impressed at all.

Shit.

"There's a credible threat against the president. All communications inside the library are down," Scott said. "If you hesitate right now, when they write the story about today, you're going to be the cop who could have stopped the president of the United States from getting killed, but who failed to act. Is that the story you want to tell your kids?"

The cop still hesitated, but Scott had seen something click in the man's eyes. Maybe the heroic cop he'd always imagined he would be was still in there somewhere.

"This is the real thing," Scott said. "A chance to make a difference. Are you going to take it or not?"

The cop handed back the credentials, and Scott could see a decision had been made. "All right, you're with me," he said. "To the security perimeter, then you talk to the Secret Service guys."

He jumped on the bike, fired it up, and flipped on his lights and siren. Scott didn't climb on, he held on to the backseat and ran with him.

The crowd parted like magic before them. Everyone gawking at the odd scene of the motorcycle cop with a plain-clothed man running behind him, a metal disc cradled under one arm.

The security detail positioned behind two rows of concrete barriers strong enough to stop a Mac truck, let alone a motorcycle, sprang into action. A combination of NYPD, SWAT, and Secret Service all gathered at the point in the barrier where the motorcycle cop aimed.

As he slowed, the most miraculous thing happened. The assembled law enforcement parted to reveal Mara running toward him.

She had a senior Secret Service agent in tow, and he was barking orders as they ran.

Mara met him at the concrete barrier. He wanted to ask how the hell she'd known to meet him there, but it didn't matter.

"Scarvan saw my watch and was confident he'd already accomplished his mission," Scott said quickly. "That means the bomb could go off any second."

Mara spotted the RF blocker. She took advantage of him being out of breath and took it from him before he could object.

"No, I'm going, Mara!" Scott shouted.

"You're spent. I have fresh legs," she said, kicking off her high-heeled shoes. "Not to mention, I'm faster than you on your best day."

Scott knew she was right, but he didn't give a shit. "No, send someone else. Goddamn it, Mara. Will you listen to me? Just this once, listen to me."

Mara smiled and it almost broke his heart. There was love in it, but so much of the smile was sadness in saying goodbye. "Love you, Dad. Now get these people out of here."

Scott reached over the barrier, trying to grab hold of her, to make her stay, to make her listen. But it was no use. She was gone.

He grieved for all of two seconds. His daughter was right; there was a job to do.

He gestured to all of the law enforcement and gathered them around. As he was accustomed to, the men and women there seemed to sense his authority. This was a man whose orders ought to be followed.

"I'm not going to sugarcoat this," he said. "There could be a massive bomb going off inside at any second. Probably dirty." This prompted chatter in the group. He held up his hand. They were all ears. He turned and pointed to the hundreds of people behind them. "These are your people. How about we get to work and save as many of them as we can?"

CHAPTER 67

Mara sprinted up the stairs, past the marble lions. A quick glance behind her confirmed the senior Secret Service agent was following behind her, waving off the SWAT snipers who likely had her in their sights. Running into the library holding a metal disc was a good way to get shot.

Without coms being up, it made things extra tricky.

As she reached the doors, she had to wait as armed men blocked her, looking at the Secret Service agent lagging behind her for guidance.

In those few seconds, she heard one, then two, then what sounded like every police siren in New York going off. She smiled. She knew her dad would get as many people to safety as possible.

"She's CIA," the agent gasped, out of breath. "There's a credible bomb threat. Get her to the Rose Reading Room. Evacuate the building. Evac Ranger, now!"

The men in front of her were well trained. No one panicked. They just got to work.

Two men in suits fell into step next to her. Together, they sprinted across the marble floor of the Astor foyer and hit the stairs, going two at a time.

Mara was faster than her new companions, even carrying the device under her arm.

She just prayed she'd be fast enough.

Asset checked his watch. He'd started the book train on its path thirty seconds ago. It was in the bowels of the building, nearly halfway to its destination.

The timing would be perfect. He was already at the steps that led up to the escape hatch. It was a simple opening mechanism, a turning wheel like one would see in a ship or submarine. Once he opened the door, an alarm would go off, but before anyone figured out what was going on, there would be bigger problems to worry about.

He estimated he didn't need to get far. Just one block. A skyscraper to put between him and the blast. Another minute, maximum. Texas, the police dog, would help clear a path. Pedestrians in New York might not get out of the way of a cop, but they'd step aside for a German shepherd.

The timing here had been a flaw in the plan. Leaving a full thirty to forty-five seconds when someone could see the book train arrive from the small opening in the librarian work area.

But the chances were low and besides, even if someone did spot it, there was nowhere to hide.

Asset spun the lock on the door and pulled the latch. There was a swoosh of air as the seal was broken. An alarm sounded, but he ignored it.

He pushed up on the outer cover and heaved it over. He and Texas emerged with dozens of protestors staring at him wide-eyed.

"Nothing to worry about, folks," he said loudly. "Routine patrol." He pulled at the lid to the opening and hefted it back into place. "Enjoy your evening."

He didn't bother gauging whether people had believed him or not. Didn't really matter. As he led Texas quickly through the crowd, he was taken by how many people were in Bryant Park. Had to be thousands. Every square inch of grass was occupied, as well as the sidewalks and open areas around the towering trees. Patterson had wanted a show of dissent for the monsters he was hosting, and he'd gotten what he'd wanted. Asset wondered how many of them would die from the blast.

He didn't dwell on it.

When all was said and done, there would be billions who had to die to reset the world order. This was just the beginning.

Using Texas as his wedge to open the crowd in front of him, he moved south toward safety.

Leaving the crowd behind him to die.

The book train carrying the bomb inched its way up the vertical portion of its journey. The weight was greater than normal, but within the system specs. The computer brain that controlled everything sent a signal as it approached a fork in the pathway. One sent it west, toward the Map Room. The other was the more used route that sent trains to the Rose Main Reading Room.

The system flawlessly activated the switch to send it to the proper location.

Neither the book train nor the bomb it carried had any malice or ill intent. Both were simply built for efficiency, designed to execute a single job.

And with all systems go, they were both going to do just that.

The system halted the book train's progress right before reaching the end of the track in the Rose Reading Room. It froze in place, cloaked in darkness, waiting, waiting.

CHAPTER 68

Mara anticipated the final cordon of security would give her trouble. And she was right.

The floor with the Rose Reading Room on it was within her credentials, but the sight of her sprinting barefoot up the stairs with a metal disc under her arm, skin glistening with sweat from exertion, negated the badge she showed them.

The Secret Service agents lagged behind her on the steps, but shouted up, "She's good to go! Evac Ranger! Now!"

They parted to let her through.

She stopped just long enough to hold up the metal disc. "This might be the only thing that will stop a bomb from going off and killing all of us," she said. "I need to get to the Rose Reading Room. Make it easy for me."

Three agents immediately ran with her, barking orders, pushing people out of the way.

Asset turned the corner on West Forty-third Street, one block north of the library. Not only that, but upwind as well. Once the bomb detonated, the radioactive fallout would travel fast.

He stood next to a subway entrance. After the explosion, he would go underground and take a train north, away from the blast area. His police uniform and Texas were the perfect cover.

He looked at his watch.

Twenty seconds.

He wondered whether the last few feet of the book train's journey would really make any difference. There was some concern whether the programing to make it stop would be interpreted by the system to just slow down and take longer. A detonation three stories down in the marble building would still be catastrophic, but just not the same.

It didn't matter. His orders had been to detonate at an exact time after sending the book train on its journey. That was precisely what he would do.

Asset looked around at the people going about their lives. No idea that everything they knew was about to change. And this was just the beginning. Asset hoped Marcus Ryker had the capability to manage the chain reaction this devastation was about to set into motion.

Jacobslav Scarvan had vastly different motives from Ryker, but in the end, did it really matter? Whether the blast would start the Second Coming of Christ or the Second Age of Man as envisioned by Ryker, either way, this was a new beginning.

Birth always involved pain and blood.

Today was no exception.

He pulled out the detonator and put his thumb on the trigger, watching the second hand on his watch tick down.

Jordi cheered as his video systems came back online, one by one.

His celebration was stifled by what he saw there.

A body in the stacks next to the book train. Sprawled on the floor in a puddle of blood.

The resolution wasn't great, but his stomach turned as he realized he was looking at Rick Hallsey

Holy shit.

Of course.

"Mara! The book train! The bomb is being delivered on the book train!"

CHAPTER 69

Mara's earpiece squelched, a piercing electronic sound that made her wince.

She reached up to yank it out of her ear, but right before she did, she heard the words.

". . . book train. The bomb . . . on . . . train . . ."

She knew what Jordi was referencing.

The door to the Rose Reading Room was closed off. The various security details didn't know what to make of her and a phalanx of Secret Service agents charging down the hall.

"Clear the way!" shouted one of the agents. "Evac Ranger. Evac Ranger."

The security at the door of the Rose Reading Room charged into the hall. This time, Mara was behind the herd. They cleared the way for her like offensive linemen.

She had no time to register the pandemonium erupting in the hall as over three hundred heads of state and their spouses and guests saw the United States Secret Service swarm the president and half-push, half-carry him from the room.

Mara knew where she had to go.

She shoved to her right, parallel to the work area in the center of the room. There were no librarians behind the counter tonight. In fact, each station had a vase with a bouquet of flowers that blocked her view.

Mara shoved one of the vases aside and it smashed on the floor. She jumped through the workstation window, right where the book train station should be.

Nothing.

For a fleeting second, she wondered if they'd gotten it all wrong after all.

Was it a monstrous hoax? Scarvan's parting gift.

Another diversion?

"Other side," Jordi said in her ear.

She climbed over the workstations to the other side.

There, only ten feet away across a book storage area, packed perfectly into the book train, was a black box. The bomb.

She held up the RF blocker, hating the feeling of trusting something she couldn't see.

Especially on a day where every piece of technology seemed to have failed them.

"Is it working, Jordi?" she whispered. "Please tell me this fucking thing is working."

Asset took a deep breath. The time to press the button had come and passed.

No one was more surprised than himself at his hesitation.

He placed two fingers on the side of his neck and felt his pulse jackhammering away.

Another deep breath.

A recollection of all the pain he'd suffered in his life to get to this moment.

All the pain he'd seen in the world. Most of it at the hands of the government leaders in the room with the bomb. It was time for rebirth. It was time for renewal.

His pulse slowed. He rediscovered his center.

He lowered his hand.

Closed his eyes.

And pressed the button.

* * *

"Mara?" Jordi said.

"Yeah, Jordi?" she said, opening her eyes, realizing she didn't remember closing them.

"It's working."

She exhaled sharply. The cacophony of shouting and screams flooded over her. The Reading Room was being evacuated in something like total chaos.

"What can you tell me?"

"Some of my sensors are back up," Jordi said. "The blocker is definitely emitting a dampening shield around the bomb, device, whatever it is. We have cellular blocked. I think . . . I think we're okay."

Mara couldn't believe it. She wondered if they'd ever know how close they'd come. "What do you say we get some damn bomb squad guys on the scene?"

"Roger that. Some of my coms are back on, but not all of them," Jordi said. "Give me a sec."

Asset pressed the button again.

And then a third time.

He craned his head to the side and listened. He thought he could have heard the explosion plainly. Even felt the ground shake beneath his feet.

But there was nothing.

Without hesitation, he turned and jogged toward the garage where he'd stored a vehicle. He and Texas had to get far, far away.

His employer was not going to be pleased.

He couldn't be certain what was happening at the library, but he felt reasonably sure that Scott and Mara Roberts had somehow pressed their thumbs on the scale and ruined the plan.

At least there was the fail-safe.

While Marcus Ryker might not get to kill the entire world's political leadership in one go, he would at least still inflict a blow on civilization.

A nuclear blast in the middle of Manhattan would still create chaos.

And that was what Omega's plan required.

"Bomb secure," Jordi's voice said over the coms. "Require immediate bomb squad support in Rose Reading Room."

Scott put his hands on his knees and hung his head.

He felt dizzy and short of breath.

He realized at that moment how much he'd believed they were fighting a lost cause. How he'd assumed Scarvan and Omega had thought of everything. They'd been a step ahead of them the entire time.

"Jordi, can you patch me in with Mara?"

"Actually, yes I can," Jordi said, clearly quite pleased with himself.

"Dad?" Mara said.

"You all right?" he asked, cupping his hand to his ear to hear her better.

"You know, just another night on the job." She sounded tired, but relieved. "You?"

He grinned. His kid's spunk always impressed him. "Couldn't be better." He paused, then turned serious. "I had a bad feeling about this one," he said. "Seems like we were playing catch-up this whole time."

"Guess the end of the race is all that matters," Mara said.

"Everything happens for a reason," Scott had said to Scarvan, who had responded with *You will come to believe that one day. Maybe today.* Scott had thought he'd meant everything along the way had been his doing. Allowing himself to be caught. Asset pretending to want to help them.

There was no way he could have predicted they would stop him at the library.

Impossible.

"Dad, are you there?" Mara asked.

"Why wasn't the bomb just on a timer?" Scott asked.

"What's that?"

"Why wasn't the bomb just on a timer?" he asked again. An ice ball formed in his stomach. "In case there was a malfunction. In case there was a delay. In case the electronic signal of the countdown could be sniffed out."

"Oh God," Mara said.

He could hear in her voice that she understood just like he did. This wasn't over.

CHAPTER 70

Mara climbed over the piles of books between her and the bomb. On the side opposite to where she'd been standing was a small display window that glowed red.

2:00

As she watched, the red glow flashed five times. Then the numbers changed.

1:59

1:58

1:57

"It's counting down," Mara said. "What do I do?"

"How much time?" Scott asked.

"Started at two minutes," she said. She ran her hands over the surface of the bomb, looking for something to open. It was perfectly smooth. "1:55, 1:54."

"Get the hell out of there," Scott said. "You can't do anything."

"I can't just leave," Mara said. "Jordi?"

"Listen to your dad," he said. "Run fast toward the west end of the building. Put as much rock between yourself and the bomb as possible."

"Wait," Mara said. "Can you send it back down? Restart the book train. The stacks are far underground. It might contain the blast."

"Mara," Jordi said. "Rick's in the stacks. But he's been shot. I can't tell if he's dead or not. The escape hatch is open, though."

Mara understood what Jordi had said but couldn't process the meaning. She couldn't allow herself to. Mara glanced at the timer 1:42. There was no time.

"Send it down, Jordi," she said. "Now."

The book train kicked into gear and disappeared down the track.

"I'll get Rick," Scott said. "I promise."

"No, Dad. Wait." But it was too late. He was gone.

CHAPTER 71

Bryant Park was emptying out. Rumor had swirled about a bomb, but the die-hard protesters were standing firm.

As Scott ran toward the escape hatch, he realized those assholes were going to die where they stood unless they moved.

He ran right at an NYPD uniformed cop, smashing into him. In two seconds, he had the man's firearm out of his holster.

Two seconds after that, Scott had it pointed into the mulch bed of the bushes nearest him, firing shot after shot.

Just like in the old Westerns, the gunshots started a stampede. It was a dangerous move, but there wasn't time for anything else. Scott hoped any parents had already had the good sense to clear the area, because the rush to leave the park turned into chaos. The crowds moving faster each time he pulled the trigger.

He reached the escape hatch and threw it open.

Someone had used it already. The inner door hung open. The staircase was clear.

Scott ran down the stairs, trying not to think about how many seconds had passed since he'd started his run.

"Rick! Where are you?"

He heard a groan and ran toward it.

Rick was drenched in his own blood, clutching his stomach, already crawling to the exit.

Scott bent and lifted him in a fireman's carry. Rick screamed in pain with Scott's shoulder jammed right into his gunshot.

He staggered back to the stairs. Rick was a big man and heavy.

But he was alive. And he'd promised his daughter he'd do his best.

He dug deeper, pushed harder, gritting his teeth.

Scott yelled as he took the stairs. He couldn't stop. If he stopped he didn't know whether he'd be able to start again.

With a final push, he cleared the top of the escape hatch.

Two NYPD cops ran up and took Rick off his shoulders.

"Run!" Scott screamed. "Take him and run. Get out of the park."

The two cops carried Rick. Together they all ran away from the park.

They'd cleared the trees and stumbled onto Forty-first Street when the blast went off.

The ground jolted, sending all of them sprawling on the pavement.

A torrent of flame shot out from the escape hatch, a hundred feet long, pouring into the building facing the park like a geyser.

Glass shattered in the buildings all around them.

The trees around the park moved like straw in the wind, back and forth. Then dozens of them fell, caving in toward the center of the park.

The air filled with the sound of the trees snapping in half, the screams of people nearby, the sirens from emergency vehicles.

Then slowly, everything came to a stop.

A cloud of dust and debris rose up and spread, covering everything.

Scott wondered whether the dust was filled with radioactivity. He covered his mouth, but he knew it wouldn't do much good.

The ground beneath his feet lurched one more time, but then that, too, settled.

For a moment, Scott just stood in place. Waiting. Still not believing it was really over.

The night was filled with alarms from the buildings all around them. Fire and police sirens followed soon after.

Scott staggered forward and bent over Rick, who was sprawled out on the asphalt.

"Rick?" Scott said, rolling him over. "Rick?"

Rick's eyes fluttered open, unfocused.

"Medic!" Scott cried out. "I need a medic! C'mon, Rick. Hang in there."

"You press the button," Rick whispered. "You press the button."

Scott leaned closer, not sure what he was saying.

"Asset, you do it," Rick said. "You press the button. The nuke. Never agreed to a nuke. That's you. You press the button."

Scott thought he had heard wrong. The man was delirious. But maybe . . . just maybe . . .

Oh Jesus.

"Are you Omega?" he asked. "Rick, are you Omega?"

For a second, Rick's eyes focused and looked right at Scott. A sudden moment of clarity. He grinned wide, his teeth and lips covered in blood.

"We're going to burn down the world," he said. "You can't stop Omega. We're everywhere."

Before Scott could respond, Rick's eyes went wide. His mouth opened in a silent scream while his legs kicked and jerked. A wet, gurgling sound came from his throat.

Scott rocked back on his knees. There was nothing to do except watch. Scott felt numb at the revelation. The only thought that came to him was that if the son of a bitch in front of him didn't die in the next ten seconds, he'd strangle him with his own bare hands.

That wasn't necessary.

Rick stopped moving, his open eyes staring up blankly into the night sky.

"Dad? Dad? Are you there?"

It was Mara in the earpiece. He didn't know what to say. What to tell her. The truth eventually. It had to be the truth. But how?

He didn't have a clue.

"Dad?"

"I'm here, Mara," he said. "I'm here."

He heard her sob on the other end of the connection. "Oh God, I thought . . . when you didn't answer . . ."

Scott stood and immediately stumbled. He felt off-balance, disoriented.

"I'm fine," he said. "I'm fine."

How did he tell her?

"And Rick?" she said, her voice cracking.

He blinked back tears. Not wanting to break his little girl's heart, not once, but twice. "I got Rick out, honey," he said. "But he didn't make it. I'm so sorry."

A long pause on the line. He thought they'd been cut off. But she came back on, her voice thick with emotion. "Thank you for trying," she said. "Where is he? I want to see him."

"You can't come down here. There's no telling what the radioactivity might be," he said. It was true, but he also wanted to put off the inevitable conversation. He had to tell her in person. He had to be there for her when she found out. "I'll stay with him," he said.

"You must be by the emergency exit," she said. "I'm coming down."

"Mara, no," he said. "Listen to me. He's gone. There are thousands of people who need help right now. There's no way of telling how bad the radiation is here. There's a fight ahead of us with Omega. You need to get somewhere safe."

Nothing.

He was desperate for her to stay away. Some of the radiation likely was in the library too, but the thick walls would have stopped most of it.

There was only one way he could think to stop her from coming down.

"Honey, I'm so sorry," he said. "I have to tell you this. Rick. He was Omega. He was helping Asset. He admitted it before he died."

A long pause.

"I'm so sorry. But you can't come down here. Not for him. Do you hear me?" he said, begging. "Not for him."

Another long pause.

It was Jordi who answered, speaking softly. "She heard you," he said. "Then she turned off her earpiece. Is it true?" Jordi paused before saying, "Please tell me you were just saying that to keep her from coming down there."

Scott took a deep breath. "I wish I was, Jordi." He felt nauseated. "Maybe I should have never told her."

"Everything Rick ever touched has to be investigated," Jordi said. "You know that. It could lead us to Omega. But beyond that, she deserved to know."

"What she deserved is to not have another person she loves turn out to be nothing but lies and betrayal."

"But do you—"

Scott never heard the end of whatever he was saying. He pulled the earpiece out and shoved it into his pocket.

He walked back into Bryant Park. Intellectually, he knew he should be walking in the other direction, but had to see. The ground had heaved up from the blast, creating a berm of dirt, smashed concrete sidewalk, and fallen trees. He climbed through the wreckage until he was on top looking down.

The entire lawn area of the park had collapsed almost twenty feet into a massive sinkhole. Giant trees lay scattered in a heap, but he saw no openings. No fissures leaking smoke. No glow of hot embers.

Nor did he see any evidence of any people down in the pit.

He figured there would be some injuries from the stampede he'd caused. There'd likely be some commission convened to investigate the night where men and women would second-guess his actions. But from what he could see, it had worked. And that was enough for him.

He wondered at the scene. The engineering designed to keep the books safe from moisture and decay had saved thousands of lives.

Omega was defeated. For today.

But he knew for certain that they would try again.

The earpiece he'd removed buzzed in his pocket. Jordi's way to signal an urgent message. He dug it out and held it to his ear in case it was Mara reconnecting.

"Go ahead, I'm here," he said.

"Coms at the black site just came back on," Jordi said. "They came for Scarvan. There was a firefight."

"Anna?" Scott said. "What about Anna?"

Jordi told him what had happened, Scott's heart hammering in his chest. Before Jordi was even done, Scott had already broken into a sprint back toward Grand Central Station.

The exhaustion he'd felt only seconds before was gone, replaced with a surge of adrenaline.

Anna. He didn't want to lose her.

He reached the door to the stairwell, punched in his code.

Nothing.

"I've got it," Jordi said in his ear.

The door buzzed open.

Scott rushed through and hit the stairs, taking them three and four at a time.

As he got closer to the black site, he smelled the cordite from the gunfight in the air. Smoke wafted up.

Jordi had informed the security team on-site that Scott was coming. They opened the last doors for him and he ran through.

Bodies were strewn all over the site. Some CIA. Others dressed in tactical gear.

The fight had been brutal and in close quarters.

Then he saw her, sitting in a chair, her hair matted with blood.

He ran to her. She groaned in pain as he carefully embraced her.

"Are you shot?" he asked.

She shook her head. "Last time I was shot, it was by you," she said. "Might have a few broken ribs, is all. These assholes didn't know who they were dealing with."

He kissed her forehead, ignoring the fact that the blood pasting her hair back likely wasn't hers. Anna was a fighter. He could only imagine the defense she'd mounted.

"Scarvan . . ." Anna said.

"It's okay," Scott said. "You did your best. We'll find him again."

Anna looked at him oddly. "You think I'd let these pricks take him? I stashed him in the cleaning supplies closet. We still have him."

Scott grinned. "Now you're just showing off."

"That's what I've been up to," she said. "What happened up there? Is Mara all right?"

Scott reached out and took her hand in his. He leaned forward and gently touched their foreheads together. "She's alive. It will take a while for her to be all right, but she's alive."

Anna didn't ask for clarification. She just held him. And he let her.

For a few moments, the rest of the world didn't exist. But they both knew that wouldn't last for long. Even though the attack had been thwarted, a nuclear device had been detonated in the middle of New York City.

The second that happened, the world had changed forever.

CHAPTER 72

Mara stared down her beer, not taking her eyes off it when Hawthorn took the seat next to her.

"Did my dad send you here?" she asked.

"He may have mentioned he was meeting you here to watch the president's address," he said. "Seemed like as good a place as any."

"I'm not changing my mind."

Hawthorn ignored the comment. "I've sat at this bar a lot over the years," Hawthorn said, ordering a drink. "Quite a few times with your father." He pointed at her. "More than once when he had the same expression you have on your face right now."

They were at Old Ebbit Grill, a landmark establishment that was walking distance to the White House. All dark wood and brass, it was a mix of tourists and government workers on the job. The bar had mounted animal heads above it, some with fake antlers, adding some whimsy to the place.

Mara wasn't in the mood for whimsy. In fact, she wasn't in the mood for anything. The last five days were a whirlwind that had left her feeling both physically and emotionally hollowed out.

In the aftermath of the bombing, every law enforcement official in America had taken part in the hunt for co-conspirators. The body of Alexis Papadopoulos had been found, but the trail had stopped there. Asset was long gone. There were no other leads.

The world reeled from the new reality of a nuclear device finally being used in a terrorist act. Markets closed for three days to hold back panic selling. Still, on the fourth day, world markets plunged precipitously. But, by the end of the trading session, cooler heads prevailed, and they stabilized.

In the midst of all this, with demands on every minute of her day, Mara was processing the unthinkable. The man she'd thought she loved was the enemy. Playing her the entire time.

Her skin crawled at the thought of his touch. Of the intimacy they'd shared. Her stomach twisted at the idea that she'd nearly helped these madmen achieve their goal.

The frantic pace of the days had helped. There was no time to dwell on what it all meant. Or fixate on how her and her dad's lives had formed into this bizarre parallel, both of them deceived by the person they loved.

All she had time for was work. Even so, more than a few times each day, she had to excuse herself, find a private spot, and let the emotion pour out of her. Anger. Grief. Shame. All of it bursting out of her. Sometimes in shuddering tears, other times in blind rage, still others curled up into herself, knees to chest, beating herself up for letting it happen.

Five days. And it still felt no better.

"You saved thousands of lives," Hawthorn said. "Not a bad day at the office."

"We were lucky," Mara said.

"Maybe we were good," Hawthorn said, taking a drink of his beer.

"We were lucky," Mara insisted. "Things could have gone the other way. My mistake. My lapse in judgment could have destroyed the world."

"You're not the only one who made a mistake with Rick Hallsey," Hawthorn said. "The Secret Service hired him. Mitch Dreslan put him on the presidential detail."

"None of them were sleeping with him," she countered. That

was easier than saying she'd fallen in love with him. That she'd considered he might be the person to be with for the rest of her life.

It may have been easier for her to talk about it that way, but it caused Hawthorn to take a long drink.

"That's true, they weren't sleeping with him," he said. "But they trusted him. I trusted him. It's what makes this Omega threat so terrifying. If feels like they are everywhere."

"Which is why you want me to stay?" Mara said.

"No, it's why I need you to stay," he said. "Now more than ever."

She took another drink of her beer. "Give me a week," she said.

He smiled, the cat who knew how the game with the mouse would turn out. He raised his pint and they clinked glasses. "In a week," he said. "Good decisions happen after a week. It took about that long for me to decide to ask Francie McKee out on a second date, for example."

Mara had known Hawthorn's wife, Francie. They'd had the kind of marriage everyone around them envied. Mara had been at her funeral after she lost her battle with cancer.

"What? How could it have taken that long to ask her out?"

"I was nervous. Uncertain where it would lead. Scared to death, to be honest. And look what happened. That decision ended up creating the very best thing in my life," Hawthorn said. "Three children. Eight grandchildren. What will they all end up doing? What great things will occur because they are here on this Earth?"

"Thank goodness you asked Francie out on that second date," Mara said, smiling.

"Thank goodness, indeed."

She raised her glass again. "I miss her."

He raised his. "Not nearly as much as I do," he whispered.

Scott and Anna joined them. "What the hell are you two drinking? Pilsners? Ugh." He waved at the bartender. "Two of the hoppiest IPAs you can find, please."

Anna kissed Mara on each cheek and took the seat next to her. Scott squeezed her shoulder.

"I just saw the latest briefing," Anna said. "Seven fatalities, including the bad guys. They're adding Scarvan to the count. It's better he's dead to the rest of the world."

"Radiation levels have stabilized," Hawthorn said. "Most of the site is contained."

Scott nodded. "The blast collapsed the tunnel leading from the stacks to the main library, so no radiation escaped in that direction."

"And the escape hatch area?" Mara asked.

Hawthorn answered. "That area is the biggest problem. The people who were near it will need to be monitored for several years, but the docs are optimistic."

"They told me my exposure was similar to what astronauts experience in space," Scott said.

"When they're in space for a year," Anna said. "Don't minimize this. I know you; you'll make it a reason not to do the check-ups."

"Where's Jordi?" Mara asked. "I thought you were bringing him?"

"'Ere I am, darling," Jordi said, coming in from the adjoining room.

Mara jumped up and gave him a hug. He'd been a good friend in the last five days, helping her through the terrific struggle of dealing with Rick's betrayal. In fact, they'd all been great. The only one who'd beat her up over the whole thing was herself.

Hawthorn checked his watch. "Couple more minutes," he said.

President Patterson was scheduled to address the nation and they were all interested to hear what he had to say. All the networks were covering it and there was a rumor that a major policy initiative was to be announced. Hawthorn knew, but he was playing it close to his vest. He assured them they would find it interesting.

Mara positioned herself so she could see all of their faces.

"Before this starts, I want to thank all of you for giving me my space in the last five days," Mara said. "It's been hard to process this." She paused for a beat, pushing aside the easy dark jokes she could make, knowing they were all just a defense mechanism. She took a deep breath. "Really hard. But the support here means everything to me. Thank you."

The group lifted their glasses toward Mara and took a drink. Scott got up and hugged her, giving her a kiss on the cheek.

"You're going to be okay," he whispered.

She nodded, staying close to his shoulder to hide her tears from the rest of the group.

"I'll feel better when we find Omega and put these assholes in the ground," she said.

Scott held her tighter. "That's my girl. We'll get them. And we'll make them pay. I promise."

Mara pulled back and wiped her eyes, getting herself back together. "You're buying the next round," she said. "And we're staying here late. We'll start looking for Omega tomorrow."

"I'd love nothing more," Scott said.

"We're in," Anna and Jordi said together.

"For which part?" Mara asked.

"For the drinking late tonight and the hunting tomorrow," Anna said, sliding an arm around Scott's midsection. "I'm here for all of it."

"Everyone, the president's on," Hawthorn said.

They all turned toward the screen, huddled close together. Not because there wasn't enough space, but because right then, all of them needed to feel part of something greater than themselves. That none of them were alone. That they had found a family.

The entire restaurant fell silent as the screen changed to President Patterson sitting in the Oval Office.

CHAPTER 73

"Good evening, my fellow Americans. Five days ago, a nuclear device was detonated in the center of New York City. This terrorist act was not only an attack against America, but against the entire world. The explosion was intended to kill the collected leaders of the world present at the gala celebrating the seventy-fifth anniversary of the United Nations.

"The men who planned this attack failed.

"Due to the valiant efforts of the great men and women who make up our intelligence and law enforcement community, the bomb was removed from the New York Public Library and transferred to the subterranean book storage area under Bryant Park.

"This fast thinking contained the bomb's impact almost entirely underground."

A graphic was displayed next to the president on the screen, showing a diagram of the library's location and Bryant Park.

"I say 'almost entirely.' The area here"—he pointed to the location of the escape hatch—"and here"—he said, pointing to the section of the library where the tunnel connected the two buildings—"have significant radioactive readings and will need to be avoided completely until this risk is mitigated.

"Fortunately, very few were exposed to any significant radiation. Those who were exposed are expected to make a full recovery and not suffer from any lasting effects.

"Our nation grieves for the five innocent people who lost their lives in this event. Even as we give thanks that our casualties in this attack were not greater, we will not forget to include the fallen in our thoughts and prayers.

"The explosion and the subsequent cave-in of the stacks under Bryant Park exacted another price on our nation. Over three and a half million books, documents, maps, and other records which had been stored in the stacks have been destroyed. Many of these are irreplaceable. This loss will be felt for generations.

"As the leader of our nation, I want to be able to tell you that the threat has been neutralized. While we caught and killed the man responsible for this heinous act, the threat remains.

"This man was no lone wolf.

"He had assistance. And those who helped him must and will be brought to justice.

"Tonight, I share with the world that our evidence points to the existence of a supranational organization called Omega. This group's sole purpose is to sow discord and to eventually challenge the world order. They will use whatever means available to turn us against one another, to spur on conflict, to encourage us to become the very worst versions of ourselves.

"The government of the United States, with unanimous support of the fifteen members of the Security Council, has declared war on Omega.

"This attack will not stand.

"The United States won't allow it.

"The world won't allow it.

"Because we believe in the inherent good in humanity.

"Because we believe we can overcome the mistakes of our past and do better.

"Because we believe it is never too late to become the best version of who we can be.

"Together.

"God bless all of you. And may God bless the United States of America and the entire world."

The red light on the camera stayed on for a few seconds as President Patterson stared into the lens. When it blinked off, he let out deep breath, finally relaxing.

The people in the Oval Office clapped hesitantly, as if not sure the solemnity of the occasion allowed for it. More people came in through the doors, Cabinet members mostly, who had been listening in the outer rooms.

The applause increased as more joined in.

President Patterson held up his hand to quiet them. "Thank you, everyone. Now how about we get to work and deliver for the American people?"

This led to another short burst of applause and Patterson had to admit he liked the way it made him feel. But he knew declaring a public war on a shadowy organization like Omega was the easy part. Getting results was going to prove harder.

To assist him, he'd brought together the world's finest minds.

One of those great minds stepped forward and shook his hand. "Well done, Mr. President," he said. "Perfect delivery. This Omega group. Is that what you want my help with?"

"Exactly. I'm counting on you to help me find them and root them out. Can you do that for me? Can you do that for the world?"

Marcus Ryker smiled. "Well, Mr. President," he said. "I can guarantee that I'll try my best."

ACKNOWLEDGMENTS

Thank you to the entire team at Kensington. Steven Zacharius and Lynn Cully have created a wonderful environment where writers feel valued and respected. James Abbate pulled book one from the submissions pile and was the first early advocate of the series. Besides being a hero for that act, he's proven to be an excellent companion during site research for this book. John Scognamiglio has shepherded these books with a deft and expert hand. His experience and insight have been invaluable.

Thank you to Kristine Noble for another wonderful cover. John Son for cover copy that makes even me want to read the book again. Steve Roman, thank you for your copyedit pass. It made the book better in so many ways. Thank you to Crystal McCoy for spreading word of this series and for being such a pleasure to work with. Kensington has been a perfect home.

Thank you to my wonderful agent, Sarah Hershman, a spunky entrepreneur who gets things done. My writer friends who supported the series with their blurbs: Steve Berry, Hank Phillippi Ryan, KJ Howe, and Simon Gervais. My family and friends who have given me unwavering support throughout this crazy ride, especially my wife, Nicole, who is a source of endless encouragement for me to follow my passion.

And, most important, thank you to my amazing readers. Time is the most valuable commodity each of us possesses. I take my responsibility seriously to ensure I don't waste yours, working as hard as I can to deliver a story well told. I hope you feel I upheld my end of the bargain with this one.